PRAISE FOR F. NELSON SMITH

JACK TUESDAY

"The rapid pacing, a cast of vividly-portrayed characters and numerous elements of surprise make this story difficult to set aside."

— *BlueInk Review, Starred*

"With satisfying nods to postwar intrigue, Jack Tuesday is a thrilling police procedural novel in which a dedicated detective is subjected to dark suspicions."

— *Clarion, Foreword Reviews*

PERPETUAL CHECK

"Perpetual Check is a page-turner with a resolution readers won't see coming. It will please anyone who appreciates interesting characters and mysteries that deliver the unexpected."

— *BlueInk Review, Starred*

"Clever and surprising, Perpetual Check is a thrilling novel set during the intersection between the decline of the Soviet Union and the dawn of the computer age."

— *Clarion, Foreword Reviews*

NO STRAIGHT THING

"Ultimately heartwarming despite its macabre circumstances, No Straight Thing is an engrossing historical mystery."

— *Clarion, Foreword Reviews*

"With its vivid atmosphere and unforgettable characters, No Straight Thing is a treat for fans of suspenseful historical fiction."

— *BlueInk Reviews, Starred*

JACK TUESDAY

F. NELSON SMITH

Jack Tuesday is a work of fiction. Apart from events and locales that figure into the narrative, all names, characters, places, and incidents are the products of the author's imagination or used fictitiously. Any resemblance to persons, living or dead, is entirely coincidental.

2023 Bear Hill Publishing
Copyright © 2023 F. Nelson Smith

Published in North America by Bear Hill Publishing
Cranbrook, B.C.
Canada

www.bearhillbooks.com

Paperback ISBN 978-1-989071-33-5
Hardcover ISBN 978-1-989071-34-2
Ebook ISBN 978-1-989071-35-9

JACK TUESDAY

Dear Readers . . .

JACK TUESDAY is a retro mystery novel set in Canada, published in Canada by a Canadian company and written by a Canadian author.

We appreciate the few readers who take it upon themselves to assist us in the proofreading process and point out any errors they find. We only ask that perhaps first you do a Google search to discover if the word you feel is spelt wrong (notice 'spelt' not 'spelled') is not just a Canadian variant of that word.

Thank you.

To my daughter, Brenda, who in my time of sadness prodded a reluctant me to finish the manuscript.

"I hold it to be the inalienable right of anybody to go to hell in his own way."

Robert Frost

1

Winnipeg, Manitoba 1951

"Run!"

If anyone wondered what flows through the veins of crime bosses, Danny would say it was ice water. But the fluid oozing around his father's head where he lay sprawled on the floor wasn't water. Danny squinted with one eye closed. Curiously, the newly installed asbestos tile shining through the blood turned from green to black. *Good thing it never happened at home, on the priceless Persian carpet.* Danny imagined blood spattered on the Cézanne and let out a manic high-pitched snicker.

"Now!" Luke's rough shoulder punch knocked him off balance, jolting him into reality. "Go, Danny."

The room swam into focus, and this time, Danny gagged at the sight of Conor Jackson's limp form and the meat cleaver beside him. Realizing he still held the baseball bat, Danny shook it free from his hand as if it were an evil thing, wincing when it clattered on the tile floor. With a will of their own, his legs backed him up against the wall. He slid to the floor and wrapped both arms around his head. "Oh God, oh God. I hit him. I had to. What he'll do . . ."

"—is kill you this time." Lips twisting in pain, Luke swore loud and long, finishing with, "Dammit, Danny, stop fooling around and get your head together. You have to run."

"Run where?" The idea of leaving stirred him into a new panic. Shuddering, his eyes slid past Luke's set face and his father's prone body as if the answer were blazed across a wall somewhere.

"God, you're dense." Luke's face warped in a mixture of anger, impatience, and pain. "What you've done, he won't tolerate." Cradling the blood-soaked handkerchief wrapped around his hand, a pressure on his finger, he took two steps forwards and aimed a vicious kick at Danny's shin. He sucked his breath between his teeth at the pain, fighting a flash of resentment.

The meat cleaver. Danny relived the memory of it raised against him again. How could he have forgotten so soon? "But you need a hospital . . ."

"The sooner you're gone, the sooner I get one." Luke used his good hand to grip Danny's shoulder as if he could raise his little brother up with one hand. God, his iron grip was as solid as Gentleman Conor's. Was his strength the reason Luke was favoured? Remembering who the favourite was made Danny's innards quiver again. Having hit the wrong Jackson with the cleaver would propel the old bastard's rage to new manic proportions.

"I'll stall him." Luke left, disappearing into the hallway. "But eventually he'll send the boys out looking," he called out behind him.

Danny forced himself to his feet, barely hearing his older brother over the blood rushing through his ears so fast he thought his head might burst at any moment.

"Here." Luke stood in front of him again. "Take this. I took it from Dad's safe." He shoved a crumpled wad of cash into his chest. "Remember, don't ask anyone for help. He'll find out."

Their father stirred and gave a weak moan. The brothers looked at each other, misery conveying all the unspoken words their upbringing would never allow them to say. Clutching the loose bills to his chest, Danny stepped over his father and towards the door.

"Danny."

He turned only halfway. Something about the way Luke said his name made him queasy.

"Don't come back. Forget you even have a family."

So Danny pedalled his bike into the late afternoon. Away from the rooms behind the pool hall.

Better for him to go to Union Station on Main Street. The CPR Station was closer but would be the first place his father's muscle monkeys, Louis and Dewey, would search.

He ditched the bike in front of a butcher shop and ran the remaining two blocks, slowing to a stop near the ticket window, breath ragged. Which way? East to Toronto? West for Calgary? Gang contacts in both cities would find him in no time at all. Danny took a deep breath, fighting rising panic and poor decisions, and inspected the big departures board hoping for inspiration. Not finding anything useful, he backed out of line and weaved amongst a crush of men milling about at the far end of the waiting room, using them as concealment. He headed for the nearest bench for a break, with the nagging thought that Luke could not stall for long.

The familiar smell of old varnish and regular activity calmed him somewhat. He picked up a brochure lying on the bench beside him, gripping it with shaking hands and raising it as a shield against his face. There in bold print: 'Your country needs you.'

Danny peered over the top, more interested in making sure nobody was pushing through the crowd and heading for him. He saw men discussing a wall-sized poster displaying a montage of soldiers guiding rafts across rivers, climbing barricades, and rappelling up cliffs. Two soldiers in crisp uniforms handed out more brochures alongside another poster crying for recruits in the war between the United Nations and Korea. Enthusiastic tones made army life seem like a picnic.

Danny's thoughts zeroed in with the finest inspiration he'd had all day. His eyes rapidly moved between the poster and the brochure. It only took a moment before he rose and pushed to the front of the line.

His open relief didn't fool the sergeant manning the desk, whose sigh of enforced patience confirmed the sharp and knowing eyes beneath his cap. "How old are you, son?" Behind him, a corporal holding a clipboard inspected Danny with interest, then cemented the sergeant's opinion with a grin.

Danny pointed to the calendar behind his desk. "Eighteen yesterday, sir. May fourteenth."

The sergeant's eyes zeroed in on Danny's shirt and the drops of blood. "You look like someone in a hurry. We aren't a refuge if you're running from the police."

His heartbeat increased to a mad gallop. He forced out a chuckle. "Oh no, sir. I deliver . . . delivered for a butcher shop, and the packages always leak." He rubbed the stain with a finger. "I'm not running from the police, sir. My job is going nowhere, and there's no future here." Danny quit talking. Luke said that when telling lies, not to overdo it and volunteer too much. He mentally crossed his fingers and focused on the sergeant's cap badge. A deer. No, an African animal.

"Do you know what it is?" The sergeant asked, bringing Jack's attention back to him.

"A Springbot."

With a glint of surprise in his eyes, the sergeant half-smiled, then pulled a form towards him. "Name?"

He uncrossed his fingers. "Jackson . . ." Danny froze.

The sergeant raised his head, smiling with forced patience. "You sure you want to join, son?" His cold eyes sent a message that action, not tolerance, was a virtue in the army.

A snicker came from behind, and the corporal grinned again. Danny felt his face grow hot. His eyes fell back on the calendar over the sergeant's shoulder. "Tuesday. My name is Jackson . . . Jack Tuesday." The corporal raised a questioning eyebrow, then gazed at the sergeant as if knowing the verdict.

But the sergeant bent his head and wrote. "Mother and father's name? Address?"

"Both parents are dead, sir." It was half-true, anyway. "And until today, I lived in a room above the butcher shop. But since I quit my job . . . guess I don't have an address, sir."

The sergeant held his pencil, one end in each hand, his eyes boring into Danny's. Danny gazed straight back with well-practiced neutrality. The sergeant bent his head to fill in the blanks on the form, turned it around, and pointed. "Sign here."

Danny took the pen and signed his new name. It felt clumsy, like when forging his father's signature for school forms.

"Welcome to the Royal Canadian Dragoons. Armoured Regiment, Private. You're in the army now."

"The Dragoons," he repeated. "Yes, sir."

"And don't call me sir. I'm a sergeant." He sorted out some papers on the desk, put them in an envelope, wrote Danny's new name on the front, and handed it to him.

"Thank you, Sergeant." Danny—Jack's lungs took in a releasing breath. A smile spread over his face for the first time that day, and he nodded to the man who had just saved his life. "And I hope you get better soon."

The sergeant's fingers froze on the envelope. His other hand squeezed into a fist, then relaxed. The icy stare told Danny his remark was invasive and beyond army protocol.

"I meant . . . your arm, Sergeant." His voice trailed off. *Shit. I'm a wet rag. He'll reject me now. Stupid, stupid.*

Danny waited for the bad news, but the sergeant only let go of the envelope, and his brown khaki arm bearing three stripes pointed to the station side door. "A bus leaves at six o'clock. Check in at five o'clock. Sharp. You will get your kit at Osborne, then you're headed to Petawawa." He leaned back. "Say goodbye to your . . . friends. You won't be seeing them for a while." He beckoned over Danny's shoulder to the next man in line.

Danny checked the big station clock. He'd stand out if he didn't have a carryall filled with necessities. The Army and Navy store wasn't far, so he could hide there and buy what he needed.

Wearing a cap and carrying his new belongings, Danny joined the line of men at the side door right on the dot of five. On board the bus, he watched as the corporal came down the aisle, checking off a list on his clipboard. When he got to Danny, he sat in the aisle seat. Danny's heart sank. Had the goons found him? Would he be kicked off the bus? The sigh of pneumatics sounded as the door closed, followed by the squeal of brakes being released. The bus moved.

"Tuesday," the corporal said. It sounded strange. "What you said. . ." He nodded his head towards the sergeant sitting behind the bus driver. "His injury. How did you know?"

Used to keeping his explanation simple, Danny rubbed his face. "I notice things . . . I shouldn't have said anything. I forgot myself."

The bus slowed at the exit road, then merged into the traffic leading from the station. Danny craned his neck towards the window, searching for Louis and Dewey.

"Tuesday." The tone said *don't ignore me.* "What things?"

"The sergeant's left arm is stiff. He squeezes a ball to strengthen it and still squeezes his fingers in a reflex. There's a white strip above a tan line on his forehead, meaning he used to wear his cap lower. Maybe he injured his head. His whole left side, I think."

Danny felt the corporal's eyes inspecting him as he talked. In the end, he asked coolly, "You got any more talents the army should know about?"

Not sure of what he was after, Danny shook his head. The corporal made a note on his clipboard and went to the front of the bus. Danny saw him exchange words with the sergeant before he sat in the seat across the aisle.

Familiar streets whipped past the window. Totally isolated now, a combination of loneliness, fear, and misery cramped his stomach. Where was Petawawa? Someplace his father couldn't find him, he hoped. He thought of Luke's last words.

"Don't come back, Danny. Forget you even have a family."

2

Edmonton, Alberta 1972

"How many secrets are rattling around in your head, Officer Tuesday?"

Warmth rushed to Jack's cheeks. The doctor had outed his fake calm in what? Two minutes?

The doctor chuckled. "Police detectives should be skilled at stone-faced exteriors." He beamed over at Jack, his face splitting into a myriad of cracks. "I ask everyone that question, and you all look guilty."

Jack bit back a sarcastic comment. Instead, he forced a grin and shrugged in a *what-can-I-say* attitude.

Dr. Pavic settled back into his chair. "Tell me what you recall. Why you are here."

Not prepared for the sudden switch in conversation, Jack spoke in spurts. "It was a raid. We, my partner Brodie and I, were with the tactical team. Afterwards, or during, I'm not sure which, we had a car accident. I was driving. I survived; Brodie didn't."

"And?" The doctor raised his eyebrows. Jack growled softly to ease the lump in his throat. If he weren't careful, the cold, harsh reality that Brodie was dead would bring the too familiar anguish, which always ended with him weeping in abject misery. Only another cop would understand what it meant to lose a partner.

"No sympathy from that end, pal. Not this time." Jack ignored the voice in his head.

"I woke up in the hospital with a major concussion and minor injuries and no memory of what happened." He eyed the doctor, whose expression showed only interest, no accusation. Jack drew in a shaky breath and held it before releasing a long exhale. "They told me Brodie died from a gunshot wound to the chest. It ruptured major organs. That's all I know. If you know more, please . . . tell me." A plea close to begging.

Dr. Pavic obliged and turned to a single typed page. "You left out the part about being suspended while the police investigate." He peered at Jack over his reading glasses, expression neutral.

Jack met his eyes but said nothing. He would contribute as little as possible until he identified the lay of the land. Was the doctor's aim to help or get him to confess to killing Brodie? He was around sixty. Burly arms and shoulders showed a man once fit but softened from hours at a desk. He wore his dark hair long, but it still didn't cover the scar tissue running across the side of his head and over his right ear, which lacked part of the upper ridge.

His brown eyes stared into Jack's face. "Your stay in the hospital was near on two months. During that time, you had no recall at all? Even a small niggle of the accident or the events leading up to it?"

"Nope. Most of what I know came from Internal Affairs and the newspapers."

"Idiot."

Jack's eye twitched. *"Move along. Nothing to see there, partner."* Brodie's voice was insistent now, seeking attention.

About to open his mouth in reply, Jack pressed his lips together, realizing nobody else could hear the voice that taunted him.

"You've remembered something?" The doctor leaned forwards.

"No." What could he say? That unrelieved depression had set him to talking to his dead partner? Back in the hospital, he'd wracked his brain for answers, for any trace of memory as he pleaded, 'I need you, Brodie. You shouldn't be dead. Help me here. Tell me what I need to know.' When the response came, he was so shocked that he spent the next two days in silence, suspecting he was brain damaged. Now the voice intruded at random. It sounded so real.

"Well, you will talk, and I will listen." Dr. Pavic closed the file and leaned back; his stubby fingers peaked into a steeple. Jack's attention sharpened seeing a man experienced in interrogation. "Would you like coffee or water? I don't want you to think of me as your enemy. Rather, you only need to remember two things. You are safe, and I may be the best friend you have right now." In the doctor's gentle tone, Jack could detect no undercurrent or warning at the remark. Despite his reluctance, his spirit warmed towards him.

Jack shook his head and shifted his gaze away to inspect the office space, postponing the inevitable. No stark, modern glass and metal here. Two leather matching easy chairs. A bookcase against the wall, the books lined up behind glass doors, sorted by height into orderly ranks like soldiers. Lighter outlines on the floor disclosed someone had recently moved the furniture. Some remodelling? The overall effect projected a warm and comforting atmosphere for patients. Two diplomas on the wall, one in a foreign language and one in English from the University of British Columbia. Also, two cityscapes; the Edmonton skyline viewed from the river, and the other seemed European.

"It's Belgrade," Pavic said, following his eyes. "I attended university there."

Jack nodded again, finishing his sweep around the office furniture. "No couch inviting me to share my innermost feelings?" He didn't hide the sarcasm.

Dr. Pavic only smiled and crossed one knee over the other. "Your physical recovery seems to be complete, except for headaches?" His eyes swept over Jack's frame as if looking for signs of injury. Jack didn't have any. Not outwards, anyway.

When he nodded, Pavic added, "Don't you wish to remember?"

Jack lifted his shoulders to hide his desperation. He had to remember . . . for Brodie's sake.

"We will get acquainted here, I promise." The man smiled. Not forced, Jack noted. It signalled Dr. Pavic cared for his patients. Or was it just the doctor's expertise at work?

"What choice do I have?"

"None," Pavic admitted. His mouth pulled down, conveying consolation that they were both constrained in choice. "Deputy Chief Durand and Internal Affairs seem committed to a full investigation and requested I flag your file as urgent action." He peered at Jack as if the urgency might be his fault.

"He's only *Acting* Deputy Chief," Jack put in. Durand was the inspector of his detective squad. "Until they find a new one."

Pavic ignored Jack's correction. "So I repeat, I am here to help you recall what happened and find the reason Officer Brian Brodie is dead."

Jack winced at the stark reminder, and his chest constricted. "I want that more than you know. Brodie and I were close. We started in the force together over ten years ago. Internal Affairs as good as accused me of shooting him and causing the accident to cover it up." He clenched his fists, unable to hide his desperation. "I wouldn't . . . can't believe it."

"Is their accusation based on evidence?"

Jack gritted his teeth. "The bullet taken from Brodie came from my weapon. And they have our prints, mine on the butt and his on the barrel. Their theory is that he grabbed the barrel just before I shot him in a last-ditch attempt to stop me."

"As if I'd be so stupid."

"It does not seem sufficient proof for them to charge you outright."

"A murder charge, you mean." Jack squeezed the word out through tight throat muscles. "No. I can't see them going that far." He blew air between pursed lips, saying what he thought of the premise. "There has to be a good reason the prints are there. I would never harm Brodie, let alone shoot him."

Head to one side, Dr. Pavic's middle finger scratched behind one ear as he considered Jack's statement. "There is no personal history in your file," he abruptly altered course. "Where you were born, your parents' names, siblings. Background things that are usually present in a police file." He looked apologetic. "You may think it unnecessary, but your background helps me understand your present condition." His eyes twinkled at Jack. "I am not fond of treating police officers if knowing that makes you feel any better. You all have the idea that you should be asking the questions, not answering them. But get over it, Jack, and things will go much faster. Don't make me guess what makes you tick, as the saying goes."

"I'm an onion patch kid." The doctor's eyebrows became part of his hairline. "An orphan. Brian was my family." A sudden ache made his voice ragged. "I never knew how much I treasured our relationship until he was gone." He clamped his teeth together to stop his chin from quivering.

Dr. Pavic said nothing, and thankfully Jack assumed his technique knew enough to leave him in peace for the moment.

"And you never married? No children?" Pavic's voice was soft, inviting confidence.

"No. At least none running around who look like me." He managed a grin, apologetic for the poor joke.

"Irresponsible rowdies looking like you? When you came out of the hospital with that bush of blond hair, you looked like an alien from The Village of the Damned, green eyes and all."

Jack mentally punched Brodie and continued, "Sometimes, I'm convinced it's lucky I don't have any." It was a lie, but this was not the place to talk of hopes and dreams. "In my job, I see too many who fall on the wrong side."

Jack saw a momentary shift in the doctor's gaze as if he had caught sight of a face over his shoulder. It was so quick that Jack wondered if it was a trick of the light. He dismissed the thought and concentrated on the doctor's questions, noting how he shifted the subject from one thing to another. He seemed good at it, maybe to force his patients to blurt out information. "You were in the army before becoming a policeman."

Jack nodded, knowing it would be in the file. "First Korea, then a posting to Germany."

"Where you learned to be a smart pest." He pronounced it like *psst.* He chuckled at Jack's questioning face. "The reports say you go your own way, have a sarcastic mouth, and resist authority." Eyes twinkling as though sharing an internal fault, he peered at Jack over the paper and tapped his forefinger against his lip. He raised his palm, smiling, painting a secrets-between-us image. "My instructions tell me to concentrate on your years before the army. Is that mere curiosity, do you think?" He shut up, waiting for an answer.

"Probably wondering if I pulled wings off flies when I was a kid," Jack said, feigning boredom. Danger signals began to tingle the back of his neck.

"What strange things you have done in the midnight sun . . . ?" Brodie and his everlasting Robert Service quotes.

"Well, no matter," the doctor continued. Safe for the moment, Jack relaxed, aware a reference could slip in anytime amongst other subjects. "We have something in common."

Jack's eyebrows rose.

"Your military background. I was in the resistance during the war. In Yugoslavia." His expression sobered. He touched the side of his head over the temple, caressing the edge of his scar. "War is not pleasant."

Great, thought Jack. *I'm getting treated by a Commie.* "Am I here to get an earful of Commie logic? Does the RCMP know why you didn't stay in your own country?" Jack shot the questions at him to keep him off the subject of his past, but just the same, he was barely kidding. Hadn't a Yugoslavian been assassinated in Toronto recently? Infiltration of Communist agents into Canada was front and center now, and the Mounties had undercover police acting as students in university to single out Reds lurking there to recruit young idealists who were avid readers of Marx and Lenin.

Pavic threw back his head in a roar of laughter. "Most Canadians aren't as vocal about Communism as you are, Jack."

"Most Canadians haven't seen them at work. Nor had daily in-your-face insistence of how superior they are."

Dr. Pavic chuckled. "Yes. I agree. Tito headed the Communist Partisan's resistance, but it was not the only resistance group. I belonged to the Chetniks. We supported the Royalist Government in exile."

He watched Jack, waiting for him to say something, perhaps remarking on their shared comradeship in military life. "Didn't the Chetniks collaborate with the Nazis?" Jack immediately regretted his rudeness. Why did he care who was or wasn't a Communist over twenty years ago?

Dr. Pavic didn't hide his surprise, either at Jack's knowledge or that he had the gumption to say it aloud. "Not altogether true. Yugoslavia's war is a complicated matter of who, where, and why. Months of discussion would not even probe the top layer." His voice hardened. "But we are not here to discuss my history."

Jack nodded his acknowledgement. Still, an uneasy feeling hung on the sidelines, somewhere in the mist, like a shape not fully formed. Mentally dismissing it, he concentrated on the doctor.

"Tell me what you remember before your accident." Pavic's manner shifted again, now like buddies having a conversation over a beer. A familiar tactic—questions stated in different ways to see if answers varied, indicating he was lying.

"Not much. We attended the briefing about the raid on a biker chop shop. I vaguely remember the team's planned routine, but the raid itself draws a blank." He waited for the doctor to contribute information, helping him along, but Pavic only bent over his notepad and scribbled. Jack bent over his knees, head in his hands, then sat back and took an unsteady breath. Pavic made another note on the pad. "It's like being half-dead. I can remember before and after, so why can't I remember that day?"

"You experienced trauma, and your brain erased it to protect you. We cannot force the memory. Do you have nightmares? Flashbacks which seem unconnected and then disappear? Are you sleeping well?"

"Nothing," he said, not wanting to complain about the hours he spent mapping the ceiling. "Everything I do is to jog my memory. I go to the station as if I am going to work, hoping for some ah-ha moment."

"No girlfriends?" When Jack shook his head, Pavic's expression changed, plainly wondering about other preferences.

Jack wasted no time protesting. "I've had a few."

"A few dozen," Brodie snickered in his ear.

Jack's lips quivered, tempted to voice an open retort to his taunt. "Nothing serious," he offered instead, "not since a girl in Germany." Jack cringed. The words had come out of their own accord. Why did he mention Ursula after all this time? ". . . It didn't work out."

Jack shut his mouth and stared out the window behind the doctor. In the distance, he could see a PWA 737 turning on a flight path towards Kingsway Avenue, targeting the runway at the Municipal Airport. The silence grew. Finally, Pavic sighed, looked at his watch, and stood. "You cannot force a memory, Jack. Do something entirely different with your days. Relaxing things. Shopping. Take in a museum. Talk to ordinary people, not policemen. An idea or clue may turn up. Just write it down. Shall we say Friday at the same time for our next appointment?"

"Watch it! He's anxious to roast your butt over the fire."

"Why so soon?"

The doctor grinned at him and waggled his eyebrows like a co-conspirator. "I have made you a priority, so why not? Besides, what else have you got to do?"

Jack almost blurted out that *his* priority was proving he wasn't a corrupt cop, so he had plenty to do. However, long experience cautioned him. Durand would be front and center, needling the doctor for prompt answers. Nodding to the man about Friday, he left the office.

Downstairs, he swung through the door to the street outside at the same time as a girl coming in. Straight blond hair fell down to her shoulders, and startled blue eyes crinkled in amusement when their voices sang a duet of apologies. As Jack stood back to let her through the door, he thought she was the prettiest girl he'd seen in a long time. Her eyes looked him over, apparently liking what she saw, for she nodded in what he took to be pleasure before she ran to the elevator, high heels tapping on the tile. Flashing a dimple that showed up at the corner of her mouth, she gave him another once over as the elevator doors closed.

Jack watched until the indicator light stopped at the second floor, and he wondered, unreasonably, if she were the doctor's next patient. His training registered her description; early thirties, well dressed, even features, and eyes the colour of bright cornflowers.

Squinting against the direct sunlight, he strode to his 1969 Volvo 164 at the far end of the lot, parked there on purpose to give himself needed exercise. Inside, he grabbed his sunglasses. With no warning, his vision could go wonky on him, and dancing prisms of light would flash before his eyes, leaving him dizzy and with another headache. It had been a cold winter day near the end of March when he regained consciousness, and the aftereffects of the concussion still plagued him . . . among other things: treatments, endless questions, and the cold stares of betrayal and blame.

Jack tuned the radio to CKUA, choosing to think about the girl with blue eyes instead. Louis Armstrong's trumpet blared forth *Love Walked Right in and Drove the Shadows Away*, the notes sweet and clear. Cheered, he smiled. It seemed fitting. From the lot on 109th Street, he turned south towards the river.

Parked at the curbside, a driver let another car pass before he pulled out and followed.

3

AT the first right after the High Level Bridge, Jack drove down the tree-lined Garneau district near the university. One of the oldest areas of Edmonton, it overlooked the river valley with easy access to downtown, neighbourhood coffee houses, small shops, and a heritage theatre specializing in foreign films. He parked in his reserved tenant slot behind the three-story walk up containing his corner apartment. Large east-facing windows in his second-floor space looked out onto a quiet street and let in the early morning sun.

Pharo met him at the door, wagging his curly tail but without his usual chortle. His eyes under his wrinkled brow were expressive enough, and with the way he opened his mouth, or didn't in this case, Jack could tell he still hadn't forgotten the two months' desertion. Someone, Hawk, he supposed, had taken Pharo to a kennel in St. Albert after the accident, for which Jack was silently grateful. When he picked him up, Jack had been subjected to the Basenji smell-over, funnelling in the odours before making a decision. Finally, he stood on his hind legs, his tail swishing with a tentative wave, and Jack bent to have his face licked. Pharo put his full weight against his knee, pressing close as he looked for their way out. Now, two weeks later, Jack made sure he got plenty of attention.

At noon, Jack picked up the telephone off the wall and returned it. Did he dare chance another call to Brodie's wife? Maureen had rejected all of his calls so far. His compulsion to deliver his sympathy in person wasn't the only reason he needed her to pick up the phone. She was the only person who could answer certain questions.

He gripped the receiver again and dialled the number. She answered on the first ring. Not expecting it, he forgot to respond. Sweat broke out on his forehead.

"It's me." He stilled his shaking hand and quickly added, "Don't hang up, Maureen, Please."

"If you think you can come see Ben and me, forget it. Why keep phoning? You're not welcome here."

"Please. I'm not responsible. If you'll just let me—"

"You're wasting your breath, Jack. I'm hanging up now."

"Maureen, wait. Meet me tomorrow. Just you and me. Please."

She hesitated, which he took for indecision and hung up before she could refuse, then immediately regretted it. Maybe she'd assume he was disgusted at her continued refusal. Jack rolled his shoulders, feeling the pain of cramped muscles, telling himself he was tense and getting too worked up. Hands shaking, he slopped coffee into a cup and took it and Pharo outside to the balcony.

How could he show Maureen that he was sincere?

He picked at the ends of his short regulation-cut blond hair as if a solution might fall out like dandruff.

"You're trying too hard, Jack. She'll see through that in a second. Just meet her halfway."

Telling himself to follow Brodie's advice, he drank his coffee and tried to think of other things. Like a magnet, his eyes automatically went to the old lady's window on the top floor of the apartment across the street.

He didn't see her and felt a sudden concern. Was she unwell? He assumed she was old, for she had white hair, and he thought she might be crippled. She reminded him of those sentinels of Europe, the old ladies who policed the neighbourhood from their doorways, eyes missing nothing. Once while staring at her, he thought their eyes locked, so he'd lifted a tentative wave. Her gaze slid past him, leaving him unsure. After that, Jack watched her somewhat sneakily, with eyes partly averted, loathe to seem rude. Still, he liked to imagine they had a bond of kinship.

She must have noticed his weeks of absence, he told himself and sniggered out loud, making Pharo cock his head at him. After all, watching people was her day job, wasn't it?

A wet nose pushed into his palm. Chortling softly, Pharo pawed at his knee.

Jack rubbed his ears and grinned. "Time for a run? Okay. Forget the neighbours, and let's go back to normal." Pharo padded along behind while he collected the leash and doggie bags.

"Emily Murphy Park?" Pharo wagged his tail. "Or the Kinsmen Park? It's closer." Pharo yipped agreement.

Situated in central Alberta, Edmonton lay on the North Saskatchewan River. Historically, the river had served the fur trade, a primary conduit for trading posts scattered around where the city was now. Miles of linear parks and ravine systems divided the landscape into winter and summer recreation spots. The multicultural mix of English and Europeans reminded him of Winnipeg, the place he shunned like a dose of poison.

They took the gate under the High Level Bridge and the path down through the trees to the park. Pharo sniffed every blade of grass and dashed off in ever-widening circles, leaping at any bird he spotted. He found a tennis ball and brought it to Jack, pretending to release it before running off with it, daring him to follow. "Nope. Me, owner. You, dog."

Across the field, he saw Pharo wag his tail at a woman who patted him before walking on. Jack grinned. Pharo was wary of strangers but deigned to be polite when he didn't perceive a threat. The woman's dark hair reminded him of Ursula and his session with Dr. Pavic. The doctor was not what he'd imagined, and Jack didn't dislike him, but he wasn't about to reveal innermost moments of angst. Still, he had easily drawn Jack into mentioning Ursula. He hadn't realized she was still so close to the front of his mind.

He'd met her while stationed at Fort Beausejour in Germany. At a bar during Oktoberfest. She'd leaned up against the back wall, one arm under her elbow supporting the other that held a cigarette. When she turned her grey eyes on him, he was committed.

"Too long in the barracks, Sergeant?" Her voice, low and husky, tinged with amusement at his frank ogling and it made his spine tingle. Dark hair with bangs cut straight across her eyebrows fell to her shoulders.

"Go on, Tuesday, show her what day it is." His three mates behind him laughed and jostled him towards her. They spotted a server carrying three steins of beer in each hand, and with arms on each other's shoulders, the men followed along behind her, leaving him alone.

"What do they mean: show me what day it is?" Her English was good, except for a slight variation in pronouncing *w* as a *v*. She waved the smoke away from her face, then crushed the cigarette against the wall, letting it drop to the floor. Her hips swayed gently in her form-fitting dress as she shifted weight from one foot to the other.

"A joke. My name is Tuesday, and so every day is Tuesday for me. You can call me Jack . . . ." He sounded silly when he wanted to sound interesting. *Scheisse.*

"Hello, Jack Tuesday," she smiled up at him. "I am Ursula."

"Ursula. Any other name to go with it?"

"Do names matter?" Her grey eyes clouded over.

"Yes. What if I want to look you up? I can't wander the streets crying out 'Ursula' like I'm calling for my lost cat."

"Never mind, Jack Tuesday. We shall always set a date for our next meeting. Just before we part."

And that was the start. She'd entranced him—mysterious and beguiling all in one. She forced away any question of her history, but he didn't care. They loved each other, and that's all that mattered. Six months later, he headed for her place with a ring, ready to sign up for the house, yard, and kids. Inside, only that loud silence which shouts emptiness greeted him. Fear rippling his insides, he opened the note she'd left. Just that once, he'd wanted his instinct to be wrong.

Shattered dreams meant he chased glimpses of her which never materialized into a real person for the remainder of his tour. Jack left the army, moved to Edmonton, and after a round of unsatisfying jobs, enrolled in the Police Academy. After five years, he got a sideways promotion to Detective.

The quiet of the area brought him out of his daydreams. The park had emptied of people. Time to go home.

He searched for Pharo and found him staring at the field directly across from him, body rigid in concentration. Jack whistled—Pharo turned his head and then back to the far end. *Don't even think of chasing across there after some squirrel,* Jack thought and whistled again. The beginnings of the familiar jackhammer headache nudged around his temples. A train began its noisy rumble over the top level of the bridge.

Still haunted by the remains of memory, the sun hid behind a cloud and adrenaline coursed through him, shaking his other-worldly antennae. The hair on his neck prickled like it did before battle, paired with a tingle in the small of his back.

Relax, he told himself. *This ain't Korea. Everything is normal.*

Pharo had his nose up, testing the air, still trying to figure out the far side of the field. Needing his medication, Jack left him and increased his pace for the path home, knowing the dog would soon dash after him. A bout of vertigo turned the field into a lopsided view of green grass and blue sky. The train's horn blared in sympathy. Jack bent forwards at the waist to stop the world from spinning.

The wind tugged at his hair, and a pop echoed against the tree trunk behind him. Training drove him to the ground, breath escaping in a whoosh as he landed on his stomach. A wet nose snuffled against his cheek.

"Play dead!" Pharo dropped, jowls flat against the ground, waiting for the next command, but Jack's fright confused him. He pawed at him, sensing anxiety. Heart pounding against his ribs, Jack's indecision whether to get up and run or continue to play dead ended when a foursome carrying tennis rackets burst out of the trees. They bunched up when they saw him, curiosity and caution making them glance at each other. He rose to his knees and pretended to wrestle with Pharo, their presence more welcome than they could ever know.

Someone took a pot shot at me, he wanted to tell them. *If I hadn't bent over, I'd be dead.*

4

ON the way up the path, Jack dashed into the bushes and vomited, retching violently until not even bile spewed up. When he reached the apartment, he made himself check the street for anyone coming to finish the job. On shaky legs, he climbed the stairs and, once inside, collapsed on the couch. His mind recreated the park scene, searching for things out of place. Coming up empty, he rubbed his temples and decided this task required more focus than his foggy brain could manage right now. He rose and tossed a trembling fistful of medication down his throat.

Did he have some memory in his brain that someone didn't want him to remember? What else could it be? Jack groaned his way to his bed, laying on top of the striped blanket tightly tucked under the mattress, army style. One forearm pressed over his eyes, he spent an hour musing who wanted him dead, in between fighting an irrational urge to re-check the locks on both the balcony and hall doors. Eventually, he climbed between the sheets and fell into a fitful sleep.

Jack woke early feeling as if the bullet from the day before had found its target. Every muscle in his body ached, but today was too important to coddle himself. He found the willpower to rise and dress, exiting the building with Pharo just after seven o'clock.

A man lounging on the boulevard saw him, straightened, crumpled a paper cup, and swooped down on him. Jack recognized the skinny frame and bald head of Harry McNaughton, crime reporter. Cops called him *the General*, referring to the WW2 general, Andrew McNaughton, because of his tenacity.

"Officer Tuesday, can I have a few words?" Jack ignored him, swung right, and took the side path to the parking lot. McNaughton followed. "Officer? Care to comment? It will only take a moment."

Jack sighed and stopped to face him. "Persistent little runt, aren't you?" Sensing irritation, Pharo growled softly. "How's this? *No comment.*"

McNaughton stepped in front of Jack, adjusted the strap of his satchel over his shoulder, and grinned up at him like he was Jack's best buddy. "What about your suspension, Officer Tuesday? Care to give your point of view? Did you kill your partner?" He flushed. "Not that I believe them, Jack. But rumours spread and create new versions. I'm your chance to establish your personal statement."

Jaw clenched, Jack gave him the eye. Twenty years on the crime desk, McNaughton kept to the facts and didn't form up sensational tabloid reporting. He had to know Jack couldn't talk about his case, so what did he really want?

"My suspension is medical, nothing more. When the doctor okays me, I'll be back."

Harry's glasses shadowed his eyes, but his face looked sorrowful. After a long moment, he sighed. "Okay, if you say so. You just got out of the hospital, and ordinarily, I wouldn't bother you. . . ."

Jack raised an eyebrow, and Harry grinned.

". . . Well, unless I smelled a story." He moved in closer, and Jack turned his head to the side to avoid his coffee-fumed breath. "Listen, Jack," McNaughton continued, voice insistent, "If you ever need a friend or want information, call me. I *won't* disappoint." His eyes pierced Jack's, and his eyebrows raised like they were making their own statement. He turned and walked off.

"The man makes me itch in places I can't scratch."

Jack nodded in agreement.

Harry's last remark was strange, even for him. One minute he could be a man's best friend, and the next minute, print the off-the-cuff statements people hadn't meant to say. Now he offered support and information? Jack snorted in disbelief. *Sure you will, Harry.*

Halfway down the path, Pharo sat. Jack walked on, nodding good morning to Glen, cleaning out winter debris in the bushes alongside the building. Jack started the car and looked back at his dog.

The Basenji moseyed over to Glen, who put down his rake to pat him. Pharo wiggled around and took Glen's hand in his mouth while the building manager looked over at Jack and grinned.

"Were you telling me porkies when you said he was a police dog? He's not too eager."

"He's a killer when he gets into action," Jack said through the open window and added in a loud voice. "Maybe he could stay with you today." Pharo darted to the car. Glen bent over, snickering with each pull of his rake.

Jack drove down Whyte Avenue as far as 104th Street and turned south to the Duggan area, his expected tail following. Jack could easily evade him, but for now, the tail served his purpose of showing he had nothing to hide. Pharo recognized the familiar direction of the Brodie house and put his paws on the window, making soft squeaky noises. Let loose from the car, he bounded up the path towards the front door just as it opened. Brian's fourteen-year-old son, Ben, emerged carrying his backpack. He saw Pharo and stopped.

"Mom!" he yelled over his shoulder, hysteria in his young voice. He hefted his backpack as a shield. "Go away!" he shouted at Jack.

Hand raised, palms out, Jack stopped and faced him. "I had to come." He swallowed, aware his voice was quavering. "I have to make sure you and your Mom are alright." He drifted forwards a step.

Maureen appeared behind her son, and both came outside on the landing.

Ben's mouth twisted. "No. We don't want you here!" Anger, confusion and hurt flashed across his face. Puzzled, Pharo started to lick his hand, but the boy blinked back tears and pulled it away. Jack signalled the dog back to his side.

Maureen put her arm around Ben and looked over his head with that weary stare of someone with too much on her mind and too little sleep. "It's better if you go." Her clenched fingers on the boy's shoulder contested her outwards calm. "We have enough pain without you coming around to beg for mercy."

Shoulders slumped, Jack could only search Maureen's face, his eyebrows lifted in a query. She stared at him for a long moment and nodded. Jack took the signal and turned back to the car, Pharo sensing the tension stuck close to his leg the whole way. Though he couldn't see them, he could feel Maureen and Ben's eyes boring into him as he went.

Thirty minutes later, after ditching the tail, Jack pulled into the parking lot of the Safeway store, where Maureen was an administrative aide to the store manager. Jack rolled down the windows for Pharo before heading to the in-store coffee shop. Maureen was easily visible at a lone table by the window, her back to him.

They waited for the waitress to bring coffee and a doughnut in uncomfortable silence. She added cream and an envelope of sugar to her coffee. Her dark hair hung limply, which usually framed her face in soft waves. Wearing no makeup, there was nothing to hide the dark circles under her eyes. Sympathy and sorrow followed by renewed anger that a husband and father had been taken before his time tugged at his chest. He reached for her hand to show he cared. She snatched it back, and her mouth turned down.

"Okay, Jack. I'm here against my better judgment, but nothing you say will make up for what you've done." Her voice cracked.

"Maureen, I—"

"Why did you do it? Brian trusted you. You betrayed us." Her eyes looked into the distance behind him, and she leaned her body as far from him as she could.

"I didn't kill him, and deep down, you must know it too." Worried she might just leave, he talked fast. "I wish, more than anything, I could tell you what happened. I swear on everything holy that I'll find out, Maureen." Before he could stop himself, he blurted out, "But you have to help."

She looked into him, and her upper lip lifted at one corner.

"I can't just do zip." Jack poked a forefinger against his head. "There's got to be things I know—hidden away in my brain somewhere." He kept his voice even, determination steadying his resolve. "Someone tried to kill me last night. Which tells me I am right."

Her eyes widened. "What? How?"

"Someone took a shot at me yesterday afternoon walking Pharo in the park." Throat tight, he wanted to rush outside into the fresh air. He felt sweat wet his forehead and focused on breathing. *In. Out.*

"What Park?" Maureen asked, then scrunched her face as if a headache had come over her. "Never mind. Maybe someone wants you dead for killing Brian."

Jaw dropped, he gawked at her, and her eyes fell from his face. Blushing, she bit into the doughnut and placed it back down carefully with two hands. "A police officer's wife always says a little prayer when he leaves for his shift, against that knock on the door which might come anytime. But we never *ever* expect he isn't coming home because his best friend and partner killed him." Face screwed up, she gave a small gulp. "You were so close, the two of you. Like twins, same opinions. He said you were smarter," Maureen scoffed. "Idiot man."

Jack's insides constricted, making him feel like he was choking.

"But it amounts to nothing now, doesn't it? It only means your supposed friendship was all a lie."

"No. We were solid." He yearned to take her misery away, but how could he tell her what he didn't know himself? Only that his gut told him the alleged version wasn't the correct version. "But I can't expect you to feel anything else."

"So why are you here? No. Why am I sitting here is more like it." She shook her head, put her elbows on the table, and clasped her hands over her face.

"I hope it means you have some doubts too."

She dropped her hands from her mouth, now twisted in anger. "The worst of it is I don't know why. I need to know, Jack. Why?"

"I wish I could tell you, Maureen." Senses cramping, Jack's grip tightened around his coffee cup. He had taken friendship for granted, trusting it would prevail forever. Brian, Ben, and Maureen. How long had it been since he actually cried? Maureen must have read his expression, for she reached out her hand to his before sucking in her breath and drawing back.

He choked out a half-chuckle, half-sob. "The first day of training, he was shouting out quotes from Robert Service to urge himself on. All the time, his face split with that big, goofy grin. Drove the rest of us nuts. But it worked. We hustled just to shut him up."

Maureen snickered and pursed her lips. "He did it because it annoyed everybody." Voice wistful, her chin trembled, and she clamped her lips shut.

Encouraged by their new closeness, Jack ventured another question. "Did Brian say anything about his work? Was he okay at home? Different than usual? Please, Maureen."

She bristled but shook her head. "You know he was working more than usual."

Jack perked at the statement; his brows cinched together.

". . . But maybe you wouldn't know. You weren't coming around as much. I asked if the two of you argued, but Brian laughed and said you were both busy." She gave him a stern eye. "Well? Were you on the outs?"

"No." Jack hardened his voice to solidify the truth of the statement. "I can't trust my memory lately but I'm sure of that. There would be the usual shifts and emergency call-outs." Thinking of what she said, his heart did a slow drop. Brodie working more? On what? He thought of another woman for a moment and rejected it as fast. His marriage was solid.

Maureen began fiddling with her earring, not meeting his eyes.

"What?"

She sighed and lowered her voice like she'd been defeated somehow. "He was going to casinos."

Stunned, Jack gaped at her. "Gambling? No way."

Maureen's laugh was short. "I agree. Not much, anyway. I saw him making notes. He said he was figuring out the odds of people winning and losing at the tables." She shrugged. "It didn't make any sense. I accused him of treating me as dim-witted, and he fobbed me off. Said he couldn't talk about work."

Jack forced his mind back, searching for odd activity. Nothing stood out. He'd remembered Brodie spending more time with Maureen and Ben, but had he really been on a case instead? Had Durand given him orders to keep it quiet? It was no secret that Durand disliked Jack. "Where is his notebook now?"

Her face closed, hand reaching for her earring again.

"Maureen?"

"Brian said that you had an ability to see things better than anyone else." She sat up straight, angry again. "That doesn't make sense either. If he believed that, why not tell you about it? Why don't you know?" Eyes narrowed in accusation, she turned away. "You know what I think? He didn't want to tell you. He wanted to show you he could do things on his own without your help." Sniffing, she swiped at her nose with a napkin and crunched it up into a ball.

Her anger hammered at him, pounding him into silence. If Brian had stumbled on a case nobody knew anything about, then a brand new path had opened up. *Oh God, Brian, what were you doing?*

"Maureen, where is Brian's notebook?"

She glowered at him. "He loved you, Jack. But he was a little wary too. He said you liked everything done your way."

"No! We were partners. Always."

Her eyes raked him over, wild, speculating that this might be why he killed her husband.

"No," he softly challenged her. "The notebook. Have you got it? It could be important."

Her shoulders slumped against the chair back. "Ben is so angry, Jack. He blames you. He's not handling his father's death." She looked defensive as if he were objecting. "Why should he? He's only a kid."

A dreadful suspicion made him take her hand. "Ben has it?" His grip tightened, and her eyes widened. "If that notebook has comments about his investigation and includes someone's name, that person might come looking for it. It could be dangerous."

She freed her hand and rubbed it, her face twisting in fear. "Stop it." She stood, the chair scraping on the tile floor. "Scaring me won't work. You can't have the notebook. In fact, when they arrest you for Brian's murder, I'll be the first one to cheer." Maureen hurried off through the employees-only door.

Stabbed to the quick, Jack stared into his cup at the cold dregs and focused on their conversation. She had a point. Why hadn't Brodie shared information with his partner or anybody for that matter? Unless he did report it, and that person held it back. He checked his watch. Still only nine o'clock. He rose, gathered the coffee cups and took them to the dirty dish tray.

A young man entered the coffee area, and Jack saw the relief sweeping across his face when his eyes lit on him. Jack waited until the newcomer paid for a cup of coffee and found a table. As he came close, the man's face assumed a fake expression of curiosity.

"I'm leaving now, and my next stop will be the station. Just in case you get lost again."

"Your kind won't find a lot of friends there." He looked down at his cup, half-smiling as if he knew a secret.

"Listen, son. Next time you follow someone, take a break and follow them from the front. Even switch cars from one day to the next. And if your assignment is to follow me, concentrate on that and nothing more. If you assume guilt, you'll tag everything you see as proof. As sure as I'm standing here, you'll miss something important because it doesn't fit your preconceived ideas."

Lips pulled back in a sneer, the boy told Jack to do something physically impossible.

The temptation to lift him up by his ears and slap some manners into him was near overwhelming. Jack pulled in a deep breath and willed his eye to stop twitching.

"You should learn to control your tongue and not prejudge if you want to make it out of training. The day will come when I am back into service, and you will be a lowly constable if you don't flunk out first. And I have a long memory." His target gave him the kind of grin that said Jack had missed the butt of the joke.

"There you go." Jack turned on his heel, wondering what the rookie would report about their encounter. Then again, the tail had been obvious. *Too obvious.* The uncaring attitude and secret smile rubbed at him like sandpaper.

"Because he isn't a cop?" Brodie sounded smug.

Exactly. Jack gave Brodie the nod. Durand was too cheap to pay for a tail. But then who? The shooter from yesterday? Jack went for his car, worried about Ben. He had to confront him before someone else discovered his father's notebook.

5

LEAVING Pharo at home, Jack continued downtown to police headquarters. At the traffic stop on 99th, waiting for the red light to turn green, he saw a familiar official black sedan travelling across the avenue directly in front of him. The Chief of Police, Alex Mackie. Although he was assigned a driver, Chief Mackie often drove himself. He had been a career police officer, was loved by the entire force and respected for his leadership. Seeing the chief's jaw jutted straight out, moustache bristling, eyes boring under bushy eyebrows, Jack shivered, thankful he hadn't met him coming out of the building just as he was sneaking in. He took it as a good omen for what he was about to do.

"Risk going into that building and breaking your suspension? They'll crucify you." Brodie's warning mocked him as he slid into a visitor parking stall.

"It'll be worth it," he muttered to himself and turned off the engine. Yes, worth it, but only if he got information on the case against him. Not only was it insane, but he'd also have to face the hatred and accusations in the eyes of the men, his former workmates. One whiff of being a dirty cop brought scant sympathy from any officer, himself included. The stench attached itself to everyone in the unit. Jack took his time locking the doors and pocketing the key.

Once inside the six-story building, he scarpered behind some civilians headed for Sergeant Rollie Burton, who saw everyone and everything and presided over the front reception desk with military precision. Praying for the sighted with a hawkeye to be sightless, he made it safely through the door to the stairway and bolted up the stairs. Halfway up the first flight, weakness made him lean against the bannister until his breath recovered. On the third floor, he checked for an empty corridor before going to the squad room at the end of the hall. At his entrance, the chatter and clacking typewriters faded into silence. Every eye stared at him, and jaws gaped in unison.

"What the hell are you doing here?" Paul Wager growled from behind his desk. He tugged at the corners of his moustache, his personal tell that he was about to launch into a litany of charges. He took a breath and waded in.

"Tipped them off, didn't you? But Brodie found out the truth, and it went sideways." His voice turned persuasive, hypnotic, like he was urging a suspect. "What happened, Tuesday? You ducked out of the raid, and he followed you? Saw you hold up a civilian and steal his car? Brodie caught up, and you shot him, then dumped him in the car like a sack of garbage. Your partner. The one who trusted you to watch his back." Wager's mouth turned down in disgust. Everyone, including Jack, stared at him, entranced.

"Was he still alive? Maybe fought back—until you crashed? Accept your penalty, Tuesday. If you're lucky, they might just keep you out of general pop." Wager leaned back in his chair, twirling his pen between nicotine-stained fingers.

Hawk, Vassar, and Ackland turned from Wager to stare at Jack.

Jack held strong even though every nerve in his body shrieked out in protest. "If you say so, Wager. You think you're right, but I'd give odds you aren't."

"Oh, that's right." Vassar snickered from the sidelines. "You don't remember a thing. Convenient."

Wager ignored Vassar and continued his tirade, "That cruiser you torched on the raid. If the chief has his way, he'll get the cost deducted from your pay."

Even Jack smiled at that one.

"He's serious. You'll be in debt for a long time with your wages."

Jack raised his shoulders, uncaring. "Now you know why the captain always goes down with his ship." Someone snickered.

"Company," Hawk warned softly.

Everyone put their heads down. Jack hustled over to Hawk's desk and hunkered down behind it, half-hoping he didn't look as silly as he felt.

"*Told you,*" Brodie congratulated himself.

"Stand up, Officer Tuesday," Deputy Chief Durand's voice rang with authority. "What part of the word *suspended* don't you understand? Who let you into the building?"

Correct and pressed, Durand's narrow shoulders barely filled his always excessively tidy uniform. Face red, his body shook with rage. He gazed at his hands as if wondering how he could put them around Jack's neck, then clasped them behind his back. Dark eyes sent lightning bolts at each officer, searching for a culprit. Jack wondered how he always managed to look as though he was the master inspecting his servants.

"*Turning water into steam wherever he goes,*" Brodie offered.

Many wondered, over an after-hours beer, how Durand had made it as far as Deputy Chief of Police. Jack wondered, too, to a lesser extent, being familiar with army life and the logic of military promotions. Watching him as he rocked on his feet, he could imagine a baton stuck in the crook of his arm. His gut told him that Durand had been military once.

"*Don't question his authority. God shouted it down.*" Brodie was on a roll.

"Well?" Durand's eyes bored into him.

"Sir!" Jack obediently stood to attention, killing the desire to snap his heels together. "I hoped it might trigger a memory of what happened that day, Chief. Nobody wants the truth more than I do." Hawk shuffled his feet, and Jack shut up. The chief's mouth turned down in revulsion as if Jack had handed him a doctor's note revealing a dose of the clap.

Hawk jumped up and took Jack's arm, quickly pulling him away from the desk. "I'll see him out."

Steve Hawken was the best sergeant in their Criminal Investigation unit. Tall and slim, he presented an invincible front to running down suspects and getting convictions. Hawken's reputation earned him the nickname Hawk, and behind his back, the Bird.

Expression sour, he led the way down the stairs. "Only have yourself to blame. Idiot. Breaking suspension rules doesn't help your case."

"How did he know?" Jack asked. "Mr. Perfect Chief. So spic and span, like he expects the Governor General might invite him over at any moment. I can just see him at home. Getting into bed in his pressed pyjamas between pressed sheets."

Hawk's lips clamped tight like he was trying not to laugh. "You could ask him for a reference to his tailor. Your fashion sense compares to a warthog's."

"Hey," Jack protested.

"What was that malarkey you spouted off about hoping to regain your memory?" Hawk snorted, giving his opinion of Jack's excuse. "Or did the accident cause your brain to short circuit a few neurons too?"

Outside, Hawk turned and faced him.

"Can we talk?"

"I can't help you, Tuesday." His face set into an angry line. "You aren't too upset about Brodie's death. You may not remember the crash, but Brodie was a good cop who always had your back. He didn't deserve to die like that." His words must have triggered a new idea, for he gave Jack a searching look. "But I noticed the two of you weren't so joined at the hip as you usually were. Like you had a disagreement. Was that it? Did you get rid of him because he knew something you didn't want reported?"

The vicious accusation rocked Jack back a step. "No! We were tight. Like always."

Hawk's expression closed, shutting off a reply before Jack could think of one. "Well, in this place, you're guilty unless you have proof otherwise. Now is not a good time to ask for help."

Jack bit back a fiery retort. Antagonizing Hawk wouldn't get him anywhere. "You're wrong if you believe Brodie's murder doesn't affect me."

Hawk's head snapped around. "Murder?" He repeated, eyebrows raised.

"Yes, it was murder. But I didn't do it."

"And you remember that?" Hawk's eyes challenged him.

"I don't have to. I'd know with or without memory."

Hawk snorted and turned to walk away. Jack grabbed his arm and held on. "Hawk. Please."

The sergeant sighed and crossed his arms.

"Thanks for taking Pharo to the kennel."

Hawk's face remained immobile, waiting.

"And I need your opinion. . . . Is Wager still tight with the Rebels?"

Curiosity flared in Hawk's eyes. The Rebel Motorcycle gang were the ruling bike lords in Edmonton, a one percenter outlaw gang. Wager had the most information about their activities, and his investigations involved a lot of give and take with the gang members. Jack quickly looked around, ensuring nobody was interested in their conversation.

"I was targeted last night. Someone with a rifle in Kinsmen Park. Could you persuade Wager to ask a few of his contacts if a Rebel member tried to take me out?"

That got his attention. "What?" Hawk dropped his arms.

"It was a serious attempt, Hawk. If I hadn't bent over with a dizzy spell, the crows would be picking over what's left of my brains." His throat tightened at the memory, and he hid his trembling hands in his pockets.

"Why the Rebels? It could have been anyone." His sneer accused Jack of pulling feathers from the wind.

"Because the raid on the Rebels that night and Brodie's death are all connected somehow," Jack insisted. "Nothing else makes sense.

Something out of the ordinary happened that night. Whoever took a pot shot at me thinks I know more and am a risk."

"Quite a stretch to ask Wager then, isn't it? He'll think you're suggesting he's in tight with the Rebels, questioning his loyalty. Who's next? Me? Or maybe the entire unit? Just stop right here." He backed away from Jack as if he might be contagious. "You're on suspension. That means just wait it out at home. Getting involved will make things worse for you." He turned away and took a step back towards the building.

Jack groaned. It had all come out wrong with implications he didn't mean. He tried again. "There's more. Brodie's wife thought he might have been on a case."

Hawk paused, then turned to face Jack again. "What case?"

"I don't know. Maybe one on the quiet."

"There's been no hints of covert cases." Hawk paused, brow puckered. "Brodie working a case that even his best buddy knows nothing about?" He peered up at Jack, eyes squinting in suspicion. He tucked his bottom lip under his front teeth and looked around for anyone nearby. Giving in, he sighed. "Okay, what do you want from me?"

"Details of the evidence against me and what they gathered at the crash site. Wager said I stole a car. Whose car? Where are the witnesses?"

Hawk's mouth gaped. "I'll try to find out what they have against you, but it's all in the evidence room and snooping around in there is out."

Two officers came by, leading a suspect in handcuffs to the cell block. They circled them, darting accusing looks at Jack and curious ones at Hawk.

"Just leave, Tuesday, and don't come back." Hawk's voice was close to shouting now. "Internal Affairs are preparing a charge of murder as we speak. Wait for your day in court, just like any other citizen."

Stunned, Jack could only hope Hawk's final jab was for show.

Left staring at the familiar station door now closed to him, Jack remembered Durand's anger. Was it that Jack had violated suspension rules? Or because, as Hawk had let slip, the charge was imminent, accusing Jack of the murder of a police officer? What was the crucial evidence? Why were Internal Affairs waiting?

"They need Dr. Pavic's report, you stupid clot. So let's all play nicey-nice."

Brodie's judgement didn't help. An ominous sense that he was about to become the proverbial sacrifice began a slow, icy march through Jack's marrow.

6

LATER that same afternoon, Jack parked his car along Ben's route home and began to walk. Reluctant to confront the boy so soon after the emotional outburst that morning, he knew he had to start somewhere. Thinking of ways to approach, he watched Pharo mosey back and forth along the boulevard, outing peculiar odours and relieving himself over top of them. Every so often, he'd gaze back at Jack, either checking on him or looking for praise at his research. One block later, Pharo suddenly dashed ahead and took a flying leap at Ben, yodelling in pleasure. Laughing, Ben hugged him until he realized Pharo couldn't be alone. He straightened and watched Jack approach, rebellion front and centre.

Jack stopped in front of him and kept his voice neutral. "Can we talk?"

The boy pulled his mouth down, a picture of teenage bad temper. "My mom won't like you bugging me." He shifted his backpack, then let his arms hang straight, hands clenched in fists.

"I'm not stalking you, Ben. Your Mom would understand." Jack knew Ben would tell her, and he sincerely hoped that it was true. Still, it was necessary. Jack spread out his hands to show he meant no harm. It didn't work.

"If it wasn't for you, my dad would still be alive." His voice changed mid-sentence to a croak. "I hate you." Close to tears, the young vulnerable face looking up at him twisted Jack's insides.

"I loved him too, Ben. Inside, you know that. And I'll find out what happened if it's the last thing I do. You can help."

Ben looked at him sideways now, his curiosity overcoming the rest of his animosity. "How?" His body slumped. Perhaps now that he had rid himself of his pent-up rage, he might feel better.

In sympathy with Ben, Jack tried to look relaxed, hoping it would help him do the same. "Your dad's notebook. Your mother says you have it."

Ben's face reddened and set in mulish revolt. He made to shove past Jack. "No! It isn't yours, no matter what you tell me. Besides, I don't have it. I threw it away. Honest."

If someone assures you he is honest, Jack wanted to tell him; it surely means he isn't. The boy's raised eyebrows emphasized the lie.

Jack sighed. "Ben, this isn't a game. Holding on to it can be dangerous. What if someone comes looking for it? That person won't give up, and you and your mom will be in real trouble. At least, if I have it, I can investigate any clues it might hold."

"Get away from me!" Ben's shrill cry echoed across the street. A couple on the other side looked over in alarm. The man stepped towards them as if wondering whether he should intervene. Ben took the opportunity and escaped. Jack grinned at the couple, raised his shoulders and spread his hands in the exaggerated lament parents give about kids and their quirks. Satisfied, the couple moved on.

Ben's figure shrank farther down the street, along with Jack's hope of getting the notebook. "Want to go to the park, Buddy?" At the magic word, the dog did his dance of anticipation. Less sure, Jack hoped the bushes wouldn't include someone pointing the business end of a rifle at him.

On returning from a thankfully uneventful outing, Jack stopped at Woodward's for much-needed groceries. More from habit than enthusiasm, he added a tray of geranium pots from the gardening stand to his cart before he joined the cashier's lineup. Stowed away in the trunk, the pots with a few lonely red blossoms didn't seem as cheerful. So a liquor store was next—never mind the medical cautions about mixing medications and alcohol.

Back home, and under Pharo's expectant eye, Jack chopped up

a piece of liver, cooked it, and put it in the steel bowl, trying not to make a face. He added chopped raw carrot to the dog's pungent dinner and placed it on the floor while Pharo pushed his nose between his legs to get to it.

"Hey, easy. You know better than that," Jack chided, stepping over his dog, who had already forgotten he was there. A smile threatened to crack his serious demeanour, but the feeling was short-lived. He shuffled over to his LP vinyl collection and sorted through them until he found Billie Holiday and popped it on the turntable. He took a bottle of Pilsner outside, leaving the door open to hear *God Bless the Child*, hoping the music would inspire fresh ideas.

Investigation of a crime was like engaging in gossip, peeling back layers of wickedness to expose the guilt behind a target's smoke and mirrors. He should follow the same technique now.

Jack lowered himself into the dusty chair on the balcony, both him and it groaning. The answers were out there, but he needed to know who had them.

"Would you recognize any helpful answers even if you asked the right questions?"

"Who knows until I ask?" he shot back out loud, then clamped his lips together, hating that he was answering an imaginary partner.

Well, no mistaking today's answers, he thought after a moment. Nobody was interested in searching for Brodie's actual killer while they already had him in their lineup of one. The attempt on his life had to be connected to Brodie's death, and planning an offence was the best defence. But what offence? He had to find a crack in the story.

"Or cause a crack and see what comes tumbling out."

"Sure, Brodie. Suspension may be permanent," Jack replied, accepting the idea he was losing his mind.

"So what? You favour the alternative? Or just sit around and wait for the inevitable decision?"

Brodie was right. A void closed in at the prospect, threatening to take not only his survival but the essence of his life. Pain up the back of his neck signalled the start of a headache. He gave up thinking and took Pharo outside for his nightly bathroom break.

Inside, he dragged his body into bed and inspected shadows on the ceiling, planning his war.

7

A wet, dreary afternoon matched Jack's disposition as he drove to his Friday appointment. Dr. Pavic's receptionist, Jassy, greeted him with a brilliant smile of white, straight teeth. The slight gap between the front two added to the warmth of it and threatened to lift his spirits.

"He's waiting for you," she said in her lilting Jamaican accent. "You can go right in."

He found Dr. Pavic in the same glum state without his usual *here we are, you can trust me* face. He had his office re-arranged again, the desk and chair placed away from the window. Why?

"Must be true that these doctors are weirder than their patients."

Or maybe Pavic had a strange interview strategy to see if patients noticed the room change. How could they not? He decided not to bite in case it gave rise to another one of the doctor's probes. Jack sat down, telling himself to curb his imagination.

He watched the doctor's fingers fiddle with a pad of note paper, then pick up the picture frame beside the pad, peering at it as if he'd only just found it. He returned it to his desk. "No, it's absurd," he muttered under his breath, but Jack caught it. Eyebrows almost meeting the deep furrow between, he shook his head again, denying some inner musing, and yanked at the chair across from Jack as if rebuking himself. "If you had children," he said when he'd sat down, "you'd find you never stop worrying about them. Yesterday, someone robbed my daughter's apartment."

"She reported the robbery?" Jack responded politely but told himself a robbery couldn't be all that had upset the Doc. Why call a robbery absurd?

"Oh yes. Scared her enough to encourage her to move. Someone found her a bigger apartment on the south side somewhere. Closer to the university." Dr. Pavic looked at Jack's raised eyebrows while he reached for his cigarette pack. "Let us begin our business with something positive. Like telling me you had a memory."

"Zero on that end." Jack kept his expression neutral. "But after our last meeting, someone tried to shoot me full of holes."

Dr. Pavic's hand froze in the middle of lighting his cigarette.

"In Kinsmen Park below the High Level." Jack's voice wavered. With a deep breath, he steadied himself and described what happened while Dr. Pavic watched his face and listened without interruption.

"So, " he said when Jack finished. "Do you have any theories?" He inspected the end of his cigarette, stubbed it out and immediately lit another.

Jack needed Brodie most at this moment, trading ideas and dialogue about the attempt on his life. And the possibility of it being included in the doctor's report cautioned him. "This is confidential, right? You don't report every golden drop out of my mouth?"

"No, Jack. I assured you at the start. Internal Affairs receives only my conclusions, whether I believe you are lying or if you need further help. But the shooting may have been accidental. Target practice?"

Jack searched the doctor's eyes for signs of doubt—that he might think him paranoid.

"No responsible rifle owner would use a public park for target practice. I concede anyone can own a rifle, but shooting at someone in public? No, that attack on me was either for real or a warning." The memory sent icy tremors down his back.

"If I'd been there, I would have searched for a shell casing."

"The tennis players distracted me," he found himself answering. His brain must be more out of whack than he thought. "Probably a .303," he added, pretending he was replying aloud to his own questions.

"Tennis players?" The doctor radiated confusion.

"A group of tennis players appeared just at the crucial time to prevent another go at me."

"At worst, a contract killing, then." Dr. Pavic mashed his cigarette stub in the crystal ashtray joining the collection. The stale air in the room confirmed the doctor was a heavy smoker, and Jack breathed through his mouth. "Revenge for your police work, perhaps?"

"I can't think of a case which singles me out in particular."

"How do you know?" He smiled, his eyes reflective. "What if you have dangerous information? Perhaps connected to your present condition and lost in your memory?"

Which matched his own theory. Still, he wasn't about to admit he agreed in case it went into the doctor's report.

Dr. Pavic opened the file, read his notes then faced Jack. "I am thinking we should try hypnotism."

Images of a North Korean sergeant and a room in the camp flashed before him without warning. He pushed the image away, only for it to be replaced with another one just as bad: himself in a trance, babbling about his boyhood.

The doctor read his expression of horror. "Don't worry. Subjects are aware of what is going on. We open locked doors to see what is behind them. If you get a feeling you are not here, in this room, it is because you are in that memory. In the place where you forgot. I will tape the session, and you can listen to it after." He leaned back, his chin tilted up, and chuckled. "Your chief likes the idea. . . . He suggested you are deliberately floating along on the river of forgetfulness."

Durand's idea, then. Beads of sweat broke out on his forehead.

"Not going to happen. Doctors have already discounted hypnosis. Yes, the concussion gave me plenty of distress in the hospital at first. Anxiety, temper, but I'm told I will remember in time."

"Post traumatic amnesia. I am aware of that, Jack. To a certain extent, I agree. But hypnosis will relax you. What have we got to lose?"

"Wouldn't he like to know the answer to that question?"

Pavic peered at him, eyebrows raised. "You won't regress and confess to a secret past." He laughed outright.

Near panic at the thought made Jack thrust his hands under his legs to stop them from shaking.

The doctor's eyes narrowed, assessing. "What's wrong?"

"Nothing, Doc," he lied. "But it's a no-go. Out of the question."

Dr. Pavic leaned back in his chair, shaking his head, stubbornness tightening his mouth. After a long silence, revelation crossed his face. He looked in the file again, letting his eye scan quickly. "You were a P.O.W. in North Korea. Did they try it there? I'm sorry, Jack, but . . ."

Jack turned his head to stare out the window towards the dome of the provincial legislature grounds dominating the sky in the distance.

The doctor rustled the cigarette package, and this time Jack creased his mouth in aversion. Sighing, Pavic returned the cigarette to the box.

"As bad as my daughter. Okay. Tell me about your fellow officers, the ones you work with. About your experiences with them." His voice sharpened, no doubt exasperated by the lack of cooperation. "Hypnosis or not, you must talk, Jack. Most surely, a spontaneous remark will lead to a memory which triggers another one. Trust me. Years of experience have rewarded me with knowledge about how the mind operates."

Jack's patience snapped. "Why can't you accept my recent memory is toast and report that?" He forced a mild tone as if his objection were reasonable. "Even if there are no charges against me now, what I say can be misinterpreted. Will I effectively damn myself? It's how they work. Internal Affairs will charge me with willful murder if only to protect themselves in the public eye. You are putting me into a position where I'm damned if I do and damned if I don't."

"Pay attention, Jack." The doctor's argument was calm and persuasive. "My report is the only pertinent document. I will decide what is relevant and what is not. Internal Affairs has no case if I deny their interpretation."

"IA pestered me every minute in the hospital," Jack confessed, a growl in his voice. "My story over and over. So many times, they'll be busy until Christmas trying to find inconsistencies."

"Then, why not give it a chance, hmm? Or do you already know something that you don't want revealed?"

"Don't use that one on me, Doc. I won't agree just to prove I am not hiding anything."

Dr. Pavic chuckled, his patience unending. "Don't look so sour, Jack. I am not your enemy. In truth, I'm likely your only hope."

"This guy talks too much. Shut up, lay back and go with the flow."

Jack sighed deep into his chest. Not even the voice in his head was on his side this time. So he leaned back and started with Hawk, not hiding his admiration. A policeman's policeman who would make Chief one day. As sergeant, he was informally acting in Durand's position as Inspector. "Next is Paul Wager. A big man who looks fat, but it's mostly muscle, and he can move fast. His advantage is being light on his feet. People who've underestimated him have lived to regret it." Jack stopped, wondering if he should go on.

"But?" Pavic prodded. "You have reservations?'

"Nothing in particular puts my guard up. Might be a hangover from the army. Other ranks always held back from the brass, and Wager is too deferential to Deputy Chief Durand. But mainly . . . he openly blames me for Brian's death." He bit down on his cheek before adding, "without reservation."

The doctor took the opportunity to dive deeper. "I can tell that bit of knowledge hurts."

Jack swallowed hard and decided he'd had enough of personality readings. "The last two are Mark Ackland and Hank Vassar. We work well as a unit. Vassar is new and only needs to grow out of puberty."

Dr. Pavic raised his eyebrows at that. "And you, Jack? How would you describe yourself?"

Annoyance flared again, mainly because Jack hadn't expected the question.

"Ha. Smart mouth. Move along, folks. Nothing to see here."

"Cynical, I guess. Maybe too many years observing the military hierarchy." He shrugged, hoping he had muddied the waters enough.

"Perhaps your war experiences have made you see the world as it is, unclouded by innocence." Dr. Pavic hummed a bit more as if adjusting his mental notes. "You've missed one, I think?" He remarked at last. Gentle.

So Jack talked about Brodie, aware this was Dr. Pavic's primary interest. Their friendship from the day they entered training together, their high fives when time saw them partnered. They worked well, feeding off each other with challenges and questions when on a case. About Jack's inclusion in family outings, special holidays, and personal life.

"I'll be crying in a minute. Stop already."

What would he do now that he'd be excluded—and without Brodie? Jack kept on, unaccountably comforted by talking about him. He only omitted his theory that Brodie may have been on an investigation nobody knew anything about. That and the fact that he still talked to him. . . .

By the time his session ended, prisms of coloured lights danced at the periphery of his sight. Nauseous, the band around his head tightened with each note of Dr. Pavic's irritating humming while he jotted notes. He stood at the desk while the doctor checked his appointment book. "Next Friday," he said and pushed a card at him. "Today's session may provoke a memory. They have a way of leaping into our brains when least expected. Please phone me if one happens."

Jack ignored his plea, more interested in the photo of Dr. Pavic's daughter propped up in front of him. A face that had been at the edges of his mind all week—the girl he'd bumped into after his last interview.

8

THE long weekend stretched before him. Early on, he walked along Saskatchewan Drive. Pharo pushed against his leg, telling Jack they were buddies. The dog probably sensed his mood and anticipated another visit to the boarding kennel. Jack gave his ears an enthusiastic rub, and Pharo wiggled in ecstasy.

Although cool, the morning air had that smell of spring which promises fresh green things and coming warmth. Below and on his left, melting ice out of the Rockies drifted eastwards in the sluggish river current but would become swift in the days ahead, swelling the river banks.

"Just the kind of day for a family picnic."

The reminder that there would be no more picnics with Ben, Maureen, and Brian knifed through his midsection. Jack turned and headed for home and a shower.

He left Pharo chewing his favourite shaggy old rope and dragged his feet to the bathroom. Starting the shower, he stepped inside before the water had time to warm and braced his arms on the wall. He stayed there, head pressed against the tiles welcoming the cascade of against his shoulders until hot water turning cold again forced him out.

Dressed and feeling only slightly better, he took a bun filled with layers of bacon and egg outside to the balcony, Pharo tagging along behind.

The old lady across the street appeared at her window. She bent her upper body, turning it from one side to another, as people do when they are expecting someone. It ruined his image of a woman in perfect solitude, her loneliness absolute. Interest piqued that she might have a visitor, he leaned forwards, his spirit willing to help her spot whoever it was she was waiting for. His eyes followed hers, searching.

A moving van appeared, gears grinding. It slowed and then stopped in front of the building. Her eyes centred on it. Sudden distress knocked him back in his chair. Was she moving out? An inexplicable disappointment twisted his mouth.

"Jeez. I never thought you'd start going all maudlin."

Silly ass, he agreed. He didn't even know her, nor had she even acknowledged his presence.

A Honda, gold hatchback—his mind wrote the details—came alongside the van, then slid into a parking space. Jack watched as the Honda's driver spoke a few words to the movers and started up the path to the apartment building. She paused at the doorway to turn and inspect the neighbourhood, giving him a full view. A rush of warmth enveloped his chest, and he leaned back into the chair cheered.

It was her.

Half an hour later, timing his actions with the movers, he crossed the street and followed as they carried a load into the elevator. On the second floor, he held the door for them, accepted their thanks, and watched them disappear into the apartment at the end of the hall.

On the way outside, he stopped at the panel, which listed resident names. His fingers noted the name against the third-floor apartment number above its twin location on the ground floor.

Heading back across the street, he climbed the stairs of his apartment two at a time. He rummaged in the kitchen cupboard, filled a measuring cup with sugar, set it aside, then waited until the movers closed up their van and left. Catching Jack's energy, Pharo padded to the door. He wagged his tail in hope, then slouched back to the couch.

Doubting his own sanity, Jack didn't blame him. Covering the cup with his hand to avoid spillage, he carried it across the street and buzzed her apartment.

From inside, a voice called out what he took to be 'who is it?' though the sound was far away, too muffled to be sure.

"Delivery," he answered.

Soft footsteps padded closer, and finally, the door creaked open cautiously.

"Hi." He put one arm up against the doorjamb in what he hoped was a casual lean and held up the sugar. Following its line of flight, she took a startled step back.

"Welcome to the neighbourhood." Turning on his best grin, he pointed to the cup. "Saves you the trouble of asking your neighbours for a cup of sugar."

Eyes blue as a summer sky zoned in on him; Jack saw a flash of recognition.

"We ran into each other where my father has his office."

Jack nodded, not hiding his delight. "Right first time. Jack Tuesday." He pushed the cup at her again. "The sugar is just an excuse."

She smiled at that, exposing the dimple at the corner of her mouth. He peered over her shoulder into the room. "You look like you could use help sorting and whatnot. I can offer a muscular arm." At her hesitation, he added, "Standing before you is a willing go-for who brews a mean coffee."

"Should I check your credentials first? Ask the police?" She gave him a wide smile, but at the same time, he felt her scrutiny, giving him the once over.

Jack bowed. "At your service. But the others won't bring sugar."

"Bribery works." She stuck out her hand. "Bianca Pavic. But I suspect you already know that." Jack switched the cup to his other hand, freeing his right. Her handshake was firm and confident.

The apartment was larger than his. The walls were painted a pale beige, and the floors combined golden oak hardwood and carpet. Jack took the cup of sugar into the kitchen, updated with an avocado-coloured stove and fridge. The effect was both engaging and relaxing. Bianca indicated numerous boxes, which he stored in the second bedroom for later sorting and arranged furniture at her direction. He started with the bigger jobs, assembled the bed which the movers should have done, but happy to prove his boast, he said nothing. An air of relaxation told him they were both comfortable, easily joking and trading information. He told her he was her father's patient, presently suspended from the force, and why. She told him she taught European history at the university and moonlighted as a French language tutor.

She bent over a box, opened it and looked inside, then kicked it, sliding it towards the kitchen. "My turn," she said, her voice muffled from inside the box. "Were you always a policeman?"

"I spent time in the army. Korea, then Germany afterwards." She shot him another quick inspection. "A bit young, weren't you? Lied about your age, I expect."

"Not by much," he admitted. "The Korean War looked like an adventure." He kept his voice light, passing over it.

"Bet that didn't last long." Her bottom lip pushed out as she blew a piece of stray hair from her eyes.

They started sorting her bookcase. Tolstoy, Dickens, and Shakespeare, and enough for a row of history and language books. He picked up Orwell's *Nineteen Eighty-Four* to read the blurb on the back cover. "I don't suppose you remember much before coming to Canada?"

She took Orwell from him, staring at the title for an overlong moment. Concluding he'd been overly inquisitive, he opened his mouth to apologize when she answered, "Impressions mostly. Moving from place to place, dodging raids. A vague memory of my mother. She died during a raid." She rammed the book home with some force.

Their easy familiarity was turning sour. She was hiding a lot more emotion than she let on. Jack watched her shoulders rising up to her ears. The distress of unwanted memories, signs he recognized in himself. *Korea.*

"Unpleasant memories stick around," he said, his tone matter of fact, understanding.

"Yes." She let her forefinger roam over a row of books and then shrugged. "They belong in the past. When my father and I arrived in Canada, we made a pact that we wouldn't let the past get in the way of our future."

"My motto too." He came up behind her, put his hands on her shoulders and turned her around. "Are you hungry?" he asked, hoping to lift her mood.

Her face cleared. "Starving, now that you mention it."

"How about I go for takeout? Save making yourself a meal."

"Too tempting to refuse. And you chopped a day's labour off my move." Her eyes crinkled at him. "You aren't just another *poseur*, are you?"

He brought back two sandwiches, roast beef and egg salad, for sharing half each, and a container of cucumber and tomato salad with a Danish to finish. She had laid plates on the round, chrome kitchen table, ready for his return. So he laid out the food, and they both ate in relative silence.

When they finished, she examined him, biting her lip. Her eyes had that same gleam which reminded him of his unit commander. The *predator on the hunt* look.

"Do you catch all your fugitives, Jack?" She bent her head in the same way as her father asking his questions.

Intuition told him her question was not idle curiosity. Grimacing, he cooperated. "Most of them, fortunately."

"I was robbed of an extremely valuable painting." She rose and went to the newly stocked cupboard. Taking out two coffee mugs, she raised them at Jack inquiringly. He nodded, and she filled the cups and readied a tray of cream and sugar. Anticipating what was coming, he wanted to run but took the loaded tray from her instead and led the way to the coffee table.

She veered off to the bookcase, took out a volume and brought it back to the table, pushing the coffee tray to one side to make room. *Art of the World*, Jack read.

"Peter Paul Rubens." Leafing easily to a page from long practice, she jabbed her forefinger at an illustration. "Here it is."

Jack dutifully peered at the coloured reproduction. Two women faced each other, one holding a chubby baby, the other's hand lifted towards the baby in greeting. Lurking in the background shadows behind the woman and baby were two men, heads together. Their furtive glances past her shoulder were like bystanders witnessing something of curiosity. The painting left no doubt the baby was the focus of attention. The caption read, "Mary greets Elizabeth, mother of John the Baptist." Oil on canvas, 615 x 523. About 24 x 20 inches, he estimated. Artist: Peter Paul Rubens.

"It doesn't do justice to the real thing," Bianca said. Her nearness gave him the urge to reach up and pull her down beside him. Instead, he examined the picture again and admired the almost translucent flesh tones of the women and baby—like porcelain. He marvelled at the near photo quality old artists managed to create.

"Years of protecting it, keeping it safe from destruction and looting. It's freakish that we lost it now."

"And you've had it for how long?" He had to ask.

She jerked away from the book. "Are you asking because we might have stolen it during the war?" Her eyes dared him to agree.

"It never crossed my mind." It had.

"It's been in our family for over a century." She pointed to the book's notation below the illustration—Circa 1635. Location: In private collection. "And you won't find this item on any list of looted art. Readily available lists." Her eyebrows arched as she said the last.

He berated himself for the question. "The investigation will include a record search of known art thieves. Someone may already be in their sights." He spouted the usual words, instinct telling him to keep quiet.

"You could find it," she said, her tone matter of fact, as though she wanted him to fetch a loaf of bread on the way home. She shifted to the edge of the couch, looking pleased with herself.

"Whoa, Nelly." He laughed to cover his dismay. "I'm suspended. Sticking my nose in an active case will make it permanent."

It didn't discourage her. "Suspension gives you time to chase the robber. That painting is the last permanent link to our ancestry and it's precious to us." She leaned forwards, her chin set in a determined line. "There must be some way you can help without getting into trouble. Contacts, people who buy stolen art for private display, someone who doesn't care where it originates. They cannot sell it in public without provenance."

Involvement was out of the question, but he was intrigued despite himself. "Who is the investigating officer?"

Her shoulders lifted in a shrug. "My father told me his old friend Inspector Durand promised to put their best art expert on it. Whoever he appointed doesn't seem too anxious to get to it." Her mouth turned down.

Jack gave her his full attention. "Hold on. Your father knew the deputy chief before?"

"For a coon's age." She waved away his remark as irrelevant to the stolen Rubens. "From the war, I think."

"Durand is Yugoslavian? Be careful. . . ."

Stunned, Jack blurted, "But his name—"

"So what?" she mocked. "It isn't unusual to change your name if it's difficult for English people to say. My father would not. Besides, his doctor's degree, the name on it . . ." She stopped and gave him an annoyed grimace. "That isn't the issue, Jack. Your help is."

Jack half-conceded, not eager to damage their relationship before it started. "I'll take a stab at their progress on the case, but with small hope. Right now, I'm as popular as the measles, and I can't go near the building."

"Well, it's something." She rewarded him with a grateful smile, teeth white and even. Pulling the elastic from her ponytail, she let her hair fall to her shoulders, and Jack curled his fingers with the urge to run them through its thickness. Sighing with relief, Bianca flopped against the couch's back. "Okay, I'm done for the day."

Jack accepted his cue to leave.

At the door, he turned. "I forgot. The lady who lives upstairs. Her name is Zamborski. Do you know her?"

Her eyes squinted at him, reflecting. "Why?"

"Her apartment windows face mine. Before you drove up, she was at her window, watching the street like she was expecting you. I thought . . ." he stopped, letting her pick up the thread.

"You really are a policeman, aren't you? A woman looks out her window, and you suspect her of . . . what, intrigue?" She giggled. "Would she like to know you spy on her?"

He flushed, conceding defeat. "Okay, I'm going. My dog will be antsy by now. I'll introduce you next time."

"Next time?" A corner of her mouth turned up, affecting false modesty. "Are you hitting on me?"

He smacked his forehead. "I'm getting rusty. I thought I was being subtle."

"A cup of sugar is novel, I'll admit."

He had a new thought. "Next Saturday? Dinner and a movie. How about it?"

Her eyebrows rose, surprise lighting up her face as she swayed closer to him. "It's a date."

He stared down at her, and she lifted her face to him, which he took as permission to kiss her cheek goodbye.

Back in his apartment, Jack's buoyant mood sobered. He hadn't been wrong about the old lady expecting Bianca. Odds were that she was the person who lured Bianca to her new apartment. But why evade his question and not just say so?

"Not all roses there. Time to get serious about Durand or whatever his

real name is."

"Thanks for the reminder," Jack replied.

"Sidestep into that trap, and your suspension will be permanent or worse."

"Get lost, Brodie. I know what I'm doing."

9

WHILE eating breakfast, Jack remembered the geraniums still packed in the trunk of his car. He carried the half-dead plants out onto the balcony. Aware the exercise was only a pretense at being normal, he arranged them around, fed them fertilizer and water, and told himself they looked perky. Pharo stood on his hind legs to sniff for intruders.

"Keep your paws out of the dirt," Jack ordered, getting a mournful glance in return.

His gaze flickered to the old lady's window, wondering if she had seen his gardening efforts, then recused himself, forestalling Brodie's ridicule that his curiosity bordered on obsession. Boredom and isolation had led him into fabricating a mystery around her. A mystery which wasn't real and thrived only in his imagination.

Later that afternoon, Jack answered a curt rap at the door.

"Ah, there you are," said his neighbour from across the hall. The professor's clipped tones suggested Jack was late for class.

"May I?" Sharp brown eyes appraised Jack under bushy eyebrows, rejecting refusal. "Of course, Professor Waterman." Jack stepped aside, curious. An unwritten code amongst the residents kept them on nodding terms, friendly yet respectful of privacy.

Once inside, Pharo circled around him and sniffed, beginning with the shoes. When he switched to the trousers, Jack snapped his fingers. With a soft whine of protest, the dog padded away.

Jack apologized. "Drink?"

The professor smiled an acknowledgement. "Please, and call me Warren."

Jack brought out two bottles of Pilsner and glasses. He opened one, handed it and a glass to the professor, then sat with his own, appraising his visitor. Bow tie, dress pants. Sleeveless vest over a striped polyester shirt. Thinning hair plastered down on either side of a precise part. English, or history, Jack surmised.

"You said you're retired . . . uh, Warren?"

"I continue with private tutoring. Those working on their master's degrees. I miss the company of students." His eyes sharpened on Jack. "Didn't you attend at one time? I notice the older ones."

"Night classes in criminology when I left the army."

"I thought so." Looking smug, he lifted his beer glass in a salute, murmured cheers, and gulped at it. His eyes slid past Jack to the bookcase—at his store of vinyl LPs and elaborate stereo equipment.

"Grundig. It's German engineering. Lucky you."

"Great sound," Jack agreed, pleased the professor had recognized it. A silence settled. One ankle resting on his knee, Jack fidgeted. What did he want?

As if his message had beamed over, the professor began, "It's about the new tenant on the third floor."

"I hadn't noticed. A new student?" Odd subject, he thought. "I'm sure Glen grilled his pants off before he gave the okay. What makes you uneasy?" He kept his voice casual.

Waterman shifted his feet, shook his head, and looked at the beer dregs in his glass, trying to get a reading.

"He's no kid. I believe he belongs to a biker gang."

Jack's antenna quivered. He shifted his ankle on his knee, hiding a sudden interest.

"Why?"

"What?"

"Why do you think he belongs to a biker gang?"

Waterman raised his eyebrows as though to say it was obvious. "Tattoos, dress, big boots, his whole manner. You know, tough guy, don't-mess-with-me type. He can't have a proper job, not with greasy hair and a chain around his neck." Waterman gave a nervous titter.

"His presence in this neighbourhood worries me. What if it's to sell drugs on the campus?" He waved his hand. "I know drugs are already here, but so far, it's weed." He looked at Jack. "I came to you because you are a policeman."

Waterman had the grace to blush. "Well, you'd recognize his sort."

"He's weird. A Fusspot? Or something else?"

Jack dropped his eyes from Waterman and smiled. "Have you asked Glen?"

"I thought you might ask him. Supposing he brings trouble to our building? The police? It's legitimate for you to be interested in a biker gang member. And bearing in mind . . ." Face turning rosy, he trailed off.

Jack leaned forwards and placed his glass on the coffee table, controlling his anger. "That I am under suspicion myself right now?" He finished, imagining himself lifting the professor up by his vest for a vicious shake.

"God." Warren's forefingers rubbed his forehead. "Sorry, Jack. I have a habit of blurting out statements to get a rise out of my students. It sounds trite, but I am here because I believe you're as straight as they come."

Jack kept silent, not stooping to assert his innocence to someone as innocuous as the man before him.

"Mud sticks. People always question."

"I'll see what I can do." He wouldn't. How many promises had he given this week? Satisfied, Warren left.

Monday morning, Jack lounged in bed, drifting on a murky cloud of depression. He flopped over on his side, shielding his eyes from the sun's rays piercing the Venetian blind slats. He needed a new angle.

Like nails scraping a chalkboard, he heard his father's voice. *"Useless schite."*

The rasping curse drove him to his feet. Damned if he'd allow it. Out on his backside. Forever disgraced as a dirty cop. He stretched out on the floor and began a set of fifty push-ups. If it affected his stability or eyesight, he'd stop and do another at night. The goal was his average count of two hundred.

He refreshed in the shower, where he promised himself it was time to impress upon Ben that giving him the notebook was not negotiable.

As if sensing determination, Pharo achieved his in-the-car routine faster than usual, but Jack's resolve waned when he saw Hawk's distinctive red Trans Am barricading Brodie's driveway. He parked further along the block and slunk down, feeling like a sleazy investigator looking for immorality. It wasn't long before Hawk appeared, along with Maureen and Ben, who said something to Hawk and ran to hop into the front seat. Jack could taste his excitement at riding in the sleek car. Hawk stowed a picnic basket in the trunk, and Jack watched them all drive off in the other direction.

"Hey, what kind of a pal is that?"

Jack pulled his mouth down. *Hawk and Maureen?* He stayed where he was, disoriented with the idea, then forced his mind to deal with his own stalled plans. Reaching into the glove compartment for a pair of gloves, he shoved them into his pocket, then let Pharo out of the car and inspected the street. Nobody there. The pleasant weather had lured everyone away from yard chores to parks or the country. Telling Pharo to come, he sauntered along the sidewalk and slipped into the alleyway. Moving fast, he checked the backyards along the way and ducked behind the unkempt hedge shielding Brodie's house. "Watch," he whispered. The dog hunkered on the grass.

Gloves on, Jack twisted the back doorknob and opened the door.

"You gotta talk to that boy about leaving doors unlocked."

Jack went down the hallway from the kitchen to Ben's bedroom. A boy's room, school texts, a workbook, and comic books were strewn across the unmade bed. Jack's eyes scanned the area, guessing a boy's classic choice for a hiding place, under the mattress, the school bag on the floor under Ben's cast-off pyjamas, and the back of the closet shelf. Ditto a dresser with drawers half open. Instinct led him to a wicker bin beside the dresser lined with a brown paper bag. Beneath the paper bag was Brodie's familiar notebook.

He scanned each page, starting at the end with the last notes. Nothing stood out. Disappointed and puzzled, he considered replacing the notebook when he noticed the crumpled edges of pages farther along in the unused section. They were four pages of illegible notes. Hoping Ben hadn't looked through it enough to miss them, Jack tore the papers out, folded them into his pocket, and replaced the notebook in the bin.

Driving back home, he thought of Hawk, able to make Maureen and Ben laugh as they got into the car. Something he couldn't accomplish. And when had he ever seen Hawk smile, let alone laugh? He gripped the steering wheel hard.

"Admit you're pulling a snit because Hawk's taking out my girl. Forget it, pal, and get on with it."

It's too soon, Jack excused himself but took Brodie's advice and got down to his next task. At home, after he started the coffee pot, he sat and numbered the pages to maintain their order. Brodie's familiar squiggle brought a lump into his throat. Fingers shaking, he lifted the first page and deciphered the late February date—after they were assigned to investigate an anonymous tip on illegal betting. Jack recalled their progress. The racetrack, a prime source, was closed for the winter, so they quietly toured secondary resources: bars. Patrons arriving and departing without seeming to drink indicated they came for other reasons like placing illegal bets with the bartender or supposedly playing pinball. Cheap to install and needing little maintenance, pinball machines played a large role in generating illicit revenues. Easy enough for bar owners to accept cash from a source and launder it as trade profits. Who could prove it didn't come from pinball machines? Bar owners received a nice cut for saying it did.

Bored, both thought the whole exercise a waste of time until Jack was assigned to a rash of robberies along Jasper Avenue. Jewelry stores, news shops, and wine stores, where thieves performed quick grab and runs. With silent thanks to whomever, Jack twiddled his fingers goodbye to Brodie and encouraged him to keep slogging. Had he stumbled on information and kept it, thinking he'd make a slam dunk?

"You told me to have fun doing the grunge job."

"You kept quiet because you wanted to spring a big discovery to show me what I'd missed?" Playing games.

Jack turned Brodie's squiggles on its side, squinting at the curved marks, circles, and straight lines. Not Brodie's familiar shorthand. Jack's brows knitted together. Was it to hide a name? One recognizable? Maybe the entire town would recognize the name. Jack curled his lip. That could refer to anyone in the city, from the mayor to a provincial politician. And why would a public figure even risk being seen in suspicious circumstances? But it meant that Brodie would be tempted to find convincing proof before reporting.

Jack began pacing. Brodie worked late trying to connect the person he saw with the illegal activity. *Damn fool.* Not telling him did explain the impressions that Jack and Brodie were on the odds. He dared not imagine Brodie so foolish as to take down the perp himself to claim the collar. The unit had a strict protocol for information sharing, an unbreakable prerequisite. Doing otherwise would only bring big trouble. Grunting in frustration, Jack resumed pacing, then stopped short. *Unless . . .*

Unless someone in the unit was a dirty cop. Another reason to use a code to hide a name. Heart thumping, Jack shuffled the pages to the end and read the quote:

> *It's bully in a high-toned joint to eat and drink your fill*
> *But it's quite another matter when you . . . Pay the Bill.*

Another Robert Service. Was it only a doodle? Yes, perhaps a doodle but also a clue towards identity. A person who pretended to be grand, using someone else's money, but not for free. Forced to pay the bill, so to speak. But doing what?

"Putting on the Ritz, Jack. Putting on the Ritz."

The answer was in here somewhere, in the code. Did three squiggles represent articles? No, most people skipped articles when jotting quick notes. Jack smacked the pages down on the table. They might as well be Viking runes for all the sense they made.

10

JACK squeezed the car into the last parking space at the rear of the Riviera Hotel at Whitemud Drive and 104th Street and headed towards the bar. As soon as he opened the door, the crowd noise of holiday chatter, laughter, and the clink of glasses slammed into him at full force. Sight adjusting to the room's dim lights, he wound past the crowded tables to a slight figure at the back. His thin shoulders slumped around a glass of beer as if it were a crystal ball showing a road map to hidden treasure. Jack sat in the chair across from him.

"The man of the hour," Apple greeted him. "Been awhile, Jack."

Apple was Hugo McIntosh. Inches shy of Jack's six feet, Hugo looked even shorter, hunched over the table. He and Jack had served together in Korea and in Germany. In the beginning, both recruits, Hugo introduced himself to the barracks, emphasizing his name wasn't pronounced Mc-Intosh, but Mac-Intosh, "you know, like the apple." Later, baptized by beer, he became Apple.

Drinking had become Apple's primary medication to lull his terrible memories of Korea, and Jack made it a point to keep watch on him. "Have a beer. Near lunchtime." Lunchtime was anytime Apple drank. He held up two fingers at a server, smoothed his hair and then did up the top button of his shirt, showing he was together. "You got a new haircut," Jack obliged.

"It's called a mullet." He eyed Jack's short back and sides. "You need one. Get with the change."

Jack shook his head. "Regs. They only allow a moustache, and I don't like them."

Apple wrinkled his nose. "I heard you were in the hospital. I would've visited you, only they might have kept me there." He snickered at his wit. "What happened to you?"

"A car accident. And my memory's shot."

"Lucky you. Everybody should have stuff they don't remember." The beer arrived. Apple chugged what remained in his glass and handed it to the server. Jack laid a two-dollar bill on her tray. "You're lucky," Apple repeated. "Drink up." He raised his glass. They each sipped and contemplated each other in silence.

"Do those times haunt you, Jack?" Apple ran his finger around the rim of his glass collecting foam, then licked it clean. He added a few choice words, none of them complimentary. Apple regularly asked, and Jack always answered, "It's better to picture it happening to someone else." His own nightmares were of more recent events than Korea.

Apple nodded, but this time his eyes were steady and appraising. "You beat the bastards at their own game. I always wondered how— you made them doubt themselves like you knew something they didn't. How'd you do it, Jack? How'd you stay strong in that shitty camp?"

"Maybe because we were young and full of it. Showing them what Canadians are made of?" Jack gave Apple's arm a playful punch and repeated what he always said. "Keep it in the past."

Apple nodded as if Jack had said something profound. "Right. None of us ever signed that asshole's paper though, did we? That's what we're made of." Apple sat up straighter and smacked the table with his palm. "Is it true you been hammered out of the cops?"

"No. But suspended for something I didn't do. Your ear always hears gossip, things which aren't public or make the news." Jack searched Apple's face to ensure he was paying attention and his eyes weren't glazing over while his mind drifted into empty spaces.

"Like who's doing what and things of that nature?" Apple nodded wisely, then slapped his palm on the table again, making the glasses jump. "You hear the one about the piece of stolen art?"

Jack's eyebrows rose. "One stolen just over a week ago?"

Apple brightened. "Ha. Funny you should ask," he said as if he hadn't brought up the subject. "Whoever stole it got ripped off. It's a phony."

"Which? The robbery or the painting?"

"Yep. What I said." Apple mumbled, shaking his empty glass, his eyes drawn to Jack's like a magnet. Jack dutifully waved his arm above his head until he caught the server's eye and indicated another for his companion.

"Anything interesting about me and my partner Brodie?" He'd better get on with it before Apple and his beer got too buddy-buddy.

"Maybe." Apple slurped his drink. He gripped Jack's forearm. "Gruesome stuff about you knocking off your partner. A lot of malarkey."

His predicament had to be pretty dire when the only person who believed in him was a buddy suffering from war jitters. A rush of warmth flooded over him.

"What's the word?"

"You tell me." Apple shot him a look tinged with doubt. "You were there, weren't you?"

"So I'm told, but the accident knocked out my memory. It's a complete blank."

Apple hooted. "Were you drunk?" He brought his face closer. "Drinking on the job isn't like you. Something else bothering you?"

"Other than being blamed for murder? I've had the official version. Is there a street version?"

Apple leered at him. "The odds are four to one that you're guilty."

"Bets have been laid? Where?"

"Anywhere people can place a bet, Jack." Apple grinned, looking pleased he knew something Jack didn't. "That you're a dirty cop. A few giggle and tap the side of their nose as if it's a setup. I pay attention to the ones who only nod and stay real quiet."

"Anyone say what it's about?"

Apple paused. "Mixed up talk. Some go on about a raid on the

Rebel's chop shop near Sherwood Park." Apple caressed his beer glass. "Others claim it was in the Northwest. But they all agree that the raid went sour because it was leaked. Might be a setup. Interested, are you?"

Jack nodded, venturing whether Apple was confused. It wouldn't be the first time. If the Rebels had a tip-off, why didn't they do their usual turnabout into a bona fide body shop before the police arrived? "A setup? Anything else? Who and why?"

"Talk is that an out-of-province gang is looking to control the Rebels."

Jack blinked, confused at the switch of venue. What did a new gang have to do with the raid?

Apple continued on his line of thought. "The Rebels already have their hands full with the Airborne Regiment. So you can imagine how unhappy they are about some guy called Fingers Jackson moving in and bossing them around."

"Jackson?" A snake slithered around inside his stomach.

"Some big crime boss out of Winnipeg. They must already be on your radar, being an organized gang and all." The corner of Apple's lip turned up, scorning. "You scared?"

Jack grinned, his lips numb. Afraid he'd start gasping, he clamped his bottom teeth over his top lip, forcing his breathing to slow.

"Get back to the main subject."

"What about the raid, Apple?"

"I got an idea. Want to hear it?" Apple was on a roll. "The Rebels know they'll only be used for gang dirty work and get nothing for their trouble. So the Rebels are not happy about the takeover, and the big honcho of the gang needs a way to convince them. So he tells the cops about the chop shop and creates a big ruckus when they turn up for a raid. While the Rebels are checking over their shoulders, the gang moves in and saves them." Apple spread out his hands, palm up. "That's about it, except . . ."

"Except?" prompted Jack, all attention now. Apple's musing

sounded credible, albeit taking the winding route.

"You should ask the reporter. He knows something."

Jack blinked and traded his estimate of Apple's mentality with an urge to shake him. "Which reporter?"

"That guy who reports on crime."

"McNaughton?"

"Yeah."

McNaughton had waylaid him last week, but what information could he have that wasn't already in the papers? "Can you poke around, Apple? I need some names, leads I can follow." But his friend hunched over the table again, his mind slipping into new areas.

"I'll make it worth your while," Jack added and immediately regretted his error.

Apple jerked upright. "That isn't necessary. You taking to insults now?"

Jack flushed, humbled. "I'm sorry. Things come out of my mouth these days I never intended." He paused, then took a gamble. "It's because someone used me for target practice last week." Apple's jaw gaped open. Jack filled him in. "It would be a bonus if you heard some talk on the street, who did it, who ordered it. You know."

"Jeez, man. Okay, give me a few days. It's been nice, Jack, but I have an appointment at the Legion now." Eyes wide, Apple stared at the table, a hint that serious brainwork tended to haunt him with visions he couldn't forget.

Jack stood his ground. "One more thing."

Apple remained in a trance in that place of his own.

"Brodie's notes." Jack took the sheets from his coat pocket and shook them at him. "I have to know what it says."

Apple stirred. His hand reached out for the notes and saw the squiggles. His fist clenched, and meekness turned to stark resentment. He glared at Jack, face red with anger. Any other time, Jack might have appreciated the switch.

He shoved the papers against Jack's abdomen. "Take them back.

Work like this makes bad things happen in my head." He scrunched the pages in his fist.

"It's a code, Apple. You're the only person who can help me. I'm drowning otherwise."

"No. Stuff it. You can't make me." Apple made to throw the papers on the floor. Jack gripped his hand and applied pressure, squeezing until the man winced.

"I'm calling in a debt, Apple. Remember Kai Tae?"

Face white, Apple's lips moved. The accusation in his eyes shrank Jack's insides, so he quickly made a play to vanity instead. "Brodie made up the code himself. It'll be a snap for you."

Apple fumbled the sheets with unsteady hands, then rolled them up and shoved them in his jeans pocket. "I need a couple of days, then I'll meet you here again. Keep away from me until then."

Chest aching with tightness, Jack watched as he staggered on spongy legs towards the exit door. Bringing Kai Tae into the equation had left an indelible stain on their friendship.

Behind the bar, the bartender watched Apple stumble by before he turned a blank accusing stare in Jack's direction. A voice from his past hurled into his head, his father telling him, *You poison everything. Always have, always will."*

11

JACK picked at his supper of a thrown-together omelet and salad even though his growling stomach reminded him he hadn't eaten since morning. Ignoring Pharo's expectant face, he scraped the lot into the garbage and opted for a beer instead.

With a Pilsner in his hand, Jack spent the evening on his balcony, watching cars and people, wending home from their holiday recreation. He rose to check plant pots for moisture and saw a man in a vest and jeans walking up the path to the building entrance. Jack registered his stats. Medium height, burly arms inked with tattoos, jeans buckled under the beginnings of a beer belly, and blond hair tied back in a ponytail.

Warren Waterman's biker.

Breaking his confident stride near the doorway, he glanced up at Jack. It was an indifferent glance, no curiosity, just bold awareness with a dash of challenge. He turned and disappeared into the entrance, leaving Jack staring at the empty space, his mind calculating and sorting impressions, filing away his conclusions. At last, he smiled, knowing they were right. The biker had singled him out, but why?

Legs outstretched, Jack rubbed Pharo's ears and watched the shadows playing tag with the rays of the setting sun through the balcony rails. He checked the old lady's window and saw her leaning against the panes, peering at the street, eyes never wavering from whatever caught her attention. Jack followed her sightline to the intersection and a man standing at the traffic light standard. Stocky build, medium height, in a suit too large for him, dark blue and rumpled as though worn for days. The electricity between the old lady and the man's returning stare sent signals coursing through Jack.

He eased out of his chair and into the apartment, then took a pair of binoculars from the end table drawer. He remained just inside the shadows of the patio door and focused the binoculars on the old lady's face. A mixture of recognition, surprise, and fear danced across her features. One hand clenched the drape, and the other covered her mouth. Magnified by the glasses, the sight made him suck in his breath. One half of her face was scarred and frozen into a mask. He kept the glasses trained on her for a long moment digesting this new information while her stare remained fixed on the corner. When he remembered to focus on the man, he was gone.

"Stop with the frills, Jack. A wandering mind and all that. . . ."

Jack obeyed and put his binoculars away. Still, his imagination hadn't cooked up what he'd just witnessed. Curiosity aroused in new proportions; he promised to make her acquaintance after setting his world to rights.

The door buzzer announced a visitor. Jack peered through the eyehole at a face that told him his day was about to get worse. As soon as he opened the door, Hawk brushed past him into the room, turned, and faced him. "What the Sam hell were you doing at Maureen's place today?"

So they saw him after all. "Come right in and make yourself at home, Hawk." Jack stalled. "And why do I need your permission to visit Brodie's family?" He waved to a chair. Hawk didn't move, so Jack sat down on the couch and looked casual. "Did Maureen ask you to come here?"

"You were parked at the end of the block," Hawk said. "Like a stalker."

"Hardly," Jack laughed. "Both of us there would have made Maureen uncomfortable. So I parked, assuming you were just leaving. When you drove off together, I had my answer." Jack kept his tone reasonable.

Hawk finally sat, and Jack pressed on with his offensive. "You were the last person I thought I'd see. You were never that close to Brodie."

"The unit always takes care of the families of slain officers." The sergeant looked straight at Jack.

"Well? Did Maureen send you?"

Hawk's face reddened. "They didn't see you. But Ben told me he didn't want you anywhere near them."

He waited for Hawk to mention the notebook, but he didn't, so Jack tested the waters. "Brodie always said that I should have his notebook if anything happened to him. Ben refuses to give it up."

Hawk's lack of response told Jack what he wanted to know. Ever the investigator, hoping silence would confirm what he suspected. Again, Jack obliged. "Whatever Brodie was investigating is there, in his notes. Probably includes the killer's name."

Hawk's lips pursed with a soft hiss of air. "Give it a rest. God, you are so thick. The evidence points to you. All the more reason you should not have the notebook."

"But there's a lot of unknowns, isn't there, Hawk? Why haven't they charged me? Why won't they show me what Internal Affairs has?"

"Nobody is letting this go, Jack. I've heard IA is waiting for the shrink's report, but it's you beyond a doubt."

"I thought you had my side in this. What's changed?"

Hawk made a slight noise in his throat, which sounded like 'hah' to Jack, and his eyes slid away towards the balcony window again. But not before Jack saw an expression he couldn't read. He persuaded himself it was embarrassment.

"I can't let personal views cloud the evidence," Hawk said. A trifle piously, Jack thought.

"Their best evidence is my piece. There must have been a lot of weapons thrown around that night. How do I know someone didn't plant it? Why won't anyone let me see it?"

"That bang on the head scramble your brains?" Hawk gave an impatient scowl as if he were arguing with a dimwit. He got to his feet and went to the balcony window to stare at the street for a moment, then abruptly swung around to Jack again. "Since when does the accused handle the evidence," he shouted down directly in Jack's face, drops of spittle raining on him. "Especially with your fingerprints already plastered all over it. So you can claim they happened when you held it in the evidence room? Fairy dust, Jack."

This argument was going nowhere. Jack came back to their original issue. "Have you got the notebook?" His pointed question indirectly accused Hawk of double-dealing in his visit to Maureen, and the knowledge set Hawk's face into grim lines. A denial now would only underscore an admission.

A small smile tugged at the corner of the detective sergeant's mouth. "People work in different ways to survive, Jack."

Hawk's motherhood statement was the last straw. Jack deliberately took his time to rise and stand, staring directly into Hawk's face, daring him to continue. They stood that way for a long moment, Jack hoping, but whatever Hawk thought, he kept it to himself. There was no acknowledgement that Brodie's notes might contain information in Jack's favour. He left it, fearing added disappointment.

At last, he shrugged, went to the door and opened it in a rude invitation for Hawk to leave. Hawk obliged without another word. Jack leaned against the closed door.

Another friendship kicked to the wall.

Without Hawk on his side, the chances the rest of the unit would come around were zilch. Instead of gaining allies, Jack was isolating himself, one by one.

12

ARMS flailing in vain attempts to exit a burning car, Jack jerked out of the last remnants of sleep. This time, an Asian face leered through the flames, mocking him. Such memories rarely appeared, but yesterday's mention of Kai Tae to Apple haunted him. Seeing Apple as imperfect, Kai Tae used his power over the captives to take sadistic torture to new heights. Aware he was sliding into self-pity, Jack threw off his tangled bedsheets, did fifty push-ups, added fifty, then let a hot shower drain off the remains of tension slinking around him.

After breakfast, Jack phoned the Edmonton Journal and asked for Harry McNaughton.

"Name?"

Jack recited his phone number. "I have a story if he's interested." He at once hung up, relying on the General's curiosity. Twenty minutes later, his phone rang. "I've been thinking of our meeting last week," Jack said. "Let's get together. This morning, if you're available."

"Hang on." Jack heard a rustle of moving papers, then Harry instructing someone to put it on the editor's desk.

Harry's voice lowered to a whisper. "Do you know Faucets?"

A cafeteria and coffee bar. "The one on 104th?"

"Eleven o'clock." And McNaughton hung up. So unlike his usual wheedling method.

Was Apple right that McNaughton had information? Hope blossomed in his chest, and Jack went to get ready, spirits buoyant for once.

Before meeting Harry, Jack drove across the High Level Bridge and turned East onto Jasper Avenue to the Bay department store parking structure. He walked into the store and up the escalator to the third floor, where he inspected the furniture, tested a few chairs, and waved away a hopeful salesman. Downstairs in the men's section, he spotted the tail right off, sorting through a rack of trousers without enthusiasm. Jack headed to the fitting room with a pair and stood as if waiting for a room to open up while glancing behind him. His follower switched his eyes from Jack to his watch and turned to finger a display of shirts.

Jack dropped the trousers and slipped behind a group gathered by a pole with a flashing blue light, listening to a sales pitch on jewelry items. He continued out to the street, sprinting for a bus a half-block away. Holding onto a strap, he stooped to look out the back window. Satisfied nobody followed him, he exited the bus at the next stop and hailed a taxi.

Ten minutes early, Jack entered the small café tucked into a strip mall South of Whyte Avenue and looked around for McNaughton. He saw a skinny arm seemingly unattached to anything, waving at him from a booth beside the door to the kitchen. A good choice if you want a conversation in private. He went towards it, and Harry's familiar bald head and spare frame emerged. Two mugs of coffee were on the table with Danish buns, keeping them company.

"They're still hot," he said before Jack sat down. "They make the best toasted Danish in town. Try it."

"The best?" Jack smirked. "What can you do to ruin a Danish?"

McNaughton's fingers scraped two napkins out of the dispenser and handed one to Jack. "They make their own." As if that explained it.

Jack obediently pried a forkful away. Not too sweet. The melting butter hadn't yet ruined the crunch of the toasted side. He nodded approval to McNaughton and tried the coffee. "So, Harry. You begin by telling me what you got, and I agree to do the same. I don't remember much. Well, nothing, actually."

McNaughton's eyes drilled into Jack's for a long moment.

"Are you wearing a wire?"

Jack's jaw dropped. "Of course not. I'm suspended." But on second thought, it was a valid question and raised a new suspicion in his mind. "Are you? Is that why you're here? To get some kind of confession from me?"

McNaughton laughed wildly like someone who'd had a fright and realized it was only imagination. "No, definitely not. You'll see."

Jack caught the relief in his voice. Interested, he held his coffee and leaned against the booth. "Okay. You go first, Harry. Tell me about it."

"They organized a team to go on a raid," Harry began.

"I know that much," Jack interrupted. "Who was on the team?"

"It was over 114th Avenue, at the Industrial Park." Harry squirmed as if he had sat on something unpleasant.

Jack held up his hand, surprised. "Bremner Park? But the paper said Sherwood Park."

"If you keep interrupting with details, we'll be here all day." McNaughton waited. Jack gave him a zip-my-lip gesture. "You should know better than to read the paper. Smoke and mirrors."

Jack thought he remembered the pre-raid briefing. Had he only chosen Sherwood Park because he'd read it in the paper?

"That explains the Groat Road."

It shook him. What other parts of his memory were unreliable?

"The place alongside the Harley-Davidson dealership," Harry continued. "Both owned by that upstanding businessman we never name, but in reality, deals with the Rebels."

Jack's mind sketched what he knew. The attached body shop was the chop shop. The front end looked legitimate enough, but the building behind, supposedly a deserted warehouse, was where the stolen cars were separated from their VIN numbers. By the time the owner reported the theft, the vehicle was already en route to a foreign country.

"Quick and efficient, these people," Harry said, reading his thoughts.

A waitress arrived with a coffee pot, and they waited while she refilled their cups. McNaughton asked for a glass of water, and she nodded and moseyed her way back to the front, topping up coffee cups as she went.

"To answer your question, Jack," he continued. "It was the brand new task force team from the Northwest who commanded the raid. Apparently, they were a couple of men short, and Deputy Chief Durand nominated you and Brodie to supplement the team."

"That makes no sense." Jack couldn't help but butt in. "Why not a task force trainee? The regular force only shows up with the warrants to make the arrests."

McNaughton shrugged. "Ask Durand." He nervously fiddled with his napkin, rolling and folding it over and over. "My opinion—and this is definitely between us—it was a plan designed to fail."

"The thought crossed my mind. But how do *you* know all this?"

"I got a tip-off about the raid, but not from my usual source. A note followed by a phone call with time and place."

"Any idea who wanted you there? Raids are never advertised. Especially to the press."

"Some person, or more than one, knew what was going down and wanted me to record the balls up. And it was set up for the police to lose, no doubt about it. I'm thinking maybe the bikers tipped me off, so I'd print it and embarrass the police. But I was there to record the fireworks. Who won," McNaughton paused, ". . . and who got killed."

They sat in silence. "And did you?" Jack said finally, not able to stop the waver in his voice.

"I did." McNaughton's tone flattened, determined.

Jack held his breath and waited.

"It went bollocks from the first. I parked down the next street. It was cold, the streets icy as hell." He hunched his shoulders and shivered as if he could still feel it. "At the corner to the target site, I hunkered down behind a parked truck, pulled my toque over my ears and waited. You and Brodie arrived first, a few minutes before the task force unit. I took some pictures, but they didn't turn out." His mouth turned down. "And I didn't dare use a flash. Anyway, I've seen plenty of raid procedures, and this one looked all wrong. You and Brodie stood apart from the group, sniffing the air like a pair of lost cats. You both zipped over and joined the team, got into the huddle and had a brief conference. Afterwards, everybody kind of melted away in some coordinated direction."

Jack nodded. "The task force moves in a pattern which only makes sense to them. Let's skip that part."

"But shouldn't you and Brodie have been with the task force squad in their vehicle? Why come separately?"

Jack stared at the crumbs of the Danish on his plate as if their pattern would spell out the answer. "Because we aren't part of their task force," he ventured. "We had a different role. A diversion to stop any guards from giving the alarm. Drive a patrol car up in plain sight as if on routine night duty. Nothing unusual in two cops checking things out. Right?" Jack grinned. "I forgot about that part of the briefing."

"*Patsies, both positioned front and centre.*"

"Two police officers from the detective unit *'usual?'*" McNaughton curled his lip. "Well, I guess it worked. All quiet. Not even normal car noise from the building, no lights, nothing. Nothing to see, nothing to hear. I assumed you knew the plan." Harry paused and shifted his shoulders, looking unhappy. He darted a look at Jack from under his eyebrows, then away.

"What?" Jack encouraged.

"A surprise party. And the shooting started. Wild, like a bad western. I hugged the ground against the back fender and poked my nose around the edge. I heard shouting, confused panic noises. Then, someone dressed in black ran from the building towards your patrol car. He tried to open the door, ran around, and tried the others.

Tossed something underneath and took off.

Jack tried to keep up. It was as if someone were describing a movie, but he had difficulty picturing the scenes in real time. Especially the actors. Who was this lead actor creeping up on the squad car? He raised his eyebrows at the reporter.

"No," McNaughton answered the unstated question. "I couldn't see if he was thin or fat. Or even what group, biker, or cop or whatever."

A burst of flashing images snapped up Jack's head. *Fire.* "He torched the car."

"You remember that?"

Noise, shouting and the cold. Hanging onto someone, pulling him down the sidewalk. Blood. Heat and smoke. A car door, a person half-in, half-laying on the seat. Kneeling beside Brodie, shouting an order for an ambulance. Jack voiced whatever hodgepodge of images swept into his mind, scattering across his brain with increasing horror.

"We had a Motorola. I thumbed it and got no answer. Damn radios are useless, no range. Nobody on the other end! Blood all over. Brodie dropped his weapon. I picked it up and shoved it in my pocket . . . carried him to the car. A couple of sitting ducks." Jack halted and searched his mind while staying focused on McNaughton.

"Did any backup arrive?" He wanted to reach across the booth and shake Harry until the answers spilled out from him. "Something you said. The one who blew up the car. What made you wonder what side he was on?"

13

"*THE* way he moved. His actions. Military. A cop. The thoughts popped into my head, but I'm sure of it." Jack's eyes bored into McNaughton as he spoke. The reporter stared back, his own gaze unwavering. "Which means the entire process was dirty, Jack. In fact, Mickey Mouse cartoons are better planned."

Jack clenched his fists. The same great, gaping pit opened up in his mind. Blank. He ground his teeth at the obstruction. "Why don't I remember if anyone came? And how did I get on the Groat Road?"

Harry leaned forwards. "What I tell you, Jack, nothing can come back to me. Nobody can link the two of us. I have reasons I need to be sure."

"No promises until I hear what you're going to tell me, Harry. But you can trust me to keep your name confidential."

McNaughton's body tensed. Jack's breath caught at the back of his throat, afraid he might get up and leave.

McNaughton relaxed and shook his head. "I'm an idiot," he murmured.

"What are you afraid of? And another thing. I read every paper when I got out of the hospital and found nothing like what you just revealed. If you're telling the truth, why didn't you print it? It's front-page stuff."

Harry grimaced as if Jack had pulled a rabbit out of a hat. "Because I was ordered otherwise. Threatened with trouble if I did. Physical trouble, if you get my drift." His face reddened, then through gritted teeth he said, "Blackmail."

"What? You?"

"Something in my life I don't want mentioned. A career stopper.

Hey, nothing illegal, but no paper would hire me," he added, interpreting the expression on Jack's face. "And no, I'm not queer."

It was Jack's turn to blush. "I believe you."

McNaughton was persistent, but he didn't invent missing links or work the angles to print a sensational story. Jack decided that Harry's secret was nobody's business.

"That car that you totalled on the Groat Road, Jack. Have you ever wondered whose car you stole?"

"No, and I don't care," Jack mumbled.

"It was mine."

Jack's eyebrows rose. "You let me take it?"

McNaughton snorted. "Fat chance. I hightailed it out of there and got as far as my car. You came up behind me, dumped Brodie inside, grabbed the keys out of my hand, and knocked me flat. Not a please or thank you. Nearly ran over me to boot."

Jack waved away Harry's declaration as though of no consequence. "Brodie was alive at that point, wasn't he?"

"Hey! The least you could do is apologize."

Jack shrugged. "You had insurance, I suppose. And you still drive a car, don't you?"

McNaughton frowned, opened his mouth and shut it. He tilted his head up, peering down his nose, assessing. "You have an empty soul, you know that, Jack?"

"So, guess I drove hell-bent for leather for the university hospital, right? What happened on the Groat Road? And Brodie?" Jack hunched his shoulders against what he might hear. "Did he die in the accident? Tell me."

"Around those sharp curves in the ravines, you hit a patch of black ice under an underpass. Several cars had already snarled into a mishmash. At your speed, you wouldn't have had a hope of stopping or missing them, so you plowed into the steel road barriers instead. You saved other people at the cost of yourself." McNaughton looked sad. He reached out to Jack, then thought better of it and pulled back. "Neither you nor Brodie had seat belts fastened."

Jack lowered his face into his hands. In the silence, he heard a muffled crash from the nearby kitchen, followed by a faint remark and an angry retort. Jack pulled his hands down his cheeks and across his mouth. Familiar waves of pain darted along his forehead, bringing out beads of sweat.

"How long before anyone came? Who came?"

McNaughton nodded. "The traffic police, the ambulance. And . . ."

"Were you there?" Jack interrupted and got a nod in return.

"I made it to 114th, flagged down a car, and begged for help. About five minutes behind you. The university hospital was my guess, so I promised the driver an extra five if he caught up to you. Lucky for me, the kid took it as a big thrill and put his foot down. Got there a moment before the police closed the road."

"How'd they get there that fast?"

"They were already there at the pileup because of the black ice. The traffic on the Groat Road was slowing, but I was near enough to hear you slam into the side rails." Harry shook his head, remembering. "Your guys arrived later."

"Tell me what you saw—a reporter's first impressions."

A group came into the café and settled at the counter, the regular lunch crowd by the way they greeted each other. The waitress showed up. "Figured you might want lunch." Her expression said to order or vacate the booth. She pushed a glossy menu at them, stacked up their cups and plates, and carted them off into the kitchen. Eating being the last thing on his mind, he ignored his menu and waited for McNaughton to finish inspecting the list of items. The kitchen doors whooshed open, and the waitress appeared with pencil and pad poised.

"We'll both have grilled cheese on brown and your soup of the day," McNaughton said without consulting Jack. "Beef and barley?"

"Fine."

At a sound from Jack, she added, "Or tomato and macaroni."

"That one," he said. At least it shouldn't hit his stomach like a ball of lead.

Longing for a beer, Jack ordered two glasses of water. She nodded and packed her pad and pencil into her short black apron. Gathering their menus, she snuck away, sponge shoe soles sucking at the lino floor.

"The police kept the crowd away, so I couldn't see everything," McNaughton continued. "I showed my media creds, and they let me move up as far as the sidelines." He closed his eyes and used the fingers of both hands to rub his forehead. "I thought you were both goners." He opened his eyes and looked at Jack. "I felt sick watching it."

Jack kept his gaze on him, unable to speak.

"The medics were gathered one on each side of the wreck, checking you both. A guy with a stretcher stood behind them, waiting for the signal. The one on Brodie's side came around and looked undecided on if they should load you or wait for the cops. When they ignored Brodie, I knew it was too late. Then your guys turned up."

"Who was it?"

"Wager and Hawk. They looked over Brodie, then went to the medics and talked to them. Hawk put your gun in a bag. They put you on a gurney, and the medics looked in a hurry to get you away, but Hawk stopped them." McNaughton paused when the waitress came back with glasses of water. He took a long drink. "Wager went back to Brodie, looking at his bullet wound, I imagine."

"Wait. Did he move him?"

"No, he talked to Hawk. I assumed he couldn't account for missing weapons. Hawk searched your pockets and came up with one. It must have been Brodie's gun. You said you put it in your pocket. Then he waved to the medics, and they took off to the hospital."

Jack frowned. The waitress returned with an arm loaded. She sorted the plates out along with the cutlery, said "enjoy," and squelched away.

"They searched me without first looking in the car for Brodie's weapon?"

McNaughton nodded, spooned his soup, gingerly took a taste, and slurped the rest.

Jack examined his sandwich and put it back on the plate. "Why?"

"Why what?"

"Why didn't they search the car? The floor. The seats."

McNaughton's mouth turned down. "You wrecked my car. Written off, in fact." He stared above Jack's head, face mournful. "I loved that car."

All the more reason to search through the wreck first, Jack thought. *They searched my pockets. Why? Did one of them already know where to find it?* Common sense told him nobody could know he picked it up after Brodie dropped it. Absently, he took a spoonful of soup, then another. He lifted half of his grilled cheese and studied it.

McNaughton's eyes returned to Jack. "What's wrong?"

"I was told my weapon killed Brodie and that Brodie's fingerprints were on the barrel. Did you see anything that made that possible?"

Harry mused awhile. "I don't see how. Hawk had isolated your gun while people were milling around Brodie, taking pictures and whatever you guys do. He'd have to take your gun out of the bag and press Brodie's fingers around it. I saw nothing like that. Sorry, Jack, but they had to already be there." After a pause, he added, "Want to go for a beer after?" He gazed at Jack hopefully. "Someplace where nobody knows us."

Jack considered, then remembered his car was still in the parking structure by the Bay. "Another time, Harry. Listen, I owe you big. Let me know if you remember anything that strikes you as odd or seems out of place. Please." Jack laid a five-dollar bill on the table. "How can I contact you? Not wanting anyone to know it's me, for instance."

Fear flashed over McNaughton's face as if he, too, remembered something. "Don't attempt to reach me, Jack. I'll get in touch with you."

"I'd like to know how someone can pressure you to print false leads, Harry. Like reporting the raid was in a different place than it was?"

McNaughton looked down at the remnants of his food and shook his head. "For now, let's assume they want things peaceful while they build a case against one of their own. Wouldn't do for the public to think the service was harbouring a dirty cop now, would it?"

Jack doubted Harry's reasoning.

"Never stopped the press before. The right to know and all that crap. . . ."

Something wasn't right. A newspaper's revenue goals directly contradicted its cooperation with public institutions. Harry wasn't telling him everything.

Jack decided not to push. "If I need you, I'll leave a message from Joe Friday. We could meet here in, say, an hour. Or, if it's important, I'll leave a callback number. Use a public phone, but only give a time to meet." Jack paused. "I'm being set up here, Harry, and if—*when* I find the answer, you'll be the first to break the news."

McNaughton still looked uneasy. Then he chuckled, snorting through his nose. "Jack Tuesday. Joe Friday. I like it."

"You're a real scream, Harry." He got up to leave.

Harry opened his mouth as if he was about to say something. Jack raised his eyebrows, questioning.

McNaughton shook his head. "Nothing. Just . . . look after yourself."

Outside, Jack sought a telephone kiosk. He found the usual ad for Yellow Cab stuck on the phone and dialled the number. While he waited for his cab to appear, his mind tried to sort out the last two hours.

Suspicions about his dead Motorola on the raid raised new questions. His only other source of information would be the task force's report. Comparing their version with his own recall and Harry's story might trigger new memories. But did he dare ask to see a report? Durand would hear about it and immediately assume his memory had returned and either arrest him or put him out of action.

The more information Jack gathered, the more shaky the ground became beneath him, threatening to suck him into an ever-deepening sinkhole.

14

JACK pocketed his parkade receipt with its timestamp—in case he needed it. A dull uneasiness dogged him on the way home that McNaughton wasn't revealing everything he knew.

"Because it implicates you, pal. But why is he so eager to tell you in the first place?"

Eager, but not in revealing *all* his information. Maybe limited by the threat of blackmail, Harry gave just enough, hoping Jack ran with it.

He cooked liver for Pharo, and pasta with canned sauce for himself, adding a heap of grated parmesan to lessen the tinny taste of the can. Trying to cheer himself up, he chose a Royal Marine vinyl out of his record collection, started it up on the turntable, and stood with a glass of wine at the balcony window. Staring at the building across the street, he sipped his wine and tapped his fingers against his thigh in time to the brass beat of Alford's *Hollyrood*. His gaze moved down to the building entrance, willing Bianca to come waltzing out of it. She came across as strong-willed, independent, and confident, but vulnerable too. He winced at the thought of all the women he'd dated—each seemed like such a waste of time now. No one was able to stir him the way Ursula had. What made this one so different?

"Secrets, knucklehead. She's another mystery you can solve."

Irritated, he gulped the last of the wine, resisting the urge to call on her. She'd ask if he had news of her painting the minute he showed. He stopped the vinyl in the middle of a brass horn fanfare.

On impulse, Jack phoned the station and asked for Hawk's personal extension. After four rings, Wager answered. Disappointed, Jack tried being friendly. "Hey Wager, it's Tuesday."

"No, it's Wednesday." A snort "What do you want?"

"Gee, it must be fun to walk in his shoes."

"Hawk." Jack kept his cool.

"Not here."

Jack waited for the hang-up click, but Wager's heavy breath told him curiosity had got the better of him. "I need information. Not related to me," he added at the disapproving grunt on the other end. "That doctor who's treating me had artwork stolen. An old master's painting."

"And why is that your suspended business?"

"He wondered who Durand assigned. One of us."

"Us?" Sarcastic.

"You," Jack amended, obedient. "Occurred in the Northwest, so why Central and not them?"

"Durand? What...?" Jack heard a long pause. Probably Wager checking for listeners. "And you phoned Hawk because you think he's in charge of the investigation?" No withering put-down, which meant he was alone.

"I thought Durand might have told Hawk."

"He may have, but you don't need to know. Suspension means you stay home and play solitaire." Jack heard the dial tone.

He screwed up his face and aped Wager's last words into the dead phone, then told himself to forget it. Bianca had his card and phone number, so nothing stopped her from phoning him to ask about the painting. Maybe she didn't remember asking him.

The telephone rang, and Jack's heart leapt. *Wager changed his mind?*

"Apologies for calling this late, Jack." Dr. Pavic said.

"Not at all," Jack shifted uneasily. Apologies for a phone call usually preceded a request.

"I have a change in circumstances and must move your appointment to tomorrow." A note of urgency chimed at the end, commanding rather than suggesting.

Jack rubbed his forehead. Although tempted to nix the

appointment, he agreed, knowing Durand would find out if he didn't. Spirits sinking into his feet, if that were possible, he asked himself if he even cared about getting another black mark.

"Fighting spirit taking off for parts unknown—"

"One o'clock then," Pavic said, cutting Brodie short.

Mind still on Bianca, Jack asked, "Have you heard from the officer investigating the case about the painting?"

"How did you know about the robbery?"

"You told me," Jack reminded him, wanting to ask if he had a memory problem too.

"Hope he hasn't forgotten the important bits."

Jack sniggered to himself and listened to Pavic's breathing.

"Ahh, yes. So I did. Bianca told me of your help," he said.

"I didn't know she was your daughter then."

The doctor's muffled snort said he recognized a lie when he heard it.

"Bianca asked me to pursue the theft," Jack continued, over-explaining perhaps. "She wasn't convinced I couldn't help because of my suspension."

This time the amusement was genuine. "Yes, Bianca does not take rejection lightly."

"Well, I told her I'd try. But first, I need the name of the cop in charge of the case. Do you have it?"

"I do, Jack, but it is in my office, and I am at a phone booth. Something like Walker or Wilder."

It didn't ring any bells in Jack's brain. "Well, how about Bianca's new telephone number? I'll ask her if he's given her an update yet."

"Nice try, Jack." Pavic's tone turned terse. "It would be worth my life to give her telephone number without permission." A click cut him off. There it was again, and he wasn't wrong. A definite note of anxiety.

"More secrets. That guy is full of them."

Jack heard dancing at the door, nails clicking against the tile floor.

He got the leash from the kitchen, rolled it around his hand, and headed out. Pharo leapt ahead, past the professor coming up, and Waterman quickly pressed up against the banister to avoid being run over.

"Sorry about that, Warren," Jack apologized. "When you gotta go . . ."

The professor pressed his lips together and gave Jack a curt nod. "I suppose."

"Has the new tenant upstairs been bothering you?" Jack deliberately misunderstood his neighbour's annoyance.

"What?" The professor stood above him on the landing, alarm plain on his face.

"The biker you mentioned? I assume he keeps to himself?"

"Oh yes." Waterman ducked his head. "Perhaps my judgement was premature. We've spoken. He's completing his doctorate with a dissertation on bikers. I feel that he only dresses the part to add realism to his research. So no worries." Waterman gave Jack a self-conscious smile and continued up the stairs.

Pharo sent little chortles from the entrance, and Jack hurried down. "Okay, okay, uncross your legs."

He waited at the corner of the path while Pharo began sniffing a crooked journey towards the back parking lot. Except for a breeze whistling through the spaces between buildings, it was quiet. Scudding clouds were getting thicker, promising rain and, perhaps worse, spring snow. Jack shivered.

The few people on the street, who hunched up their shoulders and hurried along, likely shared his thoughts. Jack looked down the block, assessing whether he should go back for his jacket, and blinked as if his eyes were playing tricks. At the corner lights, the same figure he'd seen before staring at Bianca's apartment building waited to cross the street. Jack strode towards the man and stood beside him. "Hello. Chilly tonight, isn't it? Wish I'd worn my coat." He thrust his hands into his pockets.

The man turned up his jacket collar and shrank down into its folds. He was bare-headed this time—no hat, and strands of dark hair blew across his forehead. Brown eyes, which had seen too much living, swept over him and then back to his face. Jack recognized the intelligence in them.

"You are a policeman?" the man said with a foreign accent.

The abrupt question stole his words away, and Jack could only nod, struggling to keep his expression neutral.

"He's one too."

Early forties, shorter than Jack's six feet, slight build, but his clothes suggested he had lost weight. Jack was familiar enough with the style and cut of European clothing to recognize the baggy suit did not originate in Canada.

"I saw you here before," Jack chatted. "Over there." He pointed, then decided the shock approach was best with this man. "Are you acquainted with Mrs. Zamborski?"

The man's head jerked from the traffic light to zone in on Jack's face, his dark eyes snake-flat. "It is not your concern, but I am searching for a place to lease. Before I choose, I examine every place thoroughly whether I should live there." The crease between his brows deepened. "You have the usual imagination of the police." He held up his hand, palm outwards, while his face set into rigid lines.

"Where I come from, a man's imagination often leads to terrors. Do not judge me in the same manner." The man's eye twitched. He rubbed his nose with the back of his hand and directed his gaze across the street. The conversation was over.

Jack concluded this man was not often challenged for explanation.

"A dangerous man."

Jack consciously didn't watch him walk away.

As he turned back the way he came, he searched the old lady's window and was not surprised to see her watching.

***

In the morning, before his appointment with Dr. Pavic, Jack went to find Apple. Rain pelted the windshield in an unrelenting stream that barely cleared the rapid back-and-forth wipers. At the Riviera Hotel, he zippered his jacket and sprinted for the door.

"Not for a couple of days." The bartender sprayed cleaner on the counter, followed by a swipe of a white cloth. He moved along the bar, repeating his moves. "None of his drinking buddies have seen him either. Makes me wonder if he's sick or something." The man stopped cleaning and faced him. "Or else patronizing a different bar. For a change of scenery, or to avoid someone." He gave Jack a pointed stare and wiped again.

"Any idea where Apple lives?" Jack asked, hoping he wouldn't be questioned as to why he didn't know it himself.

"Do I look like a social worker?" The next spray and thump of towel accented his choice of career. He moved to the end of the bar.

The implication was plain: Apple's absence was on purpose. Had he pushed him too far? Jack sucked the insides of his cheeks.

Answers to his questions at the Legion Boxing Club premises were depressing in their sameness. Apple had disappeared.

Turning to leave the club, he spotted four loungers against the wall, watching a sparring match. He might have passed them unnoticed, except two of them nudged each other, gave him the eye, and then turned their backs. Jack started towards them, then glanced at his watch. He'd have to put them on hold if he were to keep his appointment with Dr. Pavic.

He hurried outside and got into his car, praying the four would still be there when he returned. Two men with Rebel patches on their vests came out of the Legion Club and started up their hogs. They pulled around Jack's car and stopped at the lot entrance, gunning their motorcycles, blocking him while staying in place. Jack leaned on the horn, netting him a rigid middle finger before they roared off, their bare arms oblivious to the wet weather. On Saskatchewan Drive, just before the road dipped to enter the High Level Bridge, two more flashed past him, cutting him off and forcing him to brake. What is it with bikers today?

"Where is a cop when you need one?"

"Speaking of cops, why don't you remember what happened that night and tell me?" The morning's empty search enhanced his sour mood. He banged his fist on the steering wheel in a fit of temper. "Why won't you help me out here?" *Because I'm you, stupid,* he answered himself.

Irritation with the day increased when the lot beside Dr. Pavic's building displayed a 'full' sign, forcing him to drive around the block twice before he found a spot. Spaces along the sidewalk were at a premium, packed with drivers who all had the same idea of avoiding rain and wet.

The waiting room was empty when he entered the office. Despite his parking gymnastics, he was early. Even Jassy was still at lunch. He sat. The air hummed with silence, seeming loud in his ears after the noise of traffic. Not even a rustle of papers from the inner sanctum. Was Pavic at lunch too? Or maybe in the restroom? Jack squirmed against the leather seat, uncomfortable with his guesses. If nobody was here, why was the office door not locked? The unnatural stillness increased, raising goosebumps up along his tingling forearms.

He stood and tiptoed towards the inner office as if he were afraid to interrupt the silence. Sniggering, he put his ear against the frosted glass.

"Just go in."

The odour hit him the second he cracked open the door; a distinct coppery smell. Eyes blank, Dr. Pavic stared at him from behind his desk, blood oozing from the hole in his temple.

15

HE stayed where he was, vision narrowed to the scene in front of him. Habit kicked in as the surrounding layout and details clicked like snapshots in his mind. The shot had struck the doctor's temple, the exit scattering bone and brain bits up against the wall and filing cabinet. Jack calculated the angle of the bullet, tracked from someone sitting at the desk across from him. If Pavic had been facing his shooter, the bullet should have hit him square in the forehead. Did he turn his head away at the last moment?

Dr. Pavic's hand rested on a file in front of him, making Jack wonder if it was his. It took all his strength to stay where he was and not contaminate the crime scene. Taking a deep breath, he caught a whiff of something besides blood. He twisted his head but couldn't catch the odour again. A faint touch of . . . what? He filed it away for later, knowing the answer would come by itself.

"This isn't good."

Jack could only shake his head, not wanting to follow Brodie's logical conclusion that he'd be involved. He heard a noise in the hall and backed away, blocking the view inside the room.

Jassy hurried into the office. "Sorry. I was hoping I'd get here before you." She used one hand to hold a wet umbrella, and the other unbuttoned her coat. "I got held up at the bank." His stillness grabbed at her. Her eyes shifted behind him. "Where is Dr. Pavic?" She laid the umbrella on a chair and walked closer to him, trying to peer around him.

Jack reached out and blocked her from the room. "Call 911." She pushed away to go around him. "Don't look. There's been a shooting."

"No." She squirmed out of his grasp. Her moan began as a low mewling, then progressed into a scream. Jack pulled her against him and hugged her tight. She clung to him. Her screams drifted into moans and gulping sobs, muffled by his chest.

A small crowd of office workers bunched up in the doorway to the hall. Jack closed the inner door and said over Jassy's head, "Nothing to see here, folks. Nobody leaves the building. Lock yourselves inside your offices and stay there until the police get here."

Whispering in shocked tones, people dispersed along the hall and into offices. The sound of doors closing gave way to silence once more.

Heavy boots clattered on the stairs. Two uniforms appeared, the business end of their weapons pointing the way. The elevator doors opened, and two more peeked from opposite corners.

"Hands high. Face the wall!"

Pulse quickening at being on the other end of police commands, Jack didn't argue. "Who called you?" He took a deep breath to calm his anxiety. There was no wall, so he stood in the open door, keeping his fingertips from touching the transom window. How did they get here so soon? A rough hand ran over his frame before gripping his arms and forcibly turning him around.

Jassy, clutching a tissue, eyes wide open and red-rimmed, appeared behind the officers. "Thank God you're here. Dr. Pavic. Someone . . ." she shuddered, her hand fluttering towards his office.

The officer jerked Jack's arms. "Is this the shooter?"

"Don't be silly. He's with the police. The next appointment." Her voice got shrill. "Don't stand there. Do something!"

"Ambulance is on its way," one cop said.

A police sergeant appeared beside Jack and the constable. He looked Jack up and down, then peered into the reception area. Jack could sense he was mentally photographing the room and its contents.

On cue, the elevator door opened, exposing three EMS attendants and a gurney. They looked around, saw the officer and Jack, and started forwards.

"Hold it there, guys," the sergeant ordered. Jassy watched,

bewildered. Jack wanted to tell her that the police sergeant controls the crime scene and everyone connected, calling for and briefing the detectives when they arrive. He settled for giving her a smile and nodding his head as if to tell her everything was alright. It didn't calm her. She pulled down her mouth and wiped her eyes again. The police sergeant padded to the inner office and took a quick look at Dr. Pavic. He nodded to himself, surmising the EMS weren't necessary to proclaim death and ordered them to wait outside in the hall. He turned to Jack, eyebrows lifted.

"I'm here for an appointment." Jack jerked his head towards the office. "With the victim." Out of the corner of his eye, he saw Jassy wrap her arms around her middle, hugging tight. "I got here about twelve fifty-five. The place was empty. I thought the doctor might be in his office, so I opened the door and found him."

"What's your name?" Jack told him and sensed the lot of them gawking in new suspicion. "The one who killed his partner? That Tuesday?" Not waiting for confirmation, he put on gloves, lifted the telephone receiver and dialled using a pen. Summoning the medical examiner and detectives, Jack surmised. The police sergeant tuned out and came back. "Okay, let's secure the building, the area, hallway, and right to the entrance door. Nobody in or out."

A constable took Jassy out to the hall. On the way to another office, Jack thought. *Standard procedure; separating us.* They'd ask her if she wanted a coffee or tea and soothe her nerves with kind talk.

The same sergeant snapped his fingers at him. "Show me what you touched."

"The door into the office, and the door knob. Nothing else. Oh, and I sat in a chair." He pointed. "That one."

"Touch the phone?"

Jack shook his head.

"Take the chair into the hallway and sit where I can see you." The sergeant peeked at Pavic again, his Adam's apple moving up and down as he swallowed, face a greenish tinge.

Wondering how many violent deaths he had seen, Jack gave him a sympathetic grimace as he lifted the chair. "His girl got hysterical," he said, delaying his exit out to the hallway. "It took time to calm her. I ordered the rubberneckers in the hall to lock themselves in their offices. All done before I could call 911. How did you get here so fast?" He didn't expect to get an answer, but it was worth a try.

"Dispatch sent us. Said it was an anonymous call."

"Man or woman?" he asked and got a shrug in return.

Jack's stomach churned. His moved appointment, the doctor's killing, and the anonymous police call were too coincidental. He heard Pavic's voice again, setting up the appointment. Was it a plan to accuse him of killing Pavic with planted evidence? Panic threatened to overtake him, and he took deep breaths to calm his heartbeat, wishing he'd had more time to search, crime scene be damned, simultaneously knowing he wouldn't have done it. His gaze flickered towards Pavic's office, then at the constable eyeballing him. Jack kept his face expressionless, wondering if the doctor had recorded their sessions. Jack imagined tapes loaded with unfavourable opinions. He sat in the hall where he could see inside Pavic's reception room.

Paul Wager and Hank Vassar appeared, looking damp and grumpy. *Rain must be getting worse,* thought Jack. Wager threw him a quick glance on their way inside the office. Jack heard the sergeant briefing them and his name before the voices lowered to an indistinguishable hum. Another constable was unrolling his wad of yellow tape like he was getting ready for a party.

Jack resisted the urge to bend over and hold his head. His rapid heartbeat and apprehension tightened to the point of pain. Bile rose in his throat, and he swallowed hard, imagining that he was on the verge of a heart attack. He concentrated on deep breaths, draped one arm over the chair back, then laid one ankle over the other knee, assuming a relaxed exterior. All the while, his brain churned, anticipating the incoming disaster. Thankfully, Brodie was quiet for once.

The medical examiner appeared, wet patches covering the shoulders of his raincoat. He bustled into Pavic's office, followed by equally damp crime scene experts who sorted out various pieces and cases of equipment. Given permission to enter, they disappeared inside to do their particular jobs. Jack could picture the procedure as each person worked in silence. Time ticked slowly on, and he shifted his numb posterior and stood once to renew the circulation in his legs.

After what seemed like an hour, Wager and Vassar appeared and traded places with the EMS waiting with their gurney.

"Where's the girl?" Vassar asked, and the constable pointed.

Vassar went past Jack without a word and disappeared into an office down the hall. Wager crooked his finger at Jack to come forwards into the office, pointed to a chair and settled his bulk into the other beside him.

"You're in real trouble this time." Wager flicked the pages of his notebook to a blank one and, in plain view, jotted the time and date and Jack's name. He turned and shot Jack a smug grin. "Let's talk, Tuesday. Why kill the poor bast . . . Doc? He dig out information that would get you convicted?"

"I just got here for my one o'clock. Check it out with the dickhead tailing me."

Wager stopped flipping pages. "Knock it off, Tuesday. Nobody's tailing you."

Jack told him, and Wager shook his head in disbelief, then snickered. "Chumps." An expression flashed across his face, which Jack couldn't identify. Embarrassment? Was Wager responsible?

"Who followed you today? Give me a description." Pen poised over his notebook, Wager waited.

"I didn't spot anyone today," Jack admitted. He'd been too intent on Apple to notice.

"Of course you didn't." Wager drew his words out. "You're everybody's best like for this one, Tuesday. We'll find Pavic's notes and a report, so you may as well tell us now. You could plead insanity or manslaughter."

"I only found him. He was dead when I got here."

"He was still fresh though, wasn't he, Jack? Did you meet anyone on your way up?" Wager raised an eyebrow. "Hear a shot?"

Jack sat up straight. He must be slipping. Then he remembered the faint odour near the desk. Musty? Peaty? He frowned, trying to center in on it. "Nothing. I met nobody coming in or going out. The place was quiet, the same as any place at lunch hour. Which tells me people still in their offices heard nothing either. It'd be nice if someone did, and when. I'm sure you'll ask."

Wager scowled at him. Jack didn't give him a chance to butt in. "The officers and their sergeant got here before I could call 911. He said it was an anonymous call. What time was that, then?"

"I'm asking the questions. Your record makes you numero uno." Wager twirled his pen in his fingers, and his voice got soft. "Why not just confess and save us the grief and time?"

My record? "Sod off, Wager. When nobody hears a gunshot, you conclude the killer used a suppressor. I'm set up to be the fall guy." At Wager's sudden grin, Jack shut up, realizing he had just uttered the usual suspect's lame excuse. He wanted to leave, to think. He thought of Bianca—who would break the news to her? Should he get to her first? He pulled his earlobe, wondering how to get away.

Looking sour, Vassar arrived from interviewing Jassy. "He checks out. The girl said she saw him drive around the block and enter the building. She tried to catch him on her way from the bank at the corner."

"You sure? She didn't seem like she was lying to protect him? Like she was sweet on him?"

"I tried to trip her up, but she wouldn't budge."

"Trip her up?" Jack butted in, stressing Vassar's remark. "Like giving her hints about what you wanted her to say, Vassar? Resorting to type?"

Vassar's face turned red. He bunched up his fists and turned to Wager like he was asking permission. "Why isn't he stashed in a patrol car instead of here, contaminating the scene?"

Wager ignored him.

"Again," Jack pursued his advantage. "You guys got here fast. An anonymous call. What time was that?"

Wager sighed, rose and took the sergeant, who looked annoyed, aside. When he returned, Jack saw puzzlement and indecision on his face, which disappeared the moment he met Jack's eyes.

"Well? What is it?" Jack asked.

"Dispatch never mentioned if it was a man or woman." Wager licked his lips and looked about to add a remark. Instead, he flipped open his notebook again.

"What else? Come on, I'm the one sitting here on the hot seat. If it puts me in the clear, I have a right to hear it."

Wager mumbled something under his breath, then conceded, reluctant. "There was a prior."

"Against Pavic? When?"

"Last night. Pavic came in and reported a threat. He claimed he was in danger from someone he recognized on the street. Because Pavic is our local shrink, so to speak, we promised to check on him throughout the day."

Police speak for filing his complaint under *nothing to worry about*. Jack decided not to mention Pavic's phone call. Wager's pencil hovered over his notebook.

"Dr. Pavic was afraid of being assassinated," Jack offered.

Wager never looked up from doodling. Seemingly uninterested. "Yeah? What makes you think so?"

"He made sure his desk wasn't near a window. I saw signs he'd moved his furniture more than once. Maybe to confuse a sniper?"

Wager snapped his notebook closed again. "It doesn't let you off the hook."

Jack studied his expression, his unblinking eyes. "Ah. You got something else, right? Relating to the person Pavic saw on the street."

Wager opened his mouth, then closed it, his bottom teeth clamped over his moustache, gnawing at it. He shot a quick glance at the sergeant in charge, who was watching those at work in the inner office.

"He said the guy was Yugoslavian." Wager conceded, tone grudging.

Jack remembered the doctor admitting the resistance had complicated his life. His scalp prickled. Could he be another victim of Tito's revenge?

Wager broke into his thoughts, changing the subject. "Tell me your first impressions when you opened the door." He lifted a chair, planted it in front of Jack and sat facing him.

Jack repeated his story and suggested that Pavic had seen the killer and turned aside at the last moment. "Everything points to a suppressor used on the weapon. Did you find a casing?"

Wager said nothing.

"The shooter didn't have time to pick it up, I bet," mused Jack. "A suppressor means an assassin. He may even have left the casing on purpose, as a warning."

"Did you do it, Jack?" Wager's voice rose, tone brutal and hard, just as Hawk appeared. "Shoot the poor schmuck while he was sitting across from you? Helpless?"

Jack put out his hands, palms up. "Give me the light test, Wager. My clothes too. You won't find residue." He didn't hide his relief at seeing Hawk. So much for thinking Wager had softened towards him. It was Wager's way. Both hard and soft, keeping the suspect off balance. And good at it. Jack couldn't help admiring the technique with this firsthand experience.

"What you got?" Hawk asked.

Wager stood and tucked away his notebook. "A suspect for the lockup, that's what I got." He was back to his old snarly self.

"On what grounds?"

"Reasonable grounds. This guy is giving us a bad name. Ordinary citizens look at us like we're scum. Nothing worse than one of your own turning sour. It's time the public knows we won't protect dirty cops."

Hawk turned to Jack. Before he said anything, Jack spoke, openly angry now. "You don't have reasonable grounds, and you know it. I'll be glad to come downtown. By now, the press should be parked at the front entrance."

"Can't face them?" Vassar put in.

"You'll give them the impression I'm the killer, and they'll want your names. You'll look pretty stupid when it comes out you got the wrong guy." Jack raised his eyebrows at them. "You want to handle the questions they throw at us on the way out?"

Jack mentally crossed his fingers while they exchanged glances, assessing each other's inclination to run the gauntlet.

"Eenie, Meenie, Miney, and you're Moe."

"Always in control, aren't you, Tuesday?" Wager glared. "Just can't resist directing us onto the right path."

Like a steam valve suddenly let loose at the breaking point, Jack's temper flared. "It isn't control, Wager," he lashed out. "It's faith. Faith to believe that we can even the stakes against people who bring harm and grief to good people. It's resisting the temptation to not care and become cynical to the rot—ending up indifferent to the people who need our help. Call it control if you want, but it's either that or not at all. That's the oath I took when I became a cop."

In the silence that followed, he fancied he heard Dr. Pavic laughing and blaming it on post-traumatic amnesia. Only a few hours ago, Jack wished he didn't have to meet with him. Now he missed his wry observations.

"Nobody gets a pass." Vassar raised his fingers in a Boy Scout salute.

Jack saw Hawk's fists clench. Wager shot Vassar a sour look, but his lips twitched.

"Do you need me for anything here?" Hawk asked Wager, his voice tight, controlled.

A legitimate question, but judging by Wager's expression, he took it as questioning his crime scene investigation skills.

"Sorry if I stepped on your toes, Wager," Hawk added, not looking apologetic in the least.

"You're sure eager to set him free."

"He's right about one thing. How we handle this will reflect on us all. We'd better make sure we're on the same page."

Jack relaxed for now. Once a charge of murder became public, an investigation would center on proving it to avoid an embarrassing retraction. Foregone conclusions were dangerous and prompted investigators to overlook pertinent evidence if it didn't fit their case. Why was Wager so adamant? Jack knew Wager's history included undercover work into the Rebels. Was he still connected? He wouldn't be the first agent sucked into the very culture he was investigating.

"Uptown, Tuesday. Right smart like." Wager ordered.

Jack saluted. Wager rewarded him another scowl on the way out, leaving him alone once more. He slumped in relief.

A near simultaneous lightning flash and thunder crack rattled the window and made Jack's hair stand on end.

"Steady. It's only the beginning."

16

THE rain had dwindled to an intermittent drizzle when he parked beside the Riviera Hotel and headed for the bar. Nobody had quoted him his rights, but the thought that he might need a lawyer deflated him. He thanked whoever watched him from above that his earlier search for Apple at the Legion Boxing Club meant he could not have driven across the river in time to kill Dr. Pavic. Jack left HQ with a blinding headache and Wager's promise that he'd soon be back for good.

The bartender shook his head, raising his hands in an *I-know-nothing* gesture and went back to pouring drinks. Jack asked for a glass of water and downed it with two Motrin pills.

Back in his car, he considered Apple might be sick or worse. Maybe the bikers suspected Apple had volunteered information better left unsaid. And it may mean nothing, but the increasing number of bikers Jack saw lately was a coincidence he didn't trust. The gangs were dangerous, and Apple was unprotected. The public underestimated the Rebels. They did the charitable drives, made toy runs in the neighbourhoods, spreading the impression they were only a club of fellows who liked bikes. Not so. They pedalled drugs, laundered money, dealt in prostitution, extortion, and killed without a qualm.

If rumours that a rival organization had muscled in were true, it meant violence. Gloom increasing every minute, Jack drove to the Legion Boxing Club again. Prayers answered, he spotted the familiar four men grouped around the front entrance, smoking and trading conversation. As Jack drove past to a parking space, he saw furtive movements, hands passing objects to each other with practised blurs. He turned his head away to give them time to hide whatever it was. Likely meth. They watched him as he strode towards them, with a grin on his face and hands out where they could see them.

"I'm looking for Apple. Any of you seen him?"

"Who wants him?" said a tall man hiding from the rain under the overhang. He hawked, and a wad of phlegm landed near Jack's foot. The men moved to encircle him.

Jack raised his eyebrows in surprise and puzzlement. "We're buddies from the same outfit in Korea."

The men stood straighter, interested now, and Jack followed up. "I haven't seen him in the last few days, and I'm worried he might be sick or something." Jack looked them over, one by one. Two men locked eyes.

"If he's in trouble, I can help."

The tall wall-leaner whistled like a small bird. Jack rubbed his jaw and made eye contact with a shorter man who hitched up his sagging jeans. "Please."

"You can't tell anyone else," the man responded. The wall leaner growled in protest. "You've all heard Apple talk about his friend the cop," the shorter one stated defiantly. "And what if it's true? It's not like him to disappear. What if he is sick, and it's serious? Do we want to be responsible?"

"You said he wasn't home," the tall thin man said. He threw down his cigarette in disgust and stamped on it, grinding it into the cement.

"I said he didn't answer the door. Nobody answering a door don't mean somebody ain't home. What if he can't answer? I say we tell the cop where he lives." Struck with a new idea, he turned to Jack. "How come you don't know where he lives? If you're such good friends, I mean?" The others turned expectantly.

"Apple has always liked his privacy," Jack lied. "So I never asked him. Didn't want to intrude."

They nodded in unison, and too late, Jack realized he had hinted that Apple might not want him knowing where he lived. Didn't matter if that were true. "Oh, come on," he coaxed and spread his hands, waving away any rising protective spirit between them. "It's way past that now. After seeing if he's okay, I'll forget where he lives and how I found it. You got me worried now." For a brief second, he thought of threatening them with a search and seizure of whatever was in their pockets but knew they would clam up in total solidarity.

"He moved to a new place up 96th," Shorty blurted before the others could make a sound. "Behind a bar about 66th Avenue. The first door at the top." Eyes narrowed, he closed in on Jack with his mouth producing a gift of stale beer fumes. "You better be on the up and up, Mister Man, or we'll find you. Catch my drift?"

Jack nodded but chanced one more question. "Have there been any bikers asking for him lately?"

All drew a combined intake of breath. Shorty looked scared. "God, no. Jesus. Is he in trouble with the pack?" He pulled away as if Jack had a smallpox rash over his face.

Jack kept his cool. "Not a chance."

Shorty relaxed and shoved his hands into his pockets. "We wouldn't tell nobody nothing, anyway. Especially bikers." They nodded in unison and scarpered, putting distance between themselves and Jack.

The place wasn't hard to find; the name McGrubers splayed across the front. The neighbourhood wouldn't entice the intelligent crowd; even so, the bar was larger than he expected and well-kept. Two men exited, followed by the familiar smell of ale and the click of billiard balls. Lighted signs along the front windows advertised billiards and pinball machines. Jack mentally ticked off the pubs he and Brodie were assigned to investigate back in February, and he was sure this was not one of them. After Jack was reassigned, had Brodie been here on his own? In any case, he put his judgment on reserve for now.

At the side path, he evaded rain puddles on the way around the bar, past a dumpster reeking of hops and food. The stairs and raised walkway running along the length of the second story needed a coat of paint. The first stair tread tilted when he stepped on it, and the railing wobbled sideways when he tried to steady himself. Apparently, most of the upkeep budget had blessed the building's street front. He knocked twice, put his ear to the door calling Apple's name and then peered through the blind slats at the window.

"Mr. McIntosh isn't home," said a deep melodious voice.

Jack squinted in its direction, seeing a wheelchair sticking part way out of the only other door farther along the platform. Jack bent backwards, craning his neck to see whoever occupied it. He controlled his expression at seeing no legs hanging down to the foot pedals, only shoes jutting past the seat. The entire wheelchair rolled into view, revealing a head seeming the wrong size for the body below it. As Jack neared, he saw the man wore a white shirt with a bright blue tie tucked into a fine sleeveless wool vest. Intelligent eyes with a knowing twinkle met Jack's own. His teeth were white over his short Fu Manchu beard. "You are looking for Mr. McIntosh?"

"I haven't heard him called Mr. McIntosh for a long time," Jack said. "Have you seen him?"

"Not an hour ago." Naked curiosity shone on the strange man's face and something else Jack couldn't define. "Are you a friend?" he continued.

"I like to think so." Jack stuck out his hand. "I'm Jack Tuesday." The man put his own out. He had short arms and stubby fingers. His palm was dry. "Phineas McGruber."

Phineas, thought Jack. *Who would name someone Phineas?* And McGruber. The name of the pub. "We ordinarily meet in the . . ." about to say bar, Jack ended, "Downtown."

"Ah." McGruber smiled as if he guessed Jack's omission. "Well, unless you're prepared to wait a long while, perhaps you could call another time. I don't expect he will return before late." Again, Jack saw something else in the man's eyes. A flash of suspicion.

"He knows you're a cop."

"Would you tell him I came because I'm worried about him?

Tell him I'll be in the usual place tomorrow." Jack looked deep into McGruber's eyes, sending his own message. McGruber rewarded him with a nod.

Jack grabbed a cold Pilsner and stretched out on the couch, only to get up again to answer the door. Glen handed him a note.

"A kid brought it. He wanted to slip it under your door, but I made him give it to me or take it back. Can't have kids running around the building, casing the place." Glen scratched Pharo's ears and then turned back, muttering to himself about kids and crime.

Jack unfolded the note. Thick linen stock, the writing spidery but particular. "Apartment number 307," he read. The seven had a stroke through it in the European style. "If you would be so inclined. Not later than 9:30 pm." The signature said Mira Zamborski. Jack's glance switched to his balcony door window and beyond to the apartment across the street, but he only saw reflected sunlight.

He scraped a can of dog food into the dish and broke an egg over it. Pharo eyed it, gazed up at Jack, sniffed the bowl, decided it was alright, and went at it. For his own supper, he removed the leftover steak from the fridge and the makings of a salad. Chopped onions mixed with diced potatoes sizzled in the frypan. While that was heating, Jack went to the phone and rotated the dial with a number from memory. He listened to the ring and the greeting on the other end.

"Is that my favourite redhead?" he said.

A gasp, a pause. "Jack?" the voice on the other line said in a horrified whisper. "What do you want?"

"Can you talk?"

"He's gone for the day. I am ready to leave myself. You shouldn't be calling." After a pause, she said, "How are you?"

"I need a favour, Siobhan."

He heard a slight groan. "Please don't ask me to tell you what is going on with Durand. The secretary always gets the blame when information gets out," she said, tone pleading. "You know I can't tell you."

"Relax, Siobhan. It's another case."

"What case?" she drew out, suspicious.

"A robbery in the Northwest. A painting by Peter Paul Rubens. I am looking for a detective attached to the case. A name of Wilder, or Walker. Can you peek in the directory for any similar name and his contact number?"

"Now? Can't it wait until tomorrow?"

"I need it. You only have to check the W's."

Grumbling, Siobhan said, "I'll put you on hold. Don't go away." She *tsked*.

"There's a Sergeant Lewis Wallace." She recited his phone contact. "He'd be the only one to handle a case like that." She mumbled a few names, reading off the list, and added, "He'd be your best . . . wait, Jack. You can't go nosing around into another case when you're suspended. Are you trying to get yourself fired? What's going on with you? Why are you always doing this?"

"Doing what?" Jack said, writing on a pad.

"Meddling," Siobhan hissed. "Can't you stay out of trouble for once?"

"I owe you one. I won't forget this."

"Jack!"

"Don't worry. When this is cleared up, you'll be the first person I'm taking to the MacDonald Hotel for a celebration dinner."

"Sure. I live for a man's promises. I'm hanging up now."

"I mean it, Siobhan. Thank you."

He heard her draw in her breath like a long, patient sigh. "Right, and I'm also a fool. Take care of yourself, Jack."

***

He rapped softly on Bianca's door. Silence, then that soft thump of someone leaning to put an ear against the other side. "It's Jack. Are you up for some sympathy?"

After a long pause, the door opened just wide enough for him to see her blue eyes staring at him, giving him the odd impression that she wanted to check if it was indeed him. The same worried look witnesses gave him when he showed up at their doors to ask questions. She opened the door wider and waved him in. "If you're worried about reporters, I didn't see any," he said.

"What?" She pushed the heels of her hands against her puffy eyelids. "Oh yes, them. Thank goodness. It's bad enough without them yelling silly questions at me." She pointed in the direction of the couch.

He took both her hands in his, longing to pull her in. To cradle her against his chest and stroke her head. She'd fit snugly just under his chin. The urge increased, but then he lost his nerve. "I'm so sorry for your loss. Can I do anything to help? Do you need me to call anyone for you? Someone to come and stay with you?" He cussed himself for spouting off the usual sympathies. Inadequate, but he didn't know what else to say.

She shook her head. "No, but thank you for offering. I'm not thinking straight right now. It's too . . . the shock. There's so much to do, but I . . ." her voice trailed off. Her eyes swept the room as if she might find inspiration there.

"Do they have any leads?"

A lock of hair fell over her face, and he gently tucked it behind her ear, getting a sad smile in return. "The police wanted to know about the threat." Thankfully, with no mention of it, he assumed she wasn't aware of his involvement. It forestalled questions about him finding the body.

"Yes?"

"Father had complained about a threat. He said nothing to me." She gave a brittle laugh. "And why would he? I'm only his daughter.

At least I thought I was." Realizing how it sounded, she looked up at him, eyes wide. "Well, daughters should know, shouldn't they?" She shook her head at him. "I'm not making sense, am I?"

"It's okay." Jack waited until she took a deep breath. "Who might have made the threat? A patient perhaps?"

Her attention concentrated somewhere over his shoulder, towards her bedroom. "I asked the same question. Apparently, he told the police only last night that his life was in danger, that someone was out to kill him." Her eyes flared in anger. "They said it wasn't enough. With no open threat, they had nothing to investigate."

He looked sympathetic but said nothing about the difficulty of investigating a suspicion with no substance or identity to go with it.

Her palms wiped tears from her cheeks. She looked over his shoulder again, her anger replaced by blankness.

"Do you think it had anything to do with your stolen picture?" he asked.

She turned back to him, startled at the idea. "Why would it? It's already gone, so why threaten to kill him?" Her shoulders lifted, and she waved the idea away. "I don't care anymore. Whoever has it is welcome to it."

They stood in silence.

"If there is anything I can do, you must call me." At her indifferent nod, he added, "I mean it. If you need help with the arrangements or anything else which might come up, I'm here."

"You're a good man, Jack Tuesday. I won't forget that." She shot a wan smile at him and turned to open the door, leaning her head against the jamb.

As he passed her, he gave her a brief hug, patted her shoulder and left.

He heard the click of the lock when the door closed. He pushed the elevator button for up, then turned and looked back down the hall towards her apartment. He rubbed the side of his nose, remembering the way she had twice looked down the hall. Reflexively. Another person had been behind the closed bedroom door.

"Another one who doesn't trust you, pal."

It might not be what he thought, but it set his teeth on edge. Frowning, he turned from the elevator, went to the stairwell, and started climbing.

17

A boy, mid-teens, opened the door and peered out at him between the chain and door jamb. Jack saw shoulder-length hair and suspicious eyes peering through pieces of shorter hair hanging over his forehead.

"Mrs. Zamborski?" Jack inquired.

"Let him in, Tommy," a pleasant voice said, low and musical, with a slight accent. Polish, he supposed.

A metal chain rasped, and the door opened just wide enough for Jack to enter. The boy's eyes swept over him. As soon as Jack cleared the entrance, he snapped the door shut.

Mira Zamborski rose from her chair at the window and approached him with an apologetic smile. Up close, Jack realized his imagination had been skewed. She was no withdrawn old lady. Hair not grey, but blond, with streaks of grey. The left side of her face was scarred. Her left arm bent at her side, and Jack assumed the injury included her body. Her dress, with a single strand of pearls, mirrored elegance. She extended her right hand, smooth with long tapering fingers.

"How do you do, Mr. Tuesday? At last, we meet." Her grey eyes crinkled, teasing him. Not waiting for his answer, she turned to the boy.

"Thank you, Tommy, for your help. I wish to be alone with Mr. Tuesday now while we visit."

"Are you sure, Mrs. Zamborski?" Tommy said, his eyes swept from her to Jack as if suspecting Jack might arm wrestle her to the floor. He straightened his tee shirt and stuffed his hands into his jean pockets, prepared to stay for the duration.

"I am sure. You can come back later to check." Her hand shooed him away, a smile erasing the sting.

Tommy gone, she chose a tall wingback chair beside a small table upon which stood a crystal vase filled with yellow roses. "Please sit, Mr. Tuesday. Would you like a drink. Tea?"

Jack sat. "No, I'm alright, thanks. But please call me Jack. Mr. Tuesday is so . . ."

"Formal," she agreed. The right corner of her mouth moved upwards in a smile. "You may call me Mira." One eye appeared bluer than the other. The colour and sparkle diminished by injury? She folded her hands in her lap, watching him, her expression neutral while she waited for him to finish his inspection. "You visited Bianca before coming to see me."

Jack breathed easier, happy his instinct had not failed. "I suspected you knew her."

An expression he couldn't read flitted across her face, then vanished. She nodded. "Not long, but yes."

An odd inflection, or was it just her accent, made him wonder at the reply. It suggested a double meaning, implying they had just met but knowing her as well. He decided it was her way of speaking, an older language habit.

"I want to help her. She says she has no family here. I met her when she moved in. She seems nice." *Why am I babbling?* He flushed, suspecting Mrs. Zamborski could read him.

"Yes, she will need help. Her father was all she had. And he watched out for her."

She knew him too? He resisted the urge to ask her if she had memorized the telephone directory.

She read the question on his face. "We are of the same country."

Jack's eyebrows hit his hairline. "Really?" Mentally, he slapped his head. Zamborski was her married name. The second wrong assumption.

"You were his patient, yes?"

Another surprise. Who was the detective here? She had knowledge of him while he dreamed up far-fetched tales from across the street. "Yes, how did you . . . ?"

Her face turned serious. "I know many things, Jack Tuesday, and have information sources, although I rarely leave my apartment. The police accuse you of killing your partner and put you on forced leave. Your deputy chief is a man named Michael Durand."

Other sources? The teen, Tommy, was not a possibility. So who? Rapt now, Jack straightened and stared at her.

"Whose name was once Milo Durovic." She looked at her hands. "They were in the resistance, Chetniks, Ustache, and Partisans." Her lips twisted, and she sighed, looking up at him again. "It was a long time ago. Nobody is interested in the war anymore."

"I am. What did you think of him? As a man, I mean." Jack moved his hands apologetically. "I have to tell you . . . well, we don't see eye to eye. If I'm honest, he isn't fond of me either."

"He has not changed, only his public face." She pursed her lips which puckered up the left side of her face again, making him realize his fascination with her had already overshadowed any disfigurement. "He always wished to be powerful, even before the war. You are familiar with his kind. The people who dip their fingers into many pies."

Delighted at the prospect of more information, Jack nodded his understanding.

"His chances flourished when the war came to our country. The Italians came first, strutting in with their feathered plumes and decorated uniforms. Durovic lost no time making friends with them. After they surrendered in 1943, the Nazis took over the entire country, shouting orders, with hobnailed boots echoing over the cobblestones. The Resistance groups were so disorganized. It was chaos." She twisted her palm back and forth. "A few resistance cells collaborated with the Nazis, thinking they would eliminate the Communist Partisans. Nobody knew which group was friend or enemy. In essence, the resistance fought the Nazis and each other too." She paused, then sighed. "Add collaborators and Austrian Nazi officers. Yes, chaos, brutality, and death. A vision of hell multiplied many times."

"Austrians?" Jack's eyebrows rose. He had difficulty reconciling the figure of elegance across from him with living in the chaos she described.

She nodded, sending him a small smile as if forgiving his ignorance. "Veterans of the First World War. Revenge has a long memory, and Hitler purposely used those veterans who blamed the Serbs for ending their Austro-Hungarian Empire."

Of course. The Austrian prince was assassinated in Sarajevo.

"And Durand?"

"He divided his loyalties, but it was certain that Tito and his Partisans would be the winners near the end. And Milo Durovic slinked right in there to be with Tito." Her shoulders rose, and she lapsed into silence.

"Did you know Bianca's mother as well?"

Her forehead creased in a frown as if looking into her memory. The forefinger of her left hand touched her face. "You are curious."

"I'm sorry if you thought I was staring," he said, not admitting his curiosity. It would be prying, like a child wondering why she was different. But his face grew hot, and he pushed back from the edge of embarrassment and defensive anger as if she would chide him.

At first, startled at his expression, her face cleared, realizing what she had said. "No. Are curious about *Bianca's past*." Her manner shifted to accusation. "I did not ask you here, Jack, to make light conversation. It was to warn you."

"Warn me?" Her switch in tactics increased his feeling of being tossed around in an unknown sea. He had an urge to pinch himself to prove he was awake.

"Stay away from Bianca. It will bring trouble if you do not. You must take my advice. The murder of Marko . . . Dr. Pavic makes your situation worse."

"I did not kill him, Mrs. Zamborski. So far, they suspect the killer is a newcomer . . . an assassin if you will." A new thought made him pause. Someone like the man lurking around the building last Saturday. And maybe he wasn't interested in Mrs. Zamborski. Perhaps it was Bianca or Dr. Pavic.

"A man was outside your building the day she moved in," he blurted out. Irritation at being told to stay away from Bianca made him careless, and he hit back. "You were watching him too and didn't look pleased."

Gratified by her open-mouthed surprise, then hit by remorse, he opened his own to apologize. It was too much, and rudeness had consequences. He'd just ruined his chances of hearing about Durand.

Her eyelids fell heavy, and she blew out a small puff of disappointment. She used her right hand to smooth her hair around her ear. "You are mistaken. I do not involve you with Marko's death. Only you are not aware of many treacherous events that people must not connect to you."

Jack opened his mouth, but she raised a palm outwards, halting his question. "Yes, I believe an assassin shot Marko. The UDBA, Tito's secret police, has a long arm, and they do not respect a country's boundaries."

Turning his head to gaze out the window, he imagined the man he saw on the street and nodded in agreement. Mid-forties at most, and certainly a foreigner. Jack recalled the hard edge to his voice and cold eyes, knowing Jack was a police officer. Was the man UDBA?

Mrs. Zamborksi caught his eye when he brought it back and sat deeper in her chair. "It doesn't surprise you that he sends killers to get rid of those he considers his enemies?"

"It takes one to know one."

He shook his head in denial and wondered what the connection was to him or his problem. "But Dr. Pavic couldn't be a threat, or Tito would have killed him before this."

"Unless they were searching for something and only just realized Dr. Pavic possessed it."

"If that is the reason, I hope you will not ask me to help find what it is." Jack's mind rebelled at the prospect.

"How do you suppose Tito finds these people, Jack?" She ignored his denial.

"Informants, I expect."

She nodded, and silence fell between them for a long moment. Confused, he fidgeted. Maybe she wasn't as sharp as he first thought and was using him as a sounding board for her ramblings. His attention honed in on the wall across from him at an aboriginal painting of a bird, wings spread, an eagle imagined with bold black outlines against a teal background. Daring brush strokes of tan, bright yellows, and reds. A Morriseau. The aboriginal Picasso, they called him.

"There are things I cannot tell you at present, Jack." Her firm tone sharpened his attention on her once more. "Only, you must trust me. If you wish to solve your problem with the police, start with your own people."

"I already guessed that," he told her. Exhausted from the long day, he only wanted to go back to his apartment and stop thinking. "But it doesn't help me if I don't know who. As far as Bianca is concerned, you needn't worry. I won't intrude on her mourning. But if she asks for my help, I'll accept. She asked me to look into her stolen Rubens. I can't do much anyway. Encroaching on another cop's turf is against the rules."

"Most stolen art is never found at all, Officer Tuesday." She was back to formal addresses, and Jack repressed a smile. "Just ask those who lost art, looted by the Italians and the Nazis.

"Yes, it was common knowledge in Germany."

"You were there?" He had confused her, and it gave him a childish gratification that there were things she didn't know. "Surely you are too young for the war."

He felt better at her sudden interest. "Stationed there for a time in the late 50s. There was a lot of discussion about stolen artifacts." He couldn't resist. "Bianca's father had no trouble hanging on to their

Rubens, though."

"So you think he owns looted art?" She seemed intrigued at the thought.

"No, I've already discounted it." Something he couldn't put his finger on nagged at him, though. Was it what she said, someone else had said, or what his senses had picked up? The old lady stood. *Time to go.*

"I will send Tommy, and you will come again. He lives downstairs and runs errands for me. Somehow, he has the idea that he must protect me. I pay him, so it is a reciprocal arrangement."

Jack rose and took the hand she held out. "Thank you, Mira. It's been a great pleasure. Hopefully, not for the last time."

"You are gracious for a modern young man," she smiled to show she was joking. "If I can do more to help you sort out your situation, I will."

Still holding her hand, he gazed into her face, hoping for a clue to explain the strange remark.

"Red Alert. 'Strange things done in the midnight sun.' Secrets, Jack."

Don't start with the Robert Service. He pointed over her shoulder. "You have a Norval Morrisseau. The colours are spectacular."

"Yes." She chuckled. "The poor man was likely on another binge when he painted it. Even so, it's wonderful. My husband and I were in Vancouver on holiday. We paid him full price for it, not like the people who swindled him." Her eyebrows rose. "In case you are wondering."

Jack didn't reply. His eyes lit on another smaller artwork on the opposite wall. An old master painting of three grey-bearded men sitting around a table, conferring over drinks. The dress was appropriate for the mid-1500s, he thought. An attractive old-fashioned frame suited to the period.

"Too bad that isn't an original also," she laughed, noting his gaze. "I found it in Italy, in a second-hand shop, and liked its message of peacefulness. After the war, it seemed so ordinary, so refreshing. Do you like it?"

"Yes, I do." He inspected it from where he stood. "You are right. Something about it sends out a signal of relaxation and friendship. Who did it?"

"It is unsigned," she said. "Some amateur copy of something or other, I imagine."

"Perhaps an artist on the rise. He made copies so he could practise his techniques. But whoever repaired the frame missed a spot."

"A repair?" She narrowed her eyes, staring. "Where?"

"That corner at the bottom left. The whorls in the old plaster, or whatever they used, are close but not a match."

Mira Zamborski shot him a startled glance and then moved a step nearer the picture, squinting. "It's minor, but I wish you hadn't pointed it out because now I will always see it."

"Oops." Jack echoed her small laugh. "It's still a wonderful picture." He used the useful trick of walking away, then pretending to remember something.

"Uh, the man, I mentioned, the one on the street, staring . . . you were pretty intent on him," he began.

Not fazed, she said, "Oh, that." Her emphasis on the word dismissed any importance. "He looked like my late husband. He was in the Polish Air Force, stationed in England. We met and married there after the war. It was such a shock seeing him on the street. I've grown old and am confused with too many memories. Nothing else. Good night, Jack."

Outside, a chill wind made him hunch his shoulders and quicken his pace. Bits of conversation buzzed in his mind like bees protecting a hive. Those nuggets about Durand. Knowledge of what made him tick was an advantage. Yet, the feeling of missing a reference persisted, and he blamed his tiredness for letting his attention wander to the Morriseau. The subject of art brought a fresh idea concerning Bianca's stolen Rubens, but he needed to look at her art book again.

Mira Zamborski was more of an enigma than he ever imagined.

Far from her excuse that the stranger was a look-alike to her dead husband, she had shown outright shock when she'd spotted him. *Old woman, my ass,* he thought.

18

FACE stuffed into a pillow damp from drool, he woke at the insistent ring of the telephone. Half asleep, he lurched into the hall and picked up the phone. The crisp voice of Deputy Chief Durand answered his greeting.

"I want you in the building today, Tuesday. Administrative duties only."

It took a moment for Jack to wrap his brain around the announcement.

"Answer me, Officer Tuesday."

"Yes, sir. Sorry, sir." His heart gave an involuntary leap. "Does this mean I'm reinstated?"

"No. Temporary only. You're off suspension because we are shorthanded, and you will free a person for active cases. Do not communicate with any officer other than what work requires. Do you understand?"

Today? He had to find Apple.

"Sir. I'm due at the hospital for tests, and they may take the day." He crossed his fingers, sensing Durand's irritation over the line. Now that he knew him as Milo Durovic, he wasn't so crisp and sharp, only creepy. Jack listened for a foreign accent like Dr. Pavic's but detected none.

"Practices his English in front of a mirror."

"You will need a doctor's note," the voice interrupted Brodie's musings. "So, be there tomorrow on the morning shift. Report to Personnel first thing."

"Sharp," Jack repeated and heard an exasperated snap of Durand's tongue before the dial tone.

Jack started the coffee pot and went into the bathroom. Admin duties. He'd be sitting at a desk reading numerous reports and arrest records, looking for links and anomalies. Checking with other precincts. Filing, the hours crawling on, butt weary, a walking pile of bones, which was precisely what he'd be if it continued. A new thought came along while brushing his teeth. Under the guise of work, he had a legitimate reason to read files.

Cheered, Jack had breakfast, then collected his ten-speed Schwinn bike from the basement storage. He sat on the seat, uncertain of his balance after his accident, and rode in a reassuring circle before he and Pharo set off towards Emily Murphy Park.

On his return, in an upbeat mood, he took a hot shower to relieve tight leg muscles. Invigorated and armed with a mug of coffee and his newspaper, he drifted outside to the balcony and searched the paper for McNaughton's byline, surprised there was no report of Dr. Pavic's murder. Odd, that. Jack sipped his coffee and turned his thoughts to what he'd do if Apple ignored the message left with McGruber. He checked his watch. Well, he'd soon find out.

One o'clock found him parking under a shady tree on the north side of the Riviera.

"Sorry, pal, you'll have to stay. No dogs allowed, not even you."

Pharo stuck his nose against the passenger window, pretending he hadn't heard, hoping Jack would give in. Jack wound down all four windows enough to ventilate the car.

"Watch," he ordered and left.

Entering through a back entrance, he collided with four bikers on their way out. They stood fast, not giving an inch. Nor did Jack. Finally, with an insolent stare, one moved aside. Young, dressed in biker uniform of jeans, vests, and boots, with hair pulled into ponytails, Jack tagged them as prospects; new bikers wishing to belong but not yet accepted. Still, it was odd they were here since the Riviera was a hangout for the university crowd, not the bikers.

Jack nodded at Professor Waterman holding court, surrounded

by his post-graduate students. The girls and boys were dressed alike, except the boys had sideburns to class up their long hair, while the girls had long hair and wedge shoes. Both wore multicoloured polyester shirts tucked into bell-bottom jeans. They chewed on sandwiches, beer handy beside them while eyeing open notebooks. As Jack passed, he caught Waterman telling them he wanted 'interactionist, not reactionist views,' and got wild hoots in return.

He spotted Apple at his usual table in the back. An icy stare rewarded Jack's relieved grin.

Jack sat across from him, his back to the room. "I'm glad you got my message. Don't disappear on me again. Ideas pop into my mind that you're in trouble."

"I needed more time," Apple grumbled. "But you hear me good, Jack. If you and I stay friends, don't tell me what to do. Or when."

"Apple, I will never order you around," Jack said, contrite. "I'm here for you, and that won't ever change. Using Kai's name was a cheap shot, but I'm desperate, and I'm being set up."

"You could have just asked instead of blackmailing me."

Palms up, Jack spread his hands in agreement. The server appeared. Relieved, Jack ordered a beer and another for Apple.

"Your trouble is you always take charge." Apple sat up and looked down his nose at him, mouth twisted in a sneer. Jack decided it was best to let him spew it out. "You put in your two cents, even if nobody asks for it. Back there," he jerked his head, showing where back there was, "you cheated me out of proving I could take what that bastard dished out."

That was too much. "With your wounds?" Jack protested. "The forced march near-killed you. We had to distract Kai to give you time to heal. How do you think I felt, doing nothing while he used that cane on you? Beating a wounded soldier?" Jack clenched his fists at the memory. "I wanted to kill him."

Apple stared at him and shook his head, his chin set into stubborn lines. "What about us? The rest of the guys?" his voice rose. Aware of it, he took a quick look around to see if he had attracted attention, then lowered his tone. The server came back with the drinks. Jack was glad of the respite as the man put Apple's empty glass on his tray, smiled his thanks at the bill Jack handed him and went off.

"We needed our turn," Apple continued. He pushed his glass away and gripped the edge of the table, looking at Jack with angry eyes. "But no, you were the big shot. You didn't care about us. You had to prove you could take the questioning—the caning. Put into that cell with the damned loudspeakers blasting on for hours about how great Communism is. You think we didn't have to sit and listen to them? Or take crap from the guards who accused us of being weak soldiers? Get short rations or none because we wouldn't work?"

Apple wiped away the spittle on the corners of his mouth, then took a long drink from his beer glass. "And how about when we got home? Our own army, giving us the evil eye. Lie detector tests just to prove we were still Canadian. Convincing our own government we weren't brainwashed secret agents?"

"Yes, Apple. We all got their so-called version of de-briefing."

"Ah, but you had the scars to show how they tortured you, didn't you, Jack? Did you tell them how bravely you took it for the six of us?

"It wasn't like that. They had to go through the motions, even knowing we were all okay. Just for the record. Nobody could guess what it was like. Not even close." Jack leaned forwards, looking into Apple's face. "I was the senior NCO, but we all did our part. Looking through a rear-view mirror, we think we'd act differently, but would we really? Give me a break, Apple. Holding out was our revenge on Tae. Without the rest of you there, I would have caved."

"Sure, Jack. And I'm Prince Phillip."

"It's true. We were a family."

He understood Apple struggled with frustrations of fear, helplessness, and guilt. Not wanting to admit that his injuries would never have withstood the torture, he took aim at the nearest target, completely unwilling to face that his body had failed him when he needed its strength. Still, the intensity of his accusations shook Jack. Apple's usual tirade had never been so personal.

The injustice tempted him to reach across the table and pound sense into his old friend. His thigh muscles tensed. His father's twisted face flickered before him. Was he like him? With great effort, he forced himself back into the room.

"We watched each other's sixes, Apple," he said, perhaps trying to persuade himself. He reached for his beer glass and peered into the fading layer of foam, suddenly feeling too exhausted to drink.

"Someday, Jack, we'll get square. One for the rest of us, too," he added, not altogether logical. But he pointed his index finger at Jack, wiggled his thumb over it, mouthed a bang-bang, then pointed his finger up and blew across the tip.

Jack frowned at him. "Not funny."

"I thought so." Apple snickered.

The server appeared at his elbow. "You guys need a fill-up?"

"Sure," Jack said. "Bring me a Canadian Club, neat."

"Me too." Apple grinned at Jack and pushed aside his beer glass. "Let's drink to good times with past buddies." His mind had moved on to calmer waters, and Jack breathed a silent thank you to the powers that fueled Apple's ability to switch selves.

They clinked glasses and drank. Apple smacked his lips and sniffed at his whisky.

"Tell me about Phineas McGruber."

"He owns the pub."

"I gathered that." Warmth flooded Jack's insides, not only from the fine scotch, but that their banter was on the old footing. "But he is immobile, and those stairs looked dangerous. How does he move about?"

"The stairs are that way on purpose. An early warning system. McGruber has an elevator inside. I get cheap rent for me running his errands and keeping him safe. He ain't no dummy. Don't let his disability fool you. He was born that way, but he's educated and has a good business mind. I was on the street when we met. He found me one morning, outside the front, sleeping it off."

Apple lifted his glass and downed the rest of the whisky. He treated being drunk and homeless as a part of life. At times, Jack envied him. Apple lived his life taking full ownership without wishing he'd been something different.

"We get along fine. He counsels me, and he needs me for . . . things. We're partners." Apple shot another suspicious look at Jack. "Don't come back unless I invite you. I don't need you messing up my arrangement with him. The poor guy doesn't need anything more complicating up his life either."

"Hear that? There's more to that man. What complications?"

"I'm surprised you think I would."

Apple reddened. "Well, maybe not. But you have a knack for bringing attention to people, Jack. Getting yourself out of trouble can drag other people into it. Just better not be me."

His words brought Jack's attention to full alert. Apple's eyes focused on his empty glass and avoided any contact with him.

"What's going on?"

"Nothing. Just that . . ." Apple's shoulders lifted towards his ears in an exaggerated shrug.

"Talk to me."

"Your name's got the pack's attention. It ain't smart to be on their wrong side. You're suspended with no backing from the cops. Be glad you're single—because they can't hit on any of your family. And they'd do it too."

Why would the Rebels have him in their sights? Were they responsible for his near-miss in the park? Electricity surged along his arms. A convenient way to explain his death to the public, and nobody would investigate. Who had contacts with them? It always came back to one name. Wager. But Hawk was right. Jack couldn't straight out question him. Wager would broadcast the insult, and Durand would think Jack more foolish than ever.

"There's nothing, Apple, unless my mind's hiding it from me. I rely on you to tell me what's going on." Jack heard his own desperation.

"I'll keep my ears and eyes open." Apple reached into his pants pocket, pulled out a crumpled wad of papers, and pushed them across the table. Brodie's code. The glint in his eye told Jack he hadn't quite forgiven him. "It was easy. Amateur stuff and wouldn't fool anybody."

"What did it say?" Jack spread the papers out on the table. Brodie's squiggles and Apple's notes.

"It describes someone your pal recognized. And dates, times, and amounts of money. Lots of money, in the thousands. A suitcase full."

"Is there a name?" Jack flipped through the pages, searching.

"Nothing I could make out for real. Maybe Robert Service?" Apple's voice was all business, and Jack looked up, seeing the determined soldier before they were captured, expertly reporting mission findings. "Wasn't he some writer guy up in the Yukon? Mostly about money and a lot of it. If it involved big money, no wonder he was careful about names. It doesn't do to make friendly with people in that business. Maybe your partner was more interested in what someone was into than who he was."

"Maybe. What about that initial? DC or something." Jack jiggled the pages.

"Went nowhere, didn't connect with anything else I saw."

Brodie's investigation was limited to 'information' only and nothing more. If the amounts of money Brodie recorded were large, there had to be a source, a contact. The Rebels' accountant? Follow the accountant and identify who the accountant met. *What else did you see, Brodie, and keep to yourself? Trying to make a big score?*

"Thanks, Apple. I owe you one." From a long habit when dealing with notes, he separated Apple's interpretation from Brodie's bundle, tucked it into his shirt pocket, and then stuffed the rest into his trouser pocket.

On the way out, Jack waved to the bartender, who jerked his head as though he wanted to speak to him. Instead, he tended to a customer calling him at the end of the bar. Jack went on his way, taking a detour to the men's room before leaving.

The noise reached him in the hallway. Frantic yodels that ended in screams, signalling big trouble. "Pharo." Jack broke into a run.

They jumped him as soon as he hit the outside. He had the good sense to go into a roll as his shoulder and elbow impacted the cement. It sent a jolt of searing pain through him, leaving his arm numb and his breath away. Even as pure terror overcame him, he cursed himself for being taken unawares. He raised his arms to shield his head from more injury, but it left his midsection exposed. A few grunts accompanied by heavy biker boots connected with his ribs. He rolled sideways into a fetal position, arms still groping his head. Helpless under a brutal torrent of kicks and blows, he tried defending himself with scissor kicks sideways. A yelp and curse told him his foot connected with bone, a knee or shin, and the blows intensified. Something hard hit his face, and moisture—blood—dripped into his eye.

Rough hands gripped his arm and twisted it upwards and back. A crunch followed, and he couldn't halt his cry of pain as his shoulder separated. Pharo's frantic scream reached him. Or was it his?

New shouts, this time protesting, just as the world mercifully dissolved into blackness.

19

THE smell of fear and old blood that cleaning fluid had failed to erase enveloped him.

Thwack!

Each blow of the bamboo cane was a vow to his crew that these bastards would never break him. He bit his tongue until it bled, but he wouldn't give them the satisfaction of a cry. He closed his eyes and forced his mind into a familiar place, conjuring up a brick wall.

Thwack! Count and sort.

Thwack! Place them in precise stone-mason fashion.

Thwack! Cementing with mortise.

Bricking up Kai Tae alive . . . every layer of bricks adding to the horror in the man's eyes.

"Wake up, Jack. It's okay." The voice broke his concentration. Were they being rescued? Or just a new form of indoctrination? A personal plea from the Great Leader to join their cause.

"Bugger off," he muttered.

"That's a fine way to greet visitors bearing grapes." A woman's voice answered in English. Jack opened the eye that wasn't sticky. He reached up to inspect the other, finding a bandage and swelling. He poked the puffy flesh around it and winced.

He turned his head and saw Maureen Brodie, Ben too, pale and avoiding Jack's face and bandages as if the wounds made him nauseous.

He must look as bad as he felt. "Where am I?"

"University Hospital."

Memory rushed back. Bikers, Riviera parking lot. "Pharo," he said and tried to sit up and caught his breath at the sharp pain in his ribs and chest. A bandage on one arm tight across his chest made his balance awkward.

"He's with us," Ben said.

Jack relaxed. Hawk to the rescue again.

"I was the only one he'd let near him," Ben continued. "He growled at everybody else." Jack grinned at him, and Ben's eyes dropped, but not before Jack saw dodginess or maybe a touch of uneasiness.

"Oh God," Jack said. "He'll think I've deserted him again. I have to get out of here."

"He's fine." Maureen put her hand on him. "He mopes around and keeps looking for you, of course."

Jack glanced at the hand, then at her friendly face. "Am I still unconscious? Dreaming? Why are you being nice to me?"

Maureen flushed. "I've had time to think about our talk. After ten years of friendship, Brian would have known if you were a liar and a cheat. Overlooking something like that wasn't in him. I shouldn't have accused you of betraying his trust."

"Did your change of mind have anything to do with Hawk?"

"Of course not." She huffed at the barb. "It's just . . . well, I felt miserable and realized that accusing you meant I was accusing Brian too. So I'm giving you a chance." She pushed a grape into her mouth and munched. Realizing she was eating her gift, she put them on his tray at the foot of the bed.

A nurse popped into the room. "You're awake. I'll get the doctor," she said and disappeared again.

"Mom really changed her mind when four bikers beat the crap out of you."

"Ben! Language!" Maureen rolled her eyes at Jack. "If that man hadn't come along, we'd be planning your funeral."

"Professor Waterman," Jack said.

"Pharo wouldn't go with him either," Ben added.

Although grateful that Ben's resentment had disappeared, Jack detected a touch of insincerity. He dismissed it, allowing that the boy was embarrassed, and at that age, he didn't like to parrot his mother. Maybe Hawk had put in a good word for him after all, to make up for his accusations of stalking Maureen and Ben.

"Stop with the sour lemons. They're here, aren't they?"

A doctor bustled in, and Maureen nudged Ben towards the door. "We'll be just outside until you're finished," she said.

The doctor pulled the sheets down and stuck a cold stethoscope against Jack's chest.

"I'm fine. I want out of here."

The doctor grunted and used a penlight to examine his eyes, first one and then the other. He swivelled Jack's head and peered into his ears.

"Headache? Dizzy? Nauseous? Sleepy?" Jack shook his head, then wished he hadn't.

"Not your first head injury," the doctor accused like it was a police record and Jack a repeat offender. "You were unconscious for some time. Not good." He unwrapped the bandages holding Jack's arm to his chest. "We can take these off. You had a dislocation, and we didn't want you flailing around pulling it again. Ice will help, and the swelling will go down." He pointed to Jack's eyebrow. "You'll have a scar there to impress the girls. I've ordered head ex-rays, some blood work, and some physical tests."

"I've had enough tests to choke a horse. If I was feeling any familiar effects, I'd tell you. But I'm not. Only sore. And angry."

He suddenly remembered Apple's report in his pockets. "My clothes?"

"Not so fast," the doctor said. "I've seen your history. At home, you could go to sleep and not wake up. Things can go haywire fast."

"No, I mean, I need to see my clothes. There are papers . . ."

"Check with the nurse. Maybe in a cupboard somewhere. They may even be in Emergency. In a dump, if they cut them off."

Dammit. Jack raised his arm to rub his face, and pain shot through his ribs and shoulder. The doctor grinned.

"Bruised ribs. Fortunately, they didn't break—end up puncturing a lung." He grinned like he relished the gory thought. "You must be tough boots. But no police work."

"It's only administrative duties right now," mumbled Jack.

"Maybe tomorrow," the doctor snapped and left.

Ben peeked through the door, came in, and sat beside the bed. "Mom's gone to get coffee. She said she'd get one for you, too." He helped himself to the grapes they brought.

"I need it. Thanks for taking Pharo. He's been through tough changes and doesn't understand." He saw Ben's face and bit his lip. "Sorry, Ben. I can't imagine the rough time you're having right now. I miss your dad. Probably not as much as you do, but I'm truly empty without him."

Ben turned sullen. "Mom tells me I'm the man of the house now, so I have to act like it, don't I? I can't be too sad in front of her and make it worse for her than it already is."

Jack's heart faltered, wanting to help.

"You'd make your dad proud, Ben. Being responsible and doing a good job."

Ben shrugged as if it were nothing, but his eyes lit up at Jack's words. After a brief pause, he said, "Sergeant Hawken told me you stole Dad's notebook."

"That's ridiculous. How could I?" Jack hoped his face registered surprise as if confronted by a judge who knew him guilty. Well, half-guilty.

"I thought that too," Ben said, his voice eager. "But I went right to . . . the place where I hid it to see if it was still there. When I thought about it, I decided he'd wanted to trick me, so I'd show him where it was. And I fell for it."

Holy. The boy's no fool.

"I suppose Hawk visits you a lot?" He couldn't resist.

"Yeah. He said that fellow cops look out for families after . . . after a . . ." Ben swallowed.

"We're there whenever you need us. Just call." Jack said, with visions of them spending weekends together, him acting as big brother, giving male companionship.

Ben lifted his shoulders as if he didn't care, but Jack guessed it was a front. "He's okay, I guess. But he isn't like my dad."

"Nobody is," Jack agreed. Hawk didn't realize a boy like Ben would pick up on the ruse, and trust would become an issue not forgotten. Hawk may be a good cop, but he knew squat about boys. "I'm glad he brought Pharo to you."

"It was the big guy with a moustache. I think his name is Wager. He figured you wouldn't want him at a kennel again." He opened his mouth and then shut it as if he'd wanted to say something else and thought better of it.

Ben's words penetrated into his thoughts. "Detective Wager told you he'd taken Pharo to a kennel when I was in the hospital the first time?"

Ben took in Jack's surprise, and doubt crept into his eyes. "He said he had been in a kennel, and I guessed he took him there. But how else would he know?"

"Well, it doesn't matter. I'm grateful he's with you. He's about the only pal I've got right now." Ben avoided his eyes and turned red. Once more, Jack's instinct told him something was off with Ben's attitude.

"Cream, no sugar, right?" Maureen came in, holding two paper cups of coffee. Hawk appeared behind her and took one cup. "Hey," Maureen said and laughed, looking pleased he was there.

"Thanks, just the way I like it." Hawk grinned back at her and then winked at Jack. "Caffeine probably isn't good for you right now, anyway."

Ben got up from the lone chair by the bed. "Mom, can we go now? I have homework, and I plan to have a game of frisbee with Pharo."

"Frisbee?" Jack said to fill the hesitation as Maureen looked from Ben to her coffee and then at Jack. "Pharo loves frisbee. But I have to tell you, a Basenji only brings something back to you if he feels like it. Letting you know he's your boss." Ben brightened and gave Jack a thumbs up. Jack returned it, smugly pleased at Hawk's dour expression.

"A sad thing, competing with a kid."

"The same idea as his owner," Hawk joked, but the friendly poke at Jack didn't carry up to his eyes. He lifted an arm and sniffed. "Must be my deodorant. I can clear a room faster than you can say Jack Tuesday." He smiled at Maureen and said to Ben, "Anyhow, I have to talk business with Jack, so we'll get together later, yeah?"

Clearly willing to leave, Ben walked out of the room. Maureen gave a wave to Jack and grinned at Hawk. "Enjoy your coffee," she said and hurried after him.

"You look like hell." Hawk leaned against the bed rail. He took a sip of coffee, made a face, and laid the cup beside Maureen's. He helped himself to the grapes. "Durand sends his regrets, by the way." Hawk raised his eyebrows in a fair imitation of the deputy chief with his familiar face of scorn and disbelief. "He's like a wet hornet. He's positive you did it on purpose."

Jack shifted, grimacing. "Junior wanna-be bikers did it." His eye throbbed, and so did his shoulder. He experimented with moving it and found he could bear it. His ribs were another matter, every motion like someone jabbing a boning knife into him. "It happened so fast, I forgot my moves and let them jump me. Any idea why they went after me?"

"You tell me." Hawk moved to sit beside him, inspecting Jack's bruises and bandages. "You're lucky the crop of students came when they did. I'm thinking they used you for an initiation rite, knowing there'd be no rush to rescue a suspended cop. Or do you know something they want kept secret?"

"I've got my suspicions." The word came out as slurry *esses* through Jack's swollen mouth. "Maybe Wager . . ."

"Not that again," Hawk interrupted.

"Nobody was too eager to chase the bikers, and they got away. Maybe he thinks I deserve it."

Hawk rolled his eyes.

"I can't help it, Hawk; my instincts keep prodding me. I'm getting flashes of memory of the raid, and I've decided it was a set-up." Jack kept McNaughton out of it, as promised. "They were waiting for us."

"Come on. You saying the task force was in on it?"

"No, of course not. But nobody rides with them except their own guys. Brodie and I had to use a patrol car, which somebody fired. Both of us on our own. Prime targets."

"Can't connect those dots, Jack." His eyes narrowed. "You said you get memory flashes. Care to share?" His tone was casual, uninterested. Jack recognized his technique. Make conversation while pushing his hands into his pockets as though searching for something.

Jack cautioned himself. Hawk was duty bound to tell Internal Affairs and Durand. "Only bits of disjointed pictures which drive me nuts."

"Okay. Well, let's assume the raid was a phoney. Why? And why you and Brodie?"

"Wild guesses at this point. Maureen told me Brodie was working late nights and odd hours. Supposing he saw something he shouldn't? And because we were partners, somebody assumed I was in on it and used the raid to take us both out?"

Hawk's mouth twisted up at the corner, telling Jack those were too many assumptions for him. "An insider? Is that what you're getting at? Or a warlord? With enough clout to set up phoney raids?"

"No, but supposing we had info of a deal going down with the Rebels, knowing we couldn't resist hitting on it. Wager has informants amongst the bikers. How do we know he hasn't joined their side? It wouldn't be the first time an undercover cop turned."

"Everybody had radios."

"A fat lot of good they are—out of range a block from home. A roll of coins for a call box would have been more useful. They could have used another channel without telling Brodie and me. On purpose, like."

Hawk's silence mocked this statement.

"I know, I know," Jack insisted. "But I have a hunch, and it won't go away no matter how I try." He paused, frowning at Hawk, who stayed silent. "It's got to be him."

"Who?" Wager asked from the doorway, scowling at them. He nodded to Jack. "You look like hell. Got an ID on the lowlifes who kicked your butt?"

Hawk stood up to leave. "As usual, he's out in left field. This guy sounds like a broken record. It's a wonder he remembers his name or where he lives and can find his way home alone." He winked at Wager. "We should rent him a permanent place in the hospital. He's here often enough."

"Ha ha," Jack droned, grateful that Hawk had covered the awkward pause. How long had Wager been at the door?

"What was he doing here?" Wager's eyes watched Hawk's back disappearing.

"Followed Maureen, I suppose. He's the main family rep after Brodie died."

"Nope. That honour belongs to me."

"Are you joking? I can't see Hawk running after a married woman with a kid."

Wager snickered. "Not unless he wants to . . ." He wiggled his hand back and forth. "Get in her pants."

Anger mixed with jealousy made Jack want to punch him. Pain flared up his arm from his clenched fist. "Why are you here? Hoping to see me with a toe tag?"

"Questions. I'm the guy at the scene, remember?" Wager sat in the chair Hawk had vacated and smirked like he knew the real reason for Jack's sarcasm. "Tell me how it started. You give them any provocation?"

"Anything to make you happy," Jack growled. "Probably wanna-be full-fledged Rebels and designed to look like an initiation task. Only it wasn't—because they marked me." Jack described their behaviour in the hallway. "I should have clued in then. Odds are, it's got something to do with Brodie's death and my suspension."

Wager looked at him, his expression flat. "Yeah? How's that, then?" Jack reminded himself not to play poker with this guy.

He changed his position and wished he hadn't. He sucked in his breath as pain punched his gut. "Hell," he gasped. Wager's eyes shifted to Jack's midsection.

"They were waiting for me," he said when he could speak again. "No giggling and punching, like rowdies having fun. It was too methodical." Jack gulped. "I should have been more alert. Going soft in my old age."

"So why would they target you?" Wager's lip curled in derision.

"It's connected to the night Brodie died. Don't look so snarky. Nothing else makes sense." He repeated what he told Hawk about the raid. "There you have it." He examined Wager's expression. "You didn't find any of them?"

"No, of course not."

"Not a trace. Only wacky descriptions from the pot-head students that match anyone from Dracula's mother to Trudeau's double. I should have run the lot of them in. I did get a decent one from their professor. He says he's your neighbour."

Jack nodded. "Across the hall."

"I need solid information, not hunches." He leered at Jack as if he expected nothing more. "Your pooch was kicking up quite a fuss. I found your keys and got a mouthful of teeth at the car door. I remembered Brodie's kid, so I phoned, and they agreed to take him. The professor took your car home."

Despite his animosity, Jack was touched. "I'm grateful, Wager. He'd never forgive me if he went to a kennel. Having Pharo has changed Ben's attitude. He isn't as bitter . . . gives me hope we can be friends again."

Wager grinned. "Oh, he's smitten, alright. The kid's planning ahead. He told me that if he's nice enough, maybe you'll give him your dog when you're sent down for killing his father."

Jack sank into his pillow, disappointment mixed with betrayal, remembering Ben's not quite sincere expressions of pleasure.

Wager had the grace to look away. "Durand wants you back on admin duties," he mumbled. "I've already got a load of files to keep you busy. There's a new bunch of lowlifes from Winnipeg moving into town, and I need someone to go over police reports to tie together connections."

Chills travelled upwards from Jack's feet. "Hell's Angels? And another bike war? Things are going downhill fast."

"Not the Angels. A real crime boss. Connected to the Mafia, no doubt. Rumours are already floating around about turf wars. The Rebels aren't sitting easy over it. We have to be prepared."

Wager finished and rose. "So quit lying around in bed and earn your keep."

He sketched a wave at Jack, trading places at the door with a nurse carrying a syringe on a tray as if it were a medal.

She inspected Jack's face. "That's enough company for one day. Makes you wonder who's minding the store while everyone is congregated here." She stuck him.

"Ouch. Is it you, or are all your needles flat?"

"Sissy. Not as brave as you let on."

"Where are my clothes?" He propelled himself up and swung his legs over the side of the bed.

"Probably in the cupboard, but where do you think you're going?"

"Nature calls." Jack pushed himself to his feet, and the room rotated. She steadied him.

"Need help?"

"No. Just stay in one spot, will you?"

Things swam into place and stayed put. He pointed himself towards the door to the toilet.

"I'll wait," the nurse said softly.

Back in bed and unwilling to admit getting up made him lightheaded, he puzzled over Wager. What did he know about him? A fixture in the detective unit and had even passed his sergeant's exam, although not yet given a sergeant's post. Divorced, but that wasn't unusual amongst police officers. There was a son somewhere as well. All in all, he knew next to nothing.

"Having secrets doesn't make you a dirty cop, or you'd be right up there."

Above all, what of the gang that was taking over? Pleading to whatever spirits were in his vicinity, repeating, 'please don't let it be Conor Jackson,' Jack drifted off into dreamland.

He woke up facing the wall and the clock, hands reading 8:30.

"You missed supper or dinner or whatever they call it."

Jack carefully turned his head and managed a welcome smile at Bianca, who gave him a wide smile, then a frown. "You look . . ."

"Like hell," Jack finished. "People keep telling me."

"How long will they keep you?"

"I'm outta here in the morning. How did you sneak in after visiting hours?"

"A friend. I promised to stay out of sight."

"Who told you I was here?"

"Mira Zamborski." She didn't bat an eye.

"Of course she did." Jack sighed. "The force could use her as radar." Jack took her hand, closing his own around it. "How are you managing?"

"Truth? Not well. They haven't released my father for burial. So we are clearing out the office now the police have finished messing with it." Tears filled her eyes. "Jassy is doing most of it."

He wanted to tell her about Mrs. Zamborski's warning to stay away from her, to get her reaction. He opened his mouth and said instead, "Any progress on who did it?"

She shook her head and placed her other hand on top of his. A flood of warmth went through him at her touch. "Who did this to you?"

"Bikers. But it took four of them. Nothing worse than bruised ribs and my feelings." He held up his puffy arms. "Hurts only when I laugh, cough, or breathe." That made her roll her eyes.

"So you will keep our date?"

He'd forgotten. The day after tomorrow.

"Unless you aren't well enough?"

Was there a double meaning there? "I wouldn't miss it. My eye should be purple by Saturday. I'll tell everyone you abused me."

"Right. Do I get the promised dinner first?"

A nurse came in, wheeling a trolley. "Out. Some of us have to work."

Bianca rose. "This is Kath. We were in school together." Kath nodded at Jack and pointed a forefinger at Bianca, then the door.

"Seven o'clock," Bianca told Jack, and made a face at her friend.

Jack watched her leave. She moved like a dancer, smooth and lithe.

As soon as she was gone, he was left with nothing but the silence echoing off the walls. Stark loneliness crept into his soul, and he couldn't summon anything to take its place.

20

JACK scooped up his pants from the floor of the tiny closet by the bed, searching the pockets for Brodie's pages. Nothing. Cursing, he found his shirt stiff with dried blood. The top pocket crackled when he pushed in his fingers. Giving silent thanks to the gods, he drew out the paper. But what happened to the notes in the pocket of his jeans? Did Wager find them before EMS loaded him into the ambulance?

The nurse entered with his discharge papers. He barely listened as she recited the care instructions. She handed him a prescription for painkillers. "It's codeine 30mg. Take only the recommended dose. If it doesn't do the trick, call the doctor." Making sure he understood, she left him, quoting the usual 'hope we don't see you again.'

Jack finished dressing, nearly fainting at the pain in his chest and shoulder when he bent over. Taking the simple route, he stuffed his socks into his pocket and left his shoes untied. From the bedside table drawer, he took his watch and wallet along with the pill he'd stowed after breakfast and downed it without water.

At the hospital entrance, he stopped a cabbie before he could drive away. The cabby pulled a face at the short-haul to Jack's apartment but cheered at the generous tip. Once inside, Jack snatched his extra set of car keys and drove to fetch Pharo and pick up his prescription. By the time he returned home, his body throbbed with pain. He took a codeine and stretched out on the couch. A muzzle touched his face, accompanied by a whine of sympathy. "Good boy," he said and fell asleep.

The next morning, a rap at his door interrupted him frying leftover potatoes with onions to go with his eggs and bacon. Waterman eyed him when Jack opened the door. The professor opened his mouth and closed it, holding out a set of keys instead.

"I know, I look like hell." Jack accepted the keys. "Thanks for this and also your brave intervention. I'm told your class saved my life."

"Nonsense." Waterman stood at the door, refusing to come in. "Glad we could be of service. I'll leave you to your breakfast."

He spent the day resting and nursing his aches. That evening, Jack spread out Apple's paper.

A list of dates. Jack marked the calendar to correspond. Three weeks in March, the third week just before the raid. The calendar confirmed the pattern; a Thursday, Friday, and Saturday. Popular gambling days.

He skimmed Apple's decoding, at first with excitement, then again with suspicion and the third time with outright disbelief. Enormous amounts of money gambled away by someone with Initials DC. An organization? Upwards of two hundred thousand a week. What gambler had that amount of money to play with?

"*Someone laundering money, that's who.*"

The lists included amounts won; peanuts compared with the bets. DC was someone who could afford to be a big-time loser. Jack rubbed his shoulder and realized he was slumped into his chair, pain stabbing him in the chest. He frowned, and the pain reminded him of his eye injury. Time to take a break from the papers. Mumbling to himself in self-pity, he soaked a face cloth in cold water in the bathroom and gingerly patted the cut above his eye. Most of the bruising centred on his temple. He took the cloth into the kitchen, folded it around ice cubes and held it to his head, hoping that he wouldn't look so bad when he greeted Bianca for their date. Should he take another pill? An echo of the nurse's warning chided him.

He decided the hell with it and opened a bottle of Pilsner and moved to the sofa, collecting Apple's notes along the way. He took a gulp of beer and another peek at the notes. There were itemized clothes. Suit, shoes, and a brand of gold watch which would buy his car three times over. Brodie had watched someone shopping for clothes. Why list clothes?

"High priced items in relation to a known income."

"So tell me the location," Jack ordered aloud, staring at his beer for answers. Was Edmonton the place for this type of operation? Although oil had brought in rig workers from everywhere—and gangs—it was basically a city portraying many cultural overtures. Besides the usual crime scenes: murder, theft, and minor gambling, Brodie's notes indicated big-time, organized gambling. He thought of the race track, though that wasn't open in March. Brodie had painted the surreal picture of a Las Vegas-level operation.

Or was that Apple? He had done a fantastic job decoding. *Too* fantastic. . . . Jack threw the worthless translation down in disgust. A made-up story; Apple's idea of a joke. He scrunched his hands, pretending they were around Apple's neck.

He concentrated on the initials. DC might be real. He put his fingers to his forehead and winced, forgetting his tender spots. The only part of Apple's translation that seemed useful.

"Brodie, what the hell were you playing at? Why the code?" Jack said, still hoping for an answer. He swigged the last of his beer and tried to form something out of the thoughts spinning through his head. Maybe it had been too dangerous to write reports and name the person. Someone connected with the police force?

A sudden non-stop buzz through the intercom from the front entrance made him jump. Cursing under his breath, he got up and pushed the button to stop the insistent racket, then cursed again as he realized he'd admitted an unwanted visitor. He shoved the calendar and notes into a drawer before he heard a single knock like a paw scraping down the door. He opened the door to find Hawk and a bottle of Canadian Club.

"Hey." Hawk swayed, breathing out whisky fumes.

Jack fanned the air in front of his nose. "Smells like you've got a skin full."

"It's the job. Gets a bit much at times, you know?" Hawk pushed close and snorted. "Hell yes, you know alright. I can guess what you're thinking. What am I doing here?" He chuckled and held up the bottle again. "I'm worried about you and thought I should buy you a drink. Those troubles you've got going on in your life. Get some glasses and ice"—he eyed Jack's dripping face cloth—"or squeeze that rag over the glass."

With another high giggle, he went past Jack, made for the sofa, and sprawled with his arms spread along the back. "Mmm, comfy."

"Don't be shy. Make yourself at home." Jack carried the bottle into the kitchen and sorted out the drinks. Hawk took the proffered glass when Jack returned and smacked his lips in appreciation. "Everybody's at the usual place. Most joined tables with a few Feds. They get to go home to their wives or girlfriends. So, here I am."

Esmeralda's was the customary hangout. Drinking, reciting black gallows humour, their way to cope with the stress and to jettison hard-to-forget images. Jack studied Hawk, half-envious at missing out, especially the bands. Different favourites every week: One Horse Blue, Interceptor, the Models.

His guest rolled the glass between his hands and shot Jack a baleful look. "No wife, no girlfriend, no family."

Mildly surprised, Jack's eyebrows lifted. "I assumed you had people here. No brothers or sisters?"

"Nope. Only child. From Saskatchewan." Hawk peered at Jack over the top of his glass. "How about you? Anyone in Manitoba?"

Familiar warnings coursed through Jack's body. He grimaced at his drink. "I shouldn't combine this with the pills I'm taking."

"What was the army like?"

"An opportunity for education with room and board thrown in. Prospects weren't around for the taking, so it seemed like a good idea. The Korean War had begun."

"You were in Korea?" Hawk raised his eyebrows. "Whoa. I didn't know that."

Jack shrugged. The conversation had become an inquisition, and Hawk might be more sober than he appeared.

"Hell. You were making history while the rest of us were dragging our feet, wondering what to do. Then what?"

"I tried various jobs before joining the force, but nothing satisfying." Jack took Hawk's empty glass and filled it, leaving his own more ice than whisky.

Hawk took a determined swallow as if drowning in misery. "Guess the army's where you got your urges for order and command, huh?"

"What are you talking about?"

"Come on, Jack. I know you're conducting an investigation while under suspension. You always manage to think of an alternative to standard procedure." Hawk studied his drink. "Brodie was the only one of us who didn't mind, poor guy. Thought you were the sharpest on the block, and he'd try it."

"What's he getting at?"

Stunned and offended, Jack could not think of a reply, so he just said, "Brodie?" Hawk nodded like it was common knowledge. After a moment of silence, Jack struck back.

"Okay, why are you here? This"—he pointed to Hawk's drink—"isn't like you. What the hell's going on?" Although, the amount Hawk had put away with little effects raised a question about how often he drank.

"Jeez," Hawk accused, eyebrows drawn together. "What's with you? Not everybody has underhand motives. Can't a friend be a friend and share a drink?"

Remorse flooded Jack at Hawk's frank resentment. "Yeah. Apologies. I'm starting to suspect everything." He took a deep breath. "Tell me about Saskatchewan and your family."

"Home is a small village southeast of Saskatoon called Watrous. On the doorstep of Manitou Lake, its claim to fame."

"Never heard of it." Jack rested his aching arms on his stomach, squirming to find a comfortable spot to ease the pain.

"It's a saline lake like the Dead Sea, and health nuts use it because it's packed with minerals. An ancient story claims it cured a group of Indians sick from smallpox. There's a famous dance hall, with a floor foundation of horsehair. Popular for weekend dances."

"That was your limit of excitement? A weekend dance?"

"No, Manitou Lake was for old people. Teens would spend wild weekends in Saskatoon. Wasting time until we could leave home for good." Hawk screwed up his nose. "No future. Saskatchewan Socialism: where the rich get richer, the poor get poorer, and the roads get worse. After I got a degree in commerce, I came here. What about you? Big town Winnipeg, lots of action."

Jack laughed. "Not so you'd notice. Unless an orphanage is exciting." He recited a story that he'd repeated many times.

Hawk squinted at him with eyes half-shut. "You'd never know you brought yourself up. You know, you don't, well . . . street talk."

Jack had an urge to laugh out loud. His father would have had Hawk shot for calling him lowbrow. "Strict English teachers," he said. In reality a private school. Nothing less than St. John's-Ravenscourt would suffice for Gentleman Conar's sons. "And if a soldier wants to rise in rank, he'll take courses and watch his enunciation." He couldn't resist adding, "With time and practice, the words just spill out in their proper form."

"Ohhh. Shooting a load of sarcasm now?"

Hawk only nodded, accepting Jack's worldly savvy. "Was the orphanage a dark building with lots of chimneys and porridge for breakfast? Lights out at eight o'clock or no dinner the next day? What was it called?"

Bedroom with private bath. Meals cooked by a chef. But we ate breakfast in the kitchen. Once a month, a formal dinner following a 'manager's meeting' with Wedgewood china and sterling silver cutlery . . . and suitable wines, of course. Jack swallowed hard and prepared the usual spiel.

"You've read too much Dickens. It was called St. Joseph's. Whole place burnt down in the late 50s, I heard." Again, vague anxiety tingled through Jack's arms. Was he being oversensitive?

"Arson by an ungrateful orphan?"

Jack snickered agreeably. "It was an old building—constant problems with the electricity and plumbing. No bad memories, though." It was time to turn the conversation to another topic. "Why choose the police? A university degree opens other doors."

Hawk shrugged. "A degree gives more opportunity for advancement with the police than in business. Also, extra money, and like you said, moving up in the ranks. More power."

"Oh yeah, Hawk, you're the man. I see you as the big chief one day."

Hawk looked pleased. "It's the main goal. I'll tell you a secret, Jack." Hawk tapped his forefinger on the side of his nose. "If you want to get on, you have to study the next job you're after. Watch the guy who's in it and how he operates. Planning, and cultivating the right people. Why not—?" He shut up, and his eyes slid from Jack to his whisky, at his empty glass. He managed a path into the kitchen and returned hugging the Canadian Club like a lost love and set it on the coffee table between them.

Jack stifled a yawn, which hurt his chest, and considered groaning to hint it was time for Hawk to leave.

"Ever wonder about your ancestors?" Hawk blurted out.

"Here we go. This whole visit is a probe to find your ancestors."

Jack refrained from replying by taking a healthy swig from his glass and immediately regretted it as Hawk's face swam before his gaze.

"Gave up long ago. I do wonder where Durand comes from."

"Durand? Nothing secret about that."

Jack sat up. "Tell me."

Hawk shrugged. "Forget him. Don't you wonder about your parents?"

"Don't know and don't care," Jack said. "Even my name might not be real." Half-true anyway, but again hearing his father's rant, *"Our*

heritage on the female side traces back to The Baron Coleworthy in 1766.
I'd be a peer today if not for the rule of the male line." He always glared
at Jack as though it were his fault. In truth, it was a peerage now
extinct, and the original Baron had been a wife abuser. Jack put his
fist over his mouth to cover a smile.

"You're lucky," Hawk said and continued as if it were necessary to
explain. "I was investigating a homicide, tracing a suspect through his
family relations. I realized I didn't know anything about my history,
so I started asking my dad questions."

"Exposing the skeletons?" Jack grinned. That the Bird might also
have something shameful in his past unexpectedly tickled him.

"Easy for you to say." Hawk leaned drunkenly over his knees and
looked like he wanted to cry. Surprised, Jack realized Hawk needed his
past stain free. Most people bragged when they discovered ancestors
on the murky side of the law. But Hawk's expression told a different
story.

"Well?" he asked, his curiosity heightened.

"Anything to eat around here? Peanuts?"

Jack found a bag of chips and dumped them into a bowl. "Sorry,
this is it," he said, offering it to Hawk. Getting a treat for Pharo, the
dog sniffed at it, gave him a dirty look, and went to Hawk to slobber
on his knee. Hawk ignored him and munched.

"My great-grandfather landed in Oregon somewhere in the mid-
1800s and set up a general store, ended up with lots of kids and
money. Dad's father inherited the business and had another raft of
kids."

"You must be related to half the state of Oregon by now," Jack
said, wistful.

Hawk chewed on his chip and looked thoughtful. "No idea." He
examined the quantity left in the bottle and poured another shot.
"You might even be one," he said, leaning forwards to find a sign of
relation.

"Shut up. Is that all you got? A rich family ending with you. So sad."

Hawk gazed into his glass as if searching for something at the bottom. "Do you think we can inherit insanity, Jack?"

"Hey." Jack sat up, all attention. "Are you saying your grandfather was insane?"

"Maybe," Hawk muttered, frowning. "I dunno. I got bits of info from my dad and looked up the rest."

"What rest?"

"It started when one of his daughters crawled under a train stopped at a crossing. The train started up and ran over her."

Jack winced, his mouth a round 'o'. "Where'd you find all that stuff?"

"The Mormon church."

"You're Mormon?" Jack's eyebrows rose, a vision of lying buck naked amongst multiple wives emerging.

"No, you stupid git. The Mormons put genealogy records on microfiche for people to examine. Tracing ancestors is their mission in life. They believe people can be converted even if they're dead."

"Hey, I've got land to sell in Florida," he poked, and Hawk snorted.

Jack took a handful of chips from the bowl, getting interested now. "So what else?"

"That was the first thing I found. Next, the third son, about eleven, got hold of a gun and killed his four-year-old brother."

Jack's mouth gaped. "That's horrific," he said and meant it. "But it happened a lot in those days. Every household owned weapons, and it was inevitable that the kids would find one." Those children would be Hawk's aunt and uncles.

"A few years later, my grandfather shot himself."

This new revelation should have confounded Jack, but perhaps war and police work had hardened him, or drink and drugs had altered his senses. Jack pictured Hawk sitting in front of a microfiche reader, discovering one bad account after another. He pressed his finger to his lips to stop them twitching.

"In a schoolyard." Hawk slouched over the couch armrest.

Jack's control slipped. Sound burst out of his mouth, something between a smothered laugh and a groan.

Hawk took it as the latter and nodded. "Can you imagine? I mean, in a schoolyard?"

Jack shook his head in sympathy, desperately searching for self-control. "The deaths of the others must have driven your grandfather half-crazy with grief," he said, wincing at his use of the word 'crazy.'

"And he tried to blow up the house. He lit a stick of dynamite in the kitchen."

Jack put down his glass. "You're feeding me a crock. Right?"

Hawk wasn't listening. "The theory is he tried to kill himself. But my father was upstairs and might have been killed too. Crazy old man botched it. So, he went to the schoolyard and finished the job."

"Dynamite is one way to get your kid out of bed."

Brodie's comment caught him off guard, and pain shot into his chest, and he stuffed a fist into his mouth. Unable to hold back, a brutal chortle that only someone's nightmares would conjure up emerged.

Hawk's jaw went slack, then clenched in resentment. "Not funny, Jack. Don't make fun of me."

Jack responded with a full-blown joyous horse laugh, alternately gritting his teeth in pain, then laughing again. Jack pointed a finger, laughing until Hawk finally caught on and joined in. The image of Hawk, dignity unhinged with each B-grade movie episode and unable to see its comedy, sent Jack off again.

Pharo ran from the room straight for his bed.

By night's end, Jack convinced Hawk he was too drunk to drive. He fetched a pillow and blanket, and Hawk spread them on the couch in a cockeyed semblance of order. He sat on the edge and grabbed Jack's arm. "Listen, Jack. Durand isn't a bad egg. He's just afraid."

"Of what?" On alert, Jack tried to sound bored.

"Of being destitute, people looking down on him, ridiculing him.

His father was in the military police and did something bad. They kicked him out. Durand won't say why. His father became a drunk, got violent—a disgrace. It was a tiny village, and the people made fun of him. Durand's family lost their esteem. Poor bugger."

"How d'you know this?"

Hawk laid back on the pillow with a comfortable sigh. He looked at Jack with eyes not altogether focused. "What?"

"About his father? Did Durand tell you?

"Oh yeah. Wager's his pet, isn't he? Little toady." Hawk tried spitting, which ended up as a lip splutter. He grabbed Jack's arm again. "Durand has problems eating him inside." Hawk snickered. "Worries."

"What worries?"

"I've watched him, Jack, and he's hiding a secret. Ghosts are chasing him." Hawk tried to pat the side of his nose with his forefinger but missed. "He wants power. Who doesn't? I'm going to sit behind the enormous desk. Chief, and not a man lower." His mumbles faded, and his eyes closed.

Oh no you don't. Jack shook him. Hawk's eyes popped open. "What? Morning already?" He belched, then moaned.

"You were telling me about Durand."

"Our leader." Hawk sniggered.

"His actual name is Milo Durovic. He's from Yugoslavia."

Hawk pushed himself up on his elbows, trying to focus on Jack. "You know that too?"

"You already know?" Jack said, surprised, then cursed his own loose tongue.

"No." Hawk collapsed on the sofa. His eyes slid away from Jack's. "Never heard that," he mumbled.

Jack gave up on Durand. "What about the so-called evidence against me in Brodie's death? Help me prove I didn't kill him."

"They traded . . ."

"Traded what?"

"Wager . . ." Hawk slurred, burrowing into the pillow. ". . . Got to watch him." Hawk shut his eyes and was snoring.

21

FOR his date with Bianca, Jack knotted a red silk tie and tucked the tail of his white shirt into his trousers. A red handkerchief in the top pocket of his sport jacket complemented the tie, and he decided the look would do. He tucked two codeine tablets behind the handkerchief as insurance. Still feeling pain in his midsection, he gingerly bent over to lace up his polished shoes.

At seven o'clock, Jack rang the buzzer outside Bianca's apartment. She opened the door, a bobby pin in her mouth, and waved him in.

"Nice," he said, appreciating the straight-line dress of the same blue as her eyes, the square neckline shown off by a pearl necklace. The pearls looked old, their creamy lustre putting a high price on them.

She finished with her hair. "Given that you were in a hospital bed the worse for a beating, you clean up pretty well yourself." She leaned in for a closer inspection. "Uh oh. I spot the eyes of a hangover."

"A buddy showed up last night. We began with a drink, and it turned into an all-nighter."

Jack had been up before Hawk, added extra coffee grounds to make the pot good and strong, and leaned against the kitchen counter, watching it perk. Hawk wandered in, looking like a mummy rising from the crypt. He grabbed two mugs, handed one to Jack, and they both stared wordlessly at the percolator like castaways waiting for the rescue boat.

Later, more chipper after a shower, Hawk asked, "Was I obnoxious last night? Say things I shouldn't?" His tone was casual, but Jack was aware of his eyes searching for a signal he was lying.

"Like what?"

"That's what I'm asking," Hawk shot back. "Something that sounded . . . well, off?"

Jack snorted. "You prattled on about your relatives, or ancestors, or whatever. Best laugh I've had in years." He didn't mention Hawk's drunken references before sleep. "We were both blotto. And me? Did I blab anything I shouldn't?"

"How the blazes would I know? I can't even remember what I said." Hawk's eyes still searched Jack's face with such intensity that Jack wondered if there was indeed something that Hawk had said, and he'd missed it. He kept his expression neutral while he grinned again, disturbed at his own suspicions of Hawk's motives.

"Getting paranoid about everything, pal?"

Hawk picked up on the distaste across his face.

"What? You remembered something?"

"Maureen." Jack thought fast. "You hitting on her?"

Hawk blushed. "Well, I could go for her. You think it's too soon? And I'm not sure Ben approves of me."

"Yeah. A lot too soon. Just be a friend."

Hawk had flapped his hand, showing no problem, drank his coffee and left.

"That bruise under your eye doesn't show too much," Bianca said now. "Where are we going for dinner?"

"The CN Tower for the best rack of lamb in Alberta," he said at her back as she went towards her bedroom. Jack used the time to fetch the art book. He opened it at the bookmark and examined the Rubens.

"All set." Bianca glanced from the book to Jack, a question in her eyes.

"Taking another look." He gingerly closed the cover. "I still mean to talk to the sergeant handling the case, but I forgot some details. Sorry." He slid the book back into its groove.

She opened her small evening bag, checked the inside and snapped the clasp shut. "Jack, don't mention my dad tonight. He always said that although we can't alter events, we can move forwards. He would hate that I mourn—tell me to not mope. What happens tomorrow belongs to tomorrow." She blinked once against unshed tears, then smiled up at him. "Deal?"

"Deal," he replied, wrapped her hand around the crook of his elbow and led her towards the door.

As dinner neared the dessert course, their conversation lagged. He noted she became quieter, more pensive.

"Something bothering you?" Jack pushed away a dish of crème brûlée.

Bianca blushed, looking contrite. "Truth?" She patted her mouth with the napkin, then crumpled it on the table. "Let's go to a nightclub instead of a movie." Her voice cracked, on the verge of desperation. "A place with loud jazz, noisy conversation, and people dancing. How about it?"

He tuned into her spontaneous spirit. "Great idea. You're more than just a pretty face, aren't you?" She stuck her tongue out at him. Jack searched for the server and the bill.

"We have plenty of time." Relief obvious, she eased back into her chair. "Another drink? To get in the mood?"

Long drawn-out hours later, he needed his pain medication. He had swallowed one without washing it down while watching Bianca and her unescorted solo on the dance floor. The saxophone's blues number floated across the room, filling the corners with mournful tones of aching tenderness in one moment and tearing the basest emotions from his mind the next moment.

If he closed his eyes, Ursula would be snug up against his chest while their passions drifted and merged in unison. Before his memories drew him into the middle of that empty apartment again, he got up to join Bianca and then detoured into the washroom. A splash of cold water on his face and another pill revived him. Back at the table, the band was playing *Low Prairie Blues*, one of Jack's favourites. Both arms raised, Bianca swayed by herself, in a trance beside couples drowning in their own worlds. Her carefully pinned-up hair had come loose somewhere along the way and swayed in opposition to her hips.

They were at the Blues on Whyte. Lucifer's had been his first choice, but they'd left the basement lounge after only one drink. He'd anticipated they'd leave this one too when she had darted anxious glances around the room, making him wonder if she was seeking someone. But then she smiled. "This is better. You found the perfect place."

"What would you like?" he asked.

"To forget, Jack"—a harsh tone followed up with a softer one—"but I'll settle for a Tequila Sunrise."

Their drinks served, Jack's attention went to the band's saxophone player, supported in the background by double bass and piano. Tall and skinny, he crouched over his tenor sax, making it an extension of his body, oblivious to anyone else in the room. Content, Jack had sat mesmerized until Bianca snatched at his hand, pulling him to the crowded square floor. They only danced a short time when she drifted away from him into a fantasy all her own. He let her go, embarrassed, and returned to their table. She didn't notice, and nobody else did either. Possibly they only saw another babe who drank too much.

If it was a way of forgetting, maybe he should join her. To hell with Durand, the police station, and his suspension. He focussed his one good eye on his watch, waved to the server, and pointed to his glass for a refill, wishing he were anywhere but here, despite the sax player and band.

Sympathy and puzzlement fought with each other. Compared with the Bianca he'd helped unpack, this new one had an air of reckless energy and an outwards display of living in the moment. Her actions and her grief were at odds. He could not come up with a reason for the disparity, and it taunted him. His gut told him his presence was only a distraction, her excuse to be here.

"Something else is in the mix."

À propos, the band began the following number, *I Don't Know*. He drained his whisky.

With a satisfied grunt, Bianca appeared, fiddling with her hair. She gave up and sat down.

"God, they're great, aren't they? Thank you for bringing me here. It's just the medicine I need." She didn't appear to mind that she'd been dancing by herself.

Only the thought of her father and her grief stopped the sarcastic reply he had prepared. "I aim to please." He nodded at the sax star. "I could sit and listen to him all night."

As though he'd heard, the piano player announced they were taking a break. The crowd broke into applause, and conversation resumed. The servers began making the rounds of the tables.

Jack studied Bianca's pale face, the dark circles under her eyes caused mainly by smudged mascara. "Had enough?"

She avoided his eyes, examining her fingers running along the rim of the glass. Sighing, her eyes slid back to his and gave him a lopsided grin. "I've neglected you. This week has been so awful. Waiting around for nothing. I'm not even teaching classes." She lifted her shoulders in a puzzled gesture. "I'm lost, Jack. Who am I? I have no idea anymore."

Guilt pulsed at him, and he reached out for her hand. "You're not lost, babe. Dealing with death and the fallout takes time. Your dad—"

"You don't understand," she burst out. "It's not him. It's finding out . . ." She bit her lip and stopped.

"Finding out what? I don't get it."

Bianca shook her head and looked away.

"Bianca." He tried to draw her attention back. "What's going on? Talk to me. All night long, you've been using me as a backdrop to shuttle off your moods while doing your Salome wiggle in the middle of the floor. It's about time you clued me in."

"The police think you did it." She looked ready to cry. She squeezed her eyes shut, opened them, and shot him an accusing glare. "We agreed not to discuss my father, but you just had to bring it up."

"I didn't kill him. I proved I didn't."

"How do I know that? Are you with me tonight to find out what's going on?" She leaned forwards in her chair to peer at him. "Sorry. Maybe you didn't, but why bring it up now when we are having a good time? Let the police get on with whatever it is they do."

He tightened his grip on his drink, resisting an urge to throw it across the room if only to shock her out of her evasions. "There's something else, though, isn't there? What about the man in your apartment? I saw him at your building just after you moved in. He was there again the next day."

"What are you talking about? There's no man in my apartment." Bianca's eyes rounded at him, then narrowed. The former happy gleam turned to sharp sparks of light. And something else. He imagined he saw a brief flicker of fear. Or was it a reflection from the mirrored walls and candles flickering inside glass chimneys on each table?

She did what people do when they decide the best resistance is to attack. She grabbed at her small evening bag, took out a tissue, and swiped it over her eyes, making the smears worse. He pressed his lips together to keep from laughing, knowing she'd never forgive him if he did.

"God, I'm a mess," she said, looking into her compact mirror. She rose and swayed, leaning on the table with both hands; she pulled herself up in a haughty reserve and looked down her nose at him. "I'm off to the ladies."

He almost lost his resolve and pinched his nose between his thumb and forefinger to halt a laugh.

"Don't wait, Jack. I'll take a taxi home. Thanks for the swell time."

He paced back and forth in front of the club, hoping she wouldn't take the back entrance, and tried not to look relieved when she showed up.

"I didn't bring enough cash with me for a taxi ride." Her eyes dared him to comment.

"I'm truly sorry, Bianca. I'm your friend. Maybe the only one you can trust to understand."

"Oh, great. There you go again. Assuming." She slurred over the word. "I have plenty of friends I can call on."

"Shut up while you're ahead."

"Sure. Is it safe for me to get the car, or will you run off by yourself?" She crossed her arms, evening bag tucked into the crook of her elbow. "Just get the car," she snapped, giving him the evil eye.

Jack's attempt at conversation on the way back across the river was met with stony silence, her face turned towards the passenger side window. At her street, she gave him a view of her back as she ran up the path to her building. He exited the car and hurried to catch up. "I'll call you, shall I?"

"You do that," she muttered at his attempted wit and disappeared into the building, leaving him standing on the path like an unpaid taxi driver.

Jack drove around the block and into his parking space. Out of habit, his eyes shot to the old lady's apartment window. One hand up against the drapery, she watched him, her face barely visible in the street light. He waved to her but got no response. The chill of rejection followed him into the building and up to his apartment.

Pharo greeted him with an envelope in his mouth. "Drop it," Jack commanded, getting a chortle in return as if to say that's what happens when a dog is alone for hours. Jack smoothed the wet folds, with bite marks along the edge. The envelope had the insignia of the City of Edmonton Police Service—delivered by hand and with Durand's familiar straight up and down handwriting, cramped as though paper were rationed and writing should take up brief space. Jack ripped it open.

A formal written order to report for duty on Sunday at 7 AM. Administrative duties only.

22

"WELCOME back," Sergeant Rollie Burton announced when Jack reported to him. Rollie was the Komodo dragon in his lair, a fixture at the front reception counter and close to retirement. Lack of physical exercise and too many doughnuts were turning him into a squat three-by-five frame. He inspected Jack, squirming in his unaccustomed uniform required for admin duties. "At it again, are you? I hope I'm still here to witness the day you bow to authority." His voice softened. "I'm sorry about Brodie. Anyone who says you had a hand in it has a screw loose."

"Thanks, Rollie. You are my number one fan. So far, my only fan." Jack leaned in closer. "What else?"

Burton shifted his bulk around so he was standing sideways. "They like you for the doctor killing," he said in a low voice. "But Wager can't make it stick, and so far, you're in the clear. Durand will send you to another shrink. Just in case you're faking." He turned his head to peer into Jack's eyes. "Are you?"

"No."

Burton's stare never wavered, and neither did Jack's. "Good enough for me," Burton said, finally. "You're ordered up to Personnel. Go, then hightail it back." He jerked his head towards the rear. "There's a load of reports ready for you on the desk."

Jack made a face. "Don't expect me to look inspired at the same time."

"Get used to it," Burton said. "It's only the first day. You're the mutt for anything that goes begging for attention."

"Like what?"

"Better you don't ask." Burton shot Jack a knowing grin. "But designed to inspire you to quit, maybe."

"Not happening." Jack jerked his head to point upstairs. "Personnel? Anybody up there on a Sunday?"

Burton shrugged and turned to bark an order at a constable. Jack went upstairs to the third floor, past the empty Chief's office and other executive offices, and straight down the hall to Personnel.

Stacy Pendleton was the lone civilian in the office. Hunched over a ledger, staring at an open page, her eyes darted back and forth between it and the paper in her hand. Beside her, files with rounded corners and discoloured with age made a pile-high stack on the desk.

She looked up, her finger poised over the page. Her eyes lit as they came into focus on Jack. She made a mark on the sheet and used it as a bookmark in the ledger.

"Hi, Stace. Why are you here today?"

A twenty-year veteran in Personnel, Stacy was everyone's go-to girl for information. After a brief fling five years ago, she and Jack had drifted apart with mutual agreement.

"A case of no rest for the wicked. Some bright star thought we should review Personnel records." She rolled her eyes and indicated the files. "We want to ensure no spies, gangsters, or undesirables are on the force. Apparently, the city council decided it is *public relations conscious.*"

Her grey eyes swivelled between her loaded desk and him. "No offence, Jack. Your fiasco started them off. There was a huge public backlash at the adverse publicity."

"What am I doing here?" He kept his expression neutral, but a flutter started in his middle.

She tapped the end of her pencil against her thumbnail. "Your birth certificate."

"What about it?"

"We don't have any proof of who you are. Nothing. Why is that?"

"You have my army records."

"We need information about your early life."

"Who thought that one up? My history is well known. My army records should vouch for me."

"But there must be school accounts." She grinned at him, blushing uncomfortably. "You didn't just grow up on your own, like a wild child." She gave a nervous titter.

"I was in a Catholic orphanage. Attended school in the same place. They lost the records in a fire." Jack swallowed, uneasiness making him bite his lip. Trying for innocent confusion, he laughed. "What do they hope to find out? I was the head honcho of some Mafioso when I was a child?"

"Of course not, Jack. Your record speaks for itself. Do you have anything that shows the credibility of your age and nationality?"

"My passport bears my citizenship and birthdate. That should be good enough."

She tilted an eyebrow at him. "You got a passport without a birth certificate?"

"I had other ID. Military credentials, driver's licence. SIN card. I always travelled on my army credentials, with the army, on their recognizance."

"There's no receipt in our files of a passport ID."

"That's not my fault." Jack stopped talking before he betrayed his nervousness over Durand and his suspicions. Jack wished Brodie's notes weren't so cryptic. He suddenly desired to be downstairs with Burton's files, doing penance even though every cop hated the grind. "Is it only me?" he asked her.

"What?"

"Are there incomplete records on other cops? Or is it just me?"

Stacy pressed her lips together and scratched her head with the eraser end of her pencil. "My orders are to get a record that places your birth in Canada, or else we'll start sending out official requests for information to the Manitoba government."

Jack threw up his head and curled his lip in disbelief at the threat. Stacy nodded twice. "Yes, you heard. Trust me, you don't want official requests flying around police offices. It leads to undue suspicions, and they'll surmise you weren't born in Canada." She shrugged her shoulders and grinned at him. "Not that I care a bunch. What difference does it make after all this time? Unless you're a Commie agent, born in Russia and sent here as a mole."

Jack snorted, and her grey eyes twinkled. "Which is ridiculous, isn't it? If you were a Commie agent, they'd give you impeccable credentials, right?" She reached out and touched his arm, a begging look on her face. "Try and find something. By next week? Let me know, so I can report it's being handled." Her eyes implored him to cooperate.

"Stacy," Jack said. "I'll be spinning my wheels. There isn't anything there. You can't think this is the first time I've gone through these hoops."

"Try again?" She sighed.

Resigned to making a show of cooperation, Jack lifted his arms up from the elbows and let them flop. "Okay, but don't hold your breath."

Back downstairs, he jerked a good three-inch pile of reports towards him, raging inside. The sudden investigation into his past was a new twist. Why now? Stacy's explanation about reviewing files was lame. Unless someone hoped they would find a prior which gave credence that he killed Brodie. Which meant they had zilch against him so far. But, somebody already knew there was no record prior to 1951 when he joined the Dragoons.

"Get a move on, Tuesday." Burton's voice broke into his thoughts. Jack found himself staring at the pile of reports. "Divine inspiration won't get the work done."

One of the civilian clerks called out, "Isn't it time for coffee, Sarge? Something besides the tar remover in the coffee room?"

Burton paused, then sighed. "Okay, Tuesday. You're it. Coffee run."

"What?"

"You heard me." Burton's face set stubbornly, but Jack could see he wasn't comfortable.

"Penalty duty, pal."

Jack pulled a handkerchief from his pocket, draped it over his arm like a waiter, and said, "Payment in advance, *Gentlemen*," pencil poised over a notepad. "May I take your coffee preferences?"

Burton clicked his tongue and turned away.

Coffee chore done, Jack sorted crime reports between street and house robberies, bank hold-ups, commercial break-ins, drug charges, assaults, and car theft. The object was to seek unusual details, inconsistencies and references to other charges which could point to connections with known offenders. He toiled on until he came across a report on a badly beaten pinball machine vendor. The vendor declined to name his attacker, claiming it was too dark to see. It smacked of organized crime. The vendor machine operator shorted the proceeds from the machines, and his beating sent a warning to others.

Crime bosses used the bikers to collect revenues and enforce the rules. In their spare time, bikers tended their own marijuana grow ops and mixed their T's and R's, a combination of Ritalin and Talwin.

Jack made a note, took it upstairs, and left it on Wager's desk. On the downwards trip, he encountered Durand coming. Jack backed against the bannister to make room, bending his elbow to form a salute until he remembered he wasn't wearing his cap. "Sir."

Durand nodded, passed by, and stopped a few steps above the landing. "Officer Tuesday. You have been to Personnel?"

"Yes, sir."

"Well?" He stared down at Jack from above, a scowl on his face. "Report, man."

Jack scratched his chin. "Perhaps over the years, there is a record stashed somewhere. Something which proves I exist. Besides the fat bundle that Personnel already has," he couldn't resist adding.

"Getting cocky doesn't help, DC Tuesday." Durand's emphasis on the word *DC* hinted it might not be long before he wasn't one. "The police department isn't a refuge for born-again criminals. We need only the best, with irreproachable standards. You understand me?"

"How'd he get in here then?"

"Yes, sir. I do," Jack assured him. "I meant it with all due respect, sir."

Durand's nostrils pinched like he smelled something rancid. "Whenever I hear that excuse, I suspect the person really means the opposite."

Was that a smirk at the corner of the deputy chief's mouth? Had he actually pulled off a joke? It was a new depth in Durand's character.

Halfway through the doorway, Durand turned back to Jack.

"There will be a new doctor to take Pavic's place. We aren't finished with the matter of Detective Constable Brodie."

Jack returned his stare, staying mute.

"You are an enigma, Officer Tuesday, and I suspect you have secrets we don't know about. Which I intend to flush out." Durand gave a vicious pull on the door handle and disappeared into the hallway.

At his desk again, Jack winced as a sharp pain reminded him of his bruised ribs. The pile of files loomed in front of him, taunting, promising more drudgery and lack of ideas. Now, they inspired an enormous yawn. He shook his head to shake tiredness from his brain and thought of Bianca and their failed date. Maybe if he had news about her painting.

Jack grabbed his notebook for the phone number Siobhan had given him for Sergeant Wallace.

"Gone for the day. Try tomorrow at about lunchtime. Is it urgent?"

"No." Jack gave his name and asked that Wallace phone him.

Next, he tried McNaughton and had no satisfaction there either. Finally, the day ended, and the finished reports and files landed in the out basket with a gratifying *phlup*.

On the way home, Jack stopped at the Burger King drive-in and packed his stomach with fries and a hamburger. Dejected, he ate without noticing, which he decided was lucky since the food tasted like day-old fryer grease. The coffee was passable, and he drank a refill to dull the taste of salt and vinegar in his mouth.

Turning the corner to the apartment parking lot, he spotted the mystery man crossing from Bianca's apartment building. Jack watched as he turned down the street towards the university. He still wore the baggy suit and hat, its brim lowered across his face. Jack hurriedly parked, shot out of his car, and ran to the front street. He looked in every direction, but the man had disappeared. Was it his fancy that he came from Bianca's apartment? The instinct was strong, and Jack trusted it. He was more than an ordinary visitor, or Bianca wouldn't have denied it. Who was he?

After feeding Pharo, Jack fingered through his record collection. He pulled out a band favourite and started it up. The first notes of *Take a Pair of Sparkling Eyes* from Gilbert and Sullivan's the Gondoliers blared out. Jack quickly turned the volume down so the music wouldn't lure Professor Waterman to his door. He got comfortable and spread out Apple's code interpretation for anything he might have missed. He felt a paw at his leg and saw an expectant glower. Jack sighed and collected the leash and baggies.

In the fresh air, his mind still on Brodie's notes, an idea took shape. The downside was that it required another talk with Apple. He longed to go to bed early, but Sunday might be the best time to waylay him.

Jack followed the path to the back of the pub and up the stairs. Lights spaced at intervals across the upper balcony were lit even though the day was in twilight. Probably a move to discourage any prowler who thought McGruber stashed the pub proceeds upstairs.

He knocked and heard a soft scrape inside. After a long silence, he said to the door, "It's me. We need to talk," and heard a muttered expletive. A reluctant eye peered at him through a crack.

"Come on, Apple."

Apple opened the door wider, poked out his head for a search around, and then yanked Jack inside, shutting the door firmly behind him. Jack saw a neat kitchen, a cup of coffee still steaming on the table beside the Edmonton Journal.

"Did I invite you to my place?" His set face told Jack he wouldn't get a cup of coffee. He sat on the only other chair and faced Apple. "Nice place."

"Nope. No invitation," Apple said, answering himself. "Which means no pleasure on my side." He crossed his arms over his body and declined to sit.

"Wow, this guy needs a slap 'round the earhole."

"I'm here now." Jack frowned at him. "So a little courtesy would be nice."

Apple flushed. "There's a reason, Jack. You know the company I keep. If they connect you and me . . ."

"Well, whoever you're talking about could see us together at the Riviera as drinking buddies. What's the difference?"

"Plenty. The Riviera is where you give me glad money. To make you feel better about yourself."

Jack sharpened his eye on Apple, who had the grace to blush.

"Is that so?"

"Oh crap. Want some coffee?" Apple opened the cupboard for another cup.

"No, thanks." Jack bent forwards, his forearms on his knees, and looked up at him. "I want information about your code sheets. They don't make sense."

"Not my fault." Apple stared at him, then lifted his coffee and took a sip. His hand shook, and the cup clicked against his teeth.

"The location of where that lavish gambling is happening would help."

Apple sucked his cheeks in. "Don't think he mentioned anywhere special. A racetrack?"

"In the middle of February? Don't think so."

"Oh yeah. I dunno, Jack. Give me the papers, and let me look again."

While Apple reviewed his work, Jack inspected the apartment. It smelt of fresh paint, and the small sitting area next to the kitchen was spotless. Apple's army training had carried on to keeping his quarters shipshape. A door at the end of the sitting area led to a bedroom, he supposed.

"Did you come up with anybody who matched the initials?" Apple's voice interrupted.

Jack shrugged. "Negative. I can't understand why Brodie didn't just say right out." *And tell me.*

"Would you have believed me?"

The idea stopped him in his tracks. Or maybe it would have put them in danger. *Of course, it did; otherwise, he would still be alive, and I'd have my memory.* There must be something that he already knew but hadn't connected yet? He rose to peer over Apple's shoulder at the paper as if every word had taken him in.

"I need you to tell me who's involved, Apple. I'll never admit it came from you."

Apple scrunched the sheet and pushed it at Jack. "Unless someone followed you here and now knows I'm your information tap. Beat it, Jack. Besides, I've got nothing."

Jack didn't move. "I'm not asking for information that isn't already known on the street. So, where does it happen? Has to be a place large enough but doesn't attract attention. Like a mansion in Old Glenora? People congregating for dinner or a party. Maybe a club?"

"No, not a club," Apple readily agreed. "Too many ordinary people who'd gossip. Gotta be your guess of a mansion in a pleasant neighbourhood. Ritzy people mind their own business, and the grounds would be big enough for plenty of parking."

"But how would Brodie get in there to see?"

"How should I know? That's your job. Probably dressed up and followed someone in." Apple's face turned soft as he contemplated

Jack. "You want to know about street talk? Even if you aren't a corrupt cop, the police want it that way. Watch yourself. If I'm seen with you, I'll be branded with the same iron. I owe you this warning, but consider yourself paid in full."

Jack stood. "If that's what you want, Apple." He waved an arm around. "I'm glad they set you up safe. Hell, if it gets too bad for me, you can hide me up here, and I can lie low for a while."

Eyes round and mouth open, Apple stuttered. "You and me? Here? You listening to anything I say?"

"Why not?" Jack's eyes went wide in surprise. "As far as I see, nobody would look for me up here. There's only you and McGruber. The rest of the rooms don't seem occupied. I could hide in one of those. Can I have a look at one?"

Apple grinned at Jack then and relaxed. "I get what you're doing. McGruber likes to keep those rooms for those who get too drunk to drive. They aren't apartments like this one, only a bed and bathroom." He shot over to the door and held it open. "Now get lost. If I hear anything, I'll send a message, but don't come. Remember what I said and watch your back." A buzzer startled them both.

Apple chuckled at Jack's wary expression. "My warning finally scared some sense into you? Mr. Phineas wants me." He pointed to the outside. "Adios, Jack."

Satisfied with the information gleaned from Apple, Jack checked the building and surroundings on the way out, making sure nobody was interested in him.

23

SOMETHING heavy lay on him, and his chin was wet. Jack stared down his nose at two brown eyes mooning back at him. Alarmed, he sat up and shifted Pharo off to the side. "What's wrong? Are you sick?" Jack rubbed his ears and felt his nose. It was wet. He rolled over on his back, waiting for a tummy tickle. Jack obliged.

Pharo rolled right side up and crept forwards to snuggle against him. "Are you kidding me? You just want company?" Guilt welled up as Jack looked at him. He hadn't noticed the dog's anxiety after going in and out of different houses and kennels. It was no way to treat his best friend.

So when he showed up at work with the dog in tow, Jack ignored Sergeant Burton's protests. "He'll stay under my desk, and nobody will know, Rollie. It's that, or I have a terrible headache coming on and I'm dizzy. The doctor warned me it might happen, and when it does, I'm supposed to hike myself right to the hospital."

Face red, Burton twisted his mouth. "Watch that tone, Constable." He stared Jack down, telling him who was boss, then growled. "Keep him out of sight."

Rightly chastened, Jack filled the bowl he'd brought with water and tucked it in the back against the kick plate of his desk. Pharo ducked after it and hunkered. Jack made room for his feet, pulled the stack of the night's reports towards him, and reached for the telephone receiver. Tucking it between his ear and shoulder, he rang the Edmonton Journal's number and asked for Harry McNaughton.

After a long delay, the operator said, "I'll put you through." A pause, then another voice. "You after McNaughton? Who's this?"

"Just tell him my name is Joe Friday."

"Yeah?" A grunt.

Jack's senses heightened. "Is he sick?" He untucked the receiver from his shoulder and brought it to his ear. "I've left messages for him twice now," he lied. "So, is he there?"

"Haven't seen him."

Something was wrong. Dreading the answer, Jack asked, "Did he go on vacation without telling anybody?"

"He said he had a lead on a story and would be back to meet the filing deadline. Nobody has heard from him since." There was another pause. "So, who are you? Joe, who?"

"I just give him tips. But nothing which would put him in danger. Does he usually go missing for a time without saying where?"

"No. That's why we're worried. He warned . . . oh hell, why am I telling you? If you know anything that might help us locate him, you'd better—"

Jack hung up, and a sense of foreboding shot electric sparks along his nerves. Blackmail had forced Harry's silence about what he knew. So why would the blackmailer still feel insecure? Odd. The victim was usually afraid, not the blackmailer. He pulled at his lower lip, wondering what he could do. He hadn't a clue where Harry lived or his habits.

"You going to stare at that report all day?" Burton thundered, making him jerk upright.

"Get off my case, Sarge," Jack snapped, letting his anger vent. "I'm not a rookie here." He flicked a finger at the report in front of him. "Just wondering why this sounds familiar. It'll come to me."

Unperturbed, Burton passed on by. "So will Christmas."

Home for lunch, Pharo jumped on the couch where he shouldn't be, shooting Jack a woeful look.

Alarmed, Jack bent over him. He ran his palm along his body, searching for sore spots and found none. Pharo licked his fingers and then tucked his head into his paws. Should he leave him for the rest of the day? The phone rang. Jack considered ignoring it but was glad he hadn't when Harry McNaughton whispered his name.

"Harry, where are you?"

"Listen. Meet with me, will you?" His voice wavered, fading in and out with traffic noises. Harry was definitely at a phone booth.

"The usual place? When?"

"As soon as you can. And don't bring company."

"I—" About to say he might not make it, Jack heard a dial tone. He pressed the disconnect button and dialled a number. "Pharo needs a vet."

"You're trying my patience, Tuesday. Make it quick and get back here before someone comes looking," Burton snapped out.

Pharo jumped into the car, unresisting, which raised Jack's alarm even more. At the vet clinic, Carol, the technician, came from behind the counter and bent over him. "Ah, Pharo. Where's my kiss?" Pharo rolled his eyes up at her. "We'll keep him for the afternoon. Do a range of tests to see if something catches our attention."

"I'll come back."

She nodded, and Jack gave her the phone number of Faucets just in case.

Jack sat in the end booth, facing the front of the café, and waited. Minutes later, McNaughton slid across from him. "I made sure you weren't followed."

Aside from the reporter's usual sport jacket with bulging pockets over baggy trousers, these looked as though they'd been slept in since they were new. Bloodshot eyes peered out over dark circles, his face unshaven and skin a pasty white.

"Good grief, Harry, what's happened? By the look of you, it's not good."

"I received a tip. He said it was"—he fluttered his hand—"a lead on a story."

"Where?"

"By the airport. Quiet back street, but they often are. Does it matter? Nobody showed, so I left. When I crossed the street, someone in a pickup deliberately tried to run me over. I just made it into an alleyway. When I got to my car, it was surrounded by bikers on their hogs, waiting for me. To kill me."

"Come on, Harry." Jack laid his hand on the reporter's arm. "You're well known. The papers would splash it over every front page if someone attacked you. Scaring you is one thing, but killing you is a bit much." Spoken out loud, his words weren't entirely convincing, and Harry's disappointed expression confirmed it.

He shook off Jack's hand and placed his face in both his own, shaking his head in denial. His hands scraped down his cheeks. "You don't get it, Jack. I hoped I was safe, but I know too much. My house is staked out, and I can't go back there. He won't take a chance that I'll stay quiet."

"He who? You can hide out at my place."

McNaughton's laugh verged on the edge of hysteria. "The first place they'll come looking."

Jack thought of the empty apartments above the pub. "I know someplace where they'd never find you. Let me make a phone call. A friend of mine from Korea."

"You mean your friend Apple?" McNaughton's laugh turned shrill. A few heads turned towards them.

"I know, I know. He looks like a street bum, but that's the reason you'll be safe. Nobody would ever think he'd be involved. Let me call him. He still owes me."

Harry put his face in his hands again.

Jack pushed on with what was uppermost in his mind. "You trust me, Harry?"

Harry gave him a wary stare. "I'm here, aren't I?"

"Then let me in on your information. Brodie's only a part of it, yes? You can't keep running."

Harry pulled his fingers through his hair. "I already told you to look at the evidence they got. Your gun. I saw him switch it."

"Him? Who?"

"Jesus, Jack, why can't you accept what I tell you and get on with it? I'm dying here. You're going at me like I'm in the interrogation room. There's no time for details. That new gang moving in are the ones after me. They don't like loose ends. People running around with information which could take them down isn't good for their reputation."

Jack was all attention now. "What gang?"

"The Jackson mob. They got a money laundering scheme besides everything else they get into. The bikers are their go-to guys for delivery and enforcement. Drugs . . ."

"No. Not drugs," Jack interrupted.

"What? The police have it figured out already?"

"We're on it," he said, covering up. But were they?

"Sure you are." Harry's tone was derisive. "But not who or where it's being held, I'll bet."

"Harry, you can't keep the information to yourself. Come downtown with me and tell them your story."

Harry's face lost more colour if that were possible. "No way. By now, I think you already suspect they've got someone in there all sewn up. I may as well shoot myself right now."

Jack leaned in close, arms prickling. Exasperated, he spread out his fingers as if to strangle the other man. "For God's sake, Harry. Why call me if you're going to just sit there and spout riddles? This isn't the time for guessing games. And if we have a rogue cop, who is it?"

"Okay." McNaughton let out a long breath as if ridding himself of a burden. He glanced around to ensure nobody was within earshot and froze, sucking in air through his teeth. Alarmed, Jack screwed his head around to follow Harry's gaze, but nothing seemed out of whack.

McNaughton slid out of the booth and legged it to the front door.

"Harry!" Jack grabbed the bill, threw the money at the front till, and hurried after McNaughton. Four people coming into the café blocked him. Jack punched his way between them, seconds wasted even as he ignored their protests, and spotted McNaughton at the far end of the strip, heading into an alleyway. Feeling he was in a dream sequence, running hard but getting no nearer to his goal, Jack heard a throaty yell and sped up, feet skidding around the entrance to the alley, praying against what he'd find.

"Police," he warned, and the small crowd parted willingly. McNaughton lay against a dumpster, holding his chest, blood seeping liberally through his fingers. Jack knelt beside him and pulled his hand away, lips tightening at seeing pink foaming blood. A knife wound. McNaughton wheezed a hissing gasp.

"Ambulance," Jack ordered. An excited voice said his friend had gone to phone the police and an ambulance. Jack took time to scan the five or six people standing nearby, absorbing faces, looking for that telltale, expressionless face of a killer who wanted to make sure he'd done a good job.

"Stand back along that far wall. Nobody leaves. You'll need to answer questions." Everyone obeyed. A woman started weeping, and an older man put his arm around her.

McNaughton's eyes found Jack's. He wrapped his fingers around Jack's wrist and tried to say something.

"Tell me, Harry."

"Followed you . . . to get me." He coughed, and bubbles fizzled out his mouth. "You know him . . . *sss* . . ." McNaughton let out a rasping breath, and his head lolled to the side. Jack felt his throat for a pulse, then stared down at the reporter.

"Harry. . ." Jack's voice cracked. An archetypical reporter to the end, keeping the door to his vault of information clamped shut.

Like an omen, the faint wail of a siren, getting louder by the second, came from 104th street.

He sensed someone at his shoulder. Assuming it was a rubbernecker, rage overtook him. Head bursting with heat, only his police training to stay in complete control saved him from a physical altercation. He took a deep breath, ready to turn.

"Wherever there is a body," Wager said softly. "You're on hand. Why aren't you on desk duty? I'll be interested in your explanation for this one."

"And it's pretty convenient that you're here, Wager. Have you been here all along?"

"Did you call it in?" Wager retorted, ignoring his question.

"One of them." Jack jerked his head towards the bystanders along the wall.

"I'll ask again, Tuesday. Why are you here?" Wager stared into Jack.

"At Harry's request." Jack bore down Wager's eyes, saying he was a liar. "We met in the café at the end of the strip. He was a mess. Scared witless and on the run."

"You?" Wager stated although a flicker of uncertainty crossed his face before his habitual cynical countenance covered it.

"You don't have me for this," Jack said. He nodded to the spectators. "That bunch was here seconds before me. Maybe they saw something." He confronted Wager again. "Are you following me? McNaughton was going to give me information clearing me of Brodie's death." Jack swallowed, hard put to keep his voice steady. "He spotted someone and took off like a shot. By the time I got here . . ." Jack stood up, his knees snapping. "He saw you."

"Not me." Wager shook his head, unperturbed by the accusation. Curious, even for a hardened police officer, thought Jack. Been around too many bikers and hiding his thoughts, perhaps.

The siren gave the last moan into silence. Soon two medics appeared, wheeling a gurney, medical equipment on top. Wager stopped them from going any further. Both medics stared at McNaughton, then at each other. One returned to the ambulance to report while the other perched on the gurney to wait for the inevitable investigators.

"How long do we have to stand here?" one witness ventured. Others murmured encouragement. Evidently, the novelty had deteriorated.

Jack approached them and explained that before leaving, a constable would collect their witness statements and details. A chorus of grumbles followed him back to Wager.

As if on cue, a patrol car arrived, ejecting two constables, who separated for each end of the alley and unrolled yellow tape across the entryways. Another automobile pulled up, spilling out a sergeant and other officers.

Wager crossed his arms. "Did McNaughton manage to say anything?"

"We've got a dirty cop and likely two."

"Yeah?"

"You aren't surprised . . . ? Or insulted?"

"Are you?" Wager countered.

"Not anymore." Jack narrowed his eyes, grinding his teeth in a snarl at the silent insult. "Wipe that look off your face," he snapped. "Let your bird brain clue into the facts."

Wager only looked back at him, his expression deadpan.

Jack kept his own voice flat. "Like I said, there are plenty of witnesses. So it can't be me."

"You just said you could have a partner or partners," Wager countered.

"Oh, right." Jack threw his arms up in the air. "McNaughton asks me to meet with him to tell me he knows I want to murder him and then runs away from me. Makes perfect sense."

"We could also say he wanted to blackmail you, or else he'd release the proof you're rotten."

Jack exhaled a long breath, telling himself to count to ten, started, and made it to number three. "Jesus, Wager. They could fit you up in the frame the same way. You're up to your ying-yang with info on the bikers, their pals, and associations. There has to be a reason you want me front and centre. Probably to cover *your* ass." Wanting to punch him out, Jack turned away in frustration, a terrible weakness overtaking his body. He resisted the urge to slump down and lean against the wall alongside Harry and yield to the belief that any effort to go on was futile.

"Stop chasing your ass and get thinking about serious stuff."

A scant half hour ago, he and McNaughton were in the café. Jack wished he'd hurried him along with information. Instead, he'd tried to convince him into a safe place, hoping that if McNaughton's nerves eased enough, he'd tell Jack everything. He blinked against tears, pricking his eyelids. His father always said he was a stupid schmuck, and maybe he was right. In the last weeks, he'd been wading in syrup, lost in brain fog, striving to be somewhere unknown, never able to reach his goal. Did he have knowledge that his subconscious mind fought to keep hidden? Was that why he dithered?

Two Crown Victoria patrol cars pulled up and unloaded. Everyone in the alleyway except McNaughton gave them their full attention.

Jack took a last look at him, seeming smaller, helpless, baggy clothes soaked with blood. He clenched his fists.

"You know him. . . ." Harry's words echoed in his head.

24

JACK arrived at headquarters the following morning full of self-blame to meet Sergeant Burton's scowling face. The only good news was the vet's opinion that Pharo may have scarfed food which didn't agree with him but would suffer no lasting harm.

Now, Sergeant Burton waved the front page at him. "You made the papers again." A younger Harry McNaughton's face stared back at him, his portrait rimmed in black. "A regular magnet on the murder front," Burton went on, spouting off his black humour. "We got the only DC in Canada who attracts bloodshed instead of preventing it. You trying out for the undertaker's exam, Tuesday?" His remark raised a snigger in the room.

Jack shot him a dirty look and ducked under the partition. "Pharo is fine, by the way," he growled, adding, "Did you sneak him a piece of your stinking doughnut yesterday?" He was immediately filled with remorse as Burton's mouth fell open. It was a shoddy way to get even for being ticked off. Flushing, he tried to excuse himself.

"Apologies. It's this whole mess yesterday . . ." he pointed his finger at the paper. "He was a good guy, and he shouldn't have ended up against a dumpster, bleeding to death. I didn't . . ." He stopped, throat constricting.

"I know, son." Burton placed his beefy palm on Jack's shoulder. "That's why we tell terrible jokes, so we can cope with the repulsive sights we see and can't unsee." Even though his tone was sympathetic, his eyes weren't. He lowered his voice. "Hear this, Jack. No more taking time off whenever you're bored. Work with me here. Getting me into trouble is something I won't tolerate. Put your brain to work and keep busy. That's the cure."

Jack's attention honed in on his words. What the hell? He had to trust someone. He leaned in close. "Do you ever have reason to visit the evidence room, Rollie?"

"Why?" Burton leaned in and brought his attention fully onto Jack, the way people do when they're about to get a dose of juicy gossip.

"McNaughton insisted that I need to look at the weapon that killed Brodie."

"Why?"

"He said I'd know when I saw it."

Burton's eyebrows raised up, only stopped by the wrinkle in his forehead.

"They took fingerprints, yeah?" Jack continued.

Burton nodded. "The RCs made the ID in their new lab. The fingerprints were yours."

"Can you get me in the evidence locker?"

"A risk like that?" Burton looked horrified and shook his head. "Not a chance." He plucked a piece of paper from a pile on the counter and handed it to Jack. "While you were out upholding the law, a Sergeant Wallace from North Division phoned. Said you wanted to speak to him."

Two men with briefcases appeared at the counter. Before Burton moved away, he said, "Get down to the basement. They need someone to sort old files. You're it."

Jack groaned. "Can I call Wallace first?"

Burton turned away, throwing up his hands as if to say, 'why ask me?'

Jack hung his jacket over the back of the chair, pushing aside an inch of reports, trading them for the phone.

"Wallace," answered a deep voice.

Jack introduced himself.

"That Tuesday? Suspended, aren't you?"

"I'm back. You got an opinion already formed for that?"

"No." Wallace didn't rise to the bait. "Internal Affairs works itself into a frenzy to justify their existence. You the guy at the murder scene yesterday?"

"Yeah." Jack ignored the pregnant pause from the other end, not about to get into the news from the horse's mouth scene. "My call is about the theft of that artwork by Peter Paul Rubens. A week ago?"

"You got something for me?" Wallace sounded disappointed.

"I have an informer on another break-in," Jack lied, stressing the word informer to deter Wallace from asking for names. "He claimed he got the word about a big art theft, but whoever was behind it found out it was a fake. There might be a connection."

Jack overheard the shuffling of papers, muffled swearing, and then, "Fake? That's a new one for me. You heard about that doctor's homicide? It belonged to his daughter, to both of them, I guess. They swore it was valuable and in the family for generations. At first, I thought they had engineered an insurance scam. But they said they couldn't afford the insurance."

"Strange, isn't it?"

"Right. Which got me thinking one of their own did it. Yugoslavians are always after each other," Wallace said, his statement sweeping as if every immigrant was suspect.

"Got an impression of how it went down?" Jack asked, hoping Wallace hadn't noticed his unwarranted interest.

"Is there more to this break and enter than you're telling me?"

"Nope." So much for hoping. "It's more interesting than going over reports."

"Got you on fart work, eh?" Wallace chortled and continued, "This theft is probably on behalf of a covert collector. Impossible to track. So far, I've got zip. How reliable is your rat?"

"So-so. You know. Maybe gossip. How often is art theft recovered?"

"Hardly ever, unless the customer changes his mind and offers it openly." Wallace snickered. "I wonder if the new buyer has heard it might be fake. Thanks for the tip. If I spread the gossip, someone may slink out of the woodwork."

After hanging up, Jack headed to the basement. A file clerk led him to a dark corner and a dusty four-drawer metal filing cabinet. "The top drawer is Cold Case files," she said. "Filed alphabetically. Someone wants them sorted into years. The lower drawers are a polyglot. Your job is to sort them by name and year."

Jack sneezed.

"You should have brought a duster coat. Your clothes are going to be pretty dirty." She left him while he peeked into a drawer. The smell of old paper made him sneeze again. The girl returned with a beige duster coat made for someone a lot shorter and slimmer than him. Jack got busy, intermittently thinking of Bianca, wondering if he should call on her with the excuse of news or no news on her picture, but mainly to apologize for ruining their date.

Mid-morning, he took a break. He followed the aroma of freshly brewed coffee and poured himself a cup. He took a sip and then dumped the lot into the sink. Why did department coffee taste so bad, even freshly brewed? The machine's pipes were probably full of bacteria and whatever else grew inside tubes which were never cleaned out. Rubbing his tongue back and forth against the roof of his mouth, he imagined he could already feel glutinous strings of cells growing there.

Jack took the stairs back up. At the corner of the front desk, he saw a pair of sunglasses and noisily fumbled them as he sidled for the front door.

"Stop right there," Burton said.

Jack kept his head averted. "Coffee run for the basement."

"Those are my sunglasses. Something wrong with your eyes?"

"Seeing a bright light hurts them. I don't know why everyone in the basement hasn't gone blind."

Burton snapped his fingers and held out his hand. Jack handed them over, and the sergeant rolled his eyes. "And wash your face. Smudging it with your dirty fingers won't rouse any sympathy."

Washed and on his way through the outside door, he checked his pocket to make sure he had his wallet and collided with Bianca coming in.

"Destiny says that we will forever meet in doorways." He smiled brightly at her while he held the door open for her to pass.

"Are you just leaving?" She looked flustered. "I was hoping to talk to you."

"What a coincidence." Jack took her arm and moved farther out onto the sidewalk. "I've been thinking about you. Walk with me." He pointed across the parking lot and down the street. "Just down to the coffee shop."

"I read the piece in the paper today. About that reporter. The one they call the General. Was it terrible? Yesterday, I mean." She matched her step to his.

He glanced sideways at her and slowed his pace. It was a curious remark, he thought. "I knew him for a long time. As a reporter anyway."

They stopped at the red street light.

"I want to apologize," he said to her. "About Saturday night. With the beating, drinking, and taking painkillers, you saw my worst. I forgot myself."

She gazed up at him, eyes looking right through him. The lines around her mouth and the smudged circles under her eyes were more pronounced. She was obviously having a rough time, and a sympathetic pang made him squeeze her arm.

She said nothing, only nodded, acknowledging his empathy. The light turned green, and they started across the street. "Dad's funeral is on Thursday, the day after tomorrow. I assume you want to be there. It's at two o'clock at St. Sava Orthodox Church."

"I'll find it." Jack dodged two teens laughing and not looking where they were going. "Is there any recent information? About who . . ." The rest died on his lips.

"If there is, they aren't sharing it with me," she said. An expression flitted across her face, a cross between relief and puzzlement. Was she relieved that the investigation didn't prolong the funeral and burial and delay last goodbyes? He wanted to hold her and tell her he knew the wear and tear uncertainty had on body and mind.

They arrived at the coffee shop, and he opened the door for her. She shook her head. "Things to do. Will you be there, Jack?"

"Of course. Can I help with anything? Anything at all?"

"It's well in hand." Before he could tell her about his phone call to Sgt. Wallace, she headed down the street, walking fast. And Jack slipped into the shop.

Having extracted a cup from the holder and the messiest doughnut from the box, Burton took a bite and rolled his eyes in bliss. "You're a lifesaver, Jack." He jerked his head towards the stairs. "Get back at it. This doesn't buy you any mercies."

"Sure, Rollie. Another day sucking in dust and bacteria, and I'll put in a grievance."

"Don't push it, Tuesday," Burton growled.

"The funeral of Dr. Pavic is on Thursday. I told his daughter I'd be there, and as I was Dr. Pavic's patient . . ." He let the rest hang.

Burton's mumble came behind a mouthful of doughnut. He swallowed and said, "We'll see. The Bird's going too. Maybe you can help him look for anyone suspicious. Do some work for once."

"Any gossip about who did it?"

Burton leered at him. "Wager still likes you for it." His eyebrows pushed against the wrinkle on his forehead. ". . . It's strange, though."

"What is?" Jack tried not to seem too interested.

"No chatter at all." Burton's eyebrows lowered, and the ends knitted together in a frown. "My bet is because they think it was an assassination." Burton shrugged.

"The case is getting old. After 72 hours, it looks unsolved and bad for us if the newspapers think so. Unless . . . is there evidence of an assassination?"

Burton kept his voice low. "A cartridge shell, 9 x 18. A Makarov has that ammo. What more do they need before they rank it as an assassination?" He drained his cup and made a successful goal shot in the wastebasket tucked under the end of the counter. Burton raised both arms above his head as if the goal also banished the oddness of Dr. Pavic's murder. "The killer will be long gone by now."

Jack kept his doubts to himself.

The minute he got into his apartment that night, he headed for the shower, tossing his filthy clothes into the hamper. Hot water and soap suds erased the feeling he would smell of mildew forever. At least it was his last day there. He leaned against the tiles, letting the water cascade over his aching back muscles and asked himself how much longer he could tolerate the sheer desperation of going to work. It took all his energy to pretend he didn't notice the hateful glances of the men and women. He masked the hurt with a swaggering, confident brashness, which likely cemented their universal opinions of his guilt.

"Whistling in the dark, Jack. What else can you do?"

25

A clerk appeared at Jack's side, pushing a cart laden with files. He transferred the lot to the nearest corner of his desk and left before Jack, hands full of forms, could remove the pencil clenched between his lips.

On cue, Burton appeared with a sheet of paper in his hand that he laid on top of the uppermost file. Keeping his palm flat over the page, he said, "Someone loves you, Jack. Here lies before you every file which connects to the Jackson clan in Winnipeg. It's a gang . . ."

"I know about them," Jack interrupted, trying to take deep breaths without it showing. It did nothing to slow his elevated heart rate. "Why me?"

"Your brilliant mind. You recognize the drill. Search for names. Make a grid of connections, offences, dates, places, what's their personal grift. In the end, you'll know more about them than even God. And they want it by Friday, Saturday at the latest. So no more goofing off."

Jack poked the files with his forefinger. "Is this Durand's make-work project?"

Burton's face was a model of sufferance. "I don't care a fig. Supposedly, they're forming a plan before the gang culture gets too obvious, and the Mayor brings down the hammer."

"Plan, my ass. They always wait until they're up to it in alligators."

"Be optimistic, Jack. Anything might be in those files."

Jack grabbed at the pile, looking for a specific one.

"Not there. They keep your file at Internal Affairs, eyes only."

Jack continued sorting.

"Stop wasting time, Tuesday." Burton's growl raised in volume.

"This place runs on teamwork, and so far, you aren't pulling your weight."

The heads of the two men occupying the desks in front of him dropped in unison in case Burton decided teamwork meant they should share Jack's load. But after perusing the files for a few hours, Jack decided Burton was right.

Someone did love him.

An hour before he was to leave for the funeral, Burton ordered him to take a patrol car to the maintenance shop.

Jack hid his impatience at another rookie assignment. "Dr. Pavic's funeral?" he shot Burton a reminder.

"Don't care." The sergeant shrugged it off. "Deliver the car. You can wait for it as long as it isn't all day."

Jack got the hint. He palmed the keys and left.

After dropping off the patrol car, Jack walked to the St. Sava Orthodox church on 112 Street. Unfamiliar and uncomfortable, he followed the cues of other mourners to rise and sit at the appropriate times. With most of the speakers being Slavic, Jack spent the moments he couldn't follow along admiring the colourful Eastern architecture and artwork featuring saints and martyrs surrounding the church ceiling. Judging by the size of the crowd, Dr. Pavic was a popular member of the congregation.

The funeral moved to the graveyard, and Hawk slid in next to Jack on the path as the procession slowed to the open burial. Out of place, they stayed well back on the fringe.

Hawk's eyes skimmed over each person, honing in on an expression or someone not belonging, whatever drew attention to his experienced eye. Jack watched several women gathered around Bianca, providing both comfort and protection from the cold wind. His attention wandered over the layout of the cemetery, at the rows of headstones, some with flowers wilting in front, then onto the fir trees surrounding the perimeter. A flicker of movement and he saw the familiar figure, the hat with the brim pulled down. Jack tensed, alerting Hawk, whose own focus followed along the line of Jack's. "Who is that?"

"Not sure. Someone I've seen around my apartment building."

"Should we get him?" Hawk's question was answered when the man melted away into the trees.

Jack tried to appear uninterested. "Probably not. I think he's visiting someone in the apartment across the street."

"Same place where Dr. Pavic's daughter lives?" Hawk asked, voice innocent.

"She said she didn't know him."

The priest began a prayer, and the crowd responded by lowering their heads.

Hawk grinned and whispered. "Afraid he's muscling in on you?"

"Something like that," Jack confessed.

The prayer ended, and the mourners crossed themselves.

Twenty minutes later, the body was lowered into the ground. Jack and Hawk left before others got the urge and walked along the path towards the parking lot.

"Mind giving me a ride back to the station?" Jack asked. "Do you think we can stretch the break to get some coffee? I need to talk to you."

"What's up with you, Jack?" Hawk put his hands around the coffee mug to warm them and shivered. "Sure hope winter isn't coming back. That wind is ugly."

"You're showing your age, Hawk. Spring is here. When you still patrolled the streets, you'd have on your summer uniform by now."

Hawk inspected Jack over the rim of his cup, eyes questioning. They sat in the corner of the Coffee Cup Inn close to HQ. Though the cafe was not busy, Hawk had chosen the table farthest from the window.

"Guess it's still social suicide to be seen with you," Brodie taunted.

"The day of the accident," Jack began. "On Groat Road."

"Whoa. It's still under investigation." Hawk's eyes shifted away from Jack. "How do you know I attended the scene at Groat Road?"

"McNaughton saw you."

"Of course he did. Nosy bugger."

"What went on when you arrived there? Tell me what you noticed when you searched inside the vehicle."

"If he even had searched."

Hawk peeled a serviette from the metal canister and wiped his mouth. "I wasn't first at the scene, so I can't tell you if it was contaminated." Hawk stopped, and his face took on a wary expression. "I shouldn't be saying anything."

"You and Wager didn't come together?"

Hawk shook his head.

"Who got there first?" Jack asked.

Mouth turning down, Hawk sunk into his seat. "Him."

Jack reached over to the napkin dispenser and yanked out two napkins. Carefully aligning them, he put them to the side of his cup and laid his palm on top, mainly to stop the trembling and allow him time to centre his thoughts on the accident . . . and Brodie. A sudden, piercing grief squeezed him. "Then what?"

Hawk's lips clamped together, eyeing Jack. He rose and took their cups to the front for a refill. *Giving himself time to plan?* Jack thought. Hawk took a long while to add cream and sugar to his cup.

"You're asking too much of me, Jack. You run off the deep end. I'm not there with you." Hawk swallowed hard. "They come down on you, this information never came from me, got it?"

"Fine."

"It was a mess. Worse, because it was two of our own." Hawk scratched at the varnish on the table and sucked in his cheeks like he had bitten on a lemon. "Brodie was up against the windshield, his wound in full view. You, half-hanging out the door, as if you'd tried to exit and collapsed. What bothers me now is my reaction. Confused, shocked that Brodie had been shot, not knowing what happened. It took time before I got a grip. We needed to secure the scene, and we did." Hawk moved his hands across the table as if still cleaning up the site in his mind.

"What about my weapon?" Jack coaxed.

Hawk shook his head and pressed his hand against his lips.

"Please, Hawk. A printed report isn't enough. Maybe you'll remember something that you forgot."

Hawk wiped his mouth, face pale. "Your weapon was on the seat, half-under Brodie. I bagged it, and the medics loaded Brodie into the ambulance, ready to go. Wager stopped them from loading you up and told them to wait. He found Brodie's weapon tucked in your belt." Hawk hesitated, then glared. "Why would it be there, Jack?"

His belt? Not pocket? "I wish I knew. McNaughton claims it was mine."

"McNaughton?" Hawk's voice rose to a new level. "Are we on the same page here? How would he know that?" His creased forehead said that Jack might be substituting episodes to fit the blank spots in his theory of what had happened.

"He said I put Brodie's weapon in my pocket." Jack gave him a brief version of what McNaughton had seen at the raid.

"I'd forgotten it was McNaughton's car." Hawk put his hands over his face to stifle his laugh. "Serves him right, the nosy creep. For being there in the first place." He narrowed his eyes at Jack. "What else did he tell *you* he saw from his front row seat? Did he tell everyone at the paper?"

Jack kept his expression even. "So what if they do know? The paper is cooperating with the department's ban on printing it." He shrugged as if it were beside the point. "Anyway, he said nobody knows what he told me, and I don't doubt him."

Hawk's voice lowered as though tired of the topic. "No, he couldn't." Which made Jack raise his eyebrows, inviting an explanation. Hawk obliged. "He couldn't print without evidence, or it could land them in serious trouble with the department."

Jack kept silent, resisting an urge to hint at the possibility of blackmail and start another round of questions he couldn't answer.

"Who owns the weapon doesn't affect anything. Ballistics confirmed it was the weapon used to kill Brodie," Hawk continued. "And your fingerprints are all over it."

Jack played with his napkin, folding it over and over until finally crushing it into a ball.

"There must be more."

"More what?" Jack replied, purposely misunderstanding Hawk's drift.

"Don't play with me." Hawk's voice was sharp, accusing. "You've been investigating on your own. McNaughton's information isn't the only piece you're following up on, or you aren't Jack Tuesday. What have you learned?"

"I know who our mole is."

Hawk sputtered into his coffee, swallowed, and choked when it went down the wrong way. His face turned red. Coughing fit over, he croaked, "Yeah?" His eyes narrowed, striking Jack with full force with what he could only interpret as anger. Surprised by the intensity, Jack leaned against the back of the booth.

"It's Wager."

Hawk's breath came out with a long hiss, lips vibrating into a raspberry. "That tune is getting old fast. You don't have a shred of evidence. Is it just because he's investigating you?"

"Don't reject it, Hawk. He's in the best position to get information from Durand and leak it to the bikers."

"Well, what if he is? And Wager would know he'd be the first one under suspicion. He isn't that stupid. And what about his shadow, Vasser? He's as pure as Snow White. If Wager were dirty, Vasser would call him on it. Besides, him taking information from Durand isn't likely. I'm closer to Durand than Wager is."

"Careful, Jack. Close your mouth now."

"Yes, but don't you see?" Jack ignored Brodie. Hawk's objections only made him want to offer up more arguments. "Wager can't make his information seem easy to come by. Information that only Durand knows."

Hawk's eyes narrowed dangerously. "Are you saying Durand is *feeding* him inside information?" Hawk shot out his hand, palm up, and wiggled his fingers. "Okay, give. How do you figure that?"

Jack shrugged. "I haven't got that far yet, but it's reasonable."

"Idiot."

Jack moved his mug in a circle, making wet rings on the table. "Whenever there was a leak, it's been Wager's case."

Hawk sat up and put his palms against the side of his head like he had a migraine. "You can't possibly have that information."

"I've been looking at the files."

"What files?" Hawk was all attention now.

"Every file on the gangs. I was ordered to make up a report on any connection between the Jackson gang, the bikers, and every case connected to operations in Edmonton. Finding links between people and known gang members. Which naturally includes possible leaks if I find information that only could come from us. You know the drill."

"Who gave you permission to dig into those files, Jack? Has anybody told IA?"

Jack waved away Internal Affairs. "Doesn't matter. It's a directive."

"From who?"

Why was Hawk so focused on the files? "A need-to-know thing where I'm not on the list. My guess is it's from the top down." Caution signals flashed in Jack's brain. "Hawk, listen to me. Wager had full knowledge and opportunity."

Hawk wasn't listening. He fingered his jaw, a faraway look in his eye, a combined expression Jack picked up on immediately.

"Hawk?" Another uneasy quiver shot through him. Jack went over their conversation. Something had set Hawk off, so he took a wild guess. "Durand actually ordered something that you don't know about."

Hawk still said nothing.

"Hey. Earth to Hawk."

Hawk smiled. "Did you see any reference to the Pavic case in those files?"

"None," Jack said, thrown off by the change in subject.

"Just had a wild hope—too bad. We're waiting for information from Germany before I close Pavic's case." Jack raised his eyebrows, and Hawk added, "Probably an outside assassin. It happens in Germany regularly. Tito's as bad as Stalin, hunting traitors no matter where they are." He waved away the subject as if it were nothing extraordinary. "A couple of deaths in Toronto were linked back to him."

"So you are leaning towards a political killing? Nobody else?"

"You know something you're not telling me?" Hawk's tone was abrupt, sharp.

Jack shook his head. "What? Are you suggesting I'm involved? I thought we were over this." Jack didn't hide his disappointment. Maybe Hawk had regretted giving information, for the atmosphere had changed. Was there something in those files he'd missed? The hair on Jack's neck prickled.

"No, of course not." Hawk grinned suddenly, eyes sparkling, looking sassy, at attention. He was back to the old Hawk, confident and assured. "Tell you what, Jack. I'll reserve judgment on Wager for now. If you find anything concrete in those files, I'll back you up. One hundred percent."

"Deal." Relieved, Jack's tension eased. He couldn't expect more, and at least Hawk was receptive. "I'm putting you on notice. I've been planning a stakeout just to see if I can catch him in the act. Maybe this Friday."

Hawk's mouth went slack-jawed. "Stakeout?" he finally managed. "That's nuts, even for you."

"At McGruber's Pub. It's over on . . ."

"I don't care where it is." Hawk sneered a look of disgust. "And do what? Something stupid, you idiot? You're demented."

Jack just grinned and checked his watch. "Burton's going to lecture me again. I'll be glad when I have my old job back. Maybe in homicide, and we can work together."

"Why? So I can watch you make an ass of yourself?" Hawk snorted, then gave him a punch on his shoulder. "Just as long as you don't get me killed in the process, Jack." He grinned to show it was a joke. But to Jack's sensitive ears, it didn't sound like it.

That night, he opened a Pilsner and turned on the TV, more to distract from thoughts of self-pity than for amusement. Flipping through channels, he stopped at an international swimming meet in Seattle, a forerunner to the Munich Olympics happening in September. It made him nostalgic for Grand Beach on Lake Winnipeg. The miles and miles of fine white sand and weekend nights with his pals. At this time of year, there'd be a quick dash in and out of the Lake. He would do it again, frigid water or not.

The 4x100-metre relay just finished, led by the East German team. The scoreboard flashed up, showing East Germany leading in most of the preliminaries. Jack pulled a face. Every competitor was likely loaded to the gills with steroids and other drugs. The DDR's national goal was to be number one in international sports. Communism at its finest, no matter the damage to their children's future health. Disgusted, he turned off the TV, thinking of Ursula trapped behind the wall.

At the window with his beer, he stared across the street at Bianca's apartment building. The clouds had blown away, revealing the rosy glow of the setting sun on the horizon. The winter starkness of the trees was showing gobs of green; that soft spring green which appeared at once, shouting summer is coming. Pharo had scarfed the liver Jack made for him, then stretched out along the floor in front of the couch to nap and chase his dreams. Jack had shoved his own steak, fries, and salad into his mouth without tasting, filtering through Dr. Pavic's funeral and his conversation with Hawk.

"Evaluate it with your detective's eye. Objectively."

"No doubt there, Brodie," Jack replied. It hurt that he was still on his own, and according to McNaughton, it would get worse. He could only trust his instincts, no matter where they led.

Across the street, Jack saw Tommy walk up the front path and into the building, lugging a bag of groceries. He disappeared into the foyer and used a key to open the inside door.

Dismissing his dark thoughts, Jack grabbed his coat.

26

"**WHAT** a pleasant surprise." Mrs. Zamborski graciously welcomed Jack inside. A clatter came from the kitchen area and was followed by a muttered curse. "Tommy. Mind your language, please."

Mrs. Zamborski, looking neat in a dress Jack assessed as being afternoon wear, smiled. "I can put away my groceries myself, but Tommy likes to assume that's his job."

There was a last rattle of paper, a cupboard door slamming shut, and Tommy appeared, his eyes inspecting Jack for signs of suspicious intent. Not finding anything, he scowled, sending a message there was always a next time. Jack bared his teeth at him.

"Thank you, Tommy. What would I do without you?" She patted the boy's arm. "But then you know that already."

Tommy's eyes grew soft as he smiled at her. *He really cares for her,* Jack thought.

"I can sit in the kitchen in case you might want anything else?" Tommy's eyes pivoted from Jack to Mrs. Zamborski again. Jack caught the message they exchanged.

Why does he assume she's in danger? The nerves along his arms tingled.

She gave Tommy a small nudge. "Go now. Do your homework. You may call tomorrow after school. My companion will leap to my side if I get into trouble. After all, he is a policeman."

Tommy's lip curled. His eyes swept over him as if he doubted Jack's ability to leap, then made a wide circle around him towards the door, making a noisy exit.

"Boys." Mrs. Zamborski looked amused. "All legs and arms. They have to slam through everything. Something to do with their growth spurts, I imagine." She pointed Jack to an easy chair, and he waited while she sat across from him and smoothed her dress over her knees. His manners made her nod in acknowledgement. "You attended the funeral? Was it rewarding?"

He hadn't seen her there. "I didn't really understand much of the rites."

She only nodded at him, waiting for him to continue.

"The investigation is leaning towards an assassin." He observed her closely.

"Who has disappeared," she finished, shooting him a shrewd glance. "They didn't inform the airport. Instead, they preferred to think it local."

He grinned at that and said nothing. Pursing his lips, he made up his mind.

"Deputy Chief Durand," he started, pausing.

"Yes. Milo Durovic. You want me to tell you about him." She inspected his face, her eyes penetrating. "Would it help you? I will only talk about him if it is important."

Jack laid his palms together like in prayer and nodded. "It is."

Still, she kept her eyes on him, getting inside his head as if he were transparent. Seeing his aloneness, the solitary life, his flight from his past. Cold crept up his legs, and he put his hands on his knees to stop the quiver.

"My name was Mira Dedic then. With a husband, Peter, and two children, Stefan, twelve, and Katrina, almost four." She smiled, her gaze centring above him. "Our home was a small farm southwest of Kraljevo; fortunately, not in the town itself. The Germans there were vicious, but that's another story. We imagined if we kept to ourselves, we'd be safe. But then the Italians surrendered, and everything changed. The Partisans stepped up their attacks, and more men joined them in the mountains. Other resistance groups formed under separate leaders. Some Chetnik cells joined with the Nazis to fight the

Communists, while others either organized their own bands or went to the Partisans."

Mrs. Zamborski shifted in her chair, the scars on the side of her face standing out against her paleness. Concerned, he opened his mouth to tell her to stop, afraid it would harm her to continue. She saw his hand move and shook her head. "It's alright."

"December 10, 1943. I remember the overcast sky and imagining snow in the air. I had finished a new coat for Katrina, a deep blue one. She went outside to show her father. I made bread and sang a song in the same rhythm as my kneading, happy until I realized it had gone quiet, the silence which makes you think the world paused to take a breath.

"The door burst open, and Stefan shouted, 'they're coming!' I shoved him under the bed and went to the door to warn the men in the barn. Too late. The Germans had already arranged themselves in the yard, shouting for Partisan sympathizers, ordering every man to show themselves. I saw Katrina dart underneath the wagon and prayed nobody would notice her. A Chetnik in the yard pointed out places to search. Another pushed me back into the house. Because he was Chetnik, not German, I believed he wanted me to be safe inside, but he had other ideas." She paused, her voice wavering. "He had big yellow teeth, garlic breath, and disgusting body odour. I heard rifle fire, two shots, and it could only have been Peter and our farmhand. The Chetnik laughed as if he had won the prize. I remember a great rage—kicking at him and poking at his eyes. He stopped laughing and slammed his rifle stock into my head."

Jack's shoulders tensed. Nausea rose in his throat along with the half-digested steak. He swallowed hard against the bile. Deliberately, he kept his eyes on her, clenched his fists, and did not offer useless comments about war and its horrors. Her glance at his face seemed grateful. He hoped he read it right.

"They set the livestock loose, then set everything on fire, the barn, the house, everything. Our penalty for helping the Partisans. I woke up with the bed on fire and Stefan pulling my arm, crying and shouting my name. He'd been there the whole time . . ." She stopped, her voice cracking. "I suppose I was lucky. The Chetnik left me for dead. Not wasting a bullet on me, or maybe he thought I would burn along with the house. If Stefan had not been there . . ." Her shoulders rose. "Outside, we found the bodies of Peter and our worker. When they came, Peter must have run from the barn to save Katrina. A mistake. To run means you are guilty, and they shoot immediately. Flames were leaping from the wagon where I had seen Katrina. I think I screamed and began to run to the wagon. Stefan held me back and said that she did not burn. . . . They took her."

She touched her face. "I made Stefan go to the mountains, to the Partisans. Convinced him he had to seek safety. They would protect him."

"And your daughter?" Jack whispered through stiff lips.

Still lost in her memory, she didn't answer. "I remember the snow—big flakes like lace doilies floating down and covering Stefan's footprints, pointing away from me. It seemed so important that I remember the sight of his footprints leading away to safety. Do you ever realize how silent the snow is?" She sat up straight and unseeing, viewing the past. "I tore my dress and soaked it in the snow to cover my face and ease the burning."

Her eyes focused on Jack. "But you asked about Katrina. Children were taken to Croatia in the north and the Ustache camps." She shuddered at the vision. "Or perhaps given to people in Germany because she was fair. But everyone knew most children never survived, and I prayed on my knees to die in the snow. Another family found me there. Their men helped dig graves in the field and took me with them in their wagon. We found Katrina's blue coat thrown at the side of the road. I only thought, how would she keep warm without her coat?" She sat and shook her head. "The small things that fill our minds."

Keeps you sane. Jack thought of the Korean camp.

She switched on the lamp beside her, bringing the room into focus. "The Chetnik officer in the yard who was helping the Nazis," she said, her tone flat. "He would have ordered Katrina taken. I will never forget his face. Milo Durovic."

Jack couldn't contain the strangled oath of disgust. "You said he had been Tito's man. A Partisan."

She settled her eyes on him, and Jack saw pity in them. "The Germans committed a vast killing in Kraljevo in retaliation for killing a German soldier. Thousands of innocent people were put into mass graves. After that, some Chetniks decided the price of fighting the Nazis was too high and let the Nazis use them against the Partisans." She shrugged her shoulders. "A confusing time; divided loyalties, atrocities on every side. War brought out everyone's grudges."

"Still, Durand—Durovic. . . . A Partisan or not?"

"He was," she said, voice firm, leaving no doubt. "Perhaps, in the end, the Nazis finally revolted even him. His loyalties always rested on his own welfare. He'd determine who would win in the end. Josep Broz would welcome him along with his knowledge of Nazi personnel and strategic positions."

"Okay," Jack conceded. "Then why is he here and not sitting beside Tito in his castle?"

Mrs. Zamborski smiled. "The White Palace in Belgrade, the former home of royalty, where Tito buried his lover." Her mouth turned down. "But you raise an interesting point. Why, indeed, is Michael Durand in Canada working as a police officer?"

Jack stared at her, sitting upright in her chair as though she had never seen a rough day, her dress with pearls draped around her neck, hair immaculate. Every inch the well-bred lady entertaining afternoon guests.

"Because he is still Tito's man," he said at last.

She gave him a delighted smile, like a teacher recognizing her star pupil.

"Did he finger Bianca's father to be killed?" Sizzling anger welled up inside him—a memory of Dr. Pavic's wry humour and understanding during their talks and Jack's instinct that the doctor genuinely wanted to help him. Still, odds favoured that Pavic and Durand had been compatriots in the war. She smiled at him, and he knew she had read his thoughts, flitting across his face like a movie.

"You are wondering if Dr. Pavic was also Tito's agent. Or how else did Dr. Pavic remain safe for so long?"

"You are way ahead of me on this one," Jack admitted.

She accepted the compliment graciously. "I've had more time to think."

"It also helps that you have more information than I do." He joined in with her laughter. "But I can read expressions too. It's the painting, isn't it?"

Her mouth formed a soft 'o.'

"One for you, pal."

"Dr. Pavic had to have something on Durand," he explained. "The painting hasn't been sold or advertised, so art appreciation isn't the goal."

"Especially if it's fake, and whoever took it knows it."

She neither confirmed nor denied it but returned his gaze, waiting for something. He obliged. "So what's the connection? The picture hides a message? Or is it the picture itself?"

She raised her hands, her glance rueful. "I wish I knew. But there it is. Everything which is connected with him has disappeared, so perhaps we will never know."

"Would Dr. Pavic tell Bianca? People normally say, 'if I ever disappear or die, look in such-a-such place.' She isn't a child and has a right to the truth."

It had an effect on Mrs. Zamborski. She seemed to grow taller in her chair, and Jack readied himself for the blast. "You are wrong. If you have the intention of including her in your questions, I can assure you that he wouldn't talk to her about war. He loved her and would not have included her in his dirty secrets."

"You said you didn't know her," Jack shot back.

She brushed aside his accusation like swatting a fly. "Knowing her is not necessary. I know him. And there are other reasons he would not speak to her of his past."

"What reasons?" He followed up quickly with his question, out of habit, probing, insisting.

It didn't make a dent with her. "War. Misery. Death. Anyone involved in the resistance wants to forget, not have family discussions. Never repeat the story I told you today." Her lips thinned in anger. "Anyone born during the war years should not have to deal with the memories of their family. It only pushes guilt on them, as though somehow the purpose of their lives is to assuage all the cruelty and hate their family suffered."

Her accusations hit home, and his face reddened. Still uneasy at her furious protests, he puzzled why she had chosen him. For her, his personal life remained an open book. While he watched and made-up stories about her, she had done the same but actively pursued her curiosity to find the truth.

Her not-so-gentle reprimand hung in the air between them. Their rapport had disappeared, and he would get nothing more. He rose and thanked her.

Outside, he started down the pathway to cross the street.

"Jack?" Bianca appeared from the side parking lot. "Were you looking for me?" She juggled a bag of groceries and her purse.

He only nodded and took her groceries.

"I saw you at the funeral, but you left," she said, turning towards her door.

"Work." He held the door open for her while she used her key. "But here I am now." In the elevator, she pointed at the grocery bag he carried. "I've got casseroles till next year, but no milk or fresh fruit. Would you like some coffee? Or something stronger?"

He nodded. "I'd guess you're tired of people hanging around offering sympathy."

"I prefer someone who doesn't spout advice about what I should or shouldn't do."

"I qualify." He put the grocery bag on her kitchen counter and stood at the door, watching her. She filled the percolator, spooned the coffee, plugged it in, and emptied the bag into the fridge.

"One shouldn't drink by oneself, as they say." She held up a bottle of brandy.

"They tell you anything about the investigation?" he asked as they sat side by side on the couch, the coffee and brandy on the coffee table in front of them. Bianca's look said that was his department. He took a gulp and let the warmth spread downwards. It felt good after his visit with Mrs. Zamborski.

"No, I'm assigned to admin." He read her mind. "Supposed to keep me ignorant."

"Same here," Bianca said, seeming uncaring. She gulped most of her coffee, then poured herself another cup, adding a good portion of brandy.

"You plan on knocking yourself out?"

"That would be a change. Not much sleep." She glanced at him sideways. "I lay there and think. Pretty soon, I'm having conversations and then more thinking follows until it consumes me."

"I sympathize. But there is a trick. You try to imagine the answers you get from your conversation."

"What?"

"You're having one-sided arguments and getting no replies. That someone is sound asleep, blissfully unaware of your opinions. You resent getting no answers and go on the attack again. More sleep lost. So just turn over and give him the silent treatment. Voila." He spread his hands out and grinned at her.

She examined his face as if he were something alien. "You turn off your mind? Just like that?"

Brick walls. Sadness welled up, and he considered confessing.

"What conversations keep you awake?" he said instead.

She looked into her cup, saw it was almost full and let her breath out in a hiss. "Mostly my father." She didn't raise her head but took another gulp. "The things I hated about him."

Her words dripped in the air like icicles, making him turn sideways to examine her. Her hair, draped over the side of her face, hid her expression.

"Who's different now?" he said. "Most people have only good memories of those who died. In the early days, anyway." He kept his voice even to give the impression he appreciated her honesty. "As his patient, I found your father amiable. Humourous, even." He wondered if Pavic was one of those who led a different life at home?

She reached over for the brandy and slopped some into her cup.

"Yes, he was kind, but I hated him too. The life he made me lead . . ."

Disconcerted, Jack didn't move, waiting for her to go on.

Bianca leaned against the couch and regarded the ceiling. She looked so lost he wanted to reach out and bring her close. His desire increased so that he leaned forwards. One look at her expression, and he told himself this was not the best time; that she would resist, so he gripped his coffee cup closer to stop his hands from reaching out.

"Coward. What's wrong with you, pal?"

Look at her, his mind replied. *If I grabbed her, she'd transfer all that resentment to me. She wants an ear, not love.*

"I hated my life with him," Bianca was saying, her voice even. "My memories of being dragged from one place to another before we came to Canada. Forever on the run, never remaining anywhere long enough to make a lasting relationship. Schools were always temporary. Other parents put their children first—stay in one place. My dream was a place to call home, even if we didn't have much. Instead, we were always on the wrong side of the candy store window." She shuddered and turned her head to glare in defiance at Jack.

"What else could he do?" Jack asked, then answered the question in her eyes. "On the run from Tito's men, wasn't he?"

"I suppose so. Father never talked about it."

Jack took one of her hands in his. It was cold and unresisting.

"But you teach the history of that area. You must know the Allies at Yalta agreed to send every citizen back to the Communist countries. It was a disaster. Thousands of men were executed. I read fourteen thousand put to death by Tito alone, Chetniks and anyone who wasn't Communist. You and your father were lucky to escape."

"You don't understand." Her voice was low, unrelenting. Jack pressed his lips into a thin line. The phrase used as a defence by anyone who doesn't care to hear arguments against it. He hated it. She drained the remains of her cup.

"So why don't you tell me?"

"If he really loved me, he could have left me," she burst out. "With any family, any relative, and given me a normal life. I didn't belong there. He had no business taking me. It was monstrous. I could have . . ." Her mouth clicked shut. She stared at him, eyes wide, accusing. He imagined he saw fear in her expression, and then it was gone. She squeezed her eyes shut, banishing whatever he saw behind them, then opened them and stared at him, silently begging for his agreement.

Finally, he gave in and pulled her near, kissing the top of her head when she laid it against him. There was nothing he could say. Images of her when he had first brought a cup of sugar and helped her unpack flitted through his mind. Back then, her past had not particularly bothered her. In fact, she had vowed that whatever had affected her past would not prey on her present or future. Now she bitterly resented it and her father along with it. It had been anger behind her odd conduct at the nightclub. But was it a long-held resentment that only began to fester when her father was murdered?

His arms tightened around her, holding her until he saw she had fallen asleep. He pulled a cushion towards him and gently lowered her onto it. She muttered, protesting something, but snuggled into the cushion without waking. He remained over her for a long time, watching and hearing their conversation again. Finally, he gently covered her with a throw and left.

27

A package in his hand, Rollie Burton swept by Jack's desk. "With me, Tuesday." He continued towards the front, leaving Jack no alternative but to follow. Burton's boots echoed off the concrete stairs to the basement.

"Not sorting files again," Jack protested.

"The evidence room."

Heart skipping a beat, Jack shut up. When they reached the cage, Burton said, "Be quiet and follow my lead." He rapped on the counter. "Anybody home? Coffee time is over. I haven't got all day out here."

A head popped around from behind a shelf, farther along the aisle. "Hold your water. I'm coming."

"I'm breathing my last, waiting," shouted Burton.

"Your time isn't worth a rat's ass anyhow."

Jack caught sight of a familiar buzz cut of brown hair, more silver than brown. The figure of the resident evidence keeper limped into view, wielding a cane. Jack tried to remember his name. Atkins? Aikins?

"What happened to you?" Burton asked.

Aiken, Jack decided, blushed. "Fell down the stairs."

"Your wife finally decided to get rid of you for good, did she?"

"Cute," muttered the other man. "What do you want?"

"Remember the Zamborski case?"

Jack's ears perked to attention. Zamborski? He'd never heard of a case with that name.

Aiken creased his face. "Oh yeah, Number 59.187." He narrowed his eyes at Burton. "Pretty ancient. What's your story?"

"Evidence reports someone never put back. So I need to replace it, all proper and accounted for. And I want to see the signature of the careless twit."

"Okay, give it here."

Burton's head performed a negative. "Not so fast. My neck's on the block, and it's my responsibility now. According to the rules, Aiken."

Aiken peered past him at Jack. "And what's he for? To hold your hand?"

"My witness. I want his initials saying everything is correct."

"I can do that." Aiken peered closer at Jack with an uncertain expression. "Isn't he . . . ?"

"Yes, he is," Burton snapped. "Can we just get this done? Some of us have work to do."

"Always looking to CYA, aren't you, Burton?" Aiken let them through. "Aisle 7. I have to come with you."

"I'm not blind yet, for God's sake. Stay here and save your leg." Burton stomped past him. Jack oozed through behind him.

"I'll put your names down on the clipboard. Don't leave without signing it."

Jack followed along behind as Burton searched the shelves and then halted. Tilting his head to read through his bifocals, his hand quickly shot out and found a slim box, Number 72.189. He grinned at Jack, "Here's Brodie's evidence box. A number near enough to the one we asked for." He opened the phoney package he'd shown to Aiken and pulled out a pair of gloves. Jack quickly donned them while Burton hauled down the box and slanted it towards him. "Do what you have to and be quick about it before we get fried."

Heart pounding against his chest, Jack removed the lid, seeing the familiar rectangular box inside, labelled with the time, date, place and shield number of the person who packed it. *Hawk.* It only took a few seconds to locate the evidence bag containing the weapon. Fortunately, the bag was unsealed, done when the gun was tested for fingerprints, Jack guessed. He turned it around in his hand, noted the registration number, then repacked everything in the same order he found it.

Box back where it belonged, Jack put the gloves in his pocket. Burton buried the empty envelope in a waste bin on the way out. He took the clipboard Aiken handed him at the door and scribbled an illegible squiggle beside the Zamborski file name.

Upstairs, on the main floor again, Burton faced Jack. "Well? Was all that worth the risk to my pension?"

"It is definitely not my weapon, Rollie. It's one Brodie traded in a year ago." His throat tightened, and he wondered if he would toss his biscuits right there. "Not mine," he said again. "If that gun killed Brodie, then the person who did the switch probably pulled the trigger. Or knows who did."

Disbelief, shock, and dread flickered over Burton's lined face. "No way."

Jack nodded, unable to talk.

"You claiming you knew his number?" Burton's eyes narrowed to slits, debating.

"I knew his weapon number like I know my own. Trust me. It's a thing with me. Most people never look at their registration numbers, so someone hoped nobody would notice." Jack sighed and wiped a hand over his forehead. "Now I'm wondering if that someone altered the weapon registry, too."

Burton rubbed his finger along his jaw. "Hell. I'd have given odds you were wrong about the evidence. So what do we do next?"

"We? Nothing. I won't forget this. I owe you one or two, Burton."

But Rollie wasn't giving up. "Did you see anything on the list that shakes your tree?"

"I have to figure out what it all means," he said, evading a direct reply.

A growl escaped Burton's throat. "You've got to get rid of that pickle up your butt, Jack. Keep shutting people out, and you'll be fried by the time you change your mind."

Eyes averted, Jack ignored him, then remembered something.

"What was the Zamborski case you mentioned to Aiken?"

"What? Oh, a hit and run, back in 1959. A Polish war hero. Never found out who did it, but I recall it was deliberate. He saved his wife. Pushed her out of the way, and she only broke her elbow or something. The conclusion was somebody wanted to shut them up. These refugees had enemies and sometimes met them on the street after they thought they were safe."

Burton chuckled at Jack's speculative expression. "Rest easy, Jack. They can't blame you for this one."

By nine o'clock that night, cater-corner from McGrubers, Jack sat on the ground loafing up against a mass of lilac bushes, a picture of loneliness and despair. A knit toque pulled low over his forehead, face dirty, Jack projected himself as homeless transient. Between his knees, his dirty hands cradled a grungy-looking backpack. Pharo hunched against his side, snuffling through a scattering of dead pink and purple lilac petals. Under a sign: "Need to eat. Please, be generous," was a bowl with three quarters inside.

At the bus shelter nearby, a couple inched away, putting space between them. A girl neared the bus stop and hesitated in front of Jack. "Can I pet your dog?" she asked. At Pharo's throaty disapproval, she hurried to the far end of the bus shelter and joined the couple with a murmured remark, which made them turn and shoot Jack a withering stare. When Jack heard the word "police," he smiled at them, hoping they didn't mean the threat.

"He won't hurt you none," he mumbled. "He's hungry and tired." Five minutes later, the bus pulled up, and they piled on, looking relieved.

Jack slouched back, keeping his eye on the action around McGrubers. After two hours, he began to doubt his theory. People entered and left, spilling out the sound of whistling pings from busy pinball machines along with the clack of pool balls and rumbling cheers. Nothing interesting, and the pub would close soon. He unstrapped an old sleeping bag from his backpack and sat on it, pulling one end over himself. Pharo trotted away to sniff the bushes, found a suitable spot and lifted his leg, activating Jack's own urge. Pharo returned with a satisfied trot, only increasing his need.

Mood black with disappointment, he began dismantling his props. *"Most Stakeouts are disappointing, and there's always tomorrow."*

Movement in the corner of his eye brought his attention to the street. A polished black sedan pulled up to McGrubers from the wrong side of the road. Engine idling, the passenger door opened, and two men emerged. The driver was Waterman's biker university student. The passenger, dressed in a suit costing a year of Jack's salary, waited like a pretentious VIP beside the car. The biker retrieved an attaché case from the front seat, passed it along, and then sped away.

So, definitely not just a university student, then. Jack made himself look small, his face hidden in the folds of his sleeping bag.

There was no mistake. Durand stood on the curb and waited, his eyes sweeping in every direction.

Apple darted out from the lane opening, holding out his hand, welcoming and smiling. Jack raged at his toadying. Apple reached for the attaché case, but Durand pulled back and marched briskly past him into the lane leading to the rear of McGrubers.

It was too risky to follow Durand, and when three more cars pulled up, he congratulated himself as the expelled passengers headed for the same laneway. Jack counted eight people. *Gambling tables*, he thought, in those empty apartment rooms upstairs, where there was an elevator leading downstairs for the refreshments. Private poker games were not against the law, but what other gambling equipment was upstairs?

It didn't matter. That case Durand carried had to be stuffed with money. It justified Jack's hunch formed from his visit to Apple. McGrubers was the conduit for laundered proceeds from crime.

Jack's insides boiled with heat fueled by bottled-up frustration. The pounding of his heart echoed in the blood roaring through his head.

He bared his teeth in an urge for immediate revenge at the picture of Deputy Chief Durand standing on the curb dressed like royalty. Bought at a price of a traitor to the entire police force, cheapening every cop within it.

Wait. Jack sunk into himself, cursing on the inside that he had not seen it before. Brodie's code. DC—meant for Deputy Chief, who radiated wealth in no relation to his occupation. The reason for Brodie's death. The pain in Jack's chest threatened to suck the breath from him.

Could he wait for him to leave and take his revenge? Any witness would swear it had been a homeless drifter.

"Cool it, Jack."

Pharo raised a paw to Jack's leg and stared directly into his eyes, sensing anxiety, bringing him sanity. Saved from folly by Pharo's interference, he petted him but considered investigating at the rear of McGrubers.

Movement near the side entrance alerted him. With hands in his pockets, Wager drifted out from the laneway and into the pub's front door. Jack checked his watch. It was past eleven. Inside, only the customers who'd be finishing their drinks and settling pool bets. What did Wager think he could buy at this hour? Jack silently sneered. Nothing. Just waiting for his boss.

Jack clicked his tongue. If he had any doubts about Wager, he now had his answer. Right there, across the street.

"You know better than to trust first-sight observations. How many times has it turned into the opposite?"

A black form rustled at his side, startling even Pharo, who bounded up, chortling. Heart rate hammering wildly, Jack automatically rolled to the side, up on one knee, poised to strike, hands spread in a defensive stance.

Hawk grinned up at him. "Some watchdog you have there. You're lucky it was me and not . . ." he jerked his chin to point across the street. "You'd be down and out for good."

"What the hell? What are you doing here?" Pharo remained erect, his eyes on Hawk.

"I'm watching the guard watching Durand."

"You followed Wager?"

"Who else?" Hawk curled his lip at Jack. "But I also wanted to stop you from doing something stupid and hoping you weren't here in the first place. But here you are. I may not have recognized you, but your dog gave you away. If a bum owns a dog, it'd be a Heinz 57 breed, not an unusual breed like yours. You should know better."

Jack ignored him. "You're ready to believe me now?" He kept his voice low. "About Wager?"

"I'm not that dense, Jack. I have suspicions too, but I didn't tell you for two reasons. You might have been involved, and even if you weren't, you'd have gone gung-ho on your own, leaving me on the sidelines."

"Damn it all, I would not," Jack retorted. What was it with people lately? Accusations of taking over. "I'm vocal with my ideas. So what? I've had to think fast ever since I was a kid." Hawk's eyebrows rose, mocking Jack's excuse of plagued youth. Jack waved his hand, acknowledging it. "Forget it. Why am I even telling you? What else do you know?"

"I've been after Durand for some time now, Jack. He's into serious stuff. It's connected to Fingers Jackson in Manitoba. Prostitution, gambling, pinball machines, extortion; they own it now. The bikers operate the delivery system. Durand's got a gambling addiction, and they tricked him into big losses. The only way he can pay it off is to launder their money. It's sweet. He gets to do what he loves and gets paid for it too. You've seen him in his glory tonight. He can feed his taste in clothes and other goodies. Of course, the mob gets extra information. And Durand is in no position to refuse. I don't think he'd want to refuse anyhow."

"And Wager is his messenger." A statement, not a question.

Hawk gazed down at his hands, a sad expression. "They are both here." He nodded across the street at the pub. "Why else would he stay so close? Risk being seen?"

Jack clenched his fists. "Brodie must have seen them too."

A crease between Hawk's eyebrows showed he was considering the logical conclusion. "And had him killed? Maybe." He shook his head. "But that doesn't explain your part. Brodie may have told you everything. After all, you were his partner."

"Maybe that's what the raid was for. To kill us both."

"Now you're getting into supposition. Two detectives killed during a simple raid, but nobody on the task force? That's quite a reach. The chief would be all over it without letup."

"Maybe I'm only safe because I can't remember. But somebody did take a pot shot at me in the park when I got out of the hospital." *And then beat the snot out of me . . .*

"Perhaps. But we're spinning our wheels here. Too bad your head's a blank." He leaned over to Jack, peering into his face. "Don't you remember anything at all?"

"No. If only Brodie had told me, we'd have a hope."

"How do you know he didn't tell you if you can't remember?"

"My memory loss came after the accident. I have no problem with memories before the raid."

Satisfied, Hawk peered across the street. "Wager's probably trying his luck at pinball while he waits for Durand. It could be a few hours yet." He turned back to Jack. "How long have you been here?"

"Since before nine."

"Not much to show for it," Hawk said, looking into Jack's bowl. "You need a monkey with a cup." Hawk snorted. "Do you plan to do this often?"

Jack got to his feet, groaning. "I'll be a minute," he said and headed behind a bush, sluggish muscles protesting, but needs must.

"Go home, Jack," Hawk said when he returned. "I'll take over. Durand will be finished for the night anyway."

Jack hesitated, then agreed. "The stink of dead Lilac is getting to me, anyway."

Head tilted, Hawk probed Jack's face looking for lies.

"I'm going, Hawk. I'll check in with you tomorrow." Jack packed up his gear. Unexpectedly, Pharo sat on his haunches looking at Jack, indecision in every line of his body.

"He wants to stay and protect me," Hawk ventured.

"He hates riding in a car."

"Admit it, Jack. He's weird."

"Not when it counts," Brodie's voice shot back.

By the apartment's parking lot, lamenting his habit of looking up at her window, he did anyway. No lights or twitching of the curtain. Jack's glance dropped to the street and saw the ever-elusive man entering the front entrance. Jack shifted his backpack and slowed to a saunter imitating a vagrant looking for a spot to spend the night. From the corner of his eye, he saw the man's glance pass over him before disappearing inside. Instinct and the man's urge to be unseen told Jack he didn't live there.

But he had used a key to the inside door.

28

JACK sat at his desk the next morning, questioning his existence in a life of dull routine, bringing him near to open anger. He saw himself hurling the boring reports to the floor and stomping on them like an angsty teenager. A phone message from Stacey in Personnel sent him upstairs in a mood to rebel against any new directive Durand had thought up for him.

"You must need the overtime pay," he said when he saw her.

"Dream on." She rolled her eyes. "No overtime. I'm on salary. Saturday morning is my catch-up time, then I go home. Speaking of catching up, where is that birth certificate . . . ?"

"Dream on," Jack echoed her statement. "Tell Durand you have enough history on me to fill any requirement. The end. Fini."

"Okay." She grinned at him.

"Good." Jack turned, not waiting around for a challenge.

"Just a minute,"

"Now what?"

"Did you apply for another job? At Burger King drive-in, of all places?"

"What are you going on about?"

"I got a phone call. Apparently, you had sent in an application. He inquired if you worked here. In Personnel."

Teeth grinding, Jack clenched his fists. The jackasses in Burton's unit getting their kicks.

"Oh, I get it," Stacey said, turning red. "I'm sorry."

Jack turned on his heel and stomped out.

Despite the urge to smash a couple of faces, he kept his head down until late afternoon, when he invented an excuse to visit upstairs, hoping Hawk was in.

"What are you doing here?"

"Last night?"

Hawk yawned and looked evasive. "As expected, he went home."

"We need a plan. Something that includes witnesses."

Hawk leaned back in his chair, not meeting his eyes. Alarm signals coursed up Jack's spine.

"What aren't you telling me?"

"Not now," Hawk hissed at him. "Leave before someone catches you." He opened a desk drawer, fiddled with the contents, shut the drawer again, and picked up a pencil. Jack pulled over a chair from the next desk, thumped it down before Hawk's, and sat. Face growing red, Hawk's mouth tightened into a thin line. "Get out, Jack. Now."

"I'll just wait until you tell me."

Hawk's chest heaved in a dramatic sigh. He threw his pencil down on the desk.

"You didn't get it from me," Hawk said, voice so low Jack leaned forwards to listen. "There's a plan to make Brodie the informant."

Jack gawked at him, wondering if his brain had somehow scrambled Hawk's words. "That's the stupidest . . ." Lips stiff with dread, he could barely speak. "Gossip has sunk to new levels."

"No gossip, Jack. I have an inside in IA, and I'm sure it's Durand's idea."

"Who's your inside source?"

Hawk's eyes shuttered, his lips pressed. "If you quote me, I'll deny it to hell and back."

"They can't." Jack cursed in a hard stream. "It's a monstrous lie. The guy's dead and can't defend himself. What about Maureen and Ben?" He straightened and said through clenched teeth, "I won't let them do it."

"They've got that covered. If you testify Brodie was dirty, they'll drop the charges against you. And reinstate you. It's not so bad, Jack."

For a long moment, Jack sat there, mouth opening and closing in disbelief. He half-rose to his feet, his voice rising dangerously. "They can think again. It's evil."

"Not so loud. Listen, Jack. If you refuse, both of you will get charged, and Durand will make sure it sticks, no questions asked. Hell, most people believe it already."

"I'll quit first."

"Idiot." Hawk slapped his palm on the desk. "Either way, you're screwed. Both of you will still end up in the crapper. If you accept it and stay, there's a chance to clear both your names and get Durand too."

Jack stood, his head ringing with the impact of Hawk's revelation. His mouth opened and shut like he was sucking in his last breath before sinking into a bottomless pit for the third time. "Are you encouraging me to accept?"

"My brain is numb right now. Just go back downstairs. It's a no-win, either way. You . . . we have to think, maybe come up with a plan." He didn't look hopeful.

Blind with rage and fear, Jack stumbled through the door and collided with Wager entering. He brushed past and continued down the hall towards the elevator, imagining Wager's S&W Special trained at his back the whole way. Inside the elevator, Jack turned. Wager hadn't moved, eyes still boring into him as the elevator doors closed.

Burton handed him a slip of paper when he came back. "Message. A telephone call from an RCMP sergeant in Vancouver. I forgot his name." Burton's eyes narrowed in suspicion. "What have you done now that you're wanted in Vancouver?"

Jack took the slip, not caring, pretending to examine the number. "Beats me."

Burton held him by the arm so he couldn't pass. "What's up? You look green."

Jack wanted to close his eyes against his headache. "Nothing. Hangover."

Still in a trance, Jack obediently rang the number. *Now what?*

The ringing stopped. "Yup," a voice spoke. No announcement of who or what. Prickles went up and down Jack's arm. Only a particular police branch answered phones in that manner. Covert.

Jack gave his name and the reason. "Sergeant Smith has left for the day."

"Can you tell me what it's about?"

"I'm afraid I can't do that. Tomorrow is a better day to call."

"Sunday?"

"Yes."

"It will be Monday," Jack said firmly.

"I'll tell him," the voice said and hung up.

Another stunt by someone using him as football of the week?

In Hawreluk Park, Jack brooded career possibilities while he watched Pharo nosing everything available. Apprehension hung over him like treacle, threatening to smother any self-control he had left. The torment of isolation and foreboding made him want to cry out in pain. Who would hire a disgraced cop? The possibility of having to leave the city brought up memories of riding out of Winnipeg bereft of family or friends. Is this the way of life? Perpetually on the move?

How would Maureen and Ben react if told Brodie was a traitor? Too overwhelmed and out of ideas, his spirits sagged. He calmed himself down, but then a new cause and effect leapt into his mind and off he went in a worse direction. If only he had his weapon. *Eating my gun would solve everything. Durand would slap his hands together with glee, and the record would show I was guilty of murder, treason or whatever. I can do that much for Brodie. It's finished. I'm tired of fighting.*

"*Well, well. You've lost control. Get your skates. Hell has finally frozen over.*"

"So be it," Jack replied, watching Pharo chase in wild circles around the grass, only halting to dig up a discarded wad of chewing gum. He chewed, spat it out, and continued to dash in an ever-increasing circle until finding a new wad. Jack made noises of disgust and grabbed the frisbee, throwing it as far as he could. Pharo gave a joyous leap and nabbed it. The ordinariness of their game put a layer of protection over his bitterness until, at last, he stretched out in a shaded corner of the park and closed his eyes. Not sure when he had dozed off, he came to when a paw nudged his leg. "Lie down," Jack said, keeping his eyes shut. Pharo's warning growl changed his mind.

Five men out of nowhere. Tough and menacing. Bikers. Experienced, not prospects this time. Jack slowly rose and faced them. He saw metal clasped in their hands. Knuckle dusters. They meant business and spread themselves out around him. Pharo sensed his fear and danced around Jack, sending off sharp yodels, which turned to snapping growls.

Jack stood, making sure that he made no sudden movements. His eyes looked over each one, trying to assess the leader, planning his move to disable him once he'd decided.

They said nothing. Their eyes told him he would not survive this one. Nobody else around but bystanders who would shirk any involvement with bikers. For a long moment, nobody moved. A mosquito landed on his cheek, and Jack swatted it. Like it was the signal. The leader smiled and took a step towards him. Heart tripping in his throat, Jack tensed, ready and aware that Pharo could not fight them all and would die trying.

"You'd better hold off on that." A voice—mild yet firm—came from offside, a few yards away. Burly, denim vest over his t-shirt. Jack had an impression of tattoos, blond hair tied back in a ponytail.

Waterman's Biker.

Arms up, knuckle duster ready, the leader turned with an ominous scowl, then relaxed. Beckoned to come closer, the biker obeyed instantly, showing deference. He listened, then flagged the others. Before they left, one gave a two-finger sign at Jack of 'we're not finished.'

Legs like two sticks of melted wax, Jack collapsed on the ground.

The other man came up beside him.

"Thanks." Jack pointed to the departing bikers, his burning urge to pee signalling a lingering fear. His head started the familiar ache. He stayed down, guessing his legs were unreliable. Pharo turned his attention from a possible new menace to nuzzle his nose into Jack's armpit, looking for reassurance. Jack coddled his dog's head.

"You okay?"

"Yeah. Do you know why I'm on their kill list?" Jack peered up at him. "Those guys . . . one word, and they bolted. Who the hell are you?"

"Anderson." He reached down and shook Jack's hand. "You're welcome."

"You following me?"

Anderson gave a Gallic shrug and folded his hands in front of him, standing with his feet apart, at ease. "You have a knack for getting beat up."

"Why? I mean, why are you following me?"

"To deliver an invitation to dinner."

"Who?" Jack got his legs under him and rose, shaking off Anderson's helping hand.

"You'll see when we get there." Anderson looked at his watch. "We should go now."

"I'm not going anywhere until you tell me more." Jack didn't move. Pharo shifted away and went over to Anderson, who didn't move while he sniffed his hand, then wagged his tail. Jack frowned at him. *Traitor.*

Anderson shrugged. "I didn't save your life only to kill you somewhere else. You aren't in any danger." He took a step away. "Suit yourself."

Feeling like an obstinate teen, Jack pulled a face and followed. On the way, he dusted off his pants and straightened his shirt, feeling under one arm, then sniffing the armpit.

Anderson led him to a black Mercedes with tinted windows and a leather interior. He said nothing, only stood by the driver's door until Jack could seat himself. Jack put one hand under Pharo's collar, ready to pick him up bodily and throw him into the back seat, but Pharo jumped in without hesitation. "Traitor," Jack said again, under his breath.

"I should stop at my apartment for a change of clothes." Jack probed as they drove down 87th street towards the bridge.

"Unnecessary," Anderson said shortly. "We're going to Villeneuve Airport."

"We're flying somewhere?"

Anderson shook his head.

"You're a veritable fountain of information, aren't you?" Jack waited, but Anderson turned his full attention to driving.

At 118th Avenue, Anderson drove west then north again on Highway 44 and, in thirty more minutes, arrived at the airport, constructed mainly for smaller aircraft to reduce the traffic at Edmonton Municipal. Anderson stopped at a rectangular hangar with an added L-shape, the office area, Jack suspected.

Anderson parked facing the double hangar doors, then led Jack and Pharo to an entrance door at the side of the hangar. Inside, Jack saw a red and white Beechcraft Queen Air parked in the middle of the hangar. Twin engines, nine seats. New and shiny.

"You the pilot?" asked Jack.

"If I have to be," Anderson replied.

"Make sure you don't say too much," Jack commented and was rewarded with a twitch of Anderson's lip.

His biker chaperone led the way to another door. Hand on the knob, he paused. "This will take a while. Dinner and all."

Jack refrained from asking what 'dinner and all' entailed.

Anderson patted Pharo, who tolerated a strange hand touching him. "He can stay with me . . . Pharo? I'll make sure he's okay."

Jack hesitated.

"It might be better," Anderson added. "The boss . . ." he gave another Gallic shrug.

Boss? Jack handed the leash to Anderson. "If you take him outside, keep the leash on him. He likes to play games, and I wouldn't want him on an active runway."

Anderson waved Jack through the door, closing it behind him.

He found himself alone in a small dining room, a table set for two. White tablecloth, crystal stemware, and silverware. Something about the table placement. He picked up a plate and turned it over. Wedgewood. An opened bottle of red wine stood beside a carafe. Leaning forwards, Jack read the label. Chateau Belaire. "Guess we're having beef," he said to himself, suspicion forming into unwanted certainty. He glanced down at his casual clothes, laughing silently at his unsuitable attire. He saw another door at the end and started towards it.

The door opened, and Jack came face to face with a man—dark hair, medium height, dressed in a deep blue suit, white dress shirt, and polished brown loafers. Jack gawked at him. Heart in his throat, he blinked hard against the sting behind his eyelids.

"Hello, Danny," Luke said.

29

JACK sat in uncomfortable silence while two servers, one in a chef's tall hat and white coat, brought in platters. Formal service, as always. Mind in turmoil, he decided he would maintain a maturity different from the frightened adolescent Luke had last seen running away. Two plates meant his father wasn't about to appear.

"Phooey. I wanted to see him clout you over the head at the way you're dressed."

"I'll serve." Luke waved away the chef and helper. Knife poised over the prime rib, Jack saw his little finger, the stump ending at the knuckle. Luke deftly doled out plates of beef, twice-roasted stuffed potatoes, and roasted veggies. While they ate, they talked about the past, or rather, Jack listened while Luke chatted as if he'd seen Jack only a few days ago, rather than two decades. He learned his father was no longer alive. Massive stroke, Luke said, which wasn't surprising. A short fuse, cigars, and booze.

"The two goons still hanging around?"

Luke grinned and shook his head. "Retired."

"Now you've got Anderson."

"Anderson has more class."

"Same tasks, though. He pays off the bribes, arranges the meetings, and doles out lessons for unpaid loans. And more serious business."

Luke laughed. "Some of that, but he's above breaking legs. He fixes the bigger things." Luke's face got reproachful. "I've a reputation for completing deals, Danny. Not killing." A sudden smile lit up his face. "You remember Carol Sommer?"

"Barely." Jack blinked, a fuzzy recall of a blond whose father owned a soda fountain shifted into his thoughts.

"We got married soon after you left. We have a daughter, Olivia. She's seventeen." Luke rolled his eyes. "Teens. I might strangle her before she graduates high school."

Seventeen, the same age as Jack when he left. A muscle in Luke's jaw twitched when Jack didn't laugh at his inanity. He didn't ask if Jack was married. Probably already knew.

After a dessert of lemon and prosecco sorbet, Luke rose without a word, assuming Jack would follow. A man used to command. His office seemed more chief executive than hangar workroom. A Persian silk carpet on the floor, leather chairs and couch. A large old-fashioned oak roll-up desk against one wall.

"Welcome to the place where they hatch dirty plots."

Luke went to a corner cabinet, extracted a bottle, and returned with two brandy snifters. He sat in a chair and crossed his legs, pointing to the other chair. Jack sat and leaned forwards, elbows resting on his knees, hands around the snifter, but not drinking.

"Why am I here, Luke?"

Luke looked down into his brandy, swirled his glass, and took a sip. "It's been too long, Danny. Or should I call you Jack? Or Tuesday? Where did you find that one?" Luke curled his lip, sending wrinkles up one side of his nose, and the familiar derisive expression took Jack back into the past. He reminded himself the past was not the present. He was Jack Tuesday, a police detective constable.

"How did you find me? And my name?"

Luke's eyes mocked him, and Jack saw the adult Luke, not the brother he remembered. A man reeking of confidence, in full command of himself, knowing that others obeyed him without question. "A newspaper article about returning soldiers, former POWs of the North Koreans. There was a photo of them exiting a plane with you right in the middle. Along with your name." His eyes were curious. "You were really a prisoner? Hard to believe you'd joined the army, but it answered a lot of questions."

"It solved my problem of disappearing, so Dad couldn't find me."

Luke made a choking noise, then let out a bellow. The surprise and question on Jack's face sent him into another laugh, his amusement genuine.

"What?"

Luke put his glass on the table's edge, leaned forwards, and clasped his hands. "You really think he looked for you?" He shook his head and leaned back. "He was glad you scarpered. You have no idea of how you threatened him, do you?"

Jack wondered if the shock of being here had muddled his hearing. "Are you nuts? Me threaten *him?* Haven't you got it backwards? He hated me."

"You got that part right," Luke agreed. "But you scared him." He chuckled at Jack's slack jaw, open in disbelief. "It's true. The noble Gentleman Conor. Scared. You were too smart for him, and he knew it. In time, you'd either take over from him or destroy what he built." Luke's voice lowered. "And he was right. I told you to run because I wanted you safe, but I knew I'd lose everything if you stayed too."

Luke looked Jack up and down, examining him. "You always had this . . . thing," he said. "Sure of yourself, doing everything your way. Sure of your power to achieve. And righteous. Boy, you were so righteous. Never a moment of indecision." His tone took on a bitter edge. "Everybody knew it. Dad knew that come hell or high water, eventually, you'd destroy us all." His eyes raked over Jack, calculating. "Running you off was probably the best thing that happened to you. Admit it."

As if repeatedly stabbed, bolts of pain coursed through Jack, leaking out his inner existence. On unsteady legs, he rose, took his entire glass of brandy back to the cabinet, and carefully set it down. Imprisoned in Korea, striving to prove himself yet never quite measuring up because he wasn't the orphan he pretended to be, the days he spent alone, craving a family. No *ordinariness*, only a perpetual undercover life, nursing the secret of his father's occupation.

He made his way back to the chair and faced Luke, his resentment sending electric pulses across the room to his brother, his thoughts mixed, unaware he was half-shouting. "Why didn't you just ask me to get out of your way? Let me do my thing, but support me all the same. Finish school? Maybe university? Marry, have a family, children like you have. Not cheating me out of belonging somewhere even if I didn't fit in. Never a letter for me during a mail call in Korea, a familiar face when I returned home. What about that, Luke?"

Luke raised his eyebrows. "Marry? What stopped you?" He eyed Jack, amused. "You just couldn't lie, is that it?"

"Lie? Damn you, my entire existence is a lie! You really don't know what it means to have no roots. What you have may come crashing down, so you have to move on." New betrayal, real and imagined, sucked at him. Arm muscles bunched, he came near to striking his brother.

"Next, you'll be frothing at the mouth."

"Well, Luke." Jack reached deep inside and found a scrap of control. "You inherited the throne. Protection Racket, Union bribing? Illegal gambling?" His voice grew louder, along with his anger. "Money Laundering? Drugs?" he shouted the last word, revolted.

Unperturbed, almost proud during Jack's list of activities, Luke's lips curled at the last, like he'd just had a bite of rotten fruit. His palm shot out. "You think I'm someone who destroys children and families by filthy addiction? We Do Not Peddle Drugs." Luke's eyes were as hard and cold as marbles. "No matter the prospect of profit."

Jack searched his brother's face and found no signs of deceit. "Still. Manitoba is sufficient for you, Luke. You know what I do, what my profession is. I won't let you ply your dirty rackets in my town."

Luke grinned and waved his hand as if batting away a pesky fly. "Aren't you overstating your strength, Danny? As I understand it, you can't do much to stop me. Suspended, under investigation for the murder of your partner, aren't you? An airtight case against you."

"Which you engineered, I suppose," Jack spit out. "Are you the one behind the attacks on me? Assigning someone to take pot shots at me? A beating by the Rebels?"

Luke's mouth tightened, giving Jack a small thrill at having pierced his brother's composure. "Why would I hire someone to kill you?" Luke snapped, nostrils pinched as though he was holding himself in. "I had you followed to ensure protection, and when you kept dodging him, Anderson took over. You're lucky the Rebels are under my control now, or you'd be decorating a slab in the morgue." Luke threw up his hands in exasperation. "Look, Danny, you're here because it's time to bring you home." He smiled, and Jack registered his regret. "No arguments. Let's talk. We can help each other."

"I can't help you, Luke. You've already got the deputy chief of police doing your money laundering. And I don't need your help."

Luke sat back, a smug expression on his face. "I can get you a birth certificate."

"You know about that? Of course you do. Well, I don't need one."

"How about a house? A better apartment? I own a lot of real estate in Edmonton. You can take your pick."

"How d'you deposit dirty money in the bank?"

"Easy. I trade in real estate through private companies."

Jack said nothing to that. Numbered shell companies formed to buy up real estate with laundered money. "Well, my living arrangements are just fine. Though, I imagine Durand had no problem accepting gifts."

Luke shrugged as if business was progressing nicely. "Durand is not aware of everything I have on him . . . or on his men."

"Ha. You mean Paul Wager? No surprises there, and he won't be your dirty cop much longer." Jack bit his lip and shut up. He may as well have informed Luke they were compiling a file on him.

Luke raised an eyebrow and smiled. "Always have everything figured out, don't you, brother?"

"Don't play dumb," Jack said. "Dad taught you to dig up every little detail. No bit of information is too small. Anything or anyone remotely connected with your operation."

Luke sighed like the subject wearied him. "You haven't changed. Still arrogant and overconfident."

Indecision flitted through Jack. He reminded himself that he had spotted Wager with Durand. Well, not *with* him, his mind retorted.

"Durand launders your dirty money," Jack persisted, chasing another tack.

Luke shifted in his chair. "You want another drink?"

Jack nodded, hoping a drink might loosen the atmosphere.

He forgot that his brother could always read his expression. Luke grinned. "Drinking won't make me talk," he said, and Jack flushed. "I can still keep my mouth shut."

"I'm sure," Jack said, his voice flat enough to be sarcastic.

Luke poured his drink and came back to his chair. He shook off his jacket and threw it over the back. Jack watched him, comparing him with twenty-one years before. Luke's hair was still dark, like his father's, and had no streaks of grey. Perhaps he coloured it, but Jack didn't think so. Luke was not vain. His sturdy body had become softer, and Jack saw his shirt buttons stretching over a soft pouch of stomach flab. He caught Luke's eyes on him.

"Chief Durand?" Jack coaxed.

Luke made a dismissive noise in his throat. "Wide open for blackmail." He eyed Jack, waiting for the surprise. "And how Tito uses him here in Canada."

"So what?"

"You're aware of that?" Luke didn't show any disappointment at losing a bargaining chip.

Jack shrugged. "If your plan is to trade information about Durand in exchange for me becoming your informant, it won't work."

Luke inspected the amber liquid in his snifter. "What would happen to your career if the police service found out Fingers Jackson is your brother?" He held up his right hand and wiggled his remaining digits.

Cold crept up Jack's legs into his spine as if someone had sprayed him with dry ice. He made his lips move. "Your decision?"

Luke's gaze was flat. "It doesn't pay to dodge decisions. Especially in my business. The head can't go soft." He stared into Jack's face, the menace in his statement emphasized by his blank expression.

It left Jack with no doubt about Luke's intent. He got to his feet. "If that's why I'm here, consider the message delivered. There is nothing left to say."

"Nothing?"

Jack swallowed hard, holding on to what was left of his composure. "You do what you have to do." *I'll do the same.* At the door, he turned. "Happy landings when you leave town," he said and had the satisfaction of seeing Luke's face turn red.

"Think it over, Danny." His mild tone didn't extend to his narrowed eyes. "I'll give you time to change your mind, but I won't offer again."

Anderson drove towards the city without speaking. Pharo resorted to his usual crouch in the back seat, moaning to himself at intervals, which made Jack happy that some things remained the same. They drove onto 109th Street out of the High Level Bridge exit, and Jack broke the silence.

"How long have you worked for him?"

Anderson glanced at him and then at the road again and stayed mute.

"Does he trust you?"

Anderson didn't turn his head. "A couple of years."

"He insisted he wasn't in the drug business."

"That's right. He has a strict rule about that. Anyone caught selling drugs is . . . well, let's just say we never see them again."

Jack took a long moment before he continued, debating the danger to himself against needing an ally. "Did Luke Jackson turn you, or are you still undercover?"

Anderson lurched, and the car veered dangerously towards the left side of the road and an oncoming vehicle. Cursing, he jerked the wheel back again. The other driver leaned on his horn, and Jack saw his mouth yelling obscenities. Pharo sat on his haunches and let out a yodel.

"Jesus wept," Anderson swore. He turned right at the corner, not saying another word until he reached Jack's apartment and parked. "Get out."

Jack stayed where he was.

Anderson wrapped his arms around the wheel and lowered his head against it.

"That will get you killed." He slapped the wheel and looked at Jack. "Hell. Get me killed." A growl tore out from the back of his throat. "How did you know?"

"Pharo. Conditioning, plus nature. Knowing who's a threat and who isn't." He threw a glance at Anderson. "And years of military life and cops have shown me you never let go of the quirks learned in training. You check the time too often like you've synchronized your watch with another. And your approach method to the bikers in the park. The way you plant your feet when you stand, arms slightly out, ready to draw. Controlled. Training." At Anderson's worried face, he added, "Don't worry, it's just me. I have this thing for details. Mostly, it's been a curse. It's got me into trouble more than out of it."

"You're in deep this time." Anderson's eyes were hard as marbles, along with his voice. Jack didn't miss the threat.

"I won't betray you to anyone. Least of all, my brother."

Anderson's face popped up again. "Your brother? He's your *brother?*" He slammed his palm against the wheel, cursing.

"I haven't seen him in over twenty years. Ever since they kicked me out of the family."

Anderson frowned, not convinced. "Yet he assigned me to make sure you're safe. I thought you were his informant."

Jack shook his head. "He worries about loose ends, not my safety. If my deputy chief finds out, he'll use it as counter blackmail. Luke has found out I'm in their bad books and wants me to cooperate, or he'll tell them I'm his brother, and I'll lose my job."

Anderson didn't take his eyes off him. "And will you cooperate?"

"No. I'd quit being a cop before I'd help him. If he follows through with his threat, I can still harm him. He has to go back to Winnipeg."

"He can kill you first," Anderson said.

Jack turned towards him. "That's where you come in. You're RCMP, aren't you? You can tip them off. They can cover me."

Anderson didn't reply. He looked at his watch, and Jack smiled. Anderson choked back another curse, took it off, and stuffed it into his pants pocket. "I have to get back and report. Fingers is the clock watcher, not me. He gets antsy if I'm away too long. Get out."

Jack and Pharo stood at the curb and watched Anderson speed away. Would he turn him into Luke to cement his cover? His throat tightened, fearing the worst. Still, Anderson didn't threaten him outright, so Jack believed he still might be one of the good guys. The Mercedes disappeared around the corner, and Jack finally let out his breath. Events worsened, his world corkscrewing out of control, near to collapse. He needed an ally. Someone to help lay a play to trap Wager. Hawk? But then again, could he completely trust Hawk not to betray him? He needed direct evidence, which Durand couldn't defend.

"You'd better plan what you'll do when you aren't a cop anymore." Brodie's voice followed him inside.

30

TUESDAY, Harry McNaughton's memorial, and Jack's day off. Burton nixed it and ordered him in, pointing out that he'd already taken his free time. As he prepared the day's slog of paperwork, a reporter telephoned, telling him of the time and place, adding that Harry had left special requests, Jack being one.

"Is this a joke?" Jack demanded, suspicious of everything lately.

"Sorry," the voice said. "Harry made me promise to ask you to attend his service if he met with . . ." A sigh and a long pause followed.

"I would attend anyway," Jack told him.

"Actually, would you agree to meet me personally after the service? I can't tell you why right now, but it was important to Harry."

"Of course," Jack said, his interest rising, and went to convince a reluctant Burton.

Now, seated in the chapel waiting for the service, he mused about becoming too familiar with funerals. Thoughts of not taking Harry's fear seriously enough crept into his mind at odd moments and bothered him greatly. Because everything to do with it aligned with his suspension, he accused himself of ignoring Harry's victimhood, wanting to save that role for himself. That's why lawyers don't hire themselves for clients, or doctors act as their own physicians, he told himself. Something else he'd have to live with. He hoped he'd be around long enough to find Harry's killer.

Mark Ackland shuffled into the row and took the chair next to him. "Wager's out on a call," he said, and seeing Jack's surprise, added, "He sent me." Ackland's eyes were flicking over the crowd in front of them, sorting them into categories: okay or suspicious.

"Poor guy," he continued. "Wager said he had information he

shouldn't." He turned a questioning face to Jack. "Is that what you think too?"

Puzzled at Ackland's new friendliness, Jack said, "Definitely. Harry was about to tell me when he spotted someone and ran." Jack slumped, still remembering how he tried to stop him from dashing into the street. "If he'd stayed with me, he'd be alive now. He ran without thinking." He tactfully omitted his suspicion of Wager's sudden appearance. "By the time I caught up to him, it was too late."

There was shuffling in the aisle. McNaughton's family was coming in; an older woman and some young people in their twenties. Harry's wife? Maybe a sister. And nieces and nephews. He regretted not knowing Harry that well. A poor time for regrets. The room quietened. A minister began to tell everyone why they were there.

Harry's nephew recited the usual comic memories of his uncle. After, a reporter reminisced about Harry's career and swore his dedication to telling the truth was front and center of his reporter's credo. Jack recognized the voice as the man who'd telephoned him. After two hymns, a favourite song, and blessings from the minister, it was over. Jack and Ackland stood while people filed out and then followed the line towards the aroma of coffee.

"I guess I should go over and speak to Harry's relatives," Jack hinted, trying to separate himself from Ackland so he could get close to the reporter.

Coffee in hand and inspecting other people, Ackland nodded without turning his head. "Good idea. I'll make some rounds and see if anything interesting pops up. See if his workmates have any ideas."

"Me too." Jack sounded too eager, for Ackland turned to look at him. "Two heads are better than one," he added quickly. "Check with you later."

He hurried off and got in the queue to offer his condolences to the family.

"I'm so sorry for your loss," he said and took Harry's sister's hand. Up close, he saw the resemblance; the eyes and shape of the eyebrows.

"Jack Tuesday."

"Oh yes," she said, smiling at him. "Harry mentioned you." Bright eyes behind her glasses peered into his. "He said you didn't lie about what was what."

"He said that?" It buoyed Jack's spirits like an inflated balloon. "We got along." It sounded lame. "Thank you for telling me. Because . . ." he stopped and swallowed.

"I know," she smiled at him, serene. "I'm glad he didn't die alone." Her brightness dimmed. "You must find out who did it."

"It's a promise."

"Thank you. We *will* meet again." She reached out and laid her hand on his arm. "My address and phone number are in the book."

"It would be my pleasure," he answered politely, thinking the odds of meeting again were slim to none. She smiled and turned to the next in line.

Jack returned to the refreshment table to discard his cup and saucer and ignored the plates of sandwiches and cake. His appetite had disappeared. Ackland was at the far end of the room, talking and waving his arms at a reporter who was nodding back.

"I can see tomorrow's paper already, 'A knowledgeable source says . . .'"

"Jack Tuesday?" Jack turned to face the voice. "Of course you are. I'm Benny, by the way. I phoned you."

"And here I am, as promised." Jack smiled while he stole a look around to make sure they weren't overheard. "You said Harry had something for me?" He jerked his head towards Ackland. "If Harry wanted it to stay secret, tell me now, before that guy sees you and comes over."

Benny stepped behind Jack and put his coffee cup down. He reached into his pocket with the other hand. "Shake hands with me," he said.

A cold object slipped from Benny's palm against his, quickly disappearing into Jack's pocket. It happened in rhythm and within a second. Benny smiled at him, and Jack nodded as if agreeing. "Any word on the streets about who the killer is?"

"Not even a whistle." Benny's mouth turned down at the corners.

"It's too bad Harry had a habit of keeping things to himself." Jack sighed. "Helping him wasn't easy."

"A lifetime of keeping his sources secret. Too long to break the habit. Harry was old-school, always afraid someone would get the story first."

Both silently gazed down at the floor as if Harry's bad habits were lying there discarded forever. Benny gave him a sad smile and moved away. Jack followed him for a few steps and then veered towards the exit.

"Hey, wait up." Ackland appeared next to him. "Did you learn anything?"

"Nada," he said firmly. "And I'm leaving. Burton will have a fit if I don't get back soon." But he wasn't able to get away alone.

"Me too." Outside, Ackland took a deep breath. "Thank goodness that's over. I hate funerals. I hope I never have one."

Jack snorted. "Sure. Be immortal."

"Well, you know what I mean."

They reached Jack's Volvo and stopped. His companion showed no hurry to continue towards his car. "So how're you coping?"

"Here comes the hustle for information."

"As you would expect, Mark." Did they all know about the plot to blame Brodie? Was he about to urge Jack to accept? "Unless you are aware of any info on IA's plan."

Ackland's eyebrows went into a vee. "Who knows what's in their minds? I doubt they do, themselves. Righteous bastards." He half-grinned at Jack and added, "I hope you beat them. Come out clean. We miss you."

A slight blush in his cheeks followed his words. It didn't soothe Jack like it was meant to. Was he trying to play good cop? Was it supposed to make him think people were beginning to believe he was innocent?

"That weapon with my fingerprints." Jack burst out. "It isn't my weapon. Somebody switched it."

Ackland's jaw dropped. "What?" He swallowed, eyes disbelieving. "How could you know that? It's in evidence."

Jack ignored his question. "Harry told me. Somehow, he knew. The one in evidence is one Brodie traded in about a year ago." Jack snapped his lips shut. He'd said too much, aware Ackland would tell Wager. But perhaps it would show Jack wasn't lying down. The idea cheered him a little.

Ackland was holding out his hand to him, eager to leave. Jack took it, and Ackland's other hand gripped Jack's forearm. "If you need help, Wager and I will do what we can." He squeezed Jack's elbow as if testing for ripeness. "Remember that."

Emotions off balance, Jack watched him as he strode across the parking lot to his car. He sensed Ackland's sincerity, but then, he would hardly know if Wager was an informant. Wager wasn't about to share with him.

Inside the car, Jack reached into his pocket and turned over a key to read the number etched on it. Seventeen. It looked like a luggage locker key from any train or bus station. Instinct told him that whatever it was, it would enable him to clear his name and solve Brodie's murder once and for all. Euphoria making him lightheaded, Jack threaded the key to the ring with his car keys.

"You'll finish the day's reports," Burton told him when he showed up. "If it takes until midnight. And they want that report which was due two days ago. Enough goofing off. The police service isn't being run at your convenience."

"The report was the real deal?" Jack asked. He lowered his voice. "I thought you made that up so I could look through the files—maybe I'd find something related to my case."

"Have you lost your marbles?" Burton's voice rose, turning heads their way. "Don't push my patience, Tuesday." He stalked towards the front, making noises in his throat. Jack got busy. His journey to the train station and bus station would have to wait. At six o'clock, he signed off for a half-hour dinner break, rushed home and fed Pharo. He thanked the spirits that he was going against the rush hour traffic and made it back to work in time.

By ten thirty, he was at the Greyhound bus station on Jasper Avenue, finding no fit to his key in the bank of lockers. Next, he tried the basement of the CN Tower on 104th Avenue with the same result. Tired and depressed, he headed for home, telling himself he'd check the Greyhound station on the south side tomorrow. Driving across the 105th Street Bridge below the MacDonald Hotel, he realized what he had missed. He'd forgotten about the Strathcona CPR station. Precisely as Harry planned, knowing any other searcher would forget it too. He sped up.

A station hand was shutting down for the night just as he arrived. Pulling a face, he jerked an impatient thumb over his shoulder at the bank of lockers. Jack inserted the key in locker seventeen and grunted in satisfaction as the key turned. He heard a shuffle behind him, and a chill went up his neck. Too late.

"Stand aside, Jack," a stern voice barked. "We'll take it from here."

Jack turned and faced Wager, a sheepish Ackland behind. Jack glared at him. Of course, Ackland had seen Jack pocket the key Benny had given him. Too bemused by his good luck, he'd forgotten to check for a tail during his mad dashes between depots. He focussed on Wager again, his insides twisting into ropes.

"Get lost, Wager. It's personal."

Wager put his hand on his weapon. With the other, he waved Jack aside. "My ass it is. I gave an order to move away. Holding out on evidence won't net you points. Stop making things worse for yourself."

Jack pocketed the key and thinned his lips. "Your patsy here told you Harry wanted me to have whatever it is. You seem extremely anxious to get your hands on it before anyone else. Don't you trust me to hand it over if it's police related?"

Ackland's attention went from Jack to Wager as if he had an inkling Jack was right.

Wager flushed beet red—whether in anger or guilt, Jack couldn't tell. It didn't matter. Whatever the reason, Jack was sure Wager had an ulterior motive. While he searched the man's face, Wager's fist tightened on his weapon as if to draw it. "Well, if you've nothing to hide, open it up, and we'll see. I won't ask again, Tuesday." The threat was not to be ignored.

Jack obeyed and opened the locker door, then looked inside. Considering the circumstances, his mind hovered between disappointment, relief, and triumph.

Like conjoined twins, Wager and Ackland peered over his shoulder at an empty locker.

"What are you playing at, Jack?" Wager growled.

"Kind of obvious, isn't it? We've been played. Or the train officials emptied it. It can't be me because you've been behind me every step of the way."

As one, they looked at the station attendant who stood behind them. He inspected their faces, interpreting their accusing stares, and vehemently denied anyone could have a locker opened up without proof of identification. Maybe they emptied it after twenty-four hours, like the sign states. "Come back tomorrow. I'm off duty," he said.

Wager and Ackland pulled out their shields. Grumbling, the man vanished into the office and slammed the door. The three waited in silence under a ticking railway clock.

When he came out, his righteous smirk said it all. "Even if the sign says they will empty it after twenty-four hours, it never is until days later. Either the renter emptied it, or there was nothing in it to begin with. Now, if you don't mind, I want to close up."

31

BLASTED out of bed by an early alarm clock, Jack reported for duty, shuffled paper and wrote reports automatically, and, if questioned, couldn't have said what was in them. Had Benny stripped the locker clean to give himself first crack at Harry's position? Harry's killer might also worry about the confessions he left behind. Jack mentally calculated the time Harry ran from the café and Jack's reaction, plus the delay at the café door before he found Harry. Was it enough time for the killer to search Harry's body?

He reached for the phone. Voice filled with resentment, Benny swore he'd respected Harry's last wish to the letter, nor had he told anyone about the key. Jack apologized and hung up, wondering about Wager. He may have known where Harry stashed his evidence and got to it first, then showed up with Ackland to divert suspicion from himself. But logic told him it'd be easier for Wager to destroy the evidence and watch Jack run himself ragged through the town in pursuit of nothing.

Jack tossed his pen on the desk and used the heels of his hand to rub his eyes. He got the urge to scoop everything off his desk and fling it at the wall. Nothing for it but to continue to watch McGruber's in hopes of a clue. He stood, tucked a file under his arm, and then headed for the stairs. His hope disappeared as he caught Hawk and Vassar entering the elevator. Hawk sent Jack a warning shake of his head before letting the doors slide shut.

Downstairs again, he thought about Harry's funeral and the people there. His sister had been gracious, reciting Harry's compliments. Jack remembered her remarks, and his eyes narrowed. Her last careful statement was that she was in the phone book, making sure he knew.

Heartbeats hammered against his ribs. What was her name again? He'd seen it in the funeral service handout, the one he'd thrown away right after. He grabbed the phone again.

"Benny Jones? Not here. You want to leave a message?"

"I'm after the names of Harry's relatives? His sister. I want to leave my condolences; I can't remember her name. Can you tell me from the obit?"

"Hang on."

Jack drummed his fingers on the desk, saying silent prayers, making promises to God that he would never keep, but promised them anyway.

"Chambers," a voice said into his ear. "Edina Chambers."

"Does it give a husband's name?"

"Nope. Do you need the relative's names?"

"Thanks. That's enough," Jack said. "Appreciate it."

Jack thumbed through the telephone directory. He found three E. Chambers. Two didn't answer the phone. The third one in St. Albert, just north of Edmonton, answered, and Jack recognized her soft tones immediately.

"Mrs. Chambers, this is Detective Constable Jack Tuesday. We spoke at Harry's funeral service."

"Yes, of course, I remember you." Her voice sounded amused as if she knew why he was calling her all along.

"I remember you said that we should meet again. Would it be inconvenient if it were today? This afternoon?" He tried to keep the urgency out of his voice.

"I will be home after two o'clock." He could feel her smile over the phone.

Jack hung up and sidled over to Burton. "I need to go out later this afternoon, Rollie. It's important."

Burton rolled his eyes, sighed, and pointed the end of his pencil at Jack. "Why aren't I surprised? Where is it this time?"

Jack shifted his feet and shook his head. "You won't have to lie in case someone asks. It's vital to me but better that nobody knows. Not after . . ." He let his words drift off.

"Okay, a doctor's appointment then." Burton groaned and rolled his eyes. "And be fast about it. You're making me old before my time."

Edina Chambers lived in a neat bungalow on a winding crescent in an area called Lacombe Park, near the St. Albert Hospital. She opened the door as he came up the front steps.

"I'm sorry for the short notice," Jack said as he entered the foyer. She led him into the living room.

"Please sit. Coffee or tea? I've been grocery shopping, and the kettle's about to boil."

"Coffee would be nice," he replied.

She went into the kitchen, appearing almost immediately with a tray holding cups, cream, sugar, and a French press of coffee. She disappeared again and came back with a plate of sliced pound cake.

After she poured and offered him a cake on a napkin, she sat opposite with intelligent eyes on him, waiting for him to speak.

He sipped his coffee and nodded at her in appreciation of the taste. "Harry left a key for me," he started right in, not wasting time. "It was for a locker at the south CPR station. I tried it last night, but it was empty."

"And you suppose I know," she stated simply.

"Yes, I do. At first, I thought someone beat me to the locker, but I remembered you said I'd see you again." Jack put his empty cup back on the tray. "I believe you have information. Harry was an intelligent man, and it likely runs in the family." He didn't smile, letting her see he was serious.

She remained silent, her eyes pensive, studying him, deciding.

"Harry trusted you, Officer Tuesday."

"Jack," he said, urging friendship and first names.

"Jack," she agreed. "Harry made a mistake, and I lost my only brother. I need assurance that you weren't that mistake." She drew her brows together. "He may not have told me everything."

"I understand." Jack nodded, deciding to be frank. "But know this. Bringing Harry's killer in isn't just for him. It's for me, too, because I'm caught up in the puzzle. I had an accident during a police investigation which affected my memory. Harry had information which would clear me, and someone killed him before he could tell me. Whoever did it is eager for me to join Harry. Whatever he left behind contains answers. I can't make you trust me, but if you keep it, you'll be in great danger. Giving me the information will protect you."

Edina Chambers rose and took the tray into the kitchen without another word. From the noises within, Jack wasn't sure whether she was sending him a message to leave or stay. He heard the slam of drawers and cupboards closing, then a long silence. On the verge of quietly leaving the house, Jack rose just as she came into the room carrying a thick legal-sized envelope. Her flushed face and red eyes showed her struggle to regain composure.

"The locker was a blind." She handed the package over and smiled at Jack, her eyes filled with tears near overflowing. "I needed to decide about you."

Jack didn't hide his relief. "Thank you, Mrs. Chambers."

"I am Edina. Mrs. Chambers is my mother-in-law."

He smiled and held up the package. "You won't see me again before I finish this case. When I come, it will be to tell you who killed Harry."

"I expect it," she replied and walked with him to the door.

"Still, be careful." He wrote his phone number on the back of a card and gave it to her. "If you feel threatened, call the St. Albert RCMP detachment right away."

A careful survey of the street revealed nothing suspicious, nor was there a sign of a follower. On the St. Albert Trail, back towards Edmonton, he searched for the public library sign and made a quick right turn. Inside at a study carrel, hands trembling with anticipation, he spread out the notes and a cassette tape from the envelope.

A librarian pointed out an enclosed music booth, and half an hour later, he sagged into the chair, not quite believing the treachery laid bare in Harry's revelations. Bile rose in his throat, and nausea threatened a dash for the washroom. He rubbed his fist up and down against his breastbone, easing the tightness there while his thoughts raced between betrayals, murder, revenge, and back again. Jaw clenched with raw emotion, he had to coax his brain to concentrate on protecting the notes.

Shuffling the pages into a semblance of order, he took them and the envelope to the inevitable library copy machine. Copies made, he wrote a brief note on paper filched from the machine and questioned a library clerk for the whereabouts of the nearest post office.

On the way to Edmonton, he decided what to do next. For the first time since Brodie's death, Jack had regained a measure of control.

"You got another call from that sergeant in Vancouver. What's going on, Jack?"

In no mood for Burton's tirades about the amount of work he wasn't doing, Jack shook his head and angled around him. Burton grabbed at his sleeve and held him.

"Right. I forgot to call him back. Business got out of hand yesterday." Jack kept moving.

"Stop right there. You look like murder."

Jack paused. Burton's grab at his arm had drawn attention. Two heads focussed on them. "Not here, Rollie. Later." He laid his arm in a palsy way around Burton and forced a laugh. "I'm on it. I won't even take a coffee break."

"You've already had enough time off today for five coffee breaks, breakfast, lunch, and dinner. You're the worst time-waster I've ever had the misfortune to have under me." The men watching did not smile. Jack could almost taste their resentment.

"Sorry, Sarge." Jack resisted the impulse to salute and embarrass

Burton. "I'm here for the duration. I'll even stay after my shift is over." He hoped Burton got the message.

"Always your way or no way," Burton said softly and huffed frustration out of his nose. Jack saw indecision, and then curiosity winning. "I suppose I'll have to stay until some ungodly hour to hear your excuses. Make that call to Vancouver. I'm not your secretary."

At his desk, Jack put off calling Vancouver. He had other priorities than to listen to some crazy theory the RCMP had dreamed up, somehow linking his name to it. Instead, he dialled Glen's number at the apartment, asked him to use his key to check in on Pharo, and reminded him where to find the bag of dog food. "Thanks, Glen. I owe you another one."

"I'll still be here at Christmas," Glen hinted.

Writing another note, Jack took it up to the front. He tossed it on the desk in front of Burton, shuffled past him along to the other end, and grabbed more reports before returning to his desk. His eyes slid up to watch him read the note. Burton took a startled step backwards. His eyes convulsively darted towards Jack, then away, the rigid set of his shoulders spelling disapproval. No matter. Jack needed Burton's help, but if refused, he would go it alone.

"This is not on," Burton said, pulling out his chair to sit across from Jack at the desk in the small office. "It's bound to leak out. You can't just waltz up to the chief and say you want a meeting. Five seconds flat, and it's 'round the entire building." He took a deep breath. "There must be a mistake. McNaughton made a mistake. I can't believe it."

"A mistake that got him killed? He should have published and be damned." Jack's legs sprawled out. He tipped the chair back and linked his hands behind his head, feigning composure he didn't feel. "A trap is the only way. And I need your help in arranging it. Nobody will think twice if you set it up."

"Nobody except the chief. He'll refuse. He's the chief." Burton rolled his eyes upwards as if he were speaking of God. "He won't do anything without calling a board meeting first. If nothing else, to cover his ass in case there's a public backlash."

"Not if you impress on him its ears only. Everybody knows you and the chief go back a long way. He'll listen to you." Jack rolled forwards, and the chair's front legs landed with a *thunk*. His determination rose. "You got a better idea? We have to show definitive proof. A direct admission. The alternative is to let it go on unchecked."

Burton frowned. Shoulders slumped in resignation, he stared at Jack across the table. "But can you pull it off? Will they believe you?"

Jack nodded. "Korea taught me a valuable truth. People kid themselves when they think every man has a limit to what he can endure before he breaks."

32

"*ALL* this secrecy better be worth it," Chief Mackie said, reserving a special steely glance of answerability at Jack. He gestured around the tiny room like he was slumming it. And he was. Burton had set them up in a musty room in the basement after hours. The chief was out of uniform. *Mufti did not diminish his appearance*, Jack thought. The man would radiate an air of authority no matter how he dressed. His agreement to Burton's request confirmed his attention to the knowledge of men under him.

"Get at it," he commanded.

Jack laid out his copy sheets on the table for inspection. The chief had no follow-up questions, and Jack realized with new respect that the man's brain had ingested every bit of information for immediate recall. He gave a brief glance at Jack's papers. "Copies? Where are the originals and the tape?"

"I mailed them to my attorney, along with a note, explaining that he should keep them safe."

The chief's eyes swung towards Jack, assessing him. "The tape is clear evidence? You recognized the voice?"

Jack nodded. "As I said, it's blackmail, pure and simple. That McNaughton shuts his mouth about what he knows, what he has witnessed, or he dies. McNaughton repeats the meetings he has seen— and he recognized him at the raid when he torched our squad car. He witnessed him shoot Brodie, then later again when he switched the weapon at our car accident when Brodie died." Jack's voice quavered on the last.

"Will the tape hold up in court?"

Jack shook his head. "I believe it won't. Harry is dead, and any attorney can claim he faked the tape."

"But it contains an admission that you had nothing to do with DC Brodie's death?"

Jack swallowed and nodded again.

The chief pursed his lips in a tight grimace. "Internal Affairs has arrived at the same conclusions."

"They did?" Jack's eyebrows shot up, not hiding his delight.

"I ordered them to review it again." He frowned at Jack as though accusing him of ignoring an order. Jack's grin faded.

"So they won't blame Brodie?"

"Explain that remark, Officer."

Jack told him. Burton sucked in a noisy breath. Mackie's face turned red. Jack knew he had banished all doubt.

The chief pointed to the papers, his glare setting on Burton. "You said there was a plan?"

Burton shrugged. "Getting you here was my part. The rest is up to him." He pointed his finger at Jack like it was his fault. Jack scowled at him; the familiar tone of voice Burton used with the chief explained a lot about their history. As if agreeing with Jack's assessment, the chief ignored Burton but smiled as though they shared a secret.

"Well?" The chief faced him full on, then listened as before until Jack finished. He asked questions, point by point. "You'll organize a raid on the pub, McGrubers. You'll brief those men separately as to their purpose, the expected results, and operational sequences. All the player's parts are sorted to the last detail in your mind?" He hesitated, frowning. "One slip, and it all comes down like a ton of bricks."

Jack nodded.

"How will you stop them from comparing notes?"

"By telling them that the blame rests with the other one, and the details must remain secret at all costs, or the exposure will fail. I'm confident they will play along because it's what each wants to hear. "

Chief Mackie pursed his lips, never taking his eyes off Jack. Finally, he put his hands behind his back and paced the small room. Jack's anxiety rose.

"He's going to turn it down. You're sunk, pal. He's got too much to lose."

So sure of himself, Jack hadn't prepared for refusal. Didn't consider it a possibility until now. *Shut up and wait*, he told Brodie.

The chief stopped and stared at the far wall for a full minute.

"Okay. See Durand and set the plan in motion."

Jack's lungs deflated in relief. Burton grinned and play-wiped his brow.

"But hear this, Detective Tuesday. If your plan goes sideways, I'll hang you in public."

Jack had passed the first test, but it didn't decrease his awareness of more hurdles to cross. Despite what he told the chief, people were loath to listen or agree, and he had already lost five pounds. Would they accept he couldn't take the harassment anymore and had finally caved in? He rebuked himself for overthinking. Confidence was paramount, for they would immediately spot uncertainties. He had acted his entire life and could do it again.

Durand was his biggest worry. A man whose long experience in interrogation had honed a keen sense for deceit and secrecy. Jack held back on the ultimate persuasion until Durand's doubts were at their limits.

"Fingers Jackson is my brother," Jack revealed, with the right measure of reluctance in the admission.

He enjoyed some satisfaction in Durand's shock, a mixture of surprise and disbelief turning to self-congratulation. "I knew there was something. A suspicion my head wouldn't let go." His fist struck the palm of his other hand in delight. "Experience, DC Tuesday," he gloated. "It hasn't failed me yet."

Jack cranked up a rueful shrug.

Now Anderson was driving Jack and Durand to confer with Luke. After once meeting Anderson's eyes in the rear-view mirror, Jack turned his head to the scenery, discouraging conversation. Anderson parked at the airport office, and Jack got out of the car. He suppressed his smile as Durand waited for Anderson to open the door for him.

Inside the hangar, a couple of mechanics on a ladder fiddled with the engine of the Queen Air. Jack caught Anderson's glance and gave him a small shake of his head, hoping he got the message. Without waiting for Jack, Durand strode towards Luke's office and through the door.

By the time Jack followed, Durand was already at the door. He knocked, then walked in without waiting for a reply.

"Telling you that Luke is his partner, not his boss."

Jack followed him through. Luke was already on his feet, and Jack immediately went to him, put his arms around him, and gave him a hug. Luke's eyebrows raised to his hairline. Jack grinned. Luke glanced from Durand to him, and his eyes crinkled in amusement.

Everybody sat.

"What changed your mind?" Luke's tone was pleasant, but his icy stare said he had doubts.

"I hate to admit it, but I'm sick of the grunt work, everybody's open hostility and insults. As if I'm nobody. I've been a cop for ten years, and it's led nowhere." He pursed his lips into a wry slant. "After we met, I got home and realized my life has meant zip since I was seventeen. I'm going to be forty soon, and I want what you've got. Money. A family." He gestured to the hangar. "Maybe a Queen Air." He looked at Luke, his face set into a stubborn line. "That's it. Take it or leave it."

Luke stared at him for a long moment. Jack's eyes didn't waver.

"I confess I didn't believe him either," Durand butted in. "Until he admitted you were brothers. I kept my doubts. Until now." He laughed.

Luke's cold eyes shifted to Durand, whose laugh cut off abruptly.

"How do you see yourself in this operation, Danny?"

"Danny?" Durand burst out, eyes wide.

Jack twitched. "It's best you get used to calling me Jack. It wouldn't be good if anyone else knew my name."

Luke waved his hand, his tight mouth aware of the huge mistake. Durand's smirk confirmed he'd filed the information away.

"Well?" Luke prodded.

"The betting money from the pinball machines, and the pool tables and liquor sales McGruber reports as normal revenue. I take it upstairs and gamble with it. Whatever I win is my reward."

"The money from the pinball machines is legitimate revenue . . . Jack."

"Come on, Luke. Half of the pinball machines don't even work. They're there for show. I know about the illegal betting under the counter with the bartender as a bookie." Jack smiled at Luke and shrugged. Durand's eyes switched from Luke to Jack and back to Luke.

"I already have people in that capacity." Luke challenged him.

"How about information about police surveillance?" His eyes went to Durand. "Information that is kept out of normal reports."

Durand sat up. "This is not true."

"Talk which goes on inside other districts. Task force gossip." It wasn't true, but misgivings appeared on Durand's face. He wasn't a chief whose superiority permitted him to lower himself to the level of underlings. Durand's eyes turned to Luke, expression resenting the implication his finger wasn't on the pulse of policing.

Luke kept his focus on Jack, face impassive.

"For instance, the task force is planning a raid on McGrubers." Jack paused. "I have an idea where we can turn it to our advantage and come out stronger." Their attention quickened.

"I'm listening," Luke said.

"There's one cop whose full commitment is on McGruber's gambling operations. He followed *you* there, for instance." Jack nodded at Durand.

Durand shrugged. "I gamble there occasionally. It proves nothing."

"He has more than that on you."

Durand tensed under Luke's stare, knowing Luke wouldn't hesitate if he considered Durand a threat to his operations.

"Who is it?"

"Paul Wager." Jack kept his eye on Durand and saw him relax. "That's part of my idea. In a raid, it will be easy to compromise Wager. He may get caught in the line of fire, so to speak."

"And what about you, Da . . . Jack? Why would we need you?" he baited, making sure.

Jack threw up his arms like he'd had enough. "That's your call. If this is your idea of an inquisition to prove I'm in, forget it. You're the one who invited me." Nobody said anything.

Jack let out a loud exasperated sigh as if explaining to a couple of dimwits. "Because I can set it up. Steve Hawken trusts me, and if I say that Wager needs to be taken out as a dirty cop, he'll believe me. Durand can put me in charge of the three of us. I have a plan that puts Hawk and me as players in a game. Then at a certain point, the task force comes in with Wager. I have details to work out yet, which you don't have to know. But the raid will fail."

Jack spread out his hands. "That's it. Otherwise, McGrubers is finished. You will lose a perfect setup."

When Jack got home, he traded his clothes for a T-shirt and jeans. Hands shaking uncontrollably, he poured himself a hefty Canadian Club. Pharo pushed in close beside him on the sofa while the stomach jitters, with help from the solitude and the whisky, gradually ebbed away.

First and second task finished. Next up, he needed to tell Hawk his part. But first, he'd have a little chat with Wager.

33

THEY gathered in the command room for a final review, each relating the part they were to play, radio bands confirmed and tested, and questions raised and answered until finally, only silence remained. Jack, Hawk, and Wager stood together, giving each other a last-minute once over. Each dressed in business clothes, they portrayed men on the cusp of their careers and out for a night on the town. Each wore an S&W .38 in a shoulder holster.

If the others noticed Jack's hands restlessly checking himself as if seeking equipment which wasn't there, nobody commented. Jack hoped people saw it as normal anticipation mixed with anxiety, but in reality, he kept foreseeing unknowns which would end in his failure. Unknowns always came from surprising corners. What if Luke had arranged his own unpleasant surprise? He was capable of it and had the power to overcome any force. Luke also had the advantage of prior knowledge. Jack bit the inside of his cheek. His tongue felt stuck to the roof of his mouth.

"It's duty, duty, first and last . . . there's no such word as fail."

Stop making up the quotes, Brodie. You're not helping.

"Hell's bells, Jack," Hawk said under his breath. "Get a grip before you explode."

Wager looked up from inspecting his weapon for the tenth time and frowned. "It can't be a holdover from his last raid," he said to Hawk. "He can't remember that one." He leaned in closer to Jack and inspected his face. "Or maybe it's all coming back."

"Give it a rest, Wager," Hawk interrupted. "He'll be okay once the action begins." But his glance at Jack had worry in it.

Jack nodded, looked Wager over, and said, "I'll have your back,

Wager. Count on it."

Wager flushed and turned away.

An hour later, on a side street away from the pub, Durand handed Jack the briefcase. "Give it to McGruber," he said. The task force quietly took their positions, securing the area and discouraging bystanders.

Surprised, Jack pushed it away. "That isn't the plan. You carry the briefcase and okay me with McGruber."

"Chief's orders," Durand said, his voice smooth. "I will guide the task force instead. They are new, and the chief isn't confident they're ready." He shrugged and patted his pocket. "I have the warrants when the time comes. Your brother will vouch for you."

"The task force doesn't need guiding, and you know it," snapped Jack. "What are you up to?" Eyelids drawn into slits, Jack added, "Luke won't like this if you have a plan other than the one he agreed to."

Durand waved his hand at their surroundings and hissed his disapproval. "Keep your voice down," he said. "I'm the commander here." His small eyes shifted away from Jack. "Just do your part as agreed."

Fuming, Jack joined the other two. At the front of McGrubers, Hawk and Wager each swilled a drink of beer. They loosened ties, and Wager slung his arm around Jack's shoulder as they entered the pub. Jack faced the bartender and said, "We're here by appointment."

Face impassive, the man looked Jack over before he inspected Wager and Hawk, leering over Jack's shoulder and grinning at him. Wager belched, sending out a whiff of beer.

The bartender pointed with his head. "Who're they?"

"They're with me." Jack winked at the bartender. "Lots of money."

The bartender continued to examine them. Recognition flickered in his eyes when he saw Wager, and Jack wondered if the plan would fail right off the bat, but the man stooped and lifted a phone from under the bar.

Jack's attention swept over the busy room and its customers. All the pool tables were being played, as were the pinball machines, arranged down the far L-shaped room. The door opened, and Apple appeared. Would he make a scene? Jack sucked in his breath.

Apple beckoned. "This way, gentlemen," he said, emphasizing the word gentlemen. Glaring at Jack, he silently led the way around the building. At the back stairs, he said, "After you," and stood aside as Hawk and Wager started up. He blocked Jack from following. "You on the level?"

"Is water wet?"

"I've still got my doubts." He held Jack's forearm.

"I've never been more level in my life. It's my turn at the trough. You've probably heard from the big guy already, and I'm not about to explain myself to you." Jack pushed Apple aside and took the stairs two at a time, joining Wager and Hawk on the landing above.

The room was much larger than what he expected. Renovated too. Walls had been taken down and soundproofed, and expensive carpeting installed to muffle the sound heard below. He saw roulette wheels, blackjack tables, more for poker and baccarat, and a bar extended across one end. Easy chairs, cozy resting places in front of lush window drapes spread along the front wall. Young women in miniskirts circulated with trays of drinks and canapés. All the men wore evening clothes and appeared acquainted with each other as they juggled handfuls of chips and spoke in low tones. A newcomer could assume he was in Monaco or Monte Carlo.

Wager turned wide eyes to Jack while Hawk grinned, unable to hide his delight. To Jack's dismay, they scooted off in opposite directions as if they had forgotten why they were there. Their first job was to pinpoint obstacles the task force would encounter, like weapons, guards' positions, and how to intercept them when the raid was underway. A rough calculation of attendance put them at fifty people.

"Stay alert," Brodie warned.

Jack memorized the layout, almost a replica of the pub below. Was that an office door at the far end of the L? Where were the inside stairs? Apple had mentioned an elevator. So, there were two obvious exits, plus the windows if necessary. Which door led to McGruber's suite?

"DC Tuesday. Or is it Mr. Jackson?" The wheelchair had come up behind him with no warning, and Jack recognized the melodious cultured voice, words carefully punctuated. Phineas McGruber, dressed in a fitted tuxedo jacket with satin collar, black tie, and starched white pleated shirt, looked up at him. Despite his size and proportions, he commanded the room and showed not the slightest sign he differed from anyone else there. He pointed a shortened finger towards the far wall and a teller's cubicle. "Deposit your money there. You'll get chips in return with enough for your friends. Whatever you win is yours to keep, or"—his eyes twinkled up at Jack—"you can cash in your chips without playing. However, why not enjoy a game while you are here? You never know, you may double your bets." His fingers pressed a button in front of him, and the chair turned.

"Is my brother here?"

"Unfortunately, we have another meeting for which we both must leave the premises."

"Wait . . ." But McGruber kept going, the wheels rolling smoothly over the carpet towards the far door Jack had seen earlier. Apple appeared from nowhere, darted Jack an unforgiving glance, and scurried after his boss.

Jack took the briefcase to the cashier. It slid effortlessly through the slot in the cage as though measured for it. "Surprise, surprise," Jack said and got a steely look. While the cashier stacked chips of various denominations, Jack drummed his fingers on the ledge and resisted looking at the clock. He accepted a tray of chips and searched for Hawk and Wager to share them. He found them shoulder to shoulder, mesmerized by the players at the blackjack table. Both of them shuffled their chips, grinning like idiots at each other, and Jack poked Hawk with his elbow, nodding for him to get a move on to his assigned station away from them.

Wager eagerly started away, saying as he passed Jack, "Stay out of my line of sight." A chill went up Jack's spine.

Suddenly unsure of himself and the plan, Jack grasped his chips and discarded the tray, eyeing Wager, who was sliding into a vacant chair at the poker table. Wager stacked his chips in front of him and rubbed his hands together as if he couldn't wait to begin.

Jack spent the next hour walking around the tables and observing the progression of gamblers trying their luck, some winning, most losing. He wondered how people became habitual gamblers, losing a great deal of money, convincing themselves they'd hit it lucky on the next move. As the time grew nearer for the raid to begin, he found he was sweating, loosened his jacket and, too late, remembered the danger of showing his gun holster. Cursing his lapse of concentration, he did it up again, glancing around, hoping nobody had noticed.

Just before midnight, the door opened, and four burly men walked in, easily recognizable as bikers, even though they weren't wearing the usual jeans and vest. Nor were they clad in a suit. Casual cotton trousers, over which light windbreaker jackets, zippered closed. Definitely armed. A quick glance told Jack that Wager and Hawk had also noticed them. Wager raised his hands as if to tell the table he was out, raked in his few chips, and rose. Hawk paused only a minute, then stayed put at the roulette table. Jack patted his pockets as if looking for cigarettes, then wandered to the door and outside to the balcony. He leaned against the railing, lit a cigarette, and pretended to smoke while his eyes swept the area behind the building. He glanced at his watch. No sign of the task force squad, but that meant nothing. It was still fifteen minutes to go.

At his left, there was movement in the alley. Another movement to his right and a soft curse from below. Jack stubbed his cigarette on the railing, threw the stub over the top, and then went back inside.

Bikers.

He didn't know how many but was willing to bet over four. Looks like McGruber and Luke had indeed developed a second plan to complement the agreed-on one.

He meandered over to the roulette table, bending over Hawk's shoulder as the croupier repeated the bets. "Don't bet the red," he advised him, grinning. Hawk looked up at him, and Jack added softly, "You'll end up in debt. People after you." He laughed and looked pointedly at the door leading outside.

Hawk blinked his understanding. "One last bet, buddy." He loosened his jacket, pushed his chair back a little and said, "Red." Jack didn't wait for the result but walked away as the wheel turned.

The first sign was the commotion on the front street. Faint cries of "police" and shouts penetrated the quiet hum upstairs. Men raised their heads, puzzled. The four bikers in the corners unzipped their jackets, and guns appeared in muscular hands. The commotion increased, and men palmed their chips, shooting worried glances at each other. A few made a dash towards the cashier. Wiser ones stuffed them into their pockets and headed for the exit, pushing to be the first.

The balcony door opened. "Police. Stay where you are." Mouths gaped. A girl screamed and dropped her tray of drinks.

Weapons drawn, police moved in quickly, shifting along the room, rounding up guests. "Everyone move along the front windows. Hands where we can see them." Initial surprise turned into righteous cries of innocence and objections hurled at whoever would listen.

Over the bluster, Jack heard shots from the alleyway and surmised bikers were moving in behind the police. A quick burst of returning fire from outside, then quiet. The squad had not been so careless as to leave their flank unprotected, giving Jack new respect for their training.

He was unprepared, however, for images of another raid flashing in his mind. He and Brodie on the fringes, waiting with the proper warrants to make arrests. Sensations of gunfire, Brodie going down,

Jack's unanswered cries for backup on a useless radio.

A gunshot brought him out of his daze. Two bikers laid their weapons on the floor, but the other two opened fire on the team inside.

Cries of panic and crashing of overturned furniture as gamblers dove onto the floor, the most righteous first among them. Light bulbs exploded in a shower of sparks, and the room dimmed.

Jack cursed under his breath, dreading a pitch-black room and the dangerous moment where bad things happened before the task force switched on lamps. Where was Wager? He spotted Hawk taking cover behind a table, turned on its side. Both hands gripping his pistol, he rotated back and forth, eyes searching. Jack grabbed his own gun and centred it on Hawk, waiting for him to find his quarry. One biker let out a cry, spun around, and dropped to the floor. Jack's head turned—an involuntary movement. A mere two seconds before his eyes came back to Hawk, but in that split second, the muzzle of Hawk's .38 found its aim.

As if in slow motion, he saw Hawk's face solidify in that unmistakable tell when a finger tightens on the trigger.

Jack stared down the barrel.

A rough push turned Jack a fraction, and he felt a pull at his jacket sleeve. Gunfire immediately behind his right ear deafened him and slammed Hawk against the upturned table. Disbelief on his face, Hawk stayed motionless before sliding to the floor.

Jack was right. It was Hawk. *His plan was to kill both Wager and me, then claim I killed Wager.*

Routine took over. The remaining bikers raised their arms straight up. Men rose from the floor, inspecting themselves for injury with dazed concentration. The task force flicked up their weapons, and people quickly whipped up their own hands, palms out. A few opened their mouths again, then clamped them shut. Crying quietly, the girls huddled together for comfort in the far corner.

Jack turned to see Wager rising from his knees. "Dammit, Jack.

Don't you ever listen? I told you to stay out of my line of sight."
He walked over to Hawk, and Jack followed. Hawk gazed at them,
hands against his chest. Blood oozed between his fingers. Wager sat
on the floor beside him. "Ambulance will be coming along in a few
minutes," he said, voice weary.

Hawk's cough rattled in his throat. He faced Jack, undisguised
hatred in his eyes. "You knew it all along."

Jack crouched down, overwhelming tiredness taking hold of him.
"Harry McNaughton left a tape. Of your phone calls."

Wager looked sad. "You swore Jack would get rid of me tonight.
That I'd better do it first."

Hawk tried to laugh, and his face twisted in pain. He struggled
to breathe, took a moment, then said, "I should have, but he was so
positive it was you all along, Wager. He just wouldn't listen when I
defended you." Hawk snickered a bit, then went quiet, closing his
eyes.

Wager looked from Hawk to Jack and shook his head.

The pain in Jack's bent knees made him sit down beside both men.
The stress of the night's actions settled in his midsection like a dark
weight. His head swam. The room turned lopsided, making him
nauseous. He stared farther down, blinking furiously and waited for
his head to clear. "Why'd you do it, Hawk? You had everything going
for you. Next in line for promotion, probably Deputy Chief when
they force Durand to go. So, why?"

Hawk roused himself and opened his eyes. "What does it matter
now? It's over."

"You killed Brodie," Jack forced out through his teeth.

"I told Brodie I was undercover to get evidence, but somehow
he found out I was helping Durand." Hawk coughed again. Blood
dribbled over his lips, and he swallowed, throat convulsing. "Funny
thing, I started out straight but got sucked in. Jokes on me." He
reached out and grabbed Jack's arm. "The bastard fingered men Tito
wanted killed."

The medics arrived with their cases and carts. Wager stood and beckoned them over. Jack and Wager moved away, leaving them to their patient.

"He set up Brodie's murder with Durand. Hawk took Brodie's old weapon and shot him during the raid. They assumed I knew what Brodie had learned, although I had no clue. When I survived, Hawk pinned it on me. After pressing my fingerprints on it, he switched it at the accident before the medics took me away. He didn't figure on McNaughton seeing the whole thing. McNaughton said he was being blackmailed, but not why."

"I suspected Hawk," Wager said, "and followed him, not realizing he was after McNaughton. I wasn't even aware of McNaughton's involvement then. He must have seen you together in the café. When I saw you there, I thought you were a part of it."

Around the room, constables were herding people and handing out arrest notices ignoring the protesting wails. Equipment was being dismantled under flashes of photos. Ackland and Vassar gave a thumbs up as they headed for the office and the cashier's cage with satchels to collect the money. Everything was a performance. Nothing would be in police hands for long after McGruber's lawyer showed up, waving the application and approval for a private party ostensibly to raise money for charity. All correct and signed by Durand, of course. The chief had already planned to have any newspaper accounts quashed. Jack grinned to himself at the thought of the surprise awaiting Durand, certain Hawk would not take the blame on himself.

The Medics put Hawk on a stretcher and started towards the elevator. Wager grabbed a constable and ordered him to stay beside Hawk until relieved. They needed Hawk alive to implicate Durand.

Against the protests that the raid was merely a private charity function, the police allowed the guests to leave. The sergeant shook his head. "Well-rehearsed, aren't they? But we have the pub for illegal betting. We found a cash box behind the bar downstairs with bets listed, including names. The bartender didn't bother using a code."

The police sergeant laughed. "First stupid mistake."

"That's why you went in there," Jack said to Wager. "Watching illegal betting going on."

"And you outside, watching me." Wager looked exasperated. "Jack, when are you going to realize that we are a team?"

"I don't seem to be part of one," Jack protested.

"Maybe because you think we'll fall apart without your guidance."

Although Wager's tone was without malice, it inferred an arrogant desire for power under the guise of protecting them. Luke's same inference had echoed Apple's angry tirade. Their combined weight sent Jack back on his heels. His father.

"You're not your father, Pal."

The constable who had gone with the medic came back into the room.

"What are you doing here?" Wager snapped.

"The deputy chief said he'd take care of the sergeant." The constable looked awed. "It makes you proud to see the chief looking after his men."

Wager and Jack looked at each other and dashed off, Jack blaming himself for forgetting that Durand was out there, waiting for a moment like this.

They made it outside in time to see Durand in the middle of the road, staring after the ambulance. He turned as Wager and Jack came up beside him, Jack fearing the ambulance's slow speed meant they were too late.

Durand turned, his expression regretful. "He didn't make it. This is a sad day. I tried to talk to him just before, hoping he'd tell me if anyone else was in the scheme with him. He died before he could say anything." His eyes met Jack's with a flicker of satisfaction before sadness shadowed them.

"Didn't the medics do CPR or whatever?" Wager asked, his voice neutral.

"They left him to open the doors of the ambulance. I noticed Hawk was in distress, but it was too late. He just stopped breathing." Durand slapped a fist into his open palm. "The noise in the street . . ." he waved at the bystanders gathered now, some from inside McGruber's pub. "I called over to the medics. They didn't hear." Durand put his hand up to his head. "I can't believe they left him alone, that one of them didn't stay with him."

"I can't believe it either," Jack repeated. Durand's eyes shot him a sharp reprimand. Wager's curses were long and furious. Fists clenched, he stomped away, but not before letting Durand read utter disgust on his face. Durand shrank towards Jack as if looking for protection.

"Do you suppose he suspects?" Durand asked. "You'd best monitor him."

Jack ground his teeth, seeing their chances of proving Durand's guilt shrink to zero.

"I'm not sorry he's gone," Durand was saying. "He wanted you dead when you came out of the hospital, in case your memory returned. Lucky his first attempt failed. Silly really. I stopped him from further attempts." He shrugged his shoulders, satisfied with himself.

"Liar. Shake hands with the devil, Jack."

A string of constables carrying boxes and equipment came around the front from the alley, setting off a burst of activity from the onlookers. Durand moved to the side to make room. The press, reporters and cameramen rushed in, competing for prime space, shouting questions at anyone who looked like authority. Like flies sensing rotten meat, onlookers closed in behind them, jostling each other so as not to miss any news. Helpless, too few policemen assigned to crowd control tried but failed to stop them. Again, Jack suspected Durand assigned too few police, determined to prevent a successful raid.

The reporters spotted Durand and surged at him, and the crowd swerved with them like jackals after fresh remains. Instinctively, Jack backed away from the surge, out of camera focus.

A shot rang out, and crowd pandemonium increased. People in

front turned to flee, jostling with those shoving themselves forwards. A woman screamed.

Hand to his chest, Durand took one step, then fell.

Numb, Jack stayed where he was. It seemed like an age, but only a few seconds passed while his brain processed what had happened. Springing into action, he reached Durand, whose empty eyes stared up. Jack opened Durand's jacket and saw very little blood around a smudge on his shirt at his heart. Jack's first rational thought was that Luke was leaving no loose ends.

Clicking noises brought him to the present. The news photographer was busy standing over him, snapping pictures, and Jack turned furiously on him. He snatched the camera, ready to dash it to the ground, stopping only at the horror on the man's face. Jack shoved the camera into his chest before the police constables began herding everyone off to the sidelines.

He scanned the group, looking for guilt, escape, suspicion, anything. Wager appeared beside him, pushing through a crowd that was now in a panic to make distance between the police and themselves. With one thought, Jack and Wager dove amongst them, searching for faces they might have seen close to Durand. It was hopeless, darkness already obscuring the street.

Ready to give up, Jack almost missed him.

The foreigner in the baggy suit, the man on the corner, the man who seemed to live in the apartment across the street. He was in no hurry but strolled down the sidewalk as if the chaos behind was of no interest. About to run after him, Jack halted. Another figure stepped out of a doorway and joined the foreigner. They spoke a few words, then continued to walk around the corner.

No use chasing them. He knew where to find them.

34

"YOU'VE got another call from Vancouver," Burton said the next morning. "This one from Canada Customs Agency. Into smuggling now, are you?"

"It's a doppelgänger," Jack said, uninterested.

"The whole place is buzzing with what went down last night. I'm surprised you're even here, but as long as you are . . ."

"Forget it, Rollie. I'm off the grunt work." Jack stuck out his hand. "I just came to thank you for having my back and to tell you I'm cleared of Brodie's death. Last night was a total balls up. Be ready to see me escorted from the building when the chief's finished. I can't say he didn't warn me."

Burton's sour face confirmed the general buzz that said Jack was toast. Cleared of Brodie's death and blamed for Durand's. Nobody would hear the true story about Durand to salvage the morale of the masses. The force being the masses. Part-truths might float around but would be ignored in favour of the notorious.

Burton took his eyes away and fussed over the desk. "At least phone these people in Vancouver, so they quit pestering me."

Jack gave a pointed stare at his watch. "No time. Can't be late for my firing. Do me a last favour, Rollie. Call them and say I'll phone them later on today or tomorrow first thing? Tell them I'm on an emergency case and can't get away."

"No dice. Tell them yourself."

Jack held up his hand, palm out. "I have no connection to Customs, RCMP, or anything in Vancouver. I'm not making this up."

A growling noise rumbled from Burton's throat. "One last favour then. Thank God you're out of my hair, or being fired wouldn't be your major worry."

They were in the conference room connected to Chief Mackie's office when Jack arrived. Wager, the task force squad staff sergeant, and the guy from Internal Affairs. Jack automatically looked for Hawk, getting a knowing half-smile from Wager. A secretary perched on a corner chair, ready to take the minutes.

Everybody but the secretary wore faces only seen at funerals. The staff sergeant, Jack remembered his name was Carter, stood at the front beside a flip board perched on an easel. Jack recognized the distinctive umber colour of two personnel files under the chief's hand. Someone besides him for the chop? The chief nodded at Carter, who began by describing the actions of the raid. When he came to Durand's position, the chief stopped him. "His order was to go inside with Tuesday, Wager, and Hawken. Why was he outside?"

The staff sergeant glanced at Jack, then said, "He told me Tuesday said the plan had changed."

Jack sat up, aware of the chief's accusing stare. "Not true. We needed Durand inside to prove he and Jackson were not only connected but close associates. He said Chief Mackie ordered him to command the task force squad." He looked at each face, reading silent expressions of disbelief.

"Hawk and I heard them arguing," Wager came to his rescue. He slid a glance at Carter. "Durand claimed Chief Mackie was short on faith and the team might foul up." Wager grinned at Carter's outraged expression.

"Balls," the staff sergeant said. He looked to the chief.

"All right." Under his moustache, the chief's lips tightened considerably. "We'll agree for the present that Durand lied." He gave Carter a slight shake of his head, and Carter turned back to his easel and flip charts. When he finished, Jack went through the actions inside while Wager nodded confirmation. The Internal Affairs man jotted down copious notes relating to Hawk's death. "And thanks to DC Paul Wager, I'm here now. He saved my life." Jack nodded to him.

Wager chewed his moustache and turned rosy. "Afraid Hawk would implicate him, Durand managed to divert the attendants' attention, then killed him. Post mortem will confirm he smothered a defenceless man. Absolutely callous." Wager's statement hung in the air. Nobody challenged it, only inspected their hands.

"Describe Durand's murder."

Jack took a deep breath and plunged in. He had rehearsed his story for the better part of the night. He stuck to the events leading up to the shooting, saying only what was reliable, not conjecture.

Near the end of his narrative, he paused. Wager registered his hesitation, and his interest sharpened like an electric surge. Jack took the opportunity to take a sip of water, thinking furiously. The chief's fingers drummed on the personnel file.

Jack decided. "My opinion is that Fingers Jackson ordered it, knowing Durand was ready to throw Jackson's operation under a bus to save himself. The alternative is a hit by the assassin who killed Dr. Pavic." His eyes swept around the table, past the chief's. "Durand worked for Tito. He fingered former resistance members who had defied Tito during the war." He again scanned the faces watching him. "It's common knowledge. Tito ordered more than one assassination."

The chief waved his hands like he already knew. "Go on."

"No, wait." Internal Affairs said. "Durand and Tito?"

"Durand was Yugoslavian," the chief said drily. "His real name was Milo Durovic."

The Internal Affairs man rolled his eyes and closed his notebook as if the complications had become too bizarre to follow.

A familiar chill ran up Jack's spine, wondering what else the chief knew about names. Supposing Durand had left notes?

You'd know by now, knothead.

"Dr. Pavic was in the resistance?" Wager leaned forwards, a pleased expression making his face look young. "And Durand arranged to have him shot? I figured he was assassinated, but I didn't know why."

Jack made out he was thinking it over. "I'm not positive, but it's possible," Jack said, glad the subject had swerved away from who shot Durand. "And Dr. Pavic may have known Durand during the war."

"Thick as thieves."

"Why would they know each other?" asked Wager.

"They did," countered Jack. "Knowing who was friend or enemy back then kept them alive. If Dr. Pavic let it slip that he knew about Durand and Tito, it sealed his fate."

"He'd have to have some insurance that Pavic would keep his secret." Wager shook his head, his narrowed eyes telling them he wasn't convinced Durand had killed Dr. Pavic.

The chief brought his palm down on the table, bringing everyone's attention to him. "Get back to Durand's death." All eyes centred on Jack. Carter slapped his pointer in the palm of his hand as if to say 'it's about time.'

Jack ticked points off on his fingers. "He saw himself as a powerful kingpin, all the while using his Deputy Chief title. Under that title, he laundered illegal gambling proceeds in the city for pay and was an informant and the go-between for the Jackson gang and the Rebels. We anticipated he'd arrange for permits stating that the gambling at McGrubers was a private event with all proceeds slated for charity. He wanted the raid to look like a shocking waste of police resources. Not true. The raid had one crucial goal. To find the dirty cops. We achieved that goal." He paused, then conceded his defeat. "However, I take sole responsibility for the deaths of the Deputy Chief and Sergeant Hawken."

Exhausted, Jack realized he didn't care anymore. That he wasn't in control of the verdict filled him with a sense of freedom. Craving fresh air, he rose.

"Sit down," Chief Mackie ordered. Jack sat.

"Any more questions?" The chief continued with barely a breath to spare even if anyone had. "We have a consensus on the conclusion DC Tuesday has summarized. Rather long, but there it is. We require no further action." He paused, then said, "I'll plan further meetings with various heads of departments to ensure there are no repeats. Am I clear? Each of you will receive a copy of the minutes of this meeting. You will sign your acceptance. Agreed?" His gaze swept the table, daring anyone to make a comment. Nobody did. "That's it for the time being." Chairs scraped back, and everybody rose.

"Not you two," the chief said.

Jack pulled out his chair and sat again. Wager gave a 'who, me?' expression before he sat beside Jack, his nervous eyes shifting to the files before the chief.

"There is one further item that won't appear in the minutes as of yet. You are aware there are now two vacancies resulting from the . . . action. About the first, I will agree to recommendations that DC Wager become Detective Sergeant." He paused, and Jack inwardly stiffened his spine. "And second, reinstating Detective Constable First Class Tuesday to his old position."

Jack let out his breath and wondered if the chief had specified his full ranking to remind him of who held authority over him, newly ranked Detective Sergeant Wager.

Disapproval written over his face, Wager opened his mouth, then clamped it shut.

"Detective Sergeant?" The chief's eyes sparkled beneath bushy eyebrows.

"He's . . ."

"Well?" The chief's fingers beat a rhythm on the table.

"A pain in the backside. Not a team player. Blasts off on his own like he's got an outboard motor tied to his butt, leaving us to guess what's going on. And it rubbed off on DC Brodie. He stumbled onto Durand and ran off on his own tack. It got him killed." He shot a bitter glance at Jack. "Tuesday may be innocent of his murder, but was he responsible in his own way?"

His question aimed a blow to Jack's midsection, and he folded over as if it had been a direct shot.

The chief's questioning gaze focused on Jack.

"I've been wondering about the same thing for months." Throat convulsing, Jack admitted, "A hunch will send me veering off in different directions. And knowing staff might not encourage it, I will keep it to myself. But Brodie? I always warned him to keep to the regs about secrets. I'm sure he didn't foresee it meant dealing with organized crime gangs and just went after solid evidence." Jack looked down at his hands, misery and grief eating at his insides. "His death will haunt me forever."

A stubborn set to his chin, Wager cleared his throat. "Well, anyway, maybe he requires refresher training."

"The path to team players, Sergeant Wager, is managing your men. Imagine if you were a staff sergeant or even inspector. You look for ways to enhance your men and encourage their initiatives. Even let them tilt at windmills occasionally." The chief's moustache quivered.

"On the whole, this caper was successful, and even the parts that weren't because we learned valuable lessons." He deliberately turned his eyes from one to the other, his steely gaze hardened into marbles.

He's furious now, Jack thought, cringing inside.

"I want to know the rest of it. If I'm not mistaken, you two had more on your mind when you planned to trap *Mr.* Hawken and DC Durand in the raid. Stop giving me the mushroom treatment. There are no more secrets on my watch." The chief's gaze spread between the two of them again. "Clear?"

Wager's face went beet red. It took an effort, but Jack kept his gaze steady ahead, expression neutral.

"I had to brief Detective Wager about what I found on Harry's tape. I owed it to him."

Chief Mackie held up his hand, stopping Jack. "Back up here." He steepled his fingers. "DS Hawken openly protested DC Tuesday's guilt to IA." The chief held up a finger to silence Wager, who opened his mouth, then looked at Jack.

"Backing me up made him look innocent. He wanted me free, so he could pin more evidence on me. As a last resort, he wanted me to name Brodie a dirty cop. He knew I'd quit first, which would free him to blame the both of us." *Bastard,* he thought.

"Sergeant Hawken's fingers couldn't be everywhere. So give me the name of the officer who helped him."

A silence fell over the three. Wager nodded to Jack.

"Detective Ackland," Jack offered.

Chief Mackie smiled grimly. "Go on."

Jack glanced at Wager, who kept mute, seemingly happy to let Jack hang himself. "As I said, I had to advise Detective Wager on what I discovered. We came to the same conclusion that Hawk had a helper, a minion, so to speak."

Chief Mackie impatiently shuffled his feet.

"Short version, Ackland got too friendly," Jack hurried on. "He switched from accusing me of Brodie's death to telling me I could rely on him for help. Nobody except Hawk would know Harry was being blackmailed and that he might leave me a clue to his death. Hawk had to find out if McNaughton left any documents behind with his name attached and sent Ackland to Harry's funeral to watch me. He saw a reporter hand me a locker key. Thank goodness the key was a ruse."

"And he's still in the wind. Did your plans include telling me this tidbit?" Chief Mackie asked.

"Haven't caught him red-handed. We are short in the chain of command, so no Deputy Chief to coordinate with and advise?" Wager continued. "In the meantime . . ."

Chief Mackie scowled at the lame excuse but let it go. "Does he suspect that you know?"

Wager shook his head. "I am confident he does not and also that he will continue. Whoever his handler is won't let him quit. We could arrest him or choose to leave him and use him to our benefit."

Chief Mackie rose. "I don't want him here. Better he goes on a special assignment or is sent on a course while I decide. Fix it."

As they left the boardroom together, Wager gave Jack a sideways look, then said, "You did alright, I'll give you that. Hawk was an expert in covering himself. Your tactic forced his hand."

"With your help. The chief seemed pleased. Will I get a commendation?"

"God, no."

Jack heard a soft amen.

"He might if you wrote me one?"

Wager pushed the elevator button. "You're doing it again."

Inside the elevator, they grinned at each other. Jack shuffled his feet. "I won't forget you had my back all this time."

"Knucklehead. One of the hardest jobs I ever had."

"Will we tell Maureen Brodie the truth? She will be devastated that she trusted Hawk."

"They have assigned me that task, and it will hurt. But he fooled all of us, and we're supposed to be the professionals here. I think she can take it."

Jack put his hand out to stop Wager as they left the elevator. "All the time I was suspended, I suspected you were to blame. Hawk taunted me, but in a way that encouraged me to keep believing it. That's on me. I fell for it because I respected him." Jack flushed, shuffled his feet and looked Wager squarely in the eyes. "Apologies. I jumped to conclusions."

"Well, All Saints." Wager rolled his eyes in feigned surprise. When they entered the unit room, Ackland jumped up all smiles and applauded, followed by Visser. The others joined in with calls of "well done, Tuesday." Grinning, Jack shook hands with everyone.

"Enough," Wager bellowed. "His head's plenty big already." He leaned into Jack and said quietly, "You didn't fool me back there when you rattled on about Durand's killer. I'm glad the SOB is gone, but I expect you to fill me in when you're ready."

At noon, Jack brought coffee and doughnuts back to Burton. After his help, he deserved to hear everything.

"I'll never understand what goes on in some people's heads." Burton screwed his own around the edge of the cubicle, keeping his eye on the front desk. "Especially Hawk. He already had everything going for him."

"I doubt he started out that way," Jack said. "He aimed to be Chief someday, maybe even admired Durand. He analyzed his management techniques, followed him. Somehow, he discovered Durand's corruption, temptation took over, and he joined them. He told himself his way to advancement was influence peddling and political interference."

"Well, he sealed his fate when he killed that reporter," Burton said.

"McNaughton had a nose for smelling ambiguities. I suppose Hawk saw him too often and connected the dots. He was Hawk's weak link and had to go."

"Both he and Durand tried to make you quit." Burton gave him a curious squint. "Most men would have."

"Without you, I may have. But I'm a cop." The mob. Luke's fake living would never suit him. The coldness there . . . any softness his brother held as a young man when shielding him against his father's temper had long hardened.

"There are lives that are erring and aimless, and deaths that hang by a hair."

Jack laughed out loud, fighting tears, missing Brodie. *What will I do without you?*

"You need a wife, Jack," Burton announced. "Start a family."

Jack only nodded. He had promises to honour. Dinner at the MacDonald with Siobhan. Tell Edina Chambers how Harry had saved him. And Durand's killer was still out there—unfinished business and personal.

35

FROM his window, the back fender of Bianca's gold Honda was just visible. Glancing upwards, he thought he should tell Mrs. Zamborski about Durand. *Sure. As if she doesn't already know?* The curtains parted, and Tommy stared through his hair directly at Jack's apartment building, his arms folded across his chest in his typical defensive mode, making Jack smile. Protecting Mrs. Zamborski from whatever evil he imagined might lurk outside.

His smile faded, and an instinct from out of nowhere took over. Tommy's posture, the inspection of his apartment.

Damning himself, hoping he was wrong, Jack made it out of the building and across the street. He shouldn't have waited a full day before confronting her.

"Did you know it all along, Pal?"

He sped up to join a resident going up the path and went through the door with him. Heartbeat hammering in his throat, he tiptoed on the carpeted hallway towards Bianca's door. After repeated knocking, the obvious answer shouted at him. Her car was a decoy, saying she was home. Instinct told him her absence wasn't temporary. It was too late to trigger an APB for her without explaining why he left it so long. About to turn away, he caught it, faint in the air. A whiff of something tugging at his memory. He turned back to Bianca's door. There it was, the same musky aura lingering in Dr. Pavic's office. Like coming upon old clothes packed away in the attic.

Cursing himself for a sentimental fool, he darted up the stairs to Mrs. Zamborski's apartment, fearing what awaited him. Tommy opened the door before he could knock. Jack followed him inside.

"Where is she?"

"Gone. For good." Tommy's eyes shone with tears. "I would have looked after her." His surly expression said it was Jack's fault.

"Why didn't you come and get me right away?"

"She told me not to, that you'd follow her." An expression of pride and regret fought each other, and regret won. He wiped his tears with the back of his hand and disappeared into the kitchen, returning with a large package and an envelope. "I had to wait for you and give you this. She said you would understand."

Jack took the package, instinctively noting the bare patch on the wall. Berating himself for not expecting her actions, he returned to his apartment.

Heart tripping, he read the note. It was folly to look for them. They were experts in disappearing. The painting might tell him more. Jack smiled at what she was really saying. The day he told her the frame was marred, she knew he had identified Bianca's picture. The same flaw he saw illustrated in the volume of art she had shown him. She concluded with an exquisitely worded appreciation for his patience in listening to the memories of an old lady.

Old lady, my ass. She deliberately sought him out, knowing that helping him enabled her quest for revenge.

Jack unwrapped the package, exposing her painting of three men having drinks together. He laid it on the counter, then searched for a narrow spatula in the drawer. Guiding the spatula around the crease with gentle pressure, he forced it upwards, predicting she had been careful not to damage what was underneath. A final tug and the print came away, revealing Rubens's version of 'Mary meeting Elizabeth, mother of John the Baptist.'

He held it out at arm's length. What was it supposed to tell him? He recalled her remark that the aim of the theft might not relate to its sale. He peered at it, then turned it over to examine the back covering. Did he dare? The picture was valuable; damaging it would be unforgivable. He propped the painting on the couch cushions, stepping back to admire its sheer magnificence. It was eternal, the hues muted yet alive. Rubens had captured the figures' expressions perfectly; awe, respect, worship. Spectators beholding a miracle.

Jack fetched a beer and opened it, thinking. If it wasn't a fake, why leave it behind when they could sell it on the underground? Mrs. Z had said he would find the answers there. Jack swigged another gulp of beer.

He carried the picture to the kitchen. He slid the knife along the temporary backing, and a flat ten-inch envelope came away. Inside were two old photographs and an onion skin envelope containing a yellowed square of paper—an order stamped with the official seal and a swastika and German Eagle over a signature. Jack didn't understand every word of the order in German writing, but he recognized a name: Milo Durovic. He looked at the photos. One, a Nazi officer pinning a medal on a younger but still recognizable Durand. More Nazis stood behind with glasses of champagne. Celebratory drinks with co-conspirators. Blackmail material. Enough to enrage Tito and force Durand's eviction from Canada.

The second picture was scorched around the edges, with folding lines running through it. A man sporting a neat, black beard, a woman, and two children. No question, the woman, unscarred, was Mrs. Zamborski. With a stretch, he could see the boy as older and heavier, like his father beside him, and wearing a baggy suit. That must be Stefan. The little girl, fair hair, the image was faded, and a fold creased it, but Jack knew her eyes were cornflower blue. And with a dimple at the corner of her mouth. *Bianca.*

Jack propped the artwork up and contemplated it from across the room, drinking beer and pondering the sins of war which pursued the sinners to their deaths. Durand and Dr. Pavic—bound by the past. Durand's orders that the girl be sent to a camp, Pavic rescuing her, or perhaps Durand had gifted him with the child. The facts are forever hidden now.

A knock freed him from his morbid thoughts. Professor Waterman was on the other side. "I wondered if something was wrong. You thundered past the door and down the stairs." Waterman peered at him over the top of his glasses like he'd been remiss in his homework. "Anything I can do to help?"

Jack waved him in. "No, quite the opposite. Want a beer?"

"Sure."

Jack opened two beers and handed one to Waterman, who had found the Rubens. "Is it genuine? Can't be." He straightened, taking the bottle and waving it at the picture. "Worth a fortune if it is."

"Yes, it belonged to an old friend. But a copy."

Waterman seemed relieved he didn't have to ask how Jack came by an authentic Rubens. He bent closer again. "Still, a very good copy. You're a lucky man."

"I only borrowed the picture," Jack said, wondering if it might be true. The thought cheered him.

Waterman sat down, lifted his bottle in a toast, and drank. "I wondered if you noticed our tenant upstairs has departed. Rather suddenly, which makes me think I may have been correct."

"I've forgotten why," Jack lied. "What was it again?"

"He said he was after a master's degree. Remember, I suspected he belonged to a biker gang, up to no good, and would peddle drugs at the university."

"Cutting into your business?" Jack casually drank from his beer.

"What?"

"You're selling weed to your students."

"No," Waterman sputtered, but the hand holding his beer shook.

"Don't get your shirt in a knot, Professor. Your carefree students display all the signs, and every cop in Edmonton is aware university students head to the Riviera for their stash. Most cast a blind eye, but eventually, they put on a show to remind people who is boss."

Waterman just slumped and looked at him, his eyes massive behind his lenses. Jack half-regretted pricking the professor's balloon.

Waterman sighed and gave in. He looked straight at Jack. "They're good kids and need to settle their nerves during exams." He shrugged.

"It sounds like the usual self-preserving patter of someone trying to absolve themselves of guilt, but I believe it. At least I can talk to them, warn them off hard drugs. Believe me, I don't use them as conduits. I'm not a pusher." His expression begged Jack to have mercy.

Jack took a moment, then said, "I can't say I agree, but I won't rat on you. Just be careful, Professor. You don't know who is undercover, maybe even one of your students. It wouldn't be nice to see you charged for selling skunk."

Waterman's eyes got big again. Clearly, the idea that one of his own students might report him was something that hadn't occurred to him.

Academics, Jack mentally shook his head. "Another beer?"

"No, thank you. I should go. You've given me much to reflect on."

Jack shut the door behind a shaken Waterman, and the phone rang.

Pharo sat up, looking at him. "No rest for the wicked today," Jack told him, answering the phone.

"I won't make the mistake again," Luke said without saying hello. "I never indulge in dreaming, but I made an exception for you."

"Where are you?"

"About to take off. It isn't over, Danny. Next time, I'll be ready."

"Are you going to send your fixer after me?" Was he still working for Luke? He might give him a warning if he was a target.

"You're still my brother, Danny. Your report on the raid didn't emphasize that I was the primary person behind the gambling." Luke threw in another hint, looking for affirmation, perhaps. "And you kept quiet about my location."

Luke knew the contents of the reports? Ackland back at it? "Don't think it was goodwill that I deliberately didn't mention your location. I knew you wouldn't be there, so why waste police time?" But the muscles in his jaw contracted. Luke's statement had hit a nerve. "The police force is my path. I don't fit into yours. If you return here, well, take your chances."

"You've chosen your side, Danny. I'm not after you directly. But heed your own advice about taking chances. Fair warning."

"Enjoy your flight, Luke. Forget that you and I are family."

Luke chuckled as Jack hung up.

36

FEELING at one with his job, Jack settled in. Conversations didn't cease when he entered a room or laughter halt when he walked past. Easy interactions in the unit netted fresh insight into his friendship with Hawk, revealing the truth of Hawk's cunning strategy of silently warping relationships between his fellow officers, all to promote himself. Tearing down, rather than building.

In the middle of his third day, Jack sat hunched over a case concerning a sexual assault with violence when his phone rang. He tucked the receiver between his ear and neck, reading while announcing his name.

"Detective Constable Tuesday? Jack Tuesday?" the deep voice said on the other line.

"You got him."

"Canada Customs here, in Vancouver. You are a hard man to find."

"Hell, I forgot." Jack sat up. "I mean, we've been so busy here, and I—"

"Do you mind answering a few questions, DC Tuesday? It's imperative that you answer them fully and correctly," the voice went on, not waiting for his reply. "Can you tell me where you were living in 1958?"

Jack quit trying to read the report and listen at the same time. "What is your name again?"

"MacDonald. I am with Canada Customs and Immigration at the Peace Arch Border Crossing in Surrey, British Columbia. At the moment, I am in Vancouver with an RCMP intelligence section officer. Do you want them to verify my ID?"

Jack gave the telephone his full attention. "No. I'm good. In 1958

I was with the Canadian army in Iserlohn, West Germany."

There was a rustle of paper. "Is the name Ursula Bosch familiar to you?"

Jack's heartbeat pounded into his throat. "*An* Ursula, yes. I never knew her last name. Is she . . . ?"

"I need information concerning the events of your last contact. As precisely as you remember, please."

Alarmed, Jack said, "Not until you tell me why."

Silence and breathing. "A matter of national security. I can have you brought here under guard." The threat was obvious. "Or you can trust our process. It's up to you." A pause for objections. Jack didn't. "Now, what were the events of your last contact with Ursula Bosch?"

Curiosity overcame stubbornness. "She never showed up for a date. I went to our . . . uh, I found a note. The East Germans wanted her back because she had a degree in advanced physics. Some nuclear thing. The Stasi had imprisoned her brother and used her mother to coax her back with a pledge he'd be free on her return." A memory of stale air in the empty apartment came back in a rush.

"You must understand, my love. I have to go back."

A faint hope brought beads of sweat to his forehead. "Did she get out? Has she somehow found her way to Canada?"

"Were you and she intimate?"

Jack frowned. "Okay, now you're going too far."

"Which tells me you were." Jack heard a chuckle which raised his ire.

"Has she escaped East Germany?" He held his breath.

"Not her, DC Tuesday. A member of an East German swim team defected from a competition in Seattle and made it to the border. We've had a devil of a time fobbing off the East Germans while we searched for you." There was a pause while Jack's interest faded. Small consolation knowing she was still in East Germany.

"I'm sorry. The boy tells me she has died."

Jack closed his eyes, the receiver pressed against his forehead. A vision of her laughing at him as she straightened his tie. As if it were yesterday. His depth of grief surprised him.

"Hello? DC Tuesday?"

Jack roused himself. "Am I supposed to vouch for him or something? Sorry, I can't do that."

Another chuckle. "You already have. Ursula Bosch was his mother. She sent him to find you. He's your son."

- THE END -

JACK TUESDAY

If you enjoyed this book, *or even if you didn't,* please consider leaving a review on Amazon or Goodreads.

There is no better way to support an author.

Thanks!

Use the QR code below to review on Amazon.com

Florence Nelson Smith, otherwise known as "Flee," was born in Medicine Hat and has been writing most of her life; novels, short stories, and poetry. She has an accounting designation and a degree in Economics from the University of Alberta. Besides writing, her hobbies include genealogical research and figure skating. After a career working in various cities in Alberta and British Columbia, she now resides in Red Deer, Alberta.

Follow F. Nelson Smith on Twitter @Fleesbooks

www.fnelsonsmith.com

ACKNOWLEDGEMENTS AND HISTORICAL NOTES

Huge thanks and appreciation goes to my editor, Tessa Barron, of Bear Hill Publishing, who has an inherent knowledge of words that should be expressed. As always, she is knowledgeable and merciless in achieving a good story. The worst fear of a writer is when the manuscript is first sent to an editor after numerous self-edits. Then the answer comes back with yes; she likes it but suggests a few changes. (A few pages of notes is more accurate.) Authors also do a lot of tooth grinding.

Much appreciation to Katie Barron, who dedicated her time to copy editing instead of working on her own excellent Fantasy series, available at www.bearhillbooks.com.

The Cops and Writers Facebook group kept me on track with the proper use of weapons, crime scene investigation and procedure, as did MP Mates. They shared memories of communication technology in the 1970s. My appreciation to Frank Topp, a retired Edmonton Police Service officer, for describing the location and layout of the old Edmonton Police Service building as well as the criminal issues of the time. Wayne LeRoche answered questions about the standard protocol to address police officers. Any errors and omissions made on police procedures are entirely my own, and the timing of some events was created in the interests of fiction liberty.

McGruber's Inn does not exist and is my own creation.

Many classic works of art stolen during WW2, including Rubins, are still missing, but Peter Paul Rubins's painting of 'Mary Meeting Elizabeth, mother of John the Baptist,' exists only in my imagination.

The gory history of Yugoslavia and its citizens' suffering during World War II is well documented, as is Tito's secret police tracking down and assassinating those he considered enemies, past and present. This also happened in Russian satellite areas and stemmed from an agreement made at the Yalta conference in February 1945 and Stalin's insistence that all former citizens of those countries, dispersed during WW2, would be returned. An affair with horrific and sad consequences for many.

BIKER GANGS

The Rebels was one of four outlaw biker groups from the late 1960s to the 1990s who decided that Alberta was a good place to headquarter their operations. In the 1970s and early 1980s (the golden era in Canada for independent one-percenter clubs), the Rebels were the dominant club in the Edmonton area. At the same time, the Reapers were the alpha club in Red Deer and Calgary.

The chief rival of the Rebels was the Airborne Regiment of Canada, the same regiment which was ultimately disbanded in 1995 over disgraceful behaviour in Somalia.

One night, In March 1976, the rivals had a dust-up in the parking lot of the Kingsway Inn in Edmonton. It began when an Airborne member threw a Rebels MC leather patch onto the floor when moving a chair, a huge insult in the biker world. Both groups called in reinforcements, forty for the Airborne and twenty-three for the Rebels. The Airborne members were armed with steel bars, baseball bats, nunchaku, and a blackjack. Other than a few weapons, the Rebels were unarmed.

It didn't end as the Airborne hoped.

The Edmonton Journal reported on the fight a couple days later: "A brawl early Sunday morning between members of a motorcycle gang and soldiers from the Canadian Airborne Regiment at Namao sent thirteen of the soldiers to hospital. . . ."

The Rebels claim they fought as one unit while the Airborne members fought independently. In the end, the soldiers were forced to retreat.

THE YEAR 1972

I chose 1972 as Jack's year. It was also the year I graduated from the University of Alberta. 1970s Edmonton was a fun place to live. There were no cellphones in those days, maybe a pager or two, and no shortage of places to enjoy a night out with friends. Avoiding names and admitting to nothing, here are only a few quotes from those who recall good times: I hope they stir up fond memories for those who lived and worked uptown then.

"I used to go to the Grinder a lot. Moni was the bartender. People's Pub, Lees restaurant on Whyte Ave. Side Track, Limelight (we used to call it slimelight). How about the Library Lounge (U of A), Goose Loonies, Purple Onion, Esmeralda, Cook County Saloon, Chez Pierre? Different bands every week, Cold Feet, Flying Saucers, Sons of Adam, the Chessmen, and Gary and the Pick Ups."

"My favourite downtown was the Ambassador Hotel. They had great blues bands in a really edgy basement bar. Hawkeyes, in the basement of Capital Square, had singer/songwriter lounge acts. And I worked at the Northwoods Inn. The Wintergarden Room welcomed Oscar Peterson, which was quite a coup. And not to forget, Johnny Bourgogne, the piano man, in the basement bar, the George and Dragon in the old Renworth Inn on 5th."

The year 1972 was a year for the Olympic Games. The winter Olympics were held in Sapporo, Japan. Canada received one medal, a silver won by Karen Magnussen in figure skating. The one medal tied with the Canadian Olympic team of 1936.

Anyone alive then remembers with horror the 1972 Summer Olympics in Munich, Germany. Eleven Israeli team members lost their lives in an attack by PLO terrorists, changing the meaning of the Olympics forever.

The eight-game hockey series between Canada and the USSR almost gave all of Canada a heart attack when in the last 34 seconds of the eighth game, Paul Henderson scored the winning goal. Wikipedia has an exciting recount of the series, including the last game, where Russia declared themselves the winner and Canada's hockey team stormed the ice to prevent the Red Army from leaving the arena when it arrested the Canadian Coach. I don't believe any hockey series had the drama and excitement of the 1972 eight-game series with the USSR.

More titles by

F. NELSON SMITH

NO STRAIGHT THING

Available anywhere books are sold

www.bearhillbooks.com

PERPETUAL CHECK

"Perpetual Check is a page-turner with a resolution readers won't see coming. It will please anyone who appreciates interesting characters and mysteries that deliver the unexpected."

— *BlueInk, **Starred Review***

"Clever and surprising, Perpetual Check is a thrilling novel set during the intersection between the decline of the Soviet Union and the dawn of the computer age."

— *Clarion, Foreword Reviews*

Available anywhere books are sold

www.bearhillbooks.com

CPSIA information can be obtained
at www.ICGtesting.com
Printed in the USA
BVHW070937160223
658549BV00027B/193/J

9 781989 071342